OUTSIDE

AN ECONOMIC COLLAPSE STORY

THE FIRE

PERMUTED
PRESS

BOYD CRAVEN

A PERMUTED PRESS BOOK

ISBN: 978-1-68261-766-3
ISBN (eBook): 978-1-68261-767-0

Outside the Fire:
An Economic Collapse Story
© 2018 by Boyd Craven
All Rights Reserved

PERMUTED
PRESS

Permuted Press, LLC
New York · Nashville
permutedpress.com

Published in the United States of America

CHAPTER 1

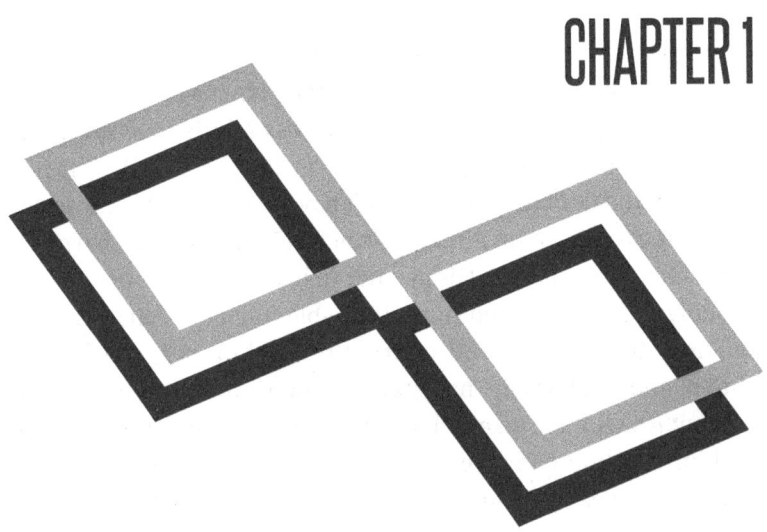

"Dad, why can't we just stop at the mall?" Amber asked.

"I need to hit the Costco before picking up your little sister," Steve told his very opinionated sixteen-year-old daughter.

"More beans and rice?" she asked with a big sigh.

"Beans, bullets, and Band-Aids," he told her with a grin and tried to poke her in the side.

She twisted at the last second and looked out the passenger side window. Steve had gotten out of work early and picked his daughter up on his way to get some preps. His wife had a surprise planned for later on, and usually, Amber would have been happy to skip sixth hour and go home early, but she looked at her father's prepping as something that was slightly embarrassing. She didn't have to worry about breaking her dad's "OPSEC," because she didn't want to even talk about the nested wooden crates in the back of the garage or the shelter built into the back of the garage floor.

"Great," she said, the sarcasm evident in her tone.

Steve was used to it, though there were plenty of days he'd have gladly traded in his daughter for a boy. He understood boys, though he'd never had any himself, just two daughters: sixteen and nine. As soon as the hormones kicked in, or they became a teen, a switch had been thrown, and his daddy's girl turned into a raging snark machine able to cut deeply with her words and body language. He knew she didn't like his prepping and thought he was a little touched in the head, but she wasn't overtly hostile. For a while, his wife Angela had been, until she saw that TSHTF didn't have to be a zombie invasion.

It was early on in their marriage before Amy had been born and Amber was two years old. His partner in his software company died suddenly, and Steve found himself unable to buy out his partner's half from the widow. She'd offered to buy him out, and he had refused, and the lawsuits had started. Almost fourteen years later, he knew it was a mistake to have tried to fight them, because he'd ran himself almost into the poorhouse trying to keep a business running and deal with angry heirs who wanted all of their shares but do none of the work.

Money had gotten extremely tight, and when the business finally folded, Steve and Angela Taylor found themselves scrimping and scraping just to make their rent on their small two-bedroom apartment in Cleveland. It had been Steve's obsessive food storage that kept their heads above water, and instead of being hostile, now his wife just did what her daughter Amber did, rolled her eyes and prayed it would never be needed again.

"You know, Amy would love to come with me to get this stuff. You used to like helping me out too," Steve said after a few moments of silence.

"That's because she's a little weirdo," Amber told him turning to face him, "but I guess...Dad, it's just that it's Friday. You guys have something planned and won't tell us, and Jennifer and I were trying to go to the mall."

"Sorry, your mother has had this planned for a while. It'd hurt her feelings if you don't go," Steve told her seriously.

"I know but...can I go see her tomorrow?" she asked.

"Tell you what, if you help me get the shopping done quick and give us no problems tonight, I'll let you take my truck tomorrow."

"What?" Amber asked, her mouth dropping open, "Daddy...."

6

She pulled tight against her seatbelt and hugged her father as much as the restraint would let her. He gave her a one-armed hug back and fought down the emotions. His little girl was growing up. She'd gotten her license and had been working on learning the main streets of Macon, Georgia, a city they'd lived in for a year and a half now. They were still the Yankees of the area, but everyone had treated them kindly and with a terror on wheels...Steve worried more about what people would do if they knew Miss Mouth had a license. The sidewalks would never be safe again.

"Hey baby, I know you're not crazy about going tonight. It's a three-day weekend, so as long as we don't have another meltdown like two weeks back, I don't have a problem with you taking my old beast out."

"I'd rather take Mom's car," she said after a second.

"You're pushing it," Steve told her.

"Ok, ok, I had to try. It's just that everyone down south here drives a truck. It'd be fun to drive the BMW once in a while."

"You remember the last time you tried to drive it? I thought we were going to have to put in a new clutch," Steve told her, poking her in the side.

She wasn't expecting it and squeaked as he hit the tickle spot. She slapped at his hand, and it turned into a one arm tickle fight. She laughed, and the world was fine again.

"I've been practicing with Mom; I'm a lot better than you last saw." Steve grinned back at her. She had no idea what she was in for.

"Daddy, there's no room for me to sit," Amy said looking at the back seat of the crew-cab pickup.

It had been piled high with bags of dried beans, lentils, rice, and underneath it, covering 2/3 of the floor between the bench seat and the front seats, were the squared buckets of Augason Farms emergency supply foods. He'd saved a ton of time by placing his order online, going to the kiosk, paying there, and wheeling things out. He thought he had enough room for little bit but....

"I got it squirt," Amber said and pushed on a large bag of rice that had slid over, exposing the seat right behind her father.

"I'm not a squirt," Amy said angrily.

"Hey now," Steve said, "we're not far from home. We're going to park the truck in the garage and head straight out with your mom, so let's not ruin this, ok?"

"I wasn't—" Amber started.

"What's the surprise, daddy?" Amy asked.

"It's your mom's surprise. I helped, but it was her idea."

Steve knew he shouldn't be sucking up to the kids so much, but he had started feeling like an outsider in the family. He was constantly worried about things he couldn't control, and his wife had quit her job at the vet after the doc made a pass at her. Angela hadn't told Steve about the first two times she'd been propositioned, but when she quit after the third time, he didn't know what he was more upset about: the doc being a letch, his wife from keeping it from him, or the fact they had been using his wife's paycheck to save up for Amber's car.

With careful planning and a surprise Christmas bonus from IT Bytes, he was able to come up with what he needed to. There had been a Jeep dealership that referred them to a small garage that restored old Jeeps, and it was the only thing that Amber and her parents could seem to agree on. Early on, Angela Taylor had gone in and bought a barely-there frame and body and had been making sizable payments as the restoration was going on. It had taken almost a year and close to ten thousand dollars, but the Jeep was almost as good as brand new. Steve just hoped she appreciated the sacrifice that both of them put towards it, hence the reason that Amber wasn't allowed to skip tonight.

The girls started talking about Amber's guy friend, and Steve winced and tried to ignore it. His first instinct was to find a hole somewhere in Mr. Abbott's field and bury the boy there, but he knew he was being overly protective, so to drown out the uncomfortable discussion, he turned on his radio, twisting the tuning knob until he found his favorite AM talk-radio station. This time of day, it was Larry Lars, a guy who reminded Steve of Don Imus from back in the day. It was a right-wing talk show for conservatives, and in Steve's opinion, one of the better places for him to listen to the news.

Today's episode was discussing the election of the new president and the protests that turned into riots in some of the larger cities. They had seen protests in downtown Macon, but they had all stayed peaceful and their family actually lived North West of town, in the suburbs. Civil unrest was what had concerned Steve the most, and since the previous November, he'd been stocking up more than usual. He didn't quite have as much of a stockpile as he wanted, but he had a lot more than his wife and daughters knew. Nobody went in the storm shelter that had the door against the back wall in the garage, and he'd been slowly building up his food and medical supplies there as well as a gun safe that his wife did know about. Just not that there were a couple more pieces and ammunition....

"...and in an effort to curb the out of control spending and deficit, the president has ordered an audit on the fed. Anybody want to guess how much of the money is left? I tell ya, it's probably gone, leveraged six ways to Sunday. Our gold reserves? Gone. All that fancy jewelry and electronics the world seems to enjoy? That's where our nation's gold supply disappeared to, loaned to the big central banks as collateral in an effort to—"

"Dad!" Amber said, shocking him out of his concentration.

"Yeah?" he asked.

"Amy was asking if Joseph could come over tomorrow, and you were zoned out."

"Sorry Ames," Steve told her, "when did you want him to stop by?"

"After lunch? He has to help his dad move something at the church," Amy said, her voice serious.

"I don't mind. After all, he's a preacher's son," Steve told her.

"Yeah, an octopus. He's all hands," Amber said.

Steve looked at her questioningly, his face starting to turn red.

"She's messing with you, Daddy. He's my friend, but he knows he's too young for Amber. She already told him no."

"Told him no to what—"

The phone interrupted the silence, and Steve turned down the radio and answered it.

"Hello?"

"Hey there, how much longer till you get here?" Angela asked, her voice sultry in her husband's ears.

"A minute, I'm almost past Clay Drive."

"Ok, just wanted to make sure you weren't late. Dave's isn't going to be open too much later."

Steve looked at the clock and saw it was 4:40 p.m. They had a good twenty minutes to get there.

"We'll make it. Just have your car running, and I'll park the truck and run like hell."

"Daddy!" Amy scolded.

Angela laughed and got off the line as they pulled into the subdivision. Their house was most of the way back, in the northeastern portion, and after a couple of turns, Steve stopped and let the girls get out. He hit the garage door button, and while the girls started getting into Angela's car, Steve parked the truck and took the garage door opener with him. He hit it as he walked out, and jogged the rest of the way to the sixteen-year-old BMW, Angela's pride and joy. It was a car she bought with her own money long before the business had been in financial trouble. She kept it immaculate and rarely drove. It had a sleek class that wasn't matched by Steve's F150, but both were diesel and part of that appealed to the prepping nature of Steve's hobby.

He got in and closed the door. He leaned over and kissed his wife deeply before she could say something and ignored the puking noises from the back seat. Angela pushed him back a little breathlessly, making a slapping motion towards him.

10

"Good afternoon ma'am, we best get a move on, if'n we're gonna make our appointment in time," Steve said, in his best imitation of a southern accent.

"You goof, how was work?" Angela asked.

"Let's go first, I'll talk to you about it after dinner."

"What's for dinner?" Amy asked.

"Where are we going? Somewhere that we can have steak?" Amber piped up.

"Your dad is cooking chicken on the grill," Angela said. "Right?"

"Yup," Steve told them. "And Mister Abbott is coming over.

"I thought we were going for a surprise?" Amy asked, a little crushed and confused.

"We are, and your sister is going to need these," Angela said handing back a set of nondescript keys.

CHAPTER 2

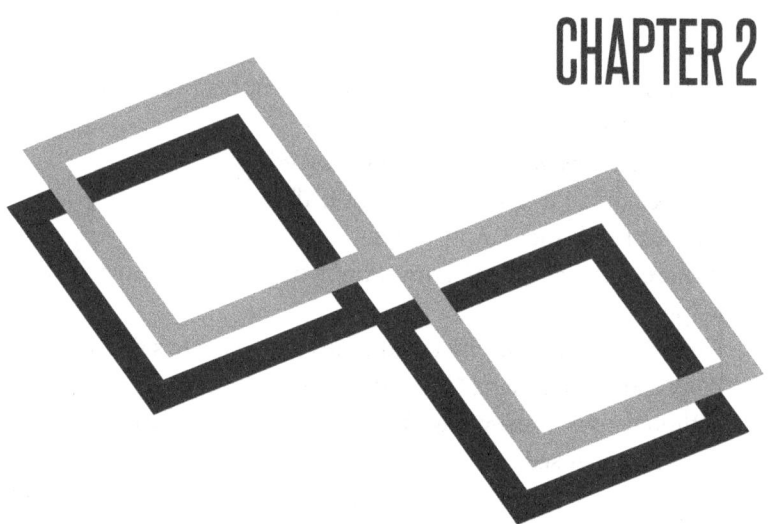

Steve had seen the word "squee" on Facebook and in text messages from his daughter. When she saw the 1990 Jeep YJ Wrangler, she educated him on what the proper usage sounded like when spoken aloud. She almost tackled her mother to the ground, her hug was so fierce. Steve watched her as Dave of Dave's Garage watched on with mild amusement. Both ladies were similar in height and build, but with his daughter growing up, Steve still heard strangers ask if they were sisters. His wife had long flowing brown hair that had loose natural curls, whereas his daughter kept hers shorter.

Still, her excitement was enough to almost knock her mother on her butt before she turned and squeezed the air out of her father and promptly burst into tears.

"What's wrong with her?" Steve asked Angela.

"She's overwhelmed, you caveman!" she chided.

"Daddy doesn't understand women. That's what Uncle Dewey says," Amy piped up.

"It's Mister Abbott," Steve told her.

"Nuh uh, he told me I can call him Uncle Dewey," Amy told her dad defiantly as Amber untangled herself and wiped her eyes looking up at her dad's face.

"I'm so sorry I've been a pain in the—"

"Don't ruin it," Angela interrupted and Amber's hand flew to her mouth.

She made a hiccupping noise and laughed, wiping her eyes again before turning to Dave.

"Is it...I mean...can I?" she asked.

"Oh yeah, got her finished for ya a week ago. I kept onto it to work out the bugs. Old girls like this, even when they get good works under the hood, they are finicky beasts. How about you let me show you what we did to her before you go cross country racing with this bad boy, huh?"

"Racing?" Amber asked.

They walked over and watched as Dave unlatched the hood and propped it open. A new motor gleamed in the sunlight. They had opted to go without the flash, because it was form over function, but a new engine and transmission had been the foundation to the powertrain.

"Is that a new Chevy three-fifty?" Amber asked.

"What's this witchcraft? How does a girl know this?" Dave asked, in mock horror.

Amber smiled at him, knowing he was baiting her, "I watched a lot of YouTube videos. I've been dreaming of having a jeep for almost three..." She started crying again and ran over and gave Dave a crushing bear hug. He held his arms out awkwardly for a second and then patted her back, giving Steve a confused look. Steve shrugged, and when Amber broke free, she didn't bother to wipe her face and turned to almost crawl into the compartment.

"It's got a carb, but I don't know which one without taking off the air filter," she said, not turning to talk to her parents, "and I think it's got either a Turbo Trans three-fifty, or a seven-hundred R4 transmission."

"Good eye," Dave told her.

"What's that?" Angela asked Steve.

"Good stuff," Steve whispered back.

Angela popped back out and closed the hood and then took her sister's hand and started walking around the Jeep. The rims and tires were new and although they hadn't put mudding tires on it, they were wide and fat enough with knobs that Steve knew she wouldn't stand out when they finally let her drive it to school.

"...and you're going to let me sit up front?" Amy asked her sister.

"Yeah, for sure squirt...and then we'll go to the mall and—"

"She can't sit up front," Angela said.

"No air bags," Dave reminded her.

She nodded, and then both girls opened the passenger side door and crawled in.

"So, Dave, how much we owe to finish this off?" Angela asked.

"How's about a hundred bucks?" Dave asked.

"I know we owe at least another three hundred or more, you put in the new instrument cluster..." Steve started saying.

"Naw, I got me a daughter. I wish she loved this kinda stuff as much as yours seems to," he said in a hoarse voice and cleared his throat a couple of times.

Steve felt his wife's hand in his, as her fingers curled around to give him a squeeze. He squeezed back and turned to see her smiling.

"Just promise me we'll talk later on about curfew and putting that tracking app on her cell phone?"

"I hate those applications—"

"Please?" Angela asked.

"Yes, ma'am," Steve said after a second.

His wife grinned and leaned in close as the two girls crawled into the front seat, now more visible in the afternoon light.

"I am going to close up, you're welcome to stick around but I promised the missus to help her out tonight and she'd skin me alive if she thinks I'm skipping out on helping her do her spring cleaning nonsense."

"Ok, I'll corral the girls and get out of your hair," Steve said and pulled out his wallet and counted out some cash, handing it to Dave.

"This is too much," Dave said.

"It's worth it, you just made our day," Steve told him.

"Well, you know where to come if you ever need it fixed. I reckon I can even fix that German toy car that Mrs. Taylor is so proud of."

"Other than regular maintenance, it's been in pretty good shape, but you bet I will," Angela said grinning.

"Deal. You folks have a good one," Dave said and turned and started walking towards the garage and office, stuffing the handful of bills into his chest pocket on his shirt.

Steve let go of his wife's hand and stretched his arms over his head. His back cracked and popped. It wasn't horribly hot yet, but it was humid. If he wanted to keep his timing right with the neighbor, he better shuck and jive.

"You want to ride home with her?" Steve asked.

"No, I've got my baby, why don't you? I'll keep Little Bit with me, just in case. You have the insurance on it?"

"Yes ma'am. I put it in the glovebox yesterday when I snuck out here and put the plates on it."

"You think of everything," she said kissing him softly.

"I'm a prepper; it's part of who I am," he said, and then jumped back when she playfully swatted at him.

The drive normally would have taken them ten minutes, but Steve texted his wife to fire up the grill to let it get warm as they took the Jeep out for a longer ride. The first results were a little bit funny. The docile six cylinder had been replaced with a Chevy small block, something that Steve knew how to work on. The problem was taking off from the stoplight. A lighter foot was needed or Amber was going to be spending her yet-to-be-earned paychecks on new tires. Still, with the windows down and the spring air whipping both of their hair back, it was hard to be critical of her driving.

Eventually, without having to be told, Amber turned onto the road leading to the subdivision and barely touched the gas as they entered. The small block and short length of the exhaust pipes and muffler still had a decent rumble to it. It wasn't as loud as a Harley, but only just. A couple people who were outside watering their lawns by hand stopped to look. A few waved, but most just stared. The Taylors were Yankees and outsiders. More so, they went to the new church and were Lutheran when the rest of their small community seemed to be Baptists or Southern Baptist. Couple all that with a funny northern accent, and it took some of them a little bit to warm up to them.

It hadn't helped that Steve and Angela were always brought up for discussion at the Home Owner's Association by two or three households that didn't like Steve's edible flower boxes that were a riot of pole beans, tomato bushes growing the smaller multi-colored tomatoes and salad mix spread throughout the boxes in front of the house. They didn't understand why the Taylors couldn't conform and plant something normal, like flowers.

Then there was the fracas involving a neighbor, Sarah Wilson, who watched from her second story window as Steve and Amy dispatched a trio of rabbits in the backyard and processed them. The furor over that was only worse than the HOA finding out that there were also three laying hens kept in the back yard as well. The neighbors were worried that the chickens were going to fly over the brick walls that separated the neighbors for privacy, or the tall chain link gate in the back that abutted Mr. Abbot's farm.

The HOA had no specific language that prevented livestock like it did pets and the Taylors were able to keep doing what they were doing, just like the way their planter box garden fit the definition of decorative plants. Overall though, the biggest infraction they got them on was putting the gate in that led to the farm, one that they were still fighting in court. None of the other houses had an entrance out of the back yard. None of them wanted one except the Taylor family.

That had always confused Steve, but he'd heard of horror stories of HOA's and people going overboard. When he'd gotten the offer to pick up and move with a generous bonus, by a headhunter, they had helped find him a nice house in a newer subdivision. He'd been able to afford it and when they made the move, it was all Steve could do not to make the cookie cutter house look like a small farm, like where he grew up in rural Ohio. As a prepper, he was glad he was able to find a house that already had a storm shelter....

"Geez Dad, I think you like sitting in this more than me," Amber said shutting off the rumbling motor as Steve stared at Clark and Sarah Wilson who had come out onto their front porch to stare at them.

"It's not just that," Steve said, and she followed his gaze to see the Wilsons.

"Oh man, gag a goat, it's Billy," Amber said getting out.

Steve saw their nineteen-year-old son had come out as well, probably curious about the rumble of the engine. The jeep did stand out in this subdivision, Most cars were darkly tinted, luxury cars. With Steve driving a twenty-year-old Ford and his wife an almost as old BMW, they didn't quite fit in. The Taylors loved not being in debt, so they kept what they had in shape and didn't care if the neighbors hated it, because Steve had been looking for property between Macon and Atlanta to start a small farmstead.

"I thought..."

"He's a creep," Amber said and slammed the door as Billy crossed the lawn.

Steve got out, closed the door to see the Wilson boy looking at the jeep with a funny look on his face. A hint of marijuana wafted over to him, and he frowned at the boy.

"Amber girl, is this baby yours?" he called after the fleeing teenager.

"Yeah, that's hers," Steve told him as his daughter disappeared in the front door.

"Hot ride. When I heard the rumble, I was like...whoa... somebody got a bike, and then I see my girl, Amber, riding up in this baby," he said running his hands across the silver metallic fleck paint on the hood.

"Don't touch, man. Just got it." Steve snapped more harshly than anticipated.

The truth was, he didn't like the kid. He'd caught him looking out the upstairs window in their houses direction more than once, and the only rooms he could see into from there, were his daughters and his bedroom if the curtains were open. He made sure they were always closed. *Creep.*

"Sorry man. If Amber wants to take me for a ride, have her call me."

"Yeah, I'll let her know," Steve said through clenched teeth as he watched the nineteen-year-old walk back towards his parents' house.

It wasn't that he was a creep, he was also a guy who was interested in his daughter, kept trying to talk to her when she clearly wasn't interested, and Steve's automatic response to any guy who wanted to date his daughter...his knuckles popped as he made a fist. Realizing it, he opened his hand and gave the Wilson's a little wave. Sarah whispered something to her husband, and they walked back inside.

"Assholes," Steve whispered as Amy came running out the front door with a large salad bowl in her hands.

"Daddy! Mom said we need to get some beans and salad for dinner tonight!"

"Ok, you saved me half the trouble, finding your momma's bowl."

She grinned and took her dad's hand impatiently and started pulling him towards the planter box. It took about three handfuls before cutting the salad greens about three inches from the dirt to fill the bowl over halfway with them before he turned her loose on picking some tomatoes. She'd gotten better at figuring out which ones were ripe. Steve hadn't made it easier by growing red ones. Some of his were purple, yellow, or tiger striped—old heirloom plants. While she was doing that, Steve picked a double handful of green beans and put them on the top.

"You're going to squish it, daddy!" Amy scolded him.

Unlike her mom and sister, 'Little Bit' Ames or Amy, had corn-silk blonde hair and seemed to have a more delicate bone structure. Amber had teased her that she was adopted until she cried and earned a grounding for it, but when Steve looked at her, he could see she was definitely a daddy's girl. She resembled Steve's mother more than she did Angela.

"No, I won't," Steve said as a man he recognized turned to start walking up to his driveway, "You take these inside to your mom to wash, then you wash up, and watch for Mister Abbott."

"Uncle Dewey!"

"Ok, scat," he said and gave her a playful shove.

She stuck her tongue out at him and then ran screaming, almost tipping the bowl as Steve playfully chased her for two steps. Once the door closed, he turned, the smile wiped off his face. His visitor was in his late fifties, his hair salt and pepper, but you could only tell that because the top of his hairline had receded to well behind his ears and tufts of it stuck out on the side in wild grizzled patches. He was well dressed, and Steve absolutely hated his guts.

"Doug, you're trespassing again," Steve said in an even tone.

"Am I? I'm on the driveway, I could go on the sidewalk if you prefer. That's public property, you know," he said, and took two steps back and stood on the concrete walkway.

"I'd prefer you go on home, but I figure you have something you wanted to tell me?"

"I heard your daughter drive in. I saw where she turned and figured I'd tell you that there's a noise ordinance against vehicles without mufflers in the HOA guidelines. Furthermore, you can't work on anything in the driveway so—"

"It's not broke down, and it has a muffler. Is that it?" Steve asked walking to within four quick steps of his nemesis.

"No," he said quietly. "There's also a rule that only two cars can be parked at any given residence at a time. You have three now," he finished with a sniff.

"That's outside in the driveway," Steve told him, "How many cars do you see in my driveway?"

"You also own a truck: a rather old and abused Ford."

He didn't snarl or swear at the man who constantly looked down his nose and was friends with the Wilsons. It was Doug and his wife, Linda Morris, who had been advocating the most to have the Taylors fined until they complied with their twisted sense of normalcy. They didn't even live on the same side of the subdivision. The Morris's lived more towards the entrance. Doug must have started walking over here immediately, or jogged, to deliver his crown jewels.

"I do, and it's parked in the garage. In fact, most of the time my wife's car is parked in there too," Steve said, noticing how good both the BMW and the Jeep looked side by side, sparkling in the spring sunlight.

"Well, at least your eyesore is out of sight. I'll have to re-read the HOA rules regarding—"

"Goodbye Doctor Toodles," Steve said and held his hand up and wiggled his fingers at the liberal college professor, "Bubye!!!"

Doug turned red in the face and opened and closed his mouth several times. It had been Angela who had overheard his hated nickname at a township meeting and had told her husband in the event in case he ever needed to use it. It had the desired effect and the professor turned and started stomping back down the road in the direction of his own house. Soft curses and threats could be heard, but he never looked back. Steve watched in amusement for a moment, feeling like he'd finally won a victory against him, when Angela called that Dwight Abbott, aka Uncle Dewey, had made it over.

CHAPTER 3

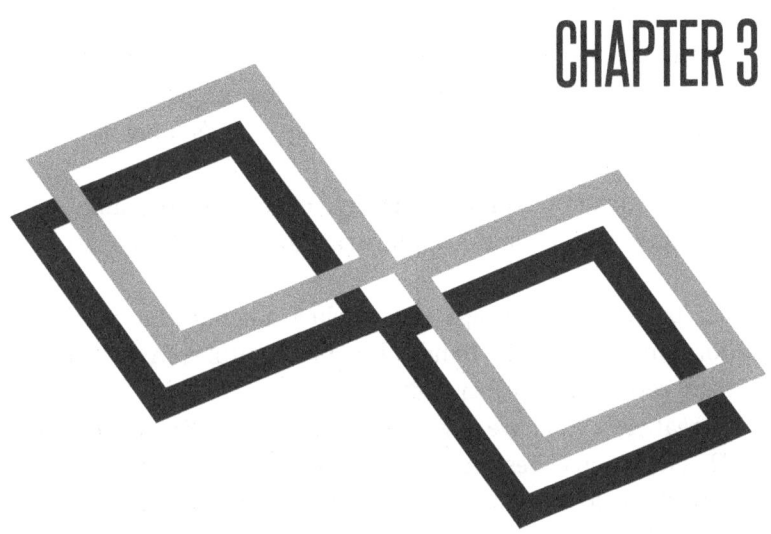

Dwight was captivated by the antics the girls were up to in the back yard. Amy had gotten permission to let her rabbit, one of the breeders, out for some salad and to let her hop around and munch grass. Her rabbit, Mister Flopps had promptly started making circles and had run from the now squealing girls chasing her. Steve took a sip of his beer and waved the smoke from the grill out of his eyes.

"I always wish I had some daughters to dote on," Dwight said after a minute.

"You want mine? No refund or return policy though," Steve joked and winced as Angela playfully kicked him under the table.

"You just want boys to be gross and do boy stuff with you. It's bad enough you turned our oldest into a grease monkey." Her words were in a playful tone, but Steve got out of range and opened the grill to flip the chicken over.

"She's not a grease monkey. She just watched a lot of YouTube. Now, if she'd actually wrenched on a car some...."

Dwight watched the back and forth, smiling. He was in his early sixties and had been a widow for the last ten years. He had often talked about his son Carter who had joined the army two years after his mother died. Steve thought about what it would be like to be a kid Amber's age and lose a parent...that was rough, and then he thought about what it would be like if he lost Angela, and he had to finish raising the girls on his own. Nope, that's a big, fat, nope sandwich there.

"Don't burn mine this time," Dwight called from the table.

"I didn't burn it last time!" Steve said as Mister Flopps ran next to Steve.

He put down the tongs and reached down and scooped the Californian rabbit up and handed him to a breathless Amy who was now staggering towards her dad.

"Great, now you have to go wash your hands," his wife told him.

"I planned on it. Besides, I need a new beer. How about you two?"

Dwight held his up to gauge how much was left and then upended the bottle and held it up. Steve took his empty and the farmer's, and as he was going inside, his wife spoke up.

"How about a glass of red wine?" Angela called.

"Mom!" Amber said. "Last time you drank red wine on a Friday, you and Dad...overslept on a Saturday!"

"Oh, the horror," Angela shot back and watched as Amber turned a furious shade of red, and Amy, who had no clue what it was about, giggled.

"So, has Jeff quit bugging you?" Angela asked Dwight.

"He called the Department of Agriculture on me last month. Did I tell you that?" Dwight asked, turning to talk about his favorite subject.

"No, what did they want?" she asked him.

"I was telling your husband about it last week, but the fools who built the subdivision next to my farm were complaining that I used manure to fertilize my fields between planting. Something about the smell coming in their windows and making them gag."

Angela snorted, glad she wasn't taking a sip of something. "So they are mad that a farm is doing farm stuff while in the middle of a farming operation?"

"Pretty much. Then they wanted to see my pigs, make sure none of them were feral or what not. I showed them and when they were done with the complaint they complimented me on how well the farm was doing, my practices, and left me alone."

"That's it?" she asked, knowing there was more.

"Naw, then your homeowner's association wrote me a letter, 'imploring me' to consider not using something so odoriferous as manure to fertilize. What do they want me to do, use the chemical crap that makes everyone cough and get sick?"

Steve walked out the back door and put a glass of red wine down in front of his wife and then handed the unopened corona to Dwight. He popped the top with an opener and tossed it on the table to the farmer who did the same and he headed back to the grill.

"What have you got him all worked up over now?" Steve asked as he opened the grill to check on things.

"I was telling her about that fool letter from Jeff Arellano," Dwight said after taking a long pull on his beer.

"Did you ever end up responding?" Steve asked him.

"I told him he could take his ideas and shove them so far up his— oh, hi, dear," Dwight said, clamming up as Amber flopped down in the open chair next to him.

"Hi Uncle Dewey. Hey, is there any chance I can try the Jeep out in your rocky field before you turn it for the summer crops?"

"No mudding," Both Taylors said in unison.

Dwight looked at them and grinned and shook his head when he faced Amber.

"Not a good place back there. I only use the big tractor back there, because if you get stuck, it's a long walk out."

"Not if you cut over to the lake stuff," Amber said.

"Amber, it's a no," Steve said, hating to be the bad guy.

She gave her dad a cool look, as if to say she'd see who won out and then shrugged and pulled out her cell phone. It had been something that Steve regretted her getting immediately, but Angela loved having her daughter only a button's touch away.

"That there was a good meal," Dwight said wiping his mouth.

Both girls had headed inside as it had gotten dark and the bugs had come out. They'd fed and watered the rabbits and chickens before Amy got on the Xbox and Amber started her texting and face timing with everyone in Bibb County.

"Thanks," Steve said, "Didn't burn it too much this time?"

"Naw, the chicken sucked. It was your wife's salad and buttered green beans that did the trick," he said, patting his stomach.

"Thank you," Angela said, at the same time as Steve said, "Hey now."

Dwight looked between the two of them and grinned. He'd seen people that were in true love, and he could tell the Taylors had that. He'd had it once himself, before cancer had split his family apart. Since the subdivision had gone in, he'd had few friends and it seemed like every neighbor was hostile to him, until one day a Yankee in a beat-up Ford had come to his yard one day asking if he could buy a couple laying hens or hatching eggs. It had been almost a year and a half ago, and a friendship was born.

"I've got the dishes," Angela said standing up, "Do you want me to run you two out another couple of beers?"

"I'd love one," Steve said, feeling slightly tipsy.

"One more should do it for me," Dwight said, "Then I gotta mosey home."

"Ok, I'll be right back," she said, taking the last of the dishes and empties and heading inside.

"She's something." Dwight said.

"I know. I got lucky she's so blind," Steve told her.

"She'd have to be blind to marry an ugly ass like yourself," Dwight said with a grin.

Angela walked back out and put the beers down, kissing her husband on the head.

"Thank you," Steve told her, and both men waited till the door closed to talk again.

"So I wanted to know if you could help me with the axel on the spreader? I hit a rock last month, and I don't know if I have to cut the bolts out or if I can just weld a fix in place."

"Did you crack the mount?" Steve asked.

"Now if I knew that, I wouldn't need your help. My hip has been...."

"Yeah, for sure! When do you want to do it?"

"I probably won't need it for a couple of weeks. I can spray it out and put it in the sun so it won't smell so bad...."

"I wish you could get away with running over the Arellano's lawn with it fully loaded," Steve said taking a big sip.

"I know, I regret selling the land, but I couldn't use it anymore and needed a new tractor. I didn't know that ten years down the road it was going to be a pain in my ass, present company excluded."

"Of course," Steve said.

"It ain't so bad. I guess if I didn't have something to complain about, I'd be dead. Hell, we all might be sooner than later."

"How so?" Steve asked, noting the abrupt subject change.

"You ever worry about the state of the world, if we might be going down the wrong path?"

The words hit Steve funny, it was the only secret he'd kept from his friend. They had moved across the country, so Steve could go to work at a new IT startup. They had done everything but make a lot of new friends, with the exception of Dwight. He didn't know if the news would put his friend off or make him think any less of him. He'd already contended with his daughter and wife's mild ridicule, and he didn't want to risk a friendship over his preps.

"All the time," Steve admitted.

"This new president...I think he's everything this country needs... and I think he might be too late."

"What do you mean?" Steve asked, a hundred possibilities and conspiracy theories running through his head.

"This whole 'Auditing the Fed' thing. We've been living in a house of cards for a long time now. It's why all these bubbles keep popping. The money is gone and only the richest of the rich have got any decent amount."

"You're worried that we're overleveraged as a country?" Steve probed.

"Not just us, the whole world. It's all funny money. I'm not a financial expert, but I know that when you have three hens, you don't tell the world you have ten and then promise a dozen eggs a day when the most you're going to get is two or three. You keep putting off your obligations and soon your chickens come home to roost."

Steve laughed immediately, understanding what his friend was talking about.

"I worry about that too. If they only went back on some kind of gold standard...."

"I know, but you know what happened to the last president who tried to do that? They killed him," Dwight said.

"Ahh man, now it's getting deep," Steve teased, but he'd already known the conspiracies his buddy believed in.

"I know, I know, I was kidding...mostly. I just worry about what's going to happen when the next bubble bursts. When the money isn't worth nothing. You can't feed your family on gold and silver coins, that's for sure. My parents and grandparents told me about the twenties where all the gold had to be turned back in for dollars, and how when the great depression hit the money wasn't worth nothing. They didn't starve none, but it was hard times."

"What did they do?" Steve asked, interested, because his thoughts ran along those same lines.

"Why, they planted more crops, hatched a few more chickens out and made do. My dad said it was many a year he didn't have no store-bought clothes, but he always had something to eat and something to wear."

"At least y'all live down here where it's warm. Up where I grew up, it got cold and froze in the wintertime."

"It gets cold down here, don't you be fooled none. It's just been warm because of that global warming hoax. Trying to fake us all out."

"Yeah, I hear that," Steve held his bottle out and clinked it against Dwight's.

"But say, if something ever happens like them books...if you ever need to...you and the family are welcome to head over to the farm."

"Thanks," Steve said with a smile. "I really appreciate that."

"Yeah well...things haven't been the same since Lucy died and Carter's been off fighting one war after another. It's good to have friends."

"Yes, it is," Steve said taking a big swallow. *Yes it is*, he repeated in his head, thinking it was time to let his friend in on his secret.

CHAPTER 4

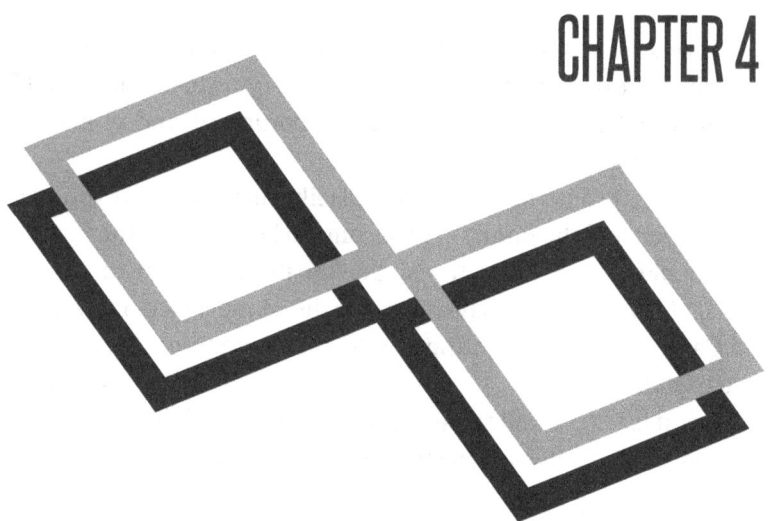

"Hey Steve, can I see you in my office when you get a sec?" Brandi, Steve's boss and owner, asked.

"Sure, now good?"

"If it doesn't throw you for a loop, I know how it is when you're coding."

"Nope," Steve said standing up, "No problemo."

He followed his boss, a woman who was closer to Dwight's age towards her glass-walled office on the North-East corner of the building. He shut the door behind her with a feeling of dread. She'd never asked to speak to him alone except when he was first hired and they were negotiating terms.

"Is...did I do something?" Steve asked.

"No, no," Brandi said motioning for him to sit, "I just wanted to go over some business stuff with you."

Feeling relieved, Steve took the chair across from her desk and sat on the edge, still feeling momentarily nervous.

"Have you been watching the news lately?" Brandi asked.

"No ma'am, I know I should but..."

"The central banks in Eastern Europe have called the losses in Greece...." she winced. "Our contract for the development of the

Omni project is going on hold until we can get paid in a currency that's good."

"Wait, the Euro is collapsing?" Steve asked, feeling thunderstruck.

Brandi picked up a remote and pushed a button. The TV on the far side of the room turned onto FBN and it showed long lines outside of buildings.

"There was Brexit, now there's been a bank run, they've suspended trading in Greece. The EU central banks are working overtime, but it's not like it's the first time it's happened...."

"You're worried about a domino effect," Steve said after a second.

"Most of our development contracts come from overseas. Over sixty percent of our income comes from EU nations—the other in Asia."

"And losing the Omni project is going to hurt bad," Steve said quietly.

Brandi nodded and then stood. Steve went to stand himself but she motioned him to sit back down. She walked over to a small wet bar on the side of the office and poured scotch in two tumblers and brought them back over.

"I don't know if you drink, but I need this," Brandi said taking a long sip.

Steve followed her lead, enjoying the smoky peaty flavor of the scotch. It did little to calm his nerves though.

"I am probably going to have to lay off a third of the developers to start, at least—"

"I hate to interrupt, but what about me?" Steve asked.

"Don't worry," Brandi said. "I have faith that things will turn around. I wanted you to know what was going on and why, so when tomorrow comes, you aren't sitting at your desk worrying yourself into an early grave. You're one of my most senior and trusted programmers. If you go, it means that IT Bytes is closing. Please, just keep it under your hat, and let me break it to them?"

"Yes ma'am," Steve said, taking another long sip.

"If this thing in China blows up though, it'll probably be hard for us to recover."

"You mean the South China Sea? The man-made islands?"

"Yes," she said, tossing back the rest of her scotch. "The president is pushing, and China is pushing back. I get not wanting to have islands with missile bases on them, but if we get into a shooting match with them, their stock markets and currency is going to go the same way as Greece's is."

Steve finished his drink and walked over to the wet bar. He rinsed his glass out and put it in the bottom of the sink there.

"I think we need to hope it doesn't, then."

"Agreed."

⚙

The layoffs happened as she had predicted, and he tried not to picture everyone's expression of horror and terror as one by one they walked in the office confused and came out near tears. Most of the crew at Mrs. Swartz company, IT Bytes, was female by some quirk, and one thing Steve had a hard time dealing with was tears. He threw himself into his work, putting in even more hours to take up some of the slack and was home later than normal. That went on for a good while, until school was almost out.

Without having to pay for Amber's Jeep anymore, Steve started buying more and more preps. He seldom shared with his wife and daughter that he'd started making extra trips to buy food, but they did notice when he started working in the garage. Already half dead from overwork and no sleep, Steve started framing a wall four feet from the back door of the back wall. He did that across 75 percent of the garage and ended it with a door that ended just short of the entryway into the house. He cut a louver into the door and then hung a small sign on it that said 'Mechanical Room' on it and started moving his boxes and crates of stored food.

The room he created was almost four feet wide and twenty feet long. At the far end was the trapdoor that led down to the three short steps to their storm shelter. Along one wall, he moved his preps. His buckets made much of the base, stacked one in front of another, and then plastic milk crates that held a lot of food in cut down five gallon Mylar bags. Each was labeled and then put out of sight. Angela was upset at first, not having as much room to park her car, but he started parking his truck behind Amber's Jeep to give her more room. It made her happy, but she knew some of what was going on.

The price of milk was the first indication that things were slipping. It had gone up by almost a third in the time between spring and summer. The real shock was when their mortgage was sold to another lender who kept asking the Taylors to refinance. It was Angela who'd found that the interest rates were creeping up. That's when she decided to allow Amy to go for a long ride with her sister in the Jeep and opened a bottle of red wine and called her husband who was half dead from exhaustion to the table.

"Honey," she said, pouring him a glass.

"Hey beautiful," Steve said and took the glass, taking a sip.

She started using her hands to work on his neck, kneading the knotted muscles until he let out a groan of pleasure.

"You're worried about work?"

"A little," he admitted. "But more, like, the creeping inflation. Losing the Omni project hurt, but it's little things that keep popping up here that are getting to me too. The uncertainty, living so close to the city. The riots...like, the whole country going insane after this election cycle."

"Why does that worry you?" she asked, already knowing the answer but wanting him to speak it out.

"Because if anything happens, we're too close to people. There's too many, and I feel like a fish out of water here. There's not enough land to grow our own food and—"

"Don't forget about Dwight," Angela said softly. "He said if things ever got bad we were welcome to head over there. He's almost a prepper himself."

Steve turned to look at his wife, who paused, "What?"

"Well, he's got a kitchen garden, grows his own food, does a ton of canning, and can practically live off the grid. That's like being a prepper, isn't it?"

"Yeah, but he's on a scale that's not even the same as what I am doing," Steve admitted. "He knows how to live when things go to hell. None of us do," he told her, his hands going up in the air.

She started on his shoulders next.

"Ok, so what's the worst that can happen? Why is today a lot worse than the others?"

"Have you been watching the news?" Steve asked her softly.

She stopped and turned on the TV in the kitchen and handed him the remote. He changed the channel and after flipping past one news station, he found another. There was what looked like a burning ship sinking, lifeboats surrounding it.

"What happened?" she asked.

"Iranian Revolutionary Guard Navy. They sent one of their fast attack crafts to play chicken with one of our boats."

"They ran into each other?" Angela asked, confused.

"No, the president and Sec-Def told Iran they weren't playing chicken anymore. Not after they ignored a boat they thought was one of theirs and had a suicide bomber on it. So...in protecting themselves, they shot the bottom out of the boat."

"That's not our guys and girls?" Angela asked, already reading the bylines on the bottom.

"No, it's not. The ship fell back to be reinforced by the carrier group. The Iranians are pissed, and it's a diplomatic mess."

"Why is that...what do you think is going to happen?" Angela said, sitting down and topping off her wineglass.

Steve took a swallow, not even tasting the wine, "At one point, our economy was three trillion dollars ahead of the game after the election. You remember that?"

"Yeah, new jobs, tax cuts, a fix to Obamacare."

"Exactly. It's slumping now. I'm just worried...there's going to be another round of layoffs at work."

"I thought you said Mrs. Swartz promised you that you'd be safe?"

"I am," Steve told her. "I just need to..."

"I know what you need," she said and poured more wine into his glass.

"Wine?"

"Drink up," Angela told him.

He did, and then she took him by the hand and led him towards the bedroom.

✦

"Why do we call this 'Lead Therapy?'" Amy asked, as the four of the Taylors had their own bench at the outdoor range set up at Dwight's property.

"Because it sends lead down range," Amber answered, before her mom could, "and it's relaxing."

Angela sent off three quick shots downrange with the Bushmaster AR-15 Steve had gotten her a few years back. She was a little cross at him when it wasn't jewelry, but he'd never taken it out himself to shoot it like she thought. She wasn't anti-gun when they got married, but didn't have the same background as her country minded husband. Once she started shooting the 5.56/.223, she soon became as much of a gun nut as her husband.

She knew he thought she had no clue about everything in the safe in the storm shelter, but she knew as much about what they had in preps as he did. As his partner, she made it her business. He would be surprised at how much she approved of his recent purchases.

33

There were now matching carbines so one for every member of the family and several matching Colt 1911s. That had been last year, this year though, he'd been stocking up on magazines and ammunition by the case. That had made her angry at first till she found one of the receipts in the safe.

She had figured out the usual buy a box at Walmart versus buying an entire case of ammunition. It was a .10 per round difference and considering how much they both loved shooting, he'd actually spent the same amount on ammunition but gotten a lot more. Still, she knew how much stress he'd been under and a Saturday at the range on the farm was good therapy. Dwight loved shooting as much as they did, though he used an old deer gun that she was sure was going to break her shoulder if she ever shot it.

For his part, Steve felt a little tension lift off of his shoulders. His wife's lovemaking had been passionate, and Amber had kept Amy out until her curfew at first McDonalds and then the park she loved to ride her bike at. They had both known their father was becoming more and more nervous, but they didn't understand why. Amber was old enough to know how much fun her dad had punching holes in the targets, and she was getting to be a good shot too.

"Can I try yours?" Amy asked Dwight as he was working the bolt on his rifle.

Everyone paused and Angela put her gun on safe to see what he would say. Steve shot his daughter a smile and mussed her hair up while Amber looked on in amusement.

"If your dad thinks it's ok," he said, after a moment, "but you're going to have to sit on my leg so you're tall enough."

She didn't mind. She was still enough of a little girl to not feel self-conscious about that. Dwight leaned back and Amy crawled on his left leg and laid back into his chest. She put the rifle against her shoulder and leaned in to make good contact like her dad showed her. She didn't put her hand anywhere near the trigger though.

"You know how to shoot this one?" Dwight asked.

She shook her head no. He showed her how to work the bolt, and when the cartridge popped out, he caught it and put it back in the gun's internal magazine. Then he showed her the safety near the rear of the gun. Then when it was time, he pulled her ear protection back a little bit and whispered into her ear. When he was done, he put it back and leaned into her as she leaned into the stock of the rifle. Steve saw that she had the gun as braced as she could and held his breath as his daughter reached out, looked through the iron sights, and slowly squeezed the trigger.

The metal target panged, as a hit rang out and Amy leaned back after she put the gun on safe. Dwight leaned back as well, and she slid off. She rolled her arm in a circle and then rubbed her shoulder a bit.

"That one's stronger than daddy's. I don't know if I like that one," she told her stunned family.

Dwight started laughing at their expressions and pretty soon Amy joined in, pointing at her sister that looked like a guppy trying to get air from the top of a tank.

"Didn't that hurt?" Angela asked.

"A little bit," Amy said, still smiling and pulled the front of her shirt down a little bit.

The recoil in the butt had left a red mark, but the slender girl was smiling, not wincing in pain.

"I thought for sure she'd—"

"Naw," Dwight said, interrupting Angela. "See, she had no expectations going in on how bad it was going to hurt, so when she shot, it didn't hurt."

"What did you whisper to her?" Steve asked him.

"That she needed to brace the gun good, and that I was going to brace her good, so it didn't launch her to the moon and back."

"I told him I'm not an astronaut, so no flying lessons for me," she said with a grin, "but I think I like yours better. I can shoot it a lot and get a little sore. This one is like ten shots of yours, daddy!"

Steve grinned. "It really is. Mine isn't really for hunting the way Mr. Abbott's gun is."

"Then why do you have it?" she asked in the innocent way little kids have about them.

"Well, for lead therapy," Amber finished off before her parents could speak, and dropped a wink at her dad.

Steve saw it and grinned. Since the Jeep had been purchased, the mostly snotty and bratty teenage girl attitude had been somewhat repressed, and a young mature woman replaced her for at least thirty minutes a day. At least, she was trying, Steve mused. He knew why too, summertime was coming, and the guy friend was trying to talk his way into taking her on a day trip to Six Flags.

"As long as lead therapy makes Daddy smile, I'm all for it. It's kinda fun! Dad, can we shoot your pistols?"

Steve's grin faltered, and Angela opened her eyes wide as the cat was let out of the bag.

"How did you know I got some pistols baby?" he asked her after a second.

"Mommy and I went shooting over here a couple of weeks ago. She said those were yours and until you taught us, not to touch them. She wanted to use her gun, and hers was in the safe, not in the case under the bed like yours."

"Oh, I see...." He looked at his wife.

She just smiled back and pulled him close and kissed him.

"I would like to learn how to shoot them too," Angela said.

"You knew? Wait, you...."

"I don't mind," Angela said, "I was scared to talk to you about it, but the little one outed the secret."

"How is it a secret, since I'm the only one who doesn't know about them?" Amber asked.

"I guess it isn't. The truth is, I know how to shoot them but I'm not as good with them as I am with a rifle like this," he said patting his AR. "Maybe we can all take a class on them, then? Together?"

They agreed, and Dwight shot him an amused look before making a finger gun and shooting it at Steve. Steve gave him a wide-eyed nod. Bullet dodged. Message received.

CHAPTER 5

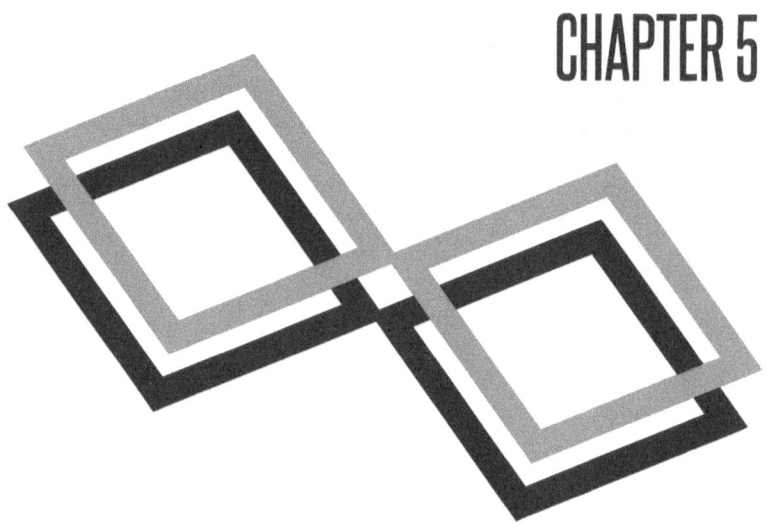

Another month passed, and not much changed except the economy worsened. Iran sent more vessels to harass US warships, and again they responded by sinking a fast attack ship that had radioed that they were coming to blow up the "Great Satan." A carrier battle group near the South China sea was repeatedly getting buzzed by the Chinese People's Liberation Army helos and fighter jets. Tensions were high, especially with the new president refusing to acknowledge the China One policy that had been in place for a long time.

To combat a new trade war, the USA had started trading more with Taiwan, forgoing Chinese imports. That had only notched up the already heightened tensions and made the already nervous Asian stock markets tremble. In Europe, it looked as if Italy and Brussels, with Germany to follow, were headed down the same path as Greece. The times scared Steve more than he liked to admit. He hadn't slowed down his preps, but hadn't increased them either. He was getting near the one year mark of food and was loading groceries from Sam's Club on his way home from work when he got an urgent text from his boss, Brandi Swartz.

He finished his loading and turned around and headed back towards IT Bytes, careful not to break any speed laws. It was almost an hour after closing and the lights were out, but one car remained in the small renovated building that had once been a mini-mall. Steve locked up his truck and headed to the front door, already pulling his keys and keycard out of his pocket. He was startled when a figure stepped out of the darkness and turned the bolt, unlocking the door. Brandi pushed it open and held the door.

"I wasn't sure if you were going to come, you didn't answer back," she said ,and closed it behind him, locking it.

"I'm sorry, I was right around the corner. I must have gotten the message while I was shopping. I rushed over without answering."

"I need you to see something," Brandi said and motioned for him to follow.

Steve did, his curiosity piqued, but he still had a bad feeling. It changed for the better when Brandi bypassed the office and directed him towards the employee lounge. He followed her on inside where the news was on, but the TV was muted. Steve looked on at shock as a US battleship smoked, a huge hole smoking on the top deck as US military choppers covered the vessel from up high. In the background, lifeboats were in the water, but as Steve gave it a closer look, he didn't recognize the emblem on the uniforms.

"It's started?" Steve asked her.

"I think so. Apparently, the Chinese thought it would be funny to buzz the ship and then turned on their radar. The news is saying that the anti-aircraft guns tore it to shreds. They've been trying to get near the ship but—"

"How did our ship get a hole in it?" Steve interrupted.

"One of their pilots retaliated, and when a smaller PLO Navy vessel showed up, they were fired upon for not responding. We had just been attacked."

"You're worried about what we talked about?" Steve asked.

"That isn't actually why I called you in; this just happened while I was waiting to hear back from you. We've had a client call who had a data breach. They are claiming it came in from our software. I need you to run down the scenario and look at the code."

Steve's mind was going a hundred miles an hour, and he mentally sighed. With the cutbacks, they had to make do with the teams they had. Was it possible that shoddy programming had left a system vulnerable? It might take more than a couple of hours to fix; it might take, with current staffing levels, weeks or months to sort it out.

"Ok, let me get the project notes, and I'll get started."

"I've already pulled them, and I'll be working alongside you on this one," Brandi said.

"I thought you always teased that the last thing you programmed was in Fortran, about a thousand years ago or something."

Brandi let out a surprised bark of a laugh and then gave Steve a scathing look. She only held it for a second before laughing out loud again.

"You're not that far off of the truth, but I stay current. Besides, I think you did more than your fair share of Fortran back in the day."

"Guilty as charged," Steve grinned, glad his boss took the joke in the context it was.

"You want to do this at your desk, or you want the big plasma in the conference room?"

Steve thought about it. "I'd rather have my setup at the desk, especially if time is of the essence."

"In this case," Brandi said, "it most definitely is. Losing government contracts, and then if word of a breach gets around...all we have is our name at this point. It's pretty dire. I feel horrible for putting this on you, but it's one of the only things I can think of, and I want to limit exposure of the breach to as few as possible. There's a lot of hurt feelings out there from the layoffs."

"I'll do my best," Steve told her quietly, then hesitated before asking, "You do know that we might not find this right away? It might not be a quick fix?"

"That's why I'm staying to help. I might not write code anymore, but I haven't forgotten how to, and I used to proof every program on the quiet before we released it."

Steve whistled. He knew she was sharp, she had once been a crack programmer...but he had no idea she was doing that. Some of their security programs and virtual firewalls had millions of lines of code. If she could read and understand that as well as he could....

"Let's get started, but first, I have to call my wife."

Angela had been frustrated but understanding of the need for him to work late. He'd had to do it often, but this was a case where he might not come home. He didn't tell her what the specific problem was, but invited her and the girls to meet him for a late dinner of pizza. In the background the girls both cheered, but Steve could tell that his long hours were starting to wear on her, even with Amber upping her game and trying to help more.

Steve was working his way through the revision history, to get a feel for when a bug might have been introduced into the program. He'd personally coded the core of this one, so he knew it well, but he hadn't worked on any of the third-party functionality and access, as that had been part of Parker Tsarnaev's group to make that happen.

Right away, he found three entries on the day of the first round of layoffs. He was talking to himself and instead of Brandi working next to him, she looked over his shoulder, her eyes going wide.

"Put that on the plasma, my old eyes...."

Steve did and she walked about ten feet away to stand in front of the twenty-foot long projected image as Steve continued to dig into the revisions. It wasn't the big plasma she was talking about, the resolution wasn't as good, but they had often used it as a training tool or for presentations...but what he found...it was the second to the last entry that confirmed it.

"The doorbell...." Brandi said, hearing the front door's buzzer.

Steve was looking in shock at what had been done, he'd hardly heard Brandi or the buzzer. One of the project leads had inserted a new line of code, essentially putting in a back door through one of the third-party applications. He even recognized the coding signature, like they weren't even trying to hide what they were doing. Probably thought IT Bytes wouldn't be around when the breach....

Steve hurried and started searching the darknet and quickly found the programmer had a profile set up on a 4chan style message board and had published the breach. He started screenshotting everything and then saw something else that made him bite his lip. The hacker had gotten a job with the same company that was being hacked. More screenshots. He could roll the revision back now to stop the plug but....

Steve ignored the smell of pizza and leaned over his keyboard and started typing lines of code furiously. He heard talking behind him and felt a hand on his shoulder, but he didn't stop. To fix things, he left the breach open and began to—

"Steve, that's a Trojan horse!" Brandi said in surprise.

"Yeah?" he asked her. "Anybody who logs in there is going to get their data wiped, but not after they send us a snapshot. This isn't simple hacking, this is corporate espionage. The only way I can think of to quickly nullify any data they got from us, is to make sure it's garbage and unusable."

He turned to see Brandi chewing on her lip as his three women stood behind her with plates of pizza in hand.

"Do it, Dad. Get the bad guys," Amy said.

"Kick some ass...I mean...butt," Amber said a second later and covered her mouth after the slip.

Angela smacked her daughter on the back of the head, but she was smiling at Steve.

"Go ahead, finish it. Make sure you record every step and make sure we have documentation to have this prosecuted."

"Already ahead of you," Steve said and sat down.

An hour later it was done. He stood up and stretched, his shoulders tight, but they popped as he twisted and turned. His back and neck were sore too.

"I can heat some pizza up for you," Angela said, walking up and putting her arms around his waist,

"That would be great," Steve told her, kissing the top of her head. "Sorry about that, I haven't had to do that in a long, long time."

"That was the craziest, most brilliant, fly by the seat of the pants programming. Where did you learn that, and how did you know where to look?" Brandi asked.

"I try to keep up to date myself. Often times, it's the script kiddies and the coders on the darknet that come up with the best breaches...so I study their methods and make sure I can defeat anything they throw at us. In this case, a woman named Calinda Braxton, a programmer under Parker is the one who did this. I don't understand why she would go to work for them and then publish the hack, but I figure that's something for the FBI to figure out, and who paid her thirty-thousand dollars to do it."

"How did you find that out?" Amber asked, bringing a warm slice from the lounge's microwave to him.

"Remember when he said he studied their methods?" Brandi asked.

"Keyboard cowboy, huh?" Amber said.

"Your dad is pretty much the badass of keyboard cowboys," Brandi answered, and then covered her mouth at the slip as well.

Amy couldn't take it, she busted up in giggles. She could read fine, and they all watched the code being generated on the big screen, but she understood the least of what was going on—just that Brandi and her mom had been talking nonstop for hours, and they had let her play one of the Xbox's in the employee lounge with unlimited supplies of pizza and pop. Even Amber joined her for a while, though she stood out there next to her mother a bit.

Steve grinned at the compliment and then looked at his phone as he was taking a big bite of a slice of pizza. 8:50 p.m. Ten minutes away from Amy's bedtime.

"I'm going to scarf this down, but are we good for tonight?"

"Yes," Brandi said, and walked over to Steve and gave him a big hug.

Steve held the pizza away so he wouldn't get it in his boss's hair and after shooting Angela a look. She winked at him, so he hugged her back with his left hand. When she pulled away, a tear had started falling down one cheek.

"Hey, what's wrong?" Steve asked, putting the pizza down.

"It's...I'm sorry, I don't want to worry you. This data breach and everything else has me emotional. You go get some rest. I'm going to head home and have a bottle of wine, if I can stay awake that long."

"It'll be ok," Amy said, "we don't worry much because my daddy tries to be ready for anything."

"Anything?" Amber asked.

"Anything and everything. You know how he is. You shouldn't worry, Mrs. Swartz. My daddy will fix it, if it's broke."

"Thank you," she said to Amy. "And thank you again. I might have seemed calm on the outside, but I was slowly coming apart on the inside," she finished, looking at Steve who had picked back up the plate and was doing his best to devour it. "And take some pizza, I already ate my fill."

"Pizza!" Amber said with a fist pump, and both girls went running for the employee lounge, followed by Brandi.

"You did pretty good. I don't know what it was, but it was good enough that your boss kept telling me that she didn't know what she'd do without you. You shouldn't worry about losing your job so much. You'll worry yourself into an early grave."

Steve finished his piece off, wiped his mouth with a napkin, and pulled his wife close for a hug. He was about to speak when both girls came running out: Amber holding two pizza boxes and Amy with a two liter of pop.

"When did we go to war with China?" Amber asked.

"Oh, crap," Steve muttered.

"What's going on?" Angela asked.

"The Navy is fighting the Chinese, they said it on TV, Mrs. Swartz is watching it."

"What do you—"

"Let's just go home," Steve told his wife.

"Ok...."

"Steve," Brandi said, walking out of the lounge, "feel free to have tomorrow off with pay. I've been running you ragged lately."

"Uh, thanks!" Steve said after a moment's hesitation as he fought down the guilt.

He knew how much more strain that would put on the others, but after a minute he realized that it really didn't matter. It was a job, and it would be here when he came back on Monday. He hoped.

"Hey...that means a three-day weekend!" Amy said "Time for more lead therapy!" she said, and held up the two liter.

Steve took it and pulled her in close for a right armed hug, and gave her head a squeeze till she squealed before letting her go.

"Just let the FBI, or police, or whoever know how to get a hold of me, or I'll talk to them on Monday."

"Sounds good. You girls take good care of your dad. He looks dead on his feet," Brandi called.

They waved and headed to the front door.

"Daddy, I'll drive your truck," Amber said holding her hand out.

"Hold on," he said and locked the door, not wanting to leave it open while Brandi was finishing things off, and then handed them to her. "You drive; I'll sleep."

CHAPTER 6

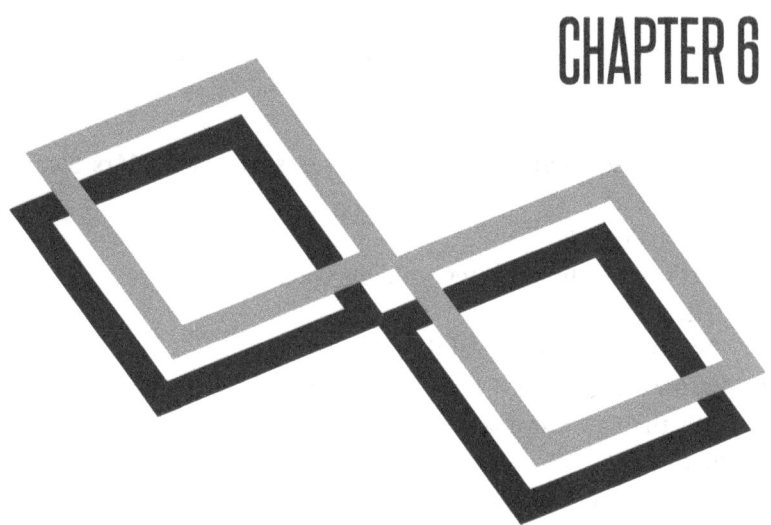

That Friday, Steve headed out to check the mail and saw the back of Doug, walking quickly away. He hurried to his mailbox and found his mail and a fat envelope with the HOA's letterhead. With a sigh, he walked back to the house and dumped everything on the kitchen table and went outside to the back patio and opened it. It was a summons to the HOA meeting later on that afternoon, signed by the president, Jeff Arellano, as well as Richard Hunter, Thomas Durazo, Matthew Fitzpatrick, and Cheryl Jacoby all from the council.

Other names like Clark and Sarah Wilson signed on as well as Doug and Linda Morris, John Hinton and Vanessa Baker. At first, he was furious but after sitting and thinking, he realized that it was the leadership council and maybe three or four households who had requested him to be at the meeting. He looked at his phone and saw he had a couple of hours before the meeting. The reasons listed? Noise ordinance violations. Nothing else.

He decided to walk over and see if he could find Dwight for an hour. He'd wandered around the house aimlessly and then settled down at the computer desk to go over some lists until Angela's cleaning fanaticism ran him to distraction. He thought about napping in the storm shelter, but the kids would have been home soon, and now he had something else to worry about.

One thing he had been doing, is watching the developments. The video coverage was spotty, but every talking head in the mainstream media was waiting to hear from the President and what was going to be done. Overnight, a submarine was sunk by a US sub and the Chinese were howling that we were provoking things worse than ever and force would be met with force. The US responded by sending all heavy tonnage in their direction, at least that's what they said on the TV.

"You headed to Dwight's?" Angela called out the back door.

"Yeah, you want to come?" he shouted back.

"No, how about you invite him over for dinner later on?"

"Sounds good," he called back and let himself out the gate.

As he was turning to latch it, he saw the curtains next door move, as if somebody had been watching from out the window. He doubted it was Billy, probably the nosier of the Wilsons, Sarah. He took off down the pathway along the back of the fences so he didn't step in the middle of a field that had corn growing in it. He didn't want to have to change again by getting covered in corn silk, if he was going to go to the meeting tonight at the neighborhood clubhouse.

It took him ten minutes to walk around to where another pathway made by truck and tractor led towards the barn. The sun was hot and his clothing started sticking to him, making him rethink whether or not he'd have to change anyways. He didn't see Dwight out working from a distance and the barn was closed up. He started towards the house. A couple of minutes later, he was knocking at the door.

Steve heard the heavy steps from Dwight long before he saw him. Dwight opened the door and motioned for him to come in. He was holding a sheaf of papers in his hand and headed back towards the kitchen table and plopped down. Steve closed the door and kicked his shoes off and joined his friend, loving the blast of air conditioning. He pulled his own papers out and recognized a torn open envelope on the table.

"You got a summons too?" Steve asked after a minute.

"Yeah, don't know what to make of it heads nor tails. It ain't signed by a lawyer, nor notarized. One of the deputies dropped it off, said they were paid to."

"Huh," Steve said and opened his up and looked at the first page again. "Mine doesn't either."

"What do you make of that?"

"It's a bunch of busybodies who are demanding we show up, and they have no legal backing for asking us. I'm half tempted to show up and tell them to blow it out their asses. What did they ask you in for, noise violations?"

"Noise, smell, improper fencing, and something about having farm animals makes people want to come over to the farm to pet them and it could be a hazard or some such."

"The Department of Ag was out here a couple of months ago, I didn't think they'd have any leg to stand on?"

"The developer has wanted more land. I refused to sell it. I think this is some sort of horseshit for them to try to push the zoning board to their way of thinking...hey, you out of work early?"

"I worked late last night so the boss gave me the day off," Steve said. "And actually...I would still be at work when they requested me to show up for the meeting...." His words trailed off thoughtfully.

"Almost like they wanted to create a paper trail but didn't want you to dance at their party?"

"You thinking what I'm thinking?" Steve asked with a grin.

"You got your fancy boots on, or the mud stomping boots?"

"Mud stomping," Steve pointed to the door where they were lined up next to Dwight's.

"Oh yeah, you walked over. How's about we take a walk through the pig waller and mosey our way up there, nice and slow like."

"We'll get hot and sweaty," Steve said after a second.

"And stinky."

◼◯◼

"Now, I'd like to go on record that—"

Both Dwight and Steve walked into the clubhouse together, a full half hour before the summons. They were lucky, because the meeting and agenda had been read already, and they were about to start the discussion. The small meeting room was half filled with about two dozen people, many of which Steve recognized. The HOA council was seated behind two folding tables that separated them from the rest of the folding chairs that had been set up, almost as if a panel of judges were addressing a crowd or a jury.

"I..." Jeff Arellano, the president of the HOA stuttered. "The meeting is already in progress, you'll both have to come back."

"Well, see here, I got me an official notice, signed by yourself and many of the folks in this room," Dwight said. holding up his sheaf of papers.

"And according to the HOA bylaws," Steve said, "you need to hold the meetings at the stated time or give notification of at least twenty-four hours that the time has been moved."

"I'm sure we gave twenty-four hours' notice," Jeff said out loud.

There was muttering in the room and Dwight looked at Steve as if to ask what he wanted to say.

"I'll go first I guess...I know I didn't get twenty-four hours' notice, because Doug there dropped this in my mailbox. It had no postage on it, so no timestamp."

"So it's just your say so," Doug said, "because I'm not sure what you're implying here. Were there any witnesses?"

"Well, you weasel dicked, poor excuse for a dried-up dog turd, you put this in my mailbox. I saw you, I had the day off...since you aren't us, or a mailman, I'm sure the post office would love to hear about you tampering with—"

"We'll not delve into name calling in this meeting, or you'll be asked to leave," Jeff said, banging a gavel, of all things, on the plastic Walmart folding table.

"And you fools had me served by a sheriff's deputy, and I happened to know this one. Said the same no-account gave him the fifty dollar fee and papers not an hour before I got it."

"Excuse me, but what's that smell?" Lucy Javier, a small mousy woman near Steve's age asked.

Both men looked down at their boots and saw the caked-on mud and pig excrement and then back up to the crowd and shrugged. Then they walked over and casually took a seat on either side of the woman. She sat there a minute and then stood up and moved to the other side of the room.

"So, would y'all like to fill us in on what we've missed so far, since we can establish that the governing body of the HOA has been deliberately trying to obfuscate the truth in this matter?" Dwight asked loudly.

Several people winced and then looked up at the plastic tables and to the President, Jeff. He looked back and forth and cleared his throat.

"Doug Morris isn't a part of our governing body. He probably got the notices out too late and the council apologizes for any mishaps that might have caused. Nevertheless, you are here now. There should be agendas on every seat. I can read it, if you want, or you can go through it yourself while we wait on you two to get caught up."

"I'll read it first," Steve said and grabbed two of them sitting on an empty seat to his right.

He handed one to Dwight and they started reading. Dwight started reading aloud after a couple moments, embellishing the written word.

"...and these lily-livered, piss ant liberal crybabies moved in next to a farm..." The crowd murmured. "And then complained that farm smells don't agree with them. And noise, well shit, I guess I done make too much noise, do I?" Dwight said turning to Steve and pushing him on the shoulder.

Steve knew he was hamming it up and playing a stereotype. It was all he could do not to bray donkey laughter at them as everyone sat in silence and listened to a crusty old man's commentary, held captive by their own tomfoolery by trying to pull a fast one on both of them. Dwight knew it well, and he made them squirm.

"...and if the roosters ain't too loud, it's all the shooting and tooting coming from my property. What'd they get you on?" He asked Steve aloud, even though it was written on the page.

"An unmuffled Jeep, considered an Off-Road Vehicle, which is against the HOA's acceptable vehicles to have parked on the property, and discharging a firearm which is against HOA ordinances."

"You're shooting guns off in your itty bitty little back yard?"

"Nope," Steve said turning the empty chair in front of him around and kicked his feet up on them. Dark, smelly, squishy stuff stuck to the chair by transference from the boots.

It was like a horror show they couldn't turn away from. Some folks got up and moved even further when the smell hit them and soon the two men had the back-left portion of the small room to themselves, though there was really no way to get away from the stink of pig shit.

"Are you quite ready?" Jeff asked after both men were silent for a good solid minute while they smirked at the busybodies.

"Sure, but I want to let ya know something," Dwight said, "Nothing here is legally binding to me. You can hem and haw, piss and moan...just know that there is nothing you can do or force me to do. I'm not part of your homeowner's covenant, nor am I contractually obligated to recognize any of this. Hell, I didn't have to show up. You can't legally compel me."

Steve spoke up. "As far as me having an unmuffled ORV, I don't. It's got a state inspection sticker, which it wouldn't be able to if it didn't have a muffler," Steve said, "and I don't shoot in my little backyard; that'd be really stupid. I go over to Dwight Abbott's," he said, hooking a thumb in his friend's direction, "where he's got enough land and setback to do it. You folks have been fighting me since I put in a gate on my fence and a whole slew of other stuff that makes no sense to fight me on. You were wrong then; you're wrong now. I think you sent out this phony summons and then changed the time when you knew he'd usually be at the auctions and I'd be at work to start a paper trail."

"That's why I called up the zoning commission while Steve and I were discussing things in the pig waller," Dwight picked up without missing a beat. "Seems that Jeff and several others have petitioned along with the developer that they want my land rezoned."

There were murmurs in the group, but they weren't all sympathetic. Some were angry that the two even had the gall to show up, let alone use their own words and rules against them.

Matthew Fitzpatrick, a man Steve thought was the HOA treasurer, leaned forward. "It was my understanding from Doug Morris and Clark and Sarah Wilson that your daughter's Jeep was out of compliance and both had said they spoke with you about how loud it was."

Steve shot them a look and none of them looked up at the two men, their focus remained on the back of the heads in front of them.

"No, that's not true and neither is the claim I shoot in my backyard. I can easily prove both claims beyond a reasonable doubt." Steve said. "Now, I have a question for the group here, because y'all seem to think my time is so useless that you are free to waste it with this clown court you are trying to run...What do you all think I do for a living?"

There were murmurs, and Sarah Wilson raised her hand. Jeff Arellano shrugged and pointed to her.

"It's something to do with farming, isn't it? The old truck and jeep?"

"Nope. Your husband is what, an attorney?" Steve shot back, knowing she was a housewife.

"CPA," she said softly.

"Ah, ok. Who else has a guess?" Steve asked.

Doug stood and turned to face them. "I really don't care what you do. You have brought about clutter and unsightliness to our neighborhood. It's not fair that you, and you alone, are bringing down our property values."

Several people murmured agreement.

"Anybody else?" Steve asked.

"You're a handyman, it's why you come and go with your truck always loaded full of supplies." A man with the name tag Richard Hunter said from behind the plastic tables.

"Ehhhhhh, wrong again." Steve said. "I'm a senior systems analyst and head programmer for a network security firm. I probably have more invested in my house than any two of you folks combined if we're talking about money. Something that Doctor Toodles there seems to be concerned about, judging about his property value concerns. See, I make more than he does. Did you know his salary is public record?"

Steve knew he was poking him deliberately, riling the man up. Part of him wondered if he could make him so angry that he'd throw a punch. He almost hoped he did, but he knew that wasn't a very Christian thought. His words though, they almost pushed the professor over the edge. He stood up again, his finger pointing and his hand shaking when Jeff slammed the gavel down on the table several times to quell the growing volume of everyone in the room.

"So, I, unlike you all, value my time. I spend it on things that are meaningful to me. Fighting you guys over things that aren't against the HOA conventions is just a waste of it. I already have my lawyers kicking your ass in court about a gate on my fence—that I own...I'm going to have them start issuing the HOA bills for every hour wasted. I know my boss bills us out at about 300 dollars an hour when she does quotes, so I'll cut you a deal. I'll only charge 200 dollars an hour next time you guys want to start a war. The governing body can figure out how to split the bill up to all the complainers next time. Sound good?"

There was a heavy silence and nobody was looking at the two of them.

"And I might be a humble ol' farmer, but they say my property is worth a couple million nowadays. I'd rather leverage it out and pay for lawyers than let any of you two-bit hucksters try to scare me into selling it."

"Two-bit hucksters, you cantankerous old—"

"Shut up, Doug," Steve said. "Don't let your mouth write checks your ass can't cash."

"What does that mean?" Sarah Wilson asked her husband loudly.

"It means if he doesn't shut up, this Yankee is gonna drag him outside and beat his ass," Clark said.

"That's barbaric," a woman in a row over said.

"Is this really your intention?" a man asked who lived one street up from Steve.

The gavel banged again, and everyone shut up.

"No," Steve said after a minute. "But I have stayed within the HOA guidelines every step of the way. I don't care if you all don't like it. I follow the rules. You can't just change the rules on a whim to force somebody's hand."

"Would you like to bet?" Jeff asked coldly.

"Love to see it enforced El Jefe," Dwight said and watched the smug smile vanish. "I'm sure I'm not the only one with access to lawyers...and now we have a whole room full of witnesses to subpoena should this go to court, so like any good public record, I'm taking a copy of the sign-in sheet before we leave."

There were several people who had enough at that point and got up and started moving to the door.

"Think we poked the bear enough?" Steve asked Dwight quietly as people started filing out, leaving the council looking shell shocked behind their cheap white tables.

"Yeah, we do anymore it'd be like beating a dead horse. Let's get."

"Do you think we went overboard?" Steve asked.

"Not really, but maybe a little. We came here to prove a point," Dwight said and started for the door.

After a moment, Steve followed. Everyone who was left in the room sat in a shocked and stunned silence as the men made sure to wipe their feet on the rug near the door before heading outside. Dwight, true to his word, took out his cell phone and snapped a picture of the sign in sheet just outside the meeting room doorway and then turned and threw a jaunty wave to Jeff before both of them went outside.

"I thought you said this would work?" Doug asked Jeff from across the table, one of the last holdouts in the room other than the governing body.

"This was deliberate?" Matthew asked Jeff, turning to the president.

"The meeting, the complaints? No, they are all true."

"No, I mean the late notices, the zoning, changing the rules on a whim?" he asked.

"I did what I had to," Doug said loudly from across the table.

"By making us," Matthew said pointing at the five behind the table, "look like a bunch of idiots?"

"You don't need my help for that," Doug snapped back.

"Watch your tone with me, Professor," Matthew said standing up.

Jeff was about to talk but he realized two things at that point. Matthew was about twenty years younger than he was, and he was a lot more imposing than the usually quiet man who sat in their weekly council meetings.

"Or what?" Doug asked.

"Or you'll find out that I'm not as polite as the Yankee. I'll knock your teeth out of your fool head and then wipe the floor with you while your wife wonders if you'll be wearing dentures the next time you kiss her."

"You can't say that to me; you threatened me. He threatened me, Jeff!" Doug pointed, but his wife was tugging on his arm, having had enough for the day.

"Matthew, this isn't helping, we don't threaten—"

"And you. You aren't a part of any government, law enforcement, or even a lawyer. You're the president of the HOA. You're a retired postman...and I notice none of you gave a reasonable explanation to Mister Taylor or refuted their allegations. To me that sounds like some sort of scam or collusion."

"This meeting is closed," Jeff said standing up.

"Is it true? Are you working with the developers to try to force Abbott to sell his land?"

"I don't answer to you, and you should watch your tone with me, son."

Matthew bristled at that and Jeff took a step back, away from him.

"Oh, yeah?"

"Let's go," Doug's wife said, dragging on his arm until he finally started moving.

"You're off the council. We don't need your help anymore," Jeff told him.

"Well, I hate to break the news to you, but you can't throw me out. I'm elected same as all of you," he said pointing to the other four. "And I think you," he said, pointing the finger at Jeff, "need to think about that. This is our community and it seems like you think you run it. I think I'll stick around a while, just to make sure things are fair."

"I'm the president of the HOA," Jeff said, trying to keep an even voice.

"For now," Matthew said, "but if what those two said was true, and you're working with the developers on some sort of scam, you'll be lucky if you don't find yourself out of an unpaid title and in jail. I'm going to give my brother a call and see what he thinks."

"Who's your brother?" Another council member asked.

"Bibb County's prosecuting attorney," Matthew said and started walking towards the door.

He paused, looking at the soiled rug and stepped around it.

"You know," he said pulling his best Colombo impression, "I don't know what stinks in here worse. The fact you didn't refute the shenanigans when it was exposed, threatened to change the rules to suit your agenda, or this rug here. As far as I can tell, 'Mister President,'" Matthew said making air quotes with his fingers, "somebody has a rug to clean, cuz I ain't getting paid to do it."

They sat there for a while as Matthew left the building.

"That didn't go as planned," Jeff muttered to himself, already wondering if the building had a carpet cleaner and whose job it was to clean up the stinky mess left behind.

CHAPTER 7

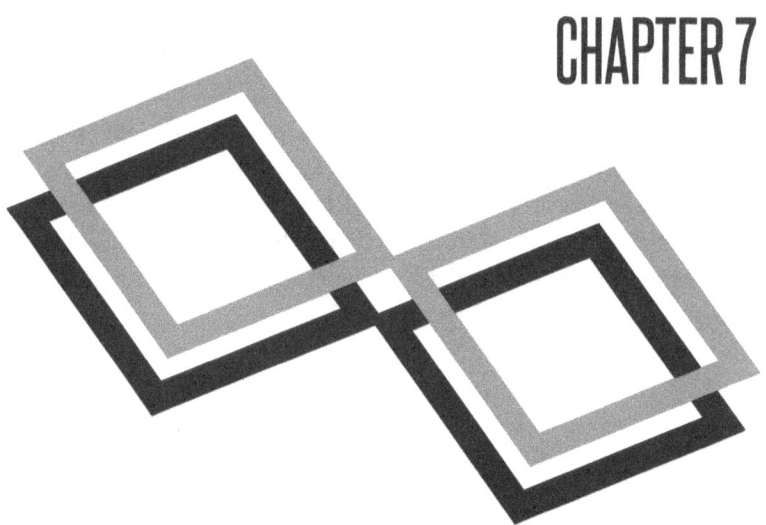

Steve had changed out of his dirty clothes and was warming up the grill with a cold beer in his hand. His little speech at the meeting felt like a win at first, but he realized too late, that he just made some folks probably double down on their dislike for him. Especially when he started making cracks about money. His guts twisted as he knew he shouldn't have, especially with his job in a precarious position because of the global economy. While he waited, he played with his laptop and checked out the news.

There was a tense standoff today with the Chinese, but no more shots fired and no more deaths. An informal cease-fire had been called for rescue operations. Internationally, stock prices were plunging, and the positive surge the US President saw when he was elected was being chipped away with the Euro tumbling in value as Greece looked like it was heading towards insolvency and fears of a new war with China.

He normally avoided politics, but he was skimming an article on how the talking heads thought the President was going to react and what that might have on international trade with Asia.

"Hello?" a voice called from the side of the house.

Steve got up and walked around to the fence that separated the front yard to the backyard. A chain-link gate had been installed here, same as the one in the back of the property. Right away he could see it was somebody from the HOA council. He racked his memory for a minute, while a feeling of dread settled in the pit of his stomach.

"Matthew?" he asked as he walked up to the fence.

"Yeah, Matthew Fitzpatrick. Your wife told me you were back this a way."

"Yeah, you want to come back?" he asked, not sure what to make of things.

"If you don't mind. I'd like to talk about the meeting."

The dread in the pit of his stomach was a cold thing. It seemed it couldn't get any worse, but somehow, it managed.

"Sure," Steve said popping the lock on the gate and pulling it open.

"Thank you," Matthew said and followed him back, both of them taking a patio chair to sit in.

The smell of the grill warming up and old grease cooking hit both men, and Matthew's stomach rumbled audibly. Steve grinned a little at that, reminding himself not to hate the man because he was associated with—

"I think what they tried to do to you and Mr. Abbott is a crock of shit."

That got his attention.

"The council didn't know?" Steve asked, a little thunderstruck and curious.

"I'm sure some of them did, but I didn't. It took me by surprise. I know I fielded a couple of phone calls about the Jeep, but I could plainly see the muffler as I walked up to your driveway. There's nothing to complain about."

"That's what I said," Steve told him. "I mean, yeah, we had a three-fifty short block put in it, and there's only so much you can muffle it when the body is so short. Not enough pipes for a huge muffler."

"How'd you manage to fit a Chevy motor into a Jeep?" Matthew asked, leaning forward.

"I had Dave's Garage do the restoration on it, and they put in the new drivetrain. I have a feeling that the Jeep and the meeting aren't the only things you wanted to talk about though, is it?"

"No," Matthew said and paused as Angela and Amber came outside, holding a platter with burger patties made up.

Both ladies were sniping at each other, but they were smiling. Amber stopped dead in her tracks when she saw who was sitting with her dad and gave him a shy wave.

"Hi, Mr. Fitz," she said, turning red.

"Amber?" he asked.

"Um...Matthew, this is my wife Angela, and you know my daughter Amber...?"

"Yeah, she used to come over after school to help Junior when his Trig class was giving him problems. I didn't know you were....well hello, little missy."

"Nice to see you again," Angela said, breaking the awkward moment, "Would you like to stay for dinner? Get you a beer?"

"Uh...beer, if it's not a hassle?"

"I got it," Amber said and took off.

"So uh...I take it Junior is Matt?" Steve asked.

"Yeah. Wow, talk about a small world. I didn't know....this is too weird," he concluded.

"I'm lost here," Steve admitted.

"Matt is her guy friend," Angela told her husband.

Steve was getting close to understanding when Matthew smacked his forehead in a comical expression.

"I see your daughter once or twice a week. She never drives the Jeep over. I didn't know she was yours...the jeep...this is...wow. That HOA meeting is such a crock of shit. I didn't know your daughter was Amber. I knew your wife looked familiar, but I always see you at the meetings. I didn't put two and two—"

"It's ok, man," Steve said putting a hand up.

The conversation stopped when Amy came running out and jumped, wrapping her arms around Matthew's waist.

"There you are, little bug!" Matthew said.

Steve turned to his wife, his eyebrows raised. She winked at him and started humming the twilight zone theme song, and they laughed. Steve realized how much of life with his family he was missing out on by being gone all the time.

"Hi Mr. Fitz, I haven't seen you in forever and ever and ever," Amy said in a breathless voice as she let him go and pulled a chair out next to her dad.

"She used to come over with Amber. It's how I knew the kids weren't up to monkey business," he said. "Hey little one, you married the preacher's boy yet?"

"His heart's been stolen away," she said dramatically and turned to watch as Amber walked out with four beers.

She set them down on the table in front of the men and turned to her mom. "Want me to grab you a glass of wine?"

"Look at you, miss helpful. What are you up to?" Angela whispered into her ear.

"Would it be ok if Matt and Mr. Fitzpatrick stay for dinner? I could cut and wash more salad, and I'll eat hot dogs instead of burgers?"

"If she's having hotdogs, I want hot dogs!" Amy said excitedly.

"Heathens," Angela said to her daughter. "Yes to wine, yes if Mr. Fitzpatrick would like to stay for dinner, and yes to hot dogs," she said to Amy.

Amber disappeared again, and Steve turned to Amy.

"Who's stolen Joseph's heart now?" he asked.

"My sister," Amy said giving them a pouty, dejected look.

It was overdone, and when Matthew chuckled, she smiled.

"Besides, my daddy won't let me get married till I'm a grown up and forty-five years old."

"That's a good thing," Matthew said and took a beer and gave it a long pull from the bottle, "I'll stay, if it's no problem," he said, "Amber is always bragging on your cooking, ma'am."

Angela smiled, pleased at that. Amber walked back out with a wine glass, bottle, and cork puller.

"Would you give my son a call?" Matthew asked her. "Tell him where to come on over?"

"Oh, he knows where I live," she said turning bright red, but she sat down at the end of the table.

"I feel like there's a secret life going on while I'm away at work sometimes," Steve admitted.

"Me too," Matthew said. "It's been me and Matty alone for a few years now. He's old enough to stick around the house if I have to work late, but I always worry about him."

"Divorced?" Steve asked.

"Widowed," Matthew told him and took a long drink.

"Sorry," Steve said softly, standing up to grab the platter full of meat.

"No worries," Matthew told him. "It's been a while, and we knew it was coming."

"Still."

He waved him off, "Need a hand?" he asked after a moment.

"Naw, just going to grill these up. How you like yours?"

Matt had stopped by a little bit after Dwight stopped over and the seven of them ate and talked. Angela was horrified by what her husband had done, now that she knew the reason his boots were near the back fence and he'd taken the hose to his old pair of blue jeans. They all talked about the HOA, the committee, and what felt to the Taylors and Abbott like the never-ending harassment. Both Amber and Matt kept Amy entertained, but when she rubbed her eyes and told them she was done, they both sat at the picnic table that sat off the patio on the grass alone.

Dwight and Matthew got to talking, and, for a time, they both talked about being widowers and how hard it was raising kids. Steve and Angela just sat and listened for that part, seeing another new friendship form right in front of them.

"What do you think about this Chinese thing?" Steve asked Matthew while the teenagers pretended to be invisible, not ten feet away.

"It's already a shooting match. I figure they built those islands to put bases and missiles on them. To make a claim they own all the land around the Philippines. Probably won't be long till Taiwan gets pulled in. Could get ugly, or they might back down."

I don't know," Angela said. "I don't love everything the new president is doing, but I do love that he took a hard line with China. They've been bullying everyone but us around for a while now."

"Yeah, all thanks to the former pres., the apologist in chief... Ooops," Matthew said putting his beer down, "beers and politics aren't the best of mixture."

"No more than clean carpets and pig shit," Dwight said.

Matt laughed at that and Amber looked at Dwight with a smirk. What her dad couldn't get away with, her mom would never dare correct the cranky farmer, but she knew it was burning her mom up inside. She had to bite her cheek.

"That was funny, now that I know what was going on," Matthew said. "Let's just see if they try to get me voted off the council. I'll probably know more next week."

"I wish I could have seen their faces, especially Doug's," Steve admitted.

"What's your history with him?" Matthew asked curiously.

"I don't like him," Steve told him simply.

"I'll tell you, since my husband is liable to develop Tourette's if he has to tell the story," Angela said.

"There she goes," Steve said, snagging empty beer bottles. "Want another one?"

"Sure. Just one more, though. I have to walk home tonight, but I might just roll home after the food and company," he said with a grin.

"Yeah, I want to hear this one, and get me one too while yer up!" Dwight told him.

Steve nodded and headed in.

"It was the day we were moving in. The company Steve works for hired a moving service to bring us down from Ohio. We drove down and were half a day ahead of the moving trucks, so we stayed in Atlanta for a day while they unloaded the truck into the garage and put the bulk of the furniture in the rooms. Doug and his wife came down, being all nosey, wondering who the new neighbors were and then started complaining that the truck had run over some flowers they'd planted in the median when they had to back up."

"This is over some flowers?" Matthew asked, taking a beer from Steve as he came back out with three in his hand.

"It's not just the flowers," Steve said walking over and handing a beer to Dwight before plopping in his own chair. "He pissed off the movers. We had to cut our trip short to get back there. They called the cops on the moving company and then threatened to call immigration on the guys."

"Hispanic?" Matthew asked.

"Yeah, came from somewhere else...like five generations ago. Anyways, the manager was pissed at us for not being there to deal with Doug. We got stuck in traffic, and by the time I got there, the cops had shown up."

"The funny thing is," Angela picked up where her husband left off, "when the cops looked at the tire tracks that went over the flower bed, they were too small to have been a semi-trailer."

"What's even funnier, Doug started insisting that they fine the moving company for blocking the flow of traffic."

"You live in a dead end cul de sac," Matthew said, chuckling.

"And they don't live on this road. Yeah, I know." Steve said and took a long pull from his beer, "It's lunacy. I guess Professor Toodles is friends with the neighbors and both had a conniption when they saw my gun case being moved inside. Granted, my guns weren't in the safe, they were packed in locked cases. But OH NO, GUNS!"

"This is the south. We clutch to our bible, our guns, and glory, don't cha remember that? Obama thought—"

"And now we're back to politics," Amber said, making Matt snicker.

Dwight stuck his tongue out at her, and she busted up.

"And I'm the one who's been drinking," Steve said and upended his bottle, killing it.

"Anyways, the Wilson's next door complained about that at the first meeting: the guns," Angela said.

"I remember that, it was right before I was voted on as treasurer," Matthew said. "Hey, who's that?" He pointed with his bottle.

Steve and Angela looked up to where he was pointing and they saw a face in the window of the Wilson's upstairs. It was gone with a swish of the curtains.

"That's Billy, he's the local creeper," Amber said.

"Shhh," Angela shushed. "They might hear you."

"Well, it's not like he's stopped being creepy and watching us all the time."

"What's he do, anyway?" Steve asked his daughter.

"I don't know. He's old, but still lives with his parents. Lame," Amber finished.

"I think he's nineteen," Angela said.

"He talks like he's a west coast surfer," Steve told him. "I think he plays video games and makes YouTube videos or something. Matt, you ever run across him at school when he was there?"

Matt sat up straight, and in the twilight of evening, he turned a little red as he realized that he'd have to talk to Amber's dad— something he'd been avoiding all night.

"He was quiet. They had lived in another city before they moved here, so I've only known of him. He was two grades ahead of me. We uh...older kids at school don't normally hang out with freshmen and sophomores."

"Unless it's you and me," Amber said sweetly and took his hand.

Matt's head looked like it was about to explode and he quickly pulled his hand away as Matthew and Steve cracked up, only making it worse. Matt was a senior now.

"Any creeper stories?" Angela asked.

"Not really, just that he was quiet," Matt said, trying not to meet Steve's gaze.

In truth, Steve knew his daughter was playing a game. It wasn't father versus her guy friend she liked, but more like she was playing everyone at once. She was gauging Matt's interest in her and checking to see if her dad was going to pull out guns and blow him away.

"I wish we could have a fire pit," Amber said, suddenly changing the subject.

"We can!" Dwight said standing up quickly, almost coming back down as he wobbled from his four beers.

"How?" Steve asked.

"Well, you got yourself a gate that opens up so you can come visit me now. Drag a hose out back and we'll dig you a mighty fine fire pit using the front loader on my little tractor. I bet that'll piss 'em off."

Angela burst into feminine giggles, and then covered her mouth as if to hold them in.

"Maybe once in a while, I have a feeling we won't be needing any more trouble," Steve told him.

"Up to you, my friend."

"Mom," Amy said walking outside, "I want to watch *Deadpool*, we have it on demand—"

"No," Both parents chorused as one.

Dwight grinned. "Young miss, can I beg a favor from you?"

Amber turned to him and grinned. "Sure thing, Uncle Dewey."

"I'm about ready to head in, but I think I might have had one too many," Dwight said and then downed the rest of his bottle and benched into a closed fist. "Nope, *now* I've had too much."

"Sure thing. Dad, you don't mind?" she asked.

"I don't mind," Steve told her.

"Can Matt ride with me?" she asked, a hopeful note in her voice.

Steve looked at Matthew and shrugged. He shrugged back and the men looked at Angela. She took a sip out of her wineglass and noticed everyone was looking at her.

"It was my idea. I told her earlier. Dwight must have overheard me," she hissed to Steve who grinned back at her.

"I don't care," Steve said, "but remember I know how long it takes to drive over there and back."

This time it was Amber who turned a bright red, and seeing that, Matt laughed. That stopped half a second later when she playfully slapped him across the chest with a backhand. He stood up and took the rest of his and Amber's paper plates and plastic cups to the trash can and threw them away. Dwight got up and held out a hand.

"I'm glad you're one of the good guys," he said to Matthew. "I'll see the rest of you at the church on Sunday, yeah?"

"You bet," Steve told him. "You need a hand to the Jeep?"

"I'm old and drunk, not dead and stupid," he snapped back, making the teenagers grin behind him.

"I should get headed home. Matthew," Matthew Sr. said, "Make sure you two don't get side tracked or break down somewhere. I heard that Jeep has been rebuilt top to bottom."

"Yes sir, but I'm not driving," he said lamely.

"But it'll be your fault if something happens, come on," Dwight said and grabbed Matt's shoulder for balance.

"See you," Amy shouted, and everyone said their goodbyes.

"I thought you were going to sleep?" Steve asked her as everyone but the three of them left.

"I'm tired, but I couldn't sleep, not with everyone outside. I ended up playing some Minecraft."

"So how do you go from Minecraft to asking about a movie I will never let you watch?"

"Because YouTube has commercials now," Angela finished. "Come on bug, let's help your daddy clean up, and we'll all head to bed."

"Aren't you going to stay up for Amber to come home?" she asked.

"I'll hear her; I have my stopwatch going," he said holding up his cell phone.

He didn't tell her it had died earlier, but she didn't question it. He found that out when he tried to check the time ten minutes later when he heard the low rumble of the Jeep pulling in and plugged it in before drifting off to sleep, letting his wife talk with Amber about girl stuff.

CHAPTER 8

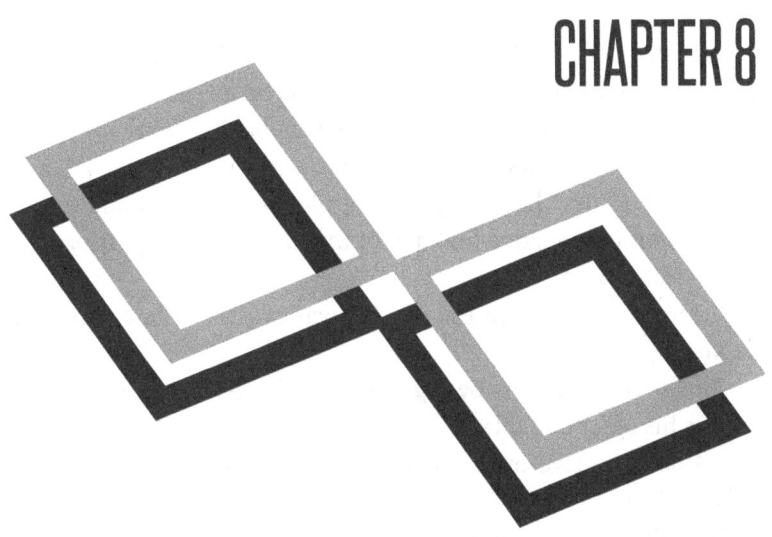

Waking up to a hangover was very low on Steve's favorite things to happen, but besides the one beer Angela had, the three guys had killed the rest of an eighteen pack of Budweiser—his other go-to beer when he wasn't drinking Corona. He rolled over, trying to focus and let out a small moan, as tiny jackhammers started pounding behind his eyes. Just out of his reach, he saw a glass of ice water and two white pills. He swung his legs off the bed and saw that they were Tylenol. For the millionth time, he sent up a prayer for having found an understanding and forgiving wife.

After he cleaned up and felt more or less human, he padded into the kitchen to the smell of frying bacon. He breathed in deep and walked in to see his daughters sitting on their knees on stools in front of the bar top that was just behind the cooktop where Angela was working. She had two skillets going at once, bacon in one and an egg concoction in another. It wasn't the food so much that had his attention, it was how his wife's shape filled out the t-shirt of his she was wearing, and how it barely came down to her thighs.

"Don't be creepy, that's Billy Wilson's job," Amber said.

"Oh hey, how are you feeling?" Angela said, putting down a spatula and wrapping her arms around Steve, giving him a hug.

"Pretty good, all things considered," he said, bending down to kiss her and noticing she'd been filching bacon already.

She pushed him back, smiling and went back to work.

"What are we doing today, Dad?" Amy asked.

"I don't know," he said, grabbing plates and beginning to put them out on the bar, one for each of them, and then repeating that with the silverware.

"Can you take me to the mall? I want to get a new game for the Xbox."

"Sure," Steve said, knowing her idea of a new game wasn't the same as his older daughter's.

"Mind if I drive over and hang out with Matt some, today?" Amber asked.

"I don't mind if your mother doesn't," Steve said.

"Just make sure his father is going to be home," Angela said, using the spatula to point at her.

"Sweet!" Amber said, pumping her fist.

"Dude," Steve said back to her in a monotone.

"Huh?" Amy asked.

"Dude," Angela said.

"Sweet!" Steve said with a little more enthusiasm.

"I think I'm lost here. What?" Amber said.

"Dude," Angela repeated.

"Sweet!" Steve almost yelled, but his head killed him.

Angela busted up laughing and started grabbing plates and dishing up the food.

"What was that about?" Amy asked.

"I don't know. When old people start acting funny, it means they are about to kiss, or go coo coo. I saw it in a movie once," she told her little sister with a straight face.

"Ohhhhh," was all Amy came up with in reply.

"It's from *Dude, Where's My Car*," Steve told the girls.

"Even the name of that movie sounds lame. So when can I go?" she asked, holding up her phone.

"How about after breakfast, and you do the dishes?"Angela asked.

"Moooom," she said in one long drawn out word.

"Whaaaaaaat?" Angela called back.

"It's not just the grownups who are weird. I hope it isn't contagious," Amy said.

Before leaving, Steve grabbed his cell phone and headed to the garage. They were taking his truck because he didn't stop at the bank to draw cash out the day before, and he wanted to stop in at Sam's Club. He'd already thumbed in his order while he waited for the girls to get ready. The food items would be ready for him to pick up while he was out. He'd hit the mall first, something about a player skin included in the new something or another for Xbox. He let the info flow right over him. He hit the button to turn on his phone now that it was fully charged and saw that the girls already had the garage door opened, and his truck was running to get the air conditioner blowing before they got out into the sunshine.

He climbed in and set his phone on the seat and started backing out when it went off. He waited till he passed the door, hit the button to close the garage and handed it over to Angela.

"Check that for me, would you? Probably Dwight texting me to see if I'm as hung over as he is."

Angela took it and swiped his code in. Then she started hitting the screen as Steve started driving down the street, pausing to swerve an impromptu basketball game some kids a little older than Amy were playing.

"Um, head to your work real quick," Angela said putting the phone face down.

"Oh no. Brandi?" He asked.

Angela nodded, but realized he was watching for the kids and hadn't seen her. "Yeah, she left three texts this morning. If we can hustle, we can get there in time."

"In time for what?"

⚡

Steve pulled in and they all got out. He held his wife's hand and she held Amy's as they crossed the parking lot of IT Bytes, noting the number of black SUV's with tinted windows. A man in a dark suit, sunglasses and an earwig was waiting at the door as they walked up. He held up a picture, then compared it to Steve and opened the door for them.

"Just you, Mister Taylor," the man said.

"Naw, that's not how it works," Steve said. "I work here. Who are you?"

The man pulled out an identification wallet and showed him. The man was Agent Walling of the FBI.

"Dad, does that mean he's a G-Man?" Amy asked.

She'd been quiet on the ride in, recognizing that her mom and dad had suddenly gone tense, turned up the radio, and whispered the whole trip here.

"Yeah, he's with the FBI," he told her, and turned to face the agent. "Agent Walling, this is my family; they're with me."

"I'm sorry sir, I was told no civilians except for you."

"Well, I'll give Brandi a call," he said pulling out his phone.

"Sir, please step inside with us, it'll only take a few moments of your time."

"No, I don't think I will," Steve said getting a bad feeling.

Technically what he'd done could be considered illegal. Purposefully planting a virus that stole data and trashed the hacker's computer. He'd done far, far worse, but he was getting some not so good vibes from Captain America here and didn't want to give up one bit of his freedom unless he was compelled.

"Sir—"

"Naw, tell your boss, or Brandi, or whoever that I'm going shopping instead. I'll be in touch."

The agent started talking into a radio mic as the door swung closed and Steve turned and gave Angela a gentle tug. They turned and headed back toward the truck.

"What was that about?" Angela asked, "I thought you said they had a question about the breach?"

"You read the texts too. I don't know why they won't let me bring you—"

"Sir," a voice shouted, and the agent they had talked to before was standing outside the door.

Brandi and another agent walked out. She looked livid, the color high in her cheeks and she walked in a stiff-legged manner that Steve had seen once. Right after her boyfriend had broken it off with her when they had first moved into the Macon area.

"Steve, it's ok. Angela, Amy, you three can come in."

He hesitated and then headed back, letting his hands drop to his side.

"What's going on?" he asked Brandi.

"We had another breach. This time, word got around."

"When?" Steve asked, suddenly nervous.

"This morning, early. The phone center woke me up about four."

"I'm sorry, my phone died, and I forgot to turn it back on—"

"Just come inside and help us, all of you. I might lose what little sanity I have left or claim early dementia."

"What's demented–ia? Is that like old timers?" Amy asked.

The agent who was walking next to Brandi cracked a small smile, and she just mussed the little girl's hair before heading back in. Steve followed and saw half a dozen agents working on the side of the office where the round of layoffs had come from first. With a sinking feeling, Steve felt his calm shattering into a thousand pieces.

"She compromised more than one system?" Steve asked.

Brandi nodded at him, a tear slipping down one cheek.

"I'm sorry, she wasn't supposed to have access to any of the other projects. Which one was it?"

"The worst one possible. We're going through all the code for the other projects now that we know what her backdoor looks like."

Steve rushed to his desk, seeing that the projector was already on. He started typing furiously and shrugged off a hand that pulled on his shoulder.

"Mister Taylor," an agent said, "we're doing this. We thought it'd be helpful if you assisted us in finding if there's any more malicious coding."

"You know what to look for. Hell, I even gave you all the information you needed to go arrest her two days ago."

The agent coughed and Brandi tapped him on the shoulder.

"What is it?" he asked her.

"She got into the main server here too, till I blocked her access. She deleted all the screenshots and had re-routed the email you sent out with the email. I contacted the FBI when I realized what was happening."

Steve sat up straight and then punched the button on his desktops DVD reader/recorder. A silver CD-R popped out and he took it, pulling a sharpie and writing EVIDENCE in block letters on it.

"You made a hardcopy backup."

"On something she couldn't erase too," he said handing the disk to Agent Waller.

"Is this all her information?"

"Yes, just like I told you. You already know where she lives, go pick her up."

"I can, now that I have something to use to compel a warrant on a Saturday."

That's when it clicked for him. They had to find a sympathetic judge and with the evidence seemingly gone or erased, all they had was a backdoor in some lines of code that probably looked like a foreign language to them. Waller whistled, and the agents hurried over to a laptop.

"Is that it? Is there anything else?"

"Can you run a search string and see if she left any more surprises?" Brandi asked, "I've done it myself three times already, but I'm not sure I would see anything at this point."

"Yeah, staring at the same code too long gets you like that. That's why we split things up into teams when we debug it."

"This is why I hired you," Brandi said, "You know how to get shit done."

✦

Amy and Angela were waiting at Steve's desk. Brandi walked over to the wet bar and grabbed a decanter of scotch and made an inquiring gesture with it. Steve shook his head and she poured herself an inch and walked back to her desk and sat down.

"How bad is it for the company?" Steve asked.

She took a long sip and then put the glass down.

"We lost the account, and while you were checking on the source coding, we had another one call and cancel their contracts with us."

"So, it's bad?" Steve asked.

"Unless we can sue the pants off of some twenty-three-year-old girl...."

"Is the company closing?" Steve asked after a minute's silence.

"I don't know how we can keep open. It was the accounts in Asia that canceled on us," Brandi told him, a fat tear running down the side of her cheek unnoticed by her.

She took another long drink, this time finishing off the scotch and put the glass down.

"Are we, I mean Monday...Um..."

"Come on in Monday. I need you most of all. I'm going to spend the afternoon calling everyone else off, unless you need someone from your team?"

"What is left? I mean...that leaves us with—"

"Nothing that can keep the business afloat. I've had several offers to buy the business. I think I might have to do that," she said as another tear fell down on the other side.

"I don't...I mean..." Steve wished his wife was in here. She would know the proper protocol.

In the south, things were different. The age gap was noticeable, but he never knew when things were proper or not.

"When I hired you on and moved you across the country, I put a year's worth of your salary on hold in case something happened. You'll still have your severance package no matter what. That's what I wanted to tell you. I don't know if I could face your family while telling you this."

Propriety be damned, Steve stood up and walked around the desk, and Brandi stood up. She wrapped her arms around him, burying her head in his shoulder and started sobbing softly. He held her for several minutes until she pushed back and reached for a tissue.

"I'll know more Monday. Hopefully some swift action by the FBI will turn things around, and I can change some minds."

"Ok," Steve said, his voice hoarse and at the edge of tears himself.

He knew moving here had been a risk, and he knew with his skills and background, he wouldn't be out of work long if something should happen. With a cushion like she was talking about, as much as he hated thinking about it, this might work out ok for him and his family. He'd have to be careful, but the other day while he was visiting with everyone he'd realized how much of their lives he wasn't a part of, and it made his chest hurt just thinking about it.

"Are you going to be ok?" Brandi asked.

Steve let out a surprised bark of laughter, "I'll be fine. We'll be fine, one way or another. Thank you, Brandi, for trusting me and for bringing us down here."

"Well, it isn't over yet," she said with a sniff, "we still have next week to figure things out."

"Next week," Steve said and nodded.

CHAPTER 9

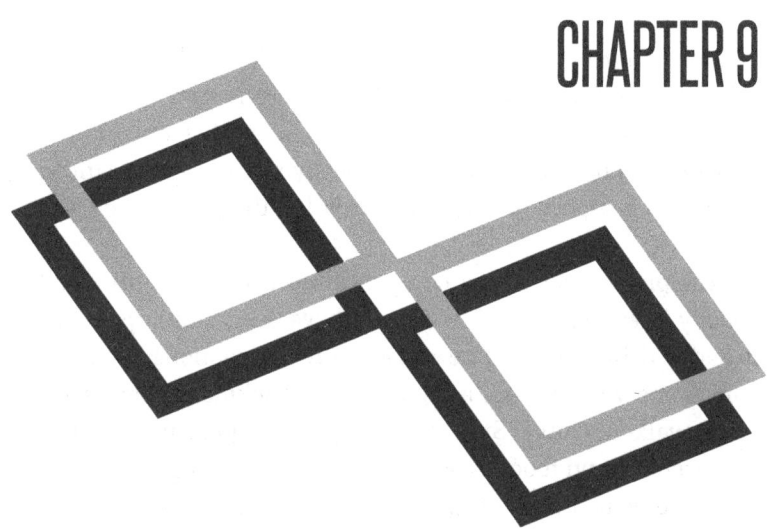

"Thank you for calling Taylor Networking," Steve said answering his new work phone.

It had been a month after the last breach that IT Bytes finally closed the doors, and in that same timeframe, he'd made moves to open his own consulting business. It didn't cost a lot of money, but time. Something he now had a lot of. He'd taken the severance package and paid his house payment for a year as well as the property taxes. That was the biggest thing he was unsure of, yet he still had a sizeable nest egg. Business had been good at first, so it was rarely touched other than the initial payments.

"Mister Taylor, my name is Robert Heath. I represent the Eleven Oaks Home Owner's Association. I was wondering if I could request a meeting with both you and your attorney present?"

Robert Heath was the lawyer the HOA had hired for the fence and gate issue. Finally, some closure.

"Sure, give my guy a call and set something up. I'll be there whenever."

"Thank you," he said and hung up.

He didn't have anything going on workwise, so he swiveled his office chair and hit the mute button on the remote for his bedroom

TV. More between the naval shenanigans between the US, Iran, and China. North Korea was even rattling its sabers now that they saw the economic impact this was causing in market uncertainty in the United States. Steve knew historically war usually meant there would be a prosperous time afterwards, but things had been getting rough fast.

The price of gas had gone up by almost seventy cents a gallon. Nobody knew why, and Steve might have been more upset by it if he had to drive a ton, but he was actually saving money by working from home with a desk, a laptop, and a rackmount server in his wife's walk-in closet. Still, utility bills had gone up last month unexpectedly and food prices were starting to get higher.

"Who was that?" Angela asked, seeing he wasn't on the phone anymore.

"The HOA's lawyer. Wants to sit down and talk. Probably going to settle with us about the fence thing."

"That was your work phone," Angela said pointing to the separate cell phone sitting on the desk.

That's when the nerves kicked in.

"How would he have that number?" Steve asked, rhetorically.

"That's what I was wondering."

"Well crap, I wonder if there's something in the HOA about home based businesses?" Steve asked her.

"There is...."

"Well shit. I don't think they can do anything about it, Billy next door does it and so do half of the people in the neighborhood."

"Selective enforcement. Still, this isn't a court of law. It's a contract."

"Damn. Yeah. Well, our guy is going to call us when they have a time set up."

"You should go shopping. Get your lists," Angela said suddenly.

"Why?" Steve asked her, suddenly curious.

"Because you're going to obsess over this and it'd be good for you and Amy to get out of the house for a little bit. It's been a rough summer for her. Her sister is never home, you're stressed out, and starting a new business isn't helping. Go buy some prepping stuff or ammo!"

"I've never heard of you actually encouraging me to buy more ammo," Steve said, fighting back a grin.

"We made really good money at IT Bytes. We set our budgets, we bought Amber a Jeep that's basically brand new with cash, you've been maxing out your IRA's and mutual funds, and yet you still had enough to do some prepping."

"Yeah, but the business isn't earning quite as much—"

"The house note and property taxes are paid a year in advance. Actually, the taxes are more like a year and a half. You've barely touched the severance pay. What would make you happy? A new gun?"

The last thing Steve expected was this, but his mind was already swirling with possibilities. She had let him off the hook earlier in the year when she found out about the AR-15s he'd gotten and had actually been impressed that his ammo buying didn't actually cost them more, he just got smarter and saved till his budget would allow him to get it by the case instead of the box. There were other projects than guns, ammo, and food he'd always wanted, and living where he did, he knew it wasn't top of the list, but if his wife was giving him free reign....

"I see that look, you have an idea," she said.

"Yeah, tell Ames that we're gonna go hit Home Depot. I have my work done for the day, and unless some kind of problem pops up, maybe we can spend a couple hours. Daddy-daughter time."

"Good. What are you going to do until then?" Angela asked, bumping her hip into his.

"Try to get out the door before you find me something else to do," Steve told her with a grin, "Actually, I want to see the shelter for a minute. I want to see if I have room for another gun safe."

"We have plenty of room in the one...unless—"

"Gotcha," Steve said goosing his wife.

She squeaked and he took off towards the garage. Amy saw part of the chase, but turned away when she found them kissing in the doorway leading into it.

"I thought you were going to talk to Dad about us doing something. You keep sucking his face and it's...gross!"

They broke their kiss and Steve walked over and scooped his daughter up. She yelped in surprise.

"I'm almost ten; put me down!" she screamed indignantly.

He walked over and laid her out on the couch, staying out of reach of flailing arms looking for revenge. Laughing, he backed up.

"Give me five and meet me in the garage. You and I are going shopping."

"Wh...where at?"

"Home Depot," Steve told her and pulled the door shut between the house and the garage.

The door did little to muffle her screaming "yes," and he imagined there was a fist pump involved. All kids were doing it lately. It was one of her favorite stores, especially in the summertime. Despite the heat, you could find a riot of flowers and all sorts of interesting things for projects she wanted to start.

The garage wasn't cooled the same way the house was, but they had one vent in here that tried to blow cold air from the air conditioner. Today it was failing. Making sure the door to the garage was still closed, he headed into his faux mechanical room. He left the lights off and walked sideways between the narrow pathway to the back where the trap door was. He pulled on it, and the lid popped up and he put a stack in front of it so it wouldn't close on accident. He walked down there and turned on the light.

Eight steps down and the steel and fiberglass shelter was almost twenty degrees cooler than the upstairs. It was easily a comfortable mid-seventies down there and the light would heat things up if he left the bare 100-watt bulb in. Steve made a mental note to buy a LED bulb to replace that one and then looked around. It was cylindrical in shape with a flat floor put in place. It was fifteen-feet long and the floor space was about five-feet wide at the narrowest point, though the walls curved out like the inside of a steel culvert. Four bunks were tucked into the space in the middle of the shelter, two to each side.

Camp chairs had been broken down and put under the bottom two bunks and then boxes of instant food were pushed into there. Boxes that held gallon jugs of water lined one wall and towards the back was the combination area. Steve had made additions to the shelter after he'd found that there was a drain in the bottom that apparently was meant to drain the structure in case of an emergency flood. When he pulled the cleanout, he got a whiff of sewer so he had closed it back down.

Now, it sported a small half bath without running water. There was a sink for brushing teeth and cleaning up, but the water would have to be brought over from the cases of water he'd been stocking. Same with flushing the toilet. He didn't know if it actually hooked into the sewer lines, not knowing how deep those were put in Georgia, but he figured in an emergency, even if it came out into a storm sewer, they had someplace to use the bathroom. Two small walls and a curtain closed off the doorway there, and on the wall opposite of the bathroom, in a cramped area, was a small cooking surface. An old Coleman stove had been set up there. Underneath the cabinet he'd not only stored his pots and pans, but several gallons of fuel.

If you were to back out of the kitchen half a step and turn towards the bunk beds and the entrance to the bunker, you'd almost run into the gun safe. It was the only thing other than the bathroom fixtures that were bolted down tight. He spun the dial and entered the combination. When it was open, he pulled out the gun he'd been practicing with as of late, one of the 1911s. He put it into a holster and then tucked it into the back of his pants. A spare magazine went into his pants pocket and after he was adjusting his belt and shirt, he was ready to go.

"Daddy, you ready yet?" Amy called down from the garage.

"Yeah, be right there," he said, closing the safe and spinning the dial, locking it.

❧

"Why are you getting all these pipes?" Amy asked for the fourth time.

Steve had the pipes cut in half so they were five-foot-long and then had threads cut onto the end.

"Can I tell you a secret?" Steve asked her.

Even the plumbing associate leaned in.

"Yes," she all but whispered.

"Remember Uncle Dewey's hand pump?"

"Yeah?" Amy asked, not for sure what his pump had to do with the pipe.

"I've got a sand point here, some special couplings, a driving cap, and the pipe is the last thing I need before I put a pump on top of the pipes, just like his pump."

"Oh, that's going to be so cool. Are we going to put it in right away?" Amy asked.

The guy from plumbing grinned and finished off the last set of threads and slid the pipe into the already heavily laden cart. "Do you need a pitcher pump for that?"

"I thought you guys didn't stock them?" Steve asked.

"We do now, we got a reset and we have all kinds of pumps now, especially with all the new pond stuff. It's a new vendor for us and you know how Home Depot is down here in Georgia."

"You get all the good stuff?" Steve asked her.

"You got it," he said and walked them over two aisles.

He helped them pick out a pitcher pump, and Steve opted for the heftier one, with better internals.

"Anything else I can help you find?" the associate asked.

"Do you know where I can find a fence post driver and a post hole digger?"

Steve and Amy were loading up groceries from Sam's when his phone started buzzing. He pulled it out and saw text messages from both his wife and Amber.

Daddy, get gas, it's going up all over the state. The news said it's gone up another forty cents today.

And then from Angela: *Call me.*

"What is it, Dad?" Amy asked.

"I dunno, your mom and sister are both blowing up my phone," he said and thumbed in Angela's number and hit send.

"Hey baby, what's going on?"

"It's...turn on the news. You know what to do about this. You've been..." Angela's voice was shaky and he could tell she was close to tears, or afraid. Probably both.

"I will. Is everything ok at home? Are you ok?"

"Yes, but it...I'm glad you're too old for the draft."

"What's going on?" Steve said, firing up the truck to get the air conditioning started on the summer heat that had slowly crept up while they were inside.

"There's a naval fight and they just closed the stock market down. Something about the Federal Reserve, and now, they say gas prices are going up."

"There's a lot of fear...." Steve said aloud.

"Yes, just come home, help me figure out what this is."

"I will babe, I love you."

"Love you too, hurry."

They both hung up and Amy looked over at her dad as he put the phone down on the dash.

"Is Mom ok?"

"Yeah, I guess the Navy is in another fight. There's some other stuff going on and gas is getting expensive."

"Oh, ok," Amy said, and then got her Kindle out.

Steve marveled at how innocent and out of the loop his daughter was. If there was a sudden suspension of trading and the Fed was involved...every conspiracy theory and fear ran through his head. Instead of speaking it aloud, he pulled out and headed towards the gas station. He almost had a full tank, a habit he'd gotten into when he lived in the frozen North and turned on the talk radio.

"...ing news...the president will be holding a press conference in an hour regarding the Chinese retaliation and sinking of the US Missile Cruiser...."

"Daddy?" Amy asked.

"Yeah, hun," he said turning the dial down.

"What happens if we get into another war? I know we're just getting out of one right now. We can't fight two at the same time, can we?"

"We're already sort of doing that," Steve admitted.

"Oh, so this would be like a third?" Amy asked, putting the Kindle face down in her lap.

"More like a fifth or sixth."

Her eyes got wide.

"Don't worry about it, Amy. As long as no nuclear weapons are used, we can take on the world. America has the biggest and best military. Even if the whole world ganged up on us, we'd still beat them."

"Does the whole world want to fight us?"

Steve mentally kicked himself.

"Nope, they'd be foolish to try."

"Oh, ok," Amy said and picked her Kindle back up and began to read.

He turned up the radio to a low level and decided to hit the gas station closest to the house, outside of town. Listening to the radio, it sounded like a ship had been attacked as it sailed too close to one of the disputed islands. The missile defense systems shot down the missile and they in turn, fired on the installation. Other islands launched and a submarine (from anybody's best guess) had fired a torpedo almost right underneath the missile cruiser. The submarine was immediately sunk and all hell broke loose. The reports started getting dicey on speculation and might-have-happened type statements, so he muted it and paid no more attention.

Almost immediately he saw that the gas stations were changing the prices. What had been about seventy cents higher on average was now over one dollar and ten cents more than it had been six months ago. He remembered seeing milk at Sam's had also been a little higher than normal, but that had been creeping up forever now. He shook his head and when Amy started singing some Miley Cyrus, he tuned her out. The only wrecking ball he cared about was the one facing the nation. He had worried about civil unrest, but maybe Dwight had been right all along. He wasn't prepping for a zombie apocalypse, just the collapse of the dollar.

Could that even be possible? He switched to the FM stations and went to the local Public Broadcasting Station. They were talking about the pitched battle in the South China Seas as he pulled into the gas station, and he left the truck running and rolled down his window and left the radio on. He started filling his gas tank as they started talking about the gas prices creeping up as tensions and market volatility were named as a reason. There was no mention of the stock market being closed early, but that's what he was listening for.

He kept a small amount of cash at home, if there was a sudden bank run, he'd need to be there fast. Still....

"...in breaking news, the President has ordered the US Navy and Airforce to maintain its space in international waters and any ship approaching them without proper identification will...this just in. Several Iranian Revolutionary Guard Naval ships have been sank as they raced towards a US..."

"Dad, can I run inside and get a candy bar?" Amy called.

"I'm almost done here," Steve called back. "I'll get you one from my stash at home."

"You have a stash of candy bars at home?"

"Sure, how do you think I can survive your mom and Amber—"

"Dad...."

Steve grinned, though his guts were starting to feel nauseated. Maybe now with a flexible schedule, it was time to up his research and get with Dwight to see what he thought of his prepping, and what his chances were. It was time to let the old farmer in on his plans if something were to happen.

CHAPTER 10

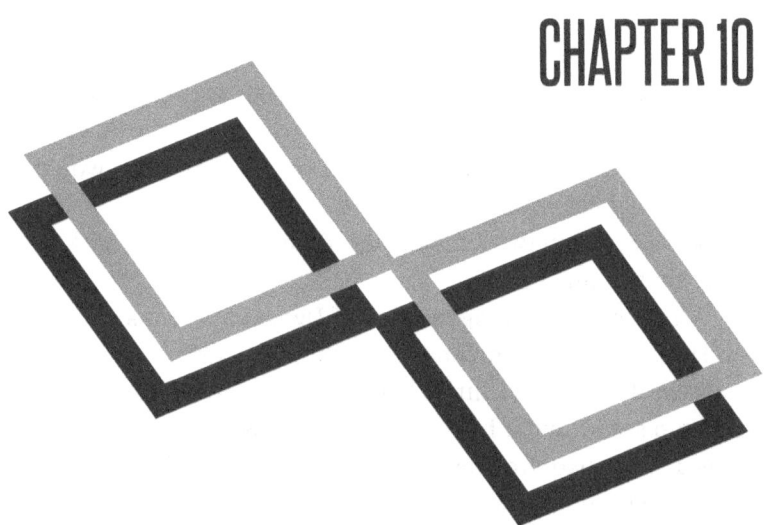

Steve and Dwight finally got a chance to sit down over a backyard barbecue and Angela had known that Steve wanted to talk to Dwight about what looked increasingly to be some scary times ahead. He'd been pretty close to being squared away with food for the four of them for a while. He'd even hinted around at church and gotten the pastor interested in prepping a little bit, but more so as a community-based idea as more and more people were having a hard time.

Inflation was starting to kick in, and though some products and services had almost doubled in prices, only the poorest of Americans were really being hurt by the pinch. Steve could see it, but he hadn't had a chance to talk to Dwight about things because the wily farmer had been getting busier with the harvest and getting ready to replant.

"Damn corn prices are low this year. This god damned global warming...everybody has good crops," Dwight snarked, reaching for a Corona that was sitting in the cooler on the back patio.

"Sorry to hear that. Didn't put you in the red, did it?" Steve asked.

"Excuse me, hon," Angela said stepping outside.

"Hey, babe."

"The girls and I are going to head out now."

"Ok, you sure you don't want to take one of the Colts?"

"No, I'm not used to carrying it yet. I'm not as comfortable with them as you are."

"Ok, you three stay out of trouble. Don't do anything I wouldn't do," Steve told her with a grin.

"Same with you two," she made a little wave and the back door swung shut behind her.

"What were you asking me again?" Dwight asked, taking a swig.

"The corn prices. Didn't put you behind, did it?"

"Naw," Dwight told him. "If I was buying something like the Monsanto seed I might have an issue, but I set aside my own corn for seed. With two growing seasons down here, I don't have any problems with that. That plus the chemical fertilizers. I don't gotta buy them none, because I make my own. Better off using what's free than spend a ton of money."

"Huh, I didn't realize you were kind of an organic farm."

"Not organic, but a lot of the same practices. I don't ask the government for permission to grow the way I do, so I don't want to ask them to come out and certify me on a piece of paper that I have to get tons of inspections and pay fees for. You might not get rich from farming, but it is a way of life."

"We just have to find you a lady friend. A crazy chicken lady who can put up with you," Steve said taking a sip.

"Yeah right. I've been alone for ten years now. I'm too old to get back on that wagon. Nuh uh, no siree."

"What about that Loretta at the church? She's been making eyes at you."

"That's because...I don't...Oh, fuck off." Dwight said turning red for the first time that Steve could ever remember.

He tried not to laugh, but a chuckle escaped before he could cut it off. After a minute, Dwight started laughing too.

"Yeah, well, she's had her hat set for me for a while now," he admitted.

"I'm sorry. I shouldn't laugh. It's just...damn, I've never seen you get touchy like that."

"My fault. She's a sore spot. The last time my son came around... it's just...I don't want him to think I'm trying to replace his mom."

"Ah, ok. Sorry, I won't bring that up."

"No, it's my hang up on things. Now I have a feeling you asked me over to pick my brain about something." Dwight told him taking another long pull.

"Oh yeah? What makes you think that?" Steve asked, curious.

"The girls always hang out when we do these shindigs. I know little Miss Amy loves to sit out here until she's either tired or bored to tears. She went willingly enough though."

"Yeah, I did want to talk to you. It's mostly about what's been going on in the world...."

He paused talking and looked up to hear a window pane push shut and the curtains swishing shut in Billy's room. He took a deep breath and then saw a light come on in the window next to it and a figure come to the window.

"They always that nosy?" Dwight asked as Sarah Wilson squinted, looking outside, probably blinded by the light in her own room.

"Yeah, pretty much," Steve said. "That's why I'm surprised none of them figured out I'm a prepper. That'd go over the neighborhood like a lead balloon."

"That's the secret? Sheeeeeeeeeeeeeeeyit, I knew that a long time ago," Dwight said.

"You did?" Steve asked, thinking he'd been easing that one in there at an opportune moment.

"Well sure. You're not a farmer, but you're interested in all things farming....you have a few hens, some rabbits with an extra couple of hutches for growing them out, and you're awful keen on learning about how to do things without refrigeration."

"Well shit, yeah. You got me," Steve admitted. "How obvious was it?"

"Pretty obvious to me, but I doubt any of these sheep around here would notice. Remember when they thought you were a handyman for always coming home with your truck loaded? At the HOA meeting? They just never paid attention to what you had in it."

"Oh, I remember," Steve said with a groan, "did you get the latest letter?"

"Yeah, and I called up El Jefe and told him that he can stuff it. Matthew told me the next day that Jeff was fit to be tied. What'd you get?"

"Threatening to sue me for running a home business as a HOA violation."

"Oh, your networking, programming, and security thing?"

"Yeah. I don't know how they found out, but it's kind of against the rules."

"What did your lawyer say?" Dwight asked.

"That if they enforce it with me, they have to do it with the rest of the community. When I pointed out to Jeff that his wife had an Etsy store, he shut up real quick." Steve said taking a big chug from his own beer.

"So if that isn't bugging ya, then what's got you dialed up?"

"The inflation, the riots, and the damn war that seems to be looming over us all."

"You're a prepper. You're ready for just about anything. Why worry?" Dwight asked.

"I think I'm pretty set on food for a while, but...you've stuck it out down here when the hurricanes knocked out power, when the stores weren't getting resupplied on time. I was wondering if you could take a look around and see what you think? I'd love to pick your brain."

"Pick away," Dwight said.

Steve stood up and grabbed his beer. "Come on, I want to show you," he said.

Dwight followed and they went in through the back door, cut through the living room, bypassing the kitchen on the right, and then hooked a short left and opened the doorway next to the hall closet leading to the garage. Steve flicked on the light and walked in. His old Ford was gleaming in the fluorescent lights.

"This is new," Dwight said, looking at the mechanical room on the left.

"Yeah, it's a little bit of camouflage," Steve said and opened the door.

Cardboard and the smell of wood from the crates wafted out. Both men walked in after Steve hit the light and illuminated this section of the garage.

"It's tight," he said and started walking towards the far end where the storm shelter was.

"This is a bit more than I expected," Dwight said, "How come the door was unlocked?"

Steve stopped and turned, looking sheepish. "Because the storm shelter is over here," he said.

"Ok, but what happens if you have a ton of hungry angry zombies and your entire food supply is attacked and removed?"

"So lock it, and give everyone a key to carry with them?" Steve asked.

"I would do that, and then find other places to stash some of this stuff. I'm assuming you have some food in the storm shelter too?"

"I do," Steve admitted and turned to walk over and unlatch the trapdoor and open it.

He headed in and Dwight followed. He whistled and looked around, turning in a full circle before taking his hat off and taking a big swallow of his beer.

"Holy shit. You got yourself a fallout shelter. How in the hell did you manage this with asshole neighbors like you got in this area?"

"Well, it's not really a fallout shelter. There are a couple of vents. One of them goes into the garage and the other goes outside. It looks like a well head stub with a cap on it, but it's screened and vented to keep critters out. Plus, there isn't that much overhead of us. Part of this is under the garage slab, but the rest is in the side yard by the gate."

"Yeah, but this wasn't a normal feature, was it? The shelter I mean?"

"The builder told me that there were three houses they had with these. Since this one was a spec house and already done, I told him we'd take it. I don't know the other two houses that got them though, they were part of the third expansion of the neighborhood."

"This is kinda cool. How'd you plumb in the bathroom over there?"

"There was a floor drain in the back corner capped off. I think it goes into the main sewer line, but it could just as well tie into the storm drain system."

Dwight walked around and sat down on one of the bottom bunks and bounced a little bit, got back up, and looked at the stacks of boxes. He raised an eyebrow and Steve motioned for him to go ahead and look. He opened the flap on one box and pulled out a gallon jug of water and then put it back down and closed the box.

"How much water?"

"Right now, fifty-four gallons," Steve said.

"So without bathing and flushing, you have enough down here for roughly ten, twelve days?"

"Yeah, roughly," Steve admitted.

"Gun safe looks secure. Bolted down?"

"Yeah. So...this is most of it. What do you think?"

Dwight sighed, rubbed his hand across his face and then looked Steve in the eye.

"You're in pretty good shape all things considered. How much food do you reckon you have?"

"A little over a year's worth, and then we have the rabbits and chickens...."

"Let's go get some more beer," Dwight said finishing off his bottle.

Steve nodded and both men headed upstairs. They dropped their empties in the sink to rinse out and recycle later and grabbed a couple more and went back out to the patio in the back. One of the chickens made a startled sound and they both looked. Nothing seemed out of order, so Steve sat down. After a moment, Dwight did too.

"So what do you think?" Steve asked after a moment.

"I mean, I sorta knew you were doing a lot of this stuff, but why ask me?"

"Your family lived through the depression, your dad and grandparents...right there," Steve said pointing with his beer.

"And you think the house of cards is going to fall down again?"

"Look at the price of gas."

"That's true. I think somebodies been siphoning a couple gallons of fuel from my tank farm by the barn. I had to put locks on the handles. Fuel's been getting more expensive, but I figured it was because of all the war uncertainty stuff."

"I'm sure that plays a big part of it, but the whole Fed. The thing has me worried too."

"Well, I think you're in better shape than just about everybody around here, except maybe me. As long as we don't get another bad drought like last year, I will probably be sitting on a ton of food if something goes crazy."

"Plus, your kitchen garden and animals."

"Yeah, but what worries me, is if something were to happen...I'm just one guy. We live outside of the city a little bit, but we're not all that far. I know Macon seems big, but when you really put on your thinking cap, we're not too far from Atlanta too. It wouldn't take much to pick the farm clean."

"Really?"

"Yeah, it looks like a lot, but you get a couple hundred people walking through, they'd clean me out of all my breeding stock and feedstock in no time flat. Sure, I have my own food I set aside, but my hope would be to protect some of my breeding stock, or trap some pigs and start over once people start to die off."

"There's an unpleasant thought."

"Yeah, just like figuring out who's been stealing gas and diesel."

"You want a hand with that?"

"What, you know how to set out traps that aren't gonna get me sued or arrested?"

"I know a couple of tricks," Steve admitted with a grin.

Steve found everything he needed from the junk drawer and in the garage and was walking with Dwight when his cell phone rang.

"Hello?" he asked.

"Hey babe, where you at?"

"Headed to Dwight's for a second."

"It's late," Angela said.

"I know, I'll fill you in when I get home. Nothing to worry about."

"You're not..."

"No, we stopped after the second beer."

"No, I can tell you're not drunk, I mean...you're not worried now. Something's different in your voice."

"Yeah, we talked about a ton of stuff, but listen, I've got my hands full. Can I talk to you in a half hour?"

"Yeah, babe. Love you, bye."

"Love you too," Steve said and then hung up.

"So tell me how this is going to work," Dwight said walking towards the barn.

"We're just going to make a simple switch with a paperclip. Might have to throw a bucket over it when it's done to waterproof it, but..."

"I've done a lot of crazy things, but I never would have thought of this."

"Did a lot of crazy things as a kid. We were on the farm for a while, that's why I know how to do some of the stuff with you, but I was a kid and never learned the important stuff."

"I'll go get the battery and horn," Dwight said and headed inside the barn.

Steve stayed outside and pulled out the supplies he'd brought from home. A few feet of black coated electrical wire from an old project, two brass thumb tacks, a large wooden clothespin they kept a supply of for potato chip bags and a roll of electrical tape. He sat down on the raised concrete pad that the fuel tanks were on and kicked his legs out, getting comfortable. He started cutting the wire to length and then stripping it with his Leatherman.

He could hear Dwight curse and then something fell with a crash. More cursing. Steve grinned and then pushed the thumbtacks in halfway in on the inside of the clothespin. He made a hook with the tip of the wire and hooked it around the thumbtacks and pressed them down tight. Then he used small strips of electrical tape to hold the wire along the outside of the clothespins with a loop and waited.

The theory was simple. He was going to hook one of the wires coming from the positive side of the battery to one end of the clothes pin. The other thumbtack and wire would be hooked up to a tractor horn he had off an older tractor, and then the other wire from the horn would go to the negative terminal on the battery. They would shove a stock in between the brass tacks on the inside of the clothespin to keep it from completing a circuit and then tie on the fishing line. When somebody stepped through the tripwire, it would dislodge the stick, the spring on the clothespin would push the tacks together and the horn would go off.

It was something he did as a kid, but he'd had an old horn from his dad's old Buick station wagon that had been slowly rusting in peace out of their garage in Ohio. Back when playing "Cowboys and Indians" wasn't a triggering term for half the country.

"I damn near busted my thumb pulling this out of the pile. Should have a charge," Dwight said walking out with a small battery.

"Great." Steve said and started hooking things up.

Dwight handed him the horn module when he got to that part and then pushed the pin up and looked around for something nonmetallic to put in it while he was going to hook it up to the battery. In the end, he double folded a piece of electrical tape with the sticky side together and put the plastic tape between the contacts and then finished hooking it up. Then he put tape around the connections, just to hold them in place.

"Want to test it?" Steve asked.

"Yeah, just a little toot," Dwight said with a grin.

Steve held onto the tape, squeezed the pin and pulled the tape out. Then the pin was allowed to close for half a heartbeat. A loud but fast beep sounded and Steve was the one smiling when he saw it startle Dwight.

"Dammit, I was ready for that, and it still got me," he said.

"Yeah. All we have to do now is find something nonmetallic to shove between the contacts and figure out where you want to set this all up."

"I can take care of that, now that I see how it's gonna work. You go ahead and get home to your wife and daughters."

"You sure?" Steve asked.

"Now that I see how it's done, I feel kinda dumb for not thinking of this myself. I'll get it moved and hidden and set it up tonight. Just call me before you come over next time, and I'll show you where not to step so you don't scare the hell out of me."

"Deal," Steve said and held his hand out.

Both men shook and he started heading home, and for the first time in a while, he didn't feel so helpless. They had discussed a plan, Dwight had offered to dig a cache spot for them, and together they would start making a backup plan in case the "Zombies" invaded.

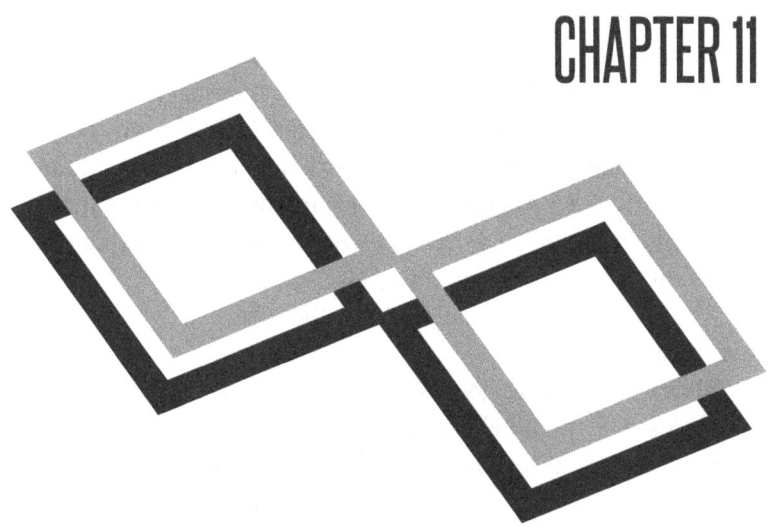

CHAPTER 11

Steve watched the daily news as the shooting match and the uneasy truce was called off. Then things got more heated. In the week since he'd shown Dwight how to make the alarm, things had started to globally deteriorate. He watched as another Iranian ship tried to get in front of a US Signal ship that monitors global communications and was subsequently run over and sunk. Global markets trembled, and the price of goods had started creeping up at a rate faster than he could imagine.

Work was steady for him. If anything, he was going to have to hire somebody on if he wanted to expand. The past week ran in waves. He had a day where he had almost nothing, then worked twenty hours straight the next day shoring up the cyber security of one of the firms that had left IT Bytes. More than once he had thought about asking Brandi if she wanted to work with him, but he had heard through the grapevine that with her buyout, she had to sign a non-compete clause. He left before that, so no such clause prevented him from working with the company. Brandi had actually funneled some business his way.

As long as everyone paid their bills, he was a little further ahead than he was when he was working with someone else, but the constant news coverage and worry was starting to test his patience. Almost nightly now, Dwight would stop out, and Angela and the two men would talk about just in case scenarios. Amy had only been all too happy to have her dad home for work now, but he was finding it hard to work when Angela wasn't keeping her busy. Steve thought it was only going to get worse after Amber started working at the restaurant a few miles down the road.

"You ready?" Steve called into the bedroom, pushing his door open.

"Dammit, Steve," Angela said, covering herself as he let himself in and closed the door behind him.

She dropped the towel and walked to the walk-in closet, her hair still wet.

"I take it as a no," Steve said admiring her form.

"You're perving on me again," Angela said.

"Isn't that how Amber and Amy happened?" he asked walking up behind her and pulling him close.

She leaned back into him for a moment, and then rubbed her wet hair on his chin, making him break his hold.

"Oh man, you play dirty," he said with a chuckle, wiping his face with his forearm.

"Dirty enough to skip church today?" she asked, turning to face him.

"No, ma'am," Steve said, but he was sorely tempted to.

"What time are we leaving?" Amber called from outside the door.

"Give me twenty minutes," Angela yelled back.

"Ok, I'll get out of your hair," Steve said backing up and walking backwards towards his desk.

"Uh huh. I don't see you hurrying to leave."

"Just admiring the view, ma'am," Steve told her with a grin.

"Admire it somewhere else. I need to get dressed and do something with my hair, and if we don't leave in twenty minutes, we're going to be late."

"Got it," Steve said and booted his laptop.

He had gotten up early to finish a couple lines of code and to do his surfing on the darknet. He knew that Angela hated when he did it because you could find anything there. Anything included subjects that weren't appropriate for polite conversation. Anything from drug deals, human smuggling, child exploitation, arms deals...and hacking. The latter is why he logged in and visited the .onion sites. He was following somebody who claimed to be from the Ukraine who was doing some probing of military satellites.

Steve thought it was absolutely insane to do something like that. It was so ballsy and difficult that he felt like the guy was wasting his time, but he was logging everything he was doing, and it made for interesting reading. He could use the methods and weaknesses found by the hackers to build better systems, and while his wife was working on not being naked and distracting, he distracted himself for a minute by looking for the latest updates.

What he saw shocked him. The North Koreans had been firing off ballistic missiles to test the new president's resolve and in return China had imposed sanctions by cutting off all coal purchases. It was going to cripple the PDRK's ability to build their military, industrial strength with little to no income. What got his attention though was Russia. The hacker had given up on getting into the US Satellites and gone after a Russian one.

He was dumping raw data through anonymous file servers, sending torrents. What he had, if it was real, was shocking. Proof that Russia was about to turn off natural gas and oil to both Europe and China. The reasons were many, but what it boiled down to was that the UN had been thumping its chest about Syria and the annexation, and the EU was talking about sanctions against Russia. Russia was exacting financial revenge on China for currency manipulation in an effort to weaken their economy while they were in a shooting match with us.

Steve knew he was no political analyst, financial expert, or even more than a slightly gifted coder who was good at trouble shooting.

Still, what he found was troubling, and they weren't even hiding these details very hard. If anybody in the EU got wind of this...it would turn bad...and quickly.

"You still coming to church?" Angela asked, startling him as she spoke and placed her hands on his neck.

"Yes ma'am," he said, standing and closing the lid on his laptop.

Both Amber and Amy stayed back after the service, sitting in the front pew with Joseph. They had been friends almost immediately when they had first found Holy Spirit Lutheran Church when they moved to Georgia almost two years ago. It had only been in the last six to eight months that Joseph suddenly realized that Amber was not only a girl, but a young woman who could soon drive. Steve smiled as he overheard his pitch to take him to Six Flags near Atlanta. Both Angela and Steve were standing in line to say their goodbyes as people made their way out of the church.

Here they felt the southern hospitality. In their subdivision, both Angela and Steve felt like their friendships were soured almost immediately by the Wilsons and Doug Morris. It wasn't the case here, even after coming for a year and a half, they were still warmly welcomed as if they were newcomers. Angela had been missing her church family more and more lately, and with Steve home now, she had been taking the opportunity to get out more, especially with the girls getting a little older and not needing constant supervision. She'd started making friends but slowly. Steve on the other hand was outgoing and forward, something she couldn't pull off as easily.

"And Mr. And Missus Taylor," Pastor James said holding his hand out.

The two men shook and then Steve took his wife Mary's hand and shook it as well.

"Thank you, Pastor. I find it interesting that you got into the Book of Matthew today," Steve said.

"It seemed very appropriate," Pastor James told him.

"Either that or the book of Revelations," both Mary and Angela chorused, and then burst out laughing at the jinx moment.

"Listen Pastor, your sermon today brought up something I wanted to talk to you about, when you get a moment."

"I can after we finish our goodbyes? Would you like to wait?"

"Sure, we might have to anyways. I think the girls are planning some sort of nefarious plan involving Joseph and Six Flags."

"Nefarious? It'd only be nefarious if Matt went along. It'd crush Joseph," Angela chided.

"It sounds like kids being kids. I'll see you two in a moment," Pastor James said smiling and gave them both a hug.

"Thanks for letting Joseph hang out with the girls. It's done a lot for his self-esteem," Mary said as soon as they walked back.

"What do you mean?" Angela asked.

"You know.... Your daughter didn't tell you?" Pastor James Johnson asked.

"No, is it something I should be concerned with?" Steve asked.

"No, no. She's just a really kind kid. Joseph was being bullied by an older kid on the bus before school let out for the summer. You know how cruel kids can be."

"Yeah, I was one once," Steve said, not sure where this was going.

"Well, you know, preacher's son. A girl in his class and a couple of boys were ragging on him a bit. Amber told them off and then took him by the hand and led him to the back of the bus with her girlfriends. Suddenly, he's sitting with the older pretty girls and it...I know it isn't very Christian of me, but it backfired on those that were picking on him."

"Big man on the bus," Angela said, touched that her daughter had done that.

"I think so. It really helped a lot, at least for him," Mary said. "It also made him...surer of himself. More confident. Anyways, I haven't had a chance to personally thank your family for that."

"Maybe that's why there's a little bit of crushing going on?" Steve asked.

"Crush?" Mary asked, an eyebrow raised.

"Now he stepped in it," Angela said with a grin. "We think Joseph is crushing on Amber a little bit and Amy is crushing on Joseph. If they weren't so innocent and young it'd be something right out of a soap opera."

"Or an old episode of *Dallas*," Mary shot back, and both ladies busted up laughing.

"I feel like, suddenly, I don't want to hear anymore," Steve said.

Pastor James stuck his fingers in his ears and made *lalalalalalalala* sounds while the ladies laughed. As soon as they noticed the very obvious eye rolls and gagging sounds of Steve and Pastor James they cut it a little bit.

"Now, you wanted to talk to me about something?" Pastor James said as he motioned for them to have a seat in the front pew.

They all sat, and Steve turned to his side a bit so he could see the pastor better, even though he was sitting on his right.

"With what's going on in the world, and what you all picked up on with the Book of Matthew's study lesson today...I think it would be prudent for you and the members of the church to prepare for hard times."

"You mean the financial meltdown and potential nuclear war with any of three countries we're trading shots with?"

Steve chuckled, not realizing how plugged in some people were. He was used to being treated like a mental defect for his prepping and crazy-sounding conspiracy theories, but right off the bat, he felt comfortable talking with the pastor about this, and it had been worrying him all day long.

"That's exactly what he's worried about," Amber said walking over. "He's got some kind of superman complex, planning to try to save the world, one damsel in distress at a time."

"There better be only one damsel in his life," Angela shot back.

"There's only one in mine," Joseph said, his voice dreamy.

Only the grownups saw Amber's rolled eyes, but she was smiling. Amy on the other hand, had her mouth opening and closing like a guppy gasping for air. Steve made a motion with his head for her to let the grownups talk.

"Hey, can I take Joseph and Amy for a ride around the block for a minute or two? He wants to check out my Jeep."

Steve looked at Mary and James who both smiled and shrugged. "I don't mind," Steve told her.

"What if I do?" Angela asked him, poking his shoulder.

"Then you can deal with it," he said and ducked as she flicked at his ear.

"Let's go before he changes his mind," Joseph said and the three of them started to run down the now empty church.

They waited until the doors closed. "You know, Pastor, I'm worried that soon the money isn't going to be worth anything anymore. It's already started out slowly and it's getting faster day by day."

"I noticed that too. I don't know what to do about it though," he said. "Donations are down, money is tight with everyone. It isn't a rich or poor thing, it's an everybody thing."

"Yes, and I think it's only going to get worse," Steve said softly.

"I fear you're correct. That's why I've gotten myself a Sam's Club card. I'd love if we had a Costco down here, it's—"

"Wait, what do you mean?" Angela asked.

"I know, right? When he said he wanted to start prepping food for us and the church, I thought he was...." Mary made a twirling motion next to her temple.

"Yeah, we've become preppers over the past two years," Pastor James said.

"Huh," Angela said, "So you do the whole beans, bullets, and Band-Aids?"

"Honey," Mary said, "It's the south. Guns are a way of life."

Steve grinned, "Pastor, in the event of hard times, would you be helping feed the church, or are you still building your family stash?"

"I've built my family stash. We don't need extravagant food, and there's three of us. As for the church, yes. I don't have much saved, but I'd like to do more with that."

Steve looked to his left at Angela who gave him a broad smile and nodded. His heart soared, suddenly he didn't feel...uncomfortable.

"Pastor, I've been into prepping for a while. I've built up my stash pretty good, but a friend pointed out to me that I've got all my eggs in one basket. I have an idea, but only if you're willing to—"

"Spit it out," Pastor James said, in his no-nonsense voice.

"In the event something happens, my biggest worry will be the roughly ninety thousand people from the Macon area. We're outside of downtown, but not too far."

"If something major ever happens, they'll head North towards Atlanta would be my guess," James said.

"I would think they'd head west towards the countryside, wouldn't they?" Mary asked the three of them.

"Anything's possible. But...I'd like to think I'd like to start prepping with our church family in mind before things are needed. It'd make me feel better, and if things go really south...I mean, we might need some of it ourselves."

"I certainly wouldn't mind the assistance. That's very generous of you. You know, we have an unused Sunday school classroom. It's the one that has the bad electrical. I haven't had a chance to finish it off yet. I've been storing the church's provisions in there. You're welcome to add to it, if you'd like."

"If that isn't too much of an intrusion," Steve said.

"No, not at all."

"Hon, I know you were nervous about pitching this idea, but I can see it might be a lifesaver. If something happens, it won't be forever. It might help people get over the gap if they aren't as ready."

"That's the other thing," Steve said and then surprised them all.

He laid out his idea, if the Pastor was willing, and he was. The next sermon would be more Matthew, and then some book of Revelations. A lot of this was just a modified hurricane prep, but every little bit would help. Then the Pastor surprised them when he suggested that he'd ask members to forgo the donations to buy their own stash of emergency food, or food for the church. Feeling much better about things, he said his goodbyes and collected the kids who were in the parking lot, the Jeep now parked next to Angela's BMW.

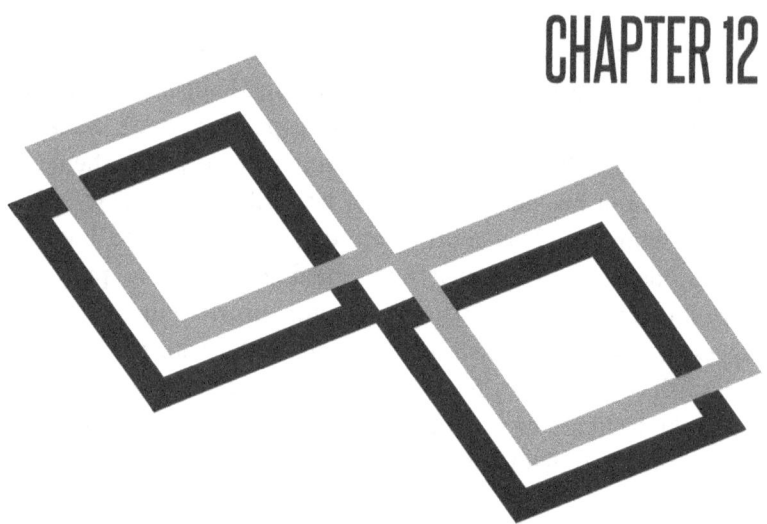

CHAPTER 12

The next week was worsening foreign relations and watching the price of all goods creeping up. Bread had gone from two dollars and eight cents a loaf to almost three dollars since the start of summer. People were visibly worried and the stock market trembled. Steve thought about how he wanted to do his backup to his backup plan. He'd been paid for the month, paid his bills for the month, and then it occurred to him. He'd asked and gotten permission from Angela when he pointed out if he was wrong, he could always donate it against taxes.

"Dad, I want to do the running with you," Amy said as he headed into the garage to fire up his truck.

"Not this time, baby," he told her, hating to say it.

"This has been a boring summer. All I want to do is get out of the house. I mean, sheesh!" Amy told him and stomped to her bedroom, slamming the door.

"I'm sorry," he called halfheartedly.

Angela had been spinning salad greens she'd gotten from the store now that it was too hot to grow their own without it bolting. She gave him a shrug.

"Want to eat before you go prepare for a Mad Max dystopian type of world?" Angela asked, nodding to the chicken breasts sizzling in olive oil with onions on a skillet.

"No thanks. I want to get rolling. I have to hit the bank first and now that I'm done working for the day, I can make it there before they close."

"What about the other place you were heading?"

"I'll know more when I get there," he told her with a grin.

"Ok, you be safe," Angela said and walked up and kissed him.

"I was disgusted before, but now it's...double!" Amy shouted from her doorway.

Both broke the kiss to look at their daughter amusedly, then Steve grabbed Angela by the waist and spun her like they were dancing and then tilted her back and kissed her deeply. Puking noises were met with that and Angela started giggling despite the kiss. He gave up and let her back up.

"I'll see you ladies later on. Have Amber text me when she gets home would you?"

"Yeah, your favorite daughter," Amy said and slammed her door again.

"What's up with her?" Steve asked, confused.

"Joseph and her had a talk—"

"Did she—"

"No, she didn't. She knows he's way too old for her. I mean, she's going to be ten soon; he's already thirteen."

Steve let out a breath he'd been holding for longer than he'd realized.

"Ok, well, I'll get her some chocolate or something on my way home."

"I don't have PMS!" Amy yelled.

Steve flinched and fled as quickly as his dignity and man card allowed, hearing his wife call goodbye. He fired up the truck and headed into town, something he was actually doing more of lately. With Dwight's help and permission, he'd buried two food grade barrels on the far side of Dwight's property to stash some dry goods that were packed in Mylar and oxygen absorbers. One of his smaller tractors, a beast almost the size of Steve's truck, easily scooped out a hole with two swipes. Then he'd rolled the nearly full barrel most of the way into it before the old farmer had gotten bored and used the bucket of the front loader to roll it in. Then they were filled in and a discrete marker was put down: a flat piece of shale.

What he was doing today was even furthering his preps, and with the price of goods constantly going up, he was now putting a plan in motion. First stop was the bank. He was pulling in when his work phone rang. He pulled over and answered it.

"...Yeah, I've specifically coded against that...yeah, I know. I saw the WikiLeaks thing too...yeah, I've known about that vulnerability for a year...oh yeah. I'll run a brute force attack as soon as I get in front of a terminal...oh...Um...8:00 p.m.? Good. Thank you for calling."

"Man," Steve said to himself after he hung up the phone, "things are really going to get interesting. Vault number eight. People didn't learn from last time."

He was always amused when a customer saw something on the news and called to inform him. In this case, it was an electronics factory in Monterey, Mexico. They had their own IT guys, but they were looking for an outside expert. The owners didn't trust anybody local. In the past, they had been taken advantage of. Steve walked into the bank, half distracted thinking about how he was going to run a simulated brute force attack on them that was obvious enough that their IT guys could see it live.

"Good afternoon sir, how can I help you?" the teller asked, as he stepped towards the ropes that made the line.

"Uh, pretty good. Dead in here, huh?" he asked looking around at the empty bank.

"Yeah, it's been quiet. What can I get for you, and your account number?"

"9703-331 is my account number, and I'd like to withdraw twenty-five thousand dollars from my savings account."

For a second, the extremely young and pretty teller did a double take at the amount and then started tapping keys. She hit a few more buttons and a printer whirred to life.

"Just need to see some ID, and because it's an amount of ten thousand dollars or more, I need you to sign an extra form for me."

"Not a problem," Steve said, already mentally prepared for this part. "Buying a new truck. I'm getting the cash discount!"

"Oh wow, I hope you're getting a good deal."

"Twenty-five thousand dollars," Steve told her with a fake grin plastered on his face.

"Oh, um..." she stammered as he signed. "You know they're going to charge you sales tax, license fees and plate transfer or new plate fees and stuff."

Steve's smile faltered and he smacked his forehead and looked at the earnest young lady.

"You know what, you're right. Make it an even thirty thousand, and that should cover it," he said, liking the sound of the round number better, one that was a decent chunk of the nest egg and severance package he got from Brandi.

She pulled the forms back and then reprinted things. As he was signing, she got a phone call. She spoke into it quietly and then took the forms when he was done.

"I'll be right back," she said.

It took her a few minutes and he was starting to think there might have been something wrong when she came back out with three stacks. She pulled the bands of each stack and ran it through a counter, three times per stack, before bundling them back up.

"I don't have an envelope big enough for three stacks. How about three envelopes?"

"Works for me," Steve said, feeling nervous.

The delay had made him wonder if he might have missed out on some new obscure banking law designed to catch money launderers. They prosecuted those like no joke, so he had no idea what they would do to people who were looking to do what he was going to do. Put a black mark on his record? Write him off as a loon?

She finished packing up his money and he put the fat stacked envelopes in his pocket. Steve felt nervous as he walked out of the bank, as if for some reason the stacks of bills suddenly weighed more. Getting his concealed carry permit had been something he'd done early on after moving from Ohio, but he'd never really done it until after the secret was out that he'd purchased the guns. Now, he hardly left the house without the comforting weight of the pistol.

With that taken care of, it was a good twenty-minute ride back in the direction of his house. His stop was a mini storage between the more built up portion of Macon and the suburbs. He still had time, if they stayed open as late as he saw on their website. If not, there was one a little bit closer to home, but he wasn't sure he wanted it closer to home. Closer to home meant more people in the area knew him by sight. He didn't want that—not yet. He pulled into the storage site with a good half hour before closing time.

"Hello, sir. Looking to get a storage unit?" The polite twentyish woman behind the counter asked, putting down a romance novel she'd been reading.

"Yes, I was wondering...would it be possible for me to rent a unit or two?"

"If you need more than one, we have larger spaces available with our inside storage?" She asked, pulling out a printed map of the units.

"Oh, let me see...hmm...See, part of it is for my daughter. She's about your age and going to college. I've been meaning to put in a small workout room but she does not want to take all her stuff, and I'd like to get her own unit."

"Oh, that's not a problem," she said pulling out a log book and set it up next to the map and started flipping.

"How big of a unit do you want to have for both?"

"Something big enough to pull in a van and store it for mine," he told her, "and maybe a ten by twelve for her?"

"Let me see..."

She flipped the map around so she could see it better and then flipped through the logbook.

"Would you like the unit to have power? Some people use them as workshops, all we ask is that it's kept swept and picked up and nothing left outside—"

"I might do some work from there," Steve said hopeful, but trying to hide it. "Yeah, how about power for both?"

"All I've got that are close by each other are these two units," she said highlighting two on the map and then turned it around so he could study them, "They're bigger than you were wanting and have power, but they are in a hard-to-back-in-and-out-of area. I could give you a discount if you want both, but being in the very back and opposite sides of the building, you'd have to drive around it to get to both doors."

Again, Steve pretended not to be excited. The units themselves on the west side of the building were twenty by twenty. The east side of the building, had units backed up to it that were ten feet wide by twenty feet deep. The smaller unit shared a back wall with the larger one.

"How much for both? I'll be paying for a year in advance."

"For both..." she turned and started punching in numbers on an adding machine, "with one month's free rent on each...plus the discount I'm going to give you...plus paying up front..."

"Do you discount for cash?" Steve asked.

The woman looked up, a devilish smile on her face.

"I do," she said. "What name should I put on the units?"

"Cash, Steve Cash," he said with a grin.

"Welcome to Little Bonnie's Mini Storage, Mister Cash. I'm Bonnie Sue. Both units with unmetered power, paid in cash a year in advance. Your total will be one-thousand seven-hundred and ninety-eight dollars."

I love America, Steve thought to himself and started counting out bills.

✛

The last stop of the evening turned out to be a dud. He'd gone to the local tractor supply store to look at covered trailers. If he was going to start doing a lot of preparing, he wanted to do so under the radar. He knew he'd have to wait a day or so to get plates and tags, but instead decided that he'd skip to what he had thought of as his fourth stop. He drove back into town and pulled into Sam's parking lot.

The door greeter gave him a wave after checking his membership card and headed back towards the aisles that held the dried goods. There's something magical about a food warehouse like this. It could feed the entire city about one whole meal from everything stocked in there. Ninety-thousand mouths. When you broke that down into smaller numbers you could feed three hundred people eighteen hundred meals, which worked out to one hundred days' worth of food, if his math was working. Maybe there was more, or less, but as he walked down the spice aisle, where they sold spices by the case, he marveled at how much there was.

"Sir, do you need a cart or flatbed?" an employee asked, startling him.

Steve looked him over while he stilled his heart rate some, and saw he was a man who looked to be in his late thirties. His skin tone suggested he was of Hispanic descent somewhere in his history, but the name tag read George. He was probably a transplant, much like Steve, and Steve figured he was as much of an outsider as he was to this area. Hell, he could probably be part American Indian, or a mixture of—

"I'm not sure," Steve admitted, "I have a weird request...and I'm trying to wrap my brain how to word it so I don't sound like a loon."

"Just spit it out," George said. "We get all types here. People running smaller grocery stores, shops, co-ops, churches, doomsday preppers, and then there are the really scary ones. You want to know who they are?"

"Who?" Steve asked in a quiet voice.

"Regular people. You have no idea what they are going to do. Regular people scare me," George said and then broke out into a grin.

"I aspire to be regular someday," Steve said, chuckling now, "but not today."

"So what can I help you find?" George asked.

"I just started working with my church, and we're going to start a mission to Guatemala," Steve lied. "To start with, I was wondering how I buy in bulk. I mean, not just in the big bags, but by the pallet?"

"Wow, I didn't peg you for a church missionary, but good on you." George said with a grin. "You just tell me what you're looking for and I'll start you out on the best way that I can."

"That's great. I think the plan is still to load up a semi piecemeal until it's full and then send the trailer south, so I don't think I'm going to have access to something like that...but what do you think about me picking up say, a pallet or two a day until they tell me to quit?"

Steve knew somewhere, he was probably going to go to hell, but it was the most plausible ruse he could come up with. Plus, a lot of the food would be going to the church first, and then his backup plan—he hoped.

"Well, if you have an idea on how much you're going to buy, you might be better off buying it now and then picking it up by the load as needed. The pricing on things is going up and people are already getting upset they can't buy a monster box of Cheetos for the same price they could a month ago."

"Has it gone up that fast here?" Steve asked.

"Yeah, I do a lot of the ordering checks. Most of the system is automated but people have been buying less lately since we started having to raise the prices. The corporate overlords will only let us eat so much of it, but the transportation costs are killing us."

That was something he hadn't thought of. How long would truckers deliver goods with the rising cost of fuel? Right here was a direct correlation between fuel and food prices. In a discounted warehouse of food....

"Wow, I uh...I don't know if I have that much of a plan yet. If I bring my personal truck and trailer, could you guys load it up with a pallet?"

"Personal truck...unless it's a one ton, I'd say be careful with the weight. For Guatemala, I'm guessing lots of grains. Rice, wheat berries, corn?"

"Yeah, some real basics. Probably a ton of spices too but that's..."

"Yeah, I've done some missionary orders before. I could look up one I did for a couple who were sending food to Haiti a couple years back? Get an idea?"

"That would be fantastic."

"It might take me a few, I have to run to the back. Want me to find you when I'm done or..."

"I'll give you my cell phone number. Give me a ring when you're ready, and I'll wander around this place and get some ideas?"

"Perfect!"

They exchanged numbers and George headed towards the back and Steve started walking the aisles. He didn't mean to, but he overheard a lot of people shopping in there. Some were talking about how the increased pricing to food, fuel and energy costs were making things more difficult. He saw one mother put away a big box of sugared cereal over her kid's loud protests to only get a big twin pack of rolled oats. It hurt his heart to see them sacrifice what they wanted versus what they could afford, but he was doing much of the same with his preps. He could go out for luxury, but didn't have that kind of budget.

Then he wandered into the middle of the store where they had everything from clothing to books, to outdoor equipment. Tables, chairs, picnic benches, camping gear, grills, stoves... and he suddenly knew what he wanted to do with that small ten by twenty foot storage unit, and although it would do storage, if he could pull it off, it would be a place like his storm shelter. A place to temporarily bug out. It would take some work...

His phone rang and he agreed on where to meet George. He found him less than a minute later and although black marker had blotted out a lot of information, quantities and old pricing was there. The couple's order was staggering and would have taken most of his chunk of money he withdrew, so he thanked George and asked if he could take it with him and come back in a day or two with a plan of his own. No sense in filling a storage unit to capacity, if construction is needed to make a fortified bolt hole.

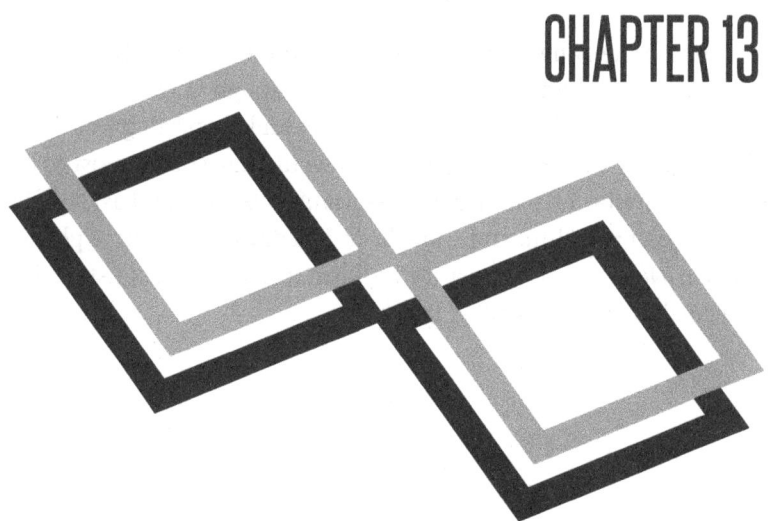

CHAPTER 13

"Dad, I want you to know something," Amber said, as they were putting bags of rice on a push cart in the church's parking lot.

"What's that, sweetie?" he asked.

"I might think you're a little weird for doing stuff like this, for us I mean...but you're...I'm proud of you."

Steve beamed at his daughter. In the last two weeks since he'd made large strides towards getting the church filled, he soon learned he had physical limitations and his back was absolutely killing him.

"Thanks kiddo," he told her. "It's the right thing to do." And besides, it'll keep the community from coming after us if the worst should happen, he finished mentally, knowing it was a selfish thought.

"Hey, when I start back to school, would you let me get a parking permit?"

"That was random," Steve said.

She grinned at her dad and kept schlepping till the cart was hard to push. She started up the ramp with it and about the halfway point Steve put his weight and muscle behind it. His back had been killing him since he overdid it a couple days ago. It was before he'd ordered the forty-dollar foldable hand cart off of Amazon. This was Amber's second trip with him.

"Hey, I was wondering if you two would be in today. Come on in!" Mary said, opening the church doors wide.

Amber took over the cart now that she didn't have to fight extra gravity from the ramp and got it over the sill and into the church.

"Yeah, I sorta fibbed to the guys at Sam's club and now I have to make good on my promise and take a good chunk worth of a semi-trailer load of food."

"Oh dear," Mary said, her eyes huge. "I don't think we can fit that much in the classroom."

"My dad has a backup plan for his backup plan," Amber said, and flipped her hair out of her eyes.

"Hi Amber, want a hand with that?" Joseph called, coming in from behind the altar where he'd been polishing brass.

"Sure!" Amber said cheerfully.

Joseph walked up and with each step, he looked between Steve and Amber and then broke out into a big grin.

"They can get it. You look like you're beat."

"I kind of am," Steve admitted.

He followed her and she sat down in the back pew.

"Where's James at?" he asked, dropping the "pastor" title in private, which James appreciated.

"He went to the office supply store. I guess the sermon was so popular that people were asking for more information on doing their own food storage. I just sort of hate that it takes global strife to get people to do something that makes sense."

"I wonder what made the LDS churches include that into their doctrine?" Steve asked her.

"I don't know, we don't really study them. James would know more..."

Mary's words trailed off as she heard teenage laughter and then the murmur of voices. A second later, both smiling, Joseph and Amber headed past them towards the door.

"We've got this; you rest up," she called.

"Ok, I'll let you young ones do it," Steve called back.

"I hate to ask, but you must have sunk a lot of money into this. Are you sure?"

"Food is the cheap part," Steve said feeling uncomfortable. Besides, I can use it as a tax write-off if nothing ever happens and we end up having to donate it."

"I can actually write you a receipt for that, we are a nonprofit after all," Mary said with a grin.

Steve hadn't thought of that and chuckled. What he told George at the supermarket warehouse wasn't all that far off from the truth after all.

"I might take you up on that by tax season," Steve said, knowing his wife would appreciate the gesture as much or more than he did.

"You were listening to the radio on your way over?" Mary asked.

"No, why?" Steve asked.

"Well, seems that fuel and part shortages are slowing down a ton of refineries, they are expecting huge price increases. It sounds like you and I were thinking a lot alike, planning ahead."

"You were the prepper in the family, weren't you?" Steve asked as the kids pushed another cartload in the doorway.

"Yes, but James was an easy convert. His family grew up hunting and fishing. He wasn't a farmer but his grandmother was a sharecropper so there was a lot of things he knew but hadn't thought of. That's why what's going on here is so..."

"Scary," Steve finished.

"Dad..." Amber called from the other room.

"I think we're being summoned," Mary said, standing.

"Yeah?" he said, and followed her.

They walked down the short hallway that was left of the main worship hall. The first three doors opened up to Sunday school rooms they were using, the last one on the left was a little larger as it was the back corner of the building that housed the church. At the very end of the hallway, was a bathroom, but it was the last door on the left they opened.

"What's up, sweetie?" Steve asked.

Amber rolled her eyes, but she had half a smile on her face, one arm wiping the sweat off her forehead.

"Is it safe to stack this all up like this? Won't it like break the floor and fall into the basement?"

Steve looked at the room, his eyes squinting. They had quite literally placed a pallet on the floor and had been stacking fifty-pound bags of rice along the back wall, forty pound bags of beans the next pallet to the left, and then lentils, textured vegetable protein, coffee, and a growing pile of canned meat.

"Oh wow, there's more here than I thought," Steve said.

"It isn't just you adding to the stockpile now," Mary said. "We've started adding some of ours and a couple trusted members of the church are working on the canned meat."

"Trusted members?" Amber asked.

"People we can trust with a secret as big as this," Joseph answered for his mother. "Operational Security. That's why we're putting a different lockset on it come Sunday before the next service."

"Yeah, we've had a couple people curious what we're doing because they've seen you and a few other people unloading stuff. I told them we're working on an outreach project and doing some remodeling," Mary answered.

"Huh, well, I hope we can all get the tax credit for this someday. I hope it's never needed," Steve told her.

"Yeah, me too," Joseph said. "Hey, Mr. Taylor, do you want me to give you a hand unloading this stuff at your house?"

The problem was, Steve thought, they weren't going back to their house. He looked over at Amber to see if she had a way out for him. She however, took his look in another direction.

"He'd be a great help," she said and Joseph grinned broadly. "I can run him home if that's ok with Mrs. Johnson?"

"Oh, I don't mind. I'm heading out in twenty minutes anyways. I can always swing by there on my way home?"

"It might take us a little longer than that. Now that we have room for more weight...."

"Don't you worry then, I don't mind. You've been driving all summer long now Amber, I trust you'll treat him with care."

"Oh, I will, don't worry," Amber said.

Dry mouthed, Steve said his goodbyes and loaded the kids into the truck.

"So, you want to see the real secret?" Amber asked him as soon as the truck started rolling.

"What?" Joseph asked.

Steve could have almost died. She hadn't misunderstood at all.

"Oh, wow. What is this place?" Joseph asked, walking into the big storage unit that was empty, ready for Steve to back the truck in.

"It's my dad's secret room," she told him, and motioned for her dad to back in.

He did and she turned on a pedestal lamp. Steve cut the truck off to combat the fumes and then pulled the door closed, leaving them in a gloomy space, empty save themselves and the truck. The room itself was plain, with unfinished green board on the walls and a cement pad.

"What do you mean secret...."

His words cut off as Amber pushed on one of the unfinished panels against the back-right wall. It swung backwards into the storage unit behind it. Steve reached in and flicked on the light he'd installed a switch for. With a flicker, fluorescent lights came on illuminating the much smaller room. At the far end, the roll-up door was hidden behind what looked like an unfinished wall. Instead of the green board on the walls in here, there were layers of cement board. It was unfinished, as evidenced of half the walls showing at

120

least three different layers of the hardy building material. A stack of cement board was leaned up against the side with the light switch and had several outlets near the floor.

"Oh snap. This is...a...uhmm...my dad was talking about this."

"An emergency fall-back location with supplies," Steve said, and pointed off to the side, a few feet away.

Pallets cut in half lined the rest of the twenty-foot wall. The amount of food inside of here wasn't as much as at the church, but it looked to be quite a bit in Joseph's eyes. It wasn't all food though. There were water-cooler jugs full of water in those funny plastic crates and what looked like camping supplies. The sound of a compressor kicking on had him turn and look. A dehumidifier kicked on in a far corner. It had a small diameter hose running from it to a small floor drain.

Joseph turned, looking in amazement and then walked over, pushing shut the door they had come in. When he did, he saw the heavy hinges on the side of the door they were on and then saw the heavy bolts to lock the door from the inside. He tested one out and then unlocked it in awe. Turning he took another look and then walked to the far side and started looking in the camp gear.

"You even have a chemical toilet," he said.

"Yeah well, it's a work in progress. If anything were to ever truly get scary, we're hoping to pull a car in here, close the door and disappear. Even if they follow us here, they would have to get the unit opened and then find this false wall," Steve told the kid, feeling vindicated that he had done something clever.

"If you're not in there though and they saw you come in, wouldn't they start looking for hidden doors and stuff?"

"Come on short stuff, let me show you," Amber said, patting him on the shoulder.

Joseph followed her back to where the truck was and she lowered the tailgate. Then she climbed up and reached up over her head and pulled on a rope hanging about eighteen inches from the ceiling. An attic ladder pulled down and she unfolded half of it, letting the rest of the stairs sit on the tailgate.

"Come on," she said and started jimmying up the ladder.

Steve almost told her to stop, the wood was going to scratch the paint, but they were already up before he could start to protest. He saw both sets of legs sitting on the edge and heard Amber explaining to Joseph about the paths they had walked in the dust up there across the flimsy plywood so it looked like they went out at the far end of the building.

"Man, with an attic access like that, you could get into any of these units," he said as he climbed down the ladder.

"Yeah, and we want to give them the best excuse to go to the far end. There's an open unit down there that's unlocked with another attic access door."

"Oh man, but what if somebody else rents it out?"

"Amber's the one who planned this escape route, why don't you ask her?" Steve said grinning as she finished her decent and was already folding the ladder back up.

"Well, daddy already had two units. The big one to hide the truck and store some stuff, which we probably will...then the hidden room. I figured if he had two, why not more? So I asked if we could rent one near the end. We left it unlocked and open."

"What if somebody comes in cuz that one's unlocked and goes up through the attic and comes in here?" he asked.

She pointed and then he understood. The same heavy bolts that held the secret room safe were installed on the inside of this unit.

"You're pretty smart. You sure you and Matt are pretty tight?" he asked.

"Excuse me?" Steve asked, jokingly bristling.

"No Dad, he doesn't...I mean...we're just friends...."

"Uh huh, nice save," Steve said with a growl, but he was actually grinning inside.

"Want to help me unload the truck?" Amber asked hopping off and all but running for the hidden room.

"She's a little too old for you," Steve told him in a softer tone.

"Oh, I know. She did something nice for me once. I know I'm in the friend zone, but I figure she'd appreciate feeling...wanted? Even if both of us know it'd never go anywhere."

"Damn. You're smarter than I was when I was younger."

"How long ago was that?" Joseph asked.

"I didn't think I figured that one out till last year."

Steve was sitting on the back patio, but had no plans on doing it for long. Late summer was hot and muggy and the bugs were horrible. Instead, he was sipping on a beer and listening for the low growl that indicated Amber was coming back. It gave him a little time to think and his back to rest.

"Hey Dad, Uncle Dewey's pig had babies. Can we go over and see them?" Amy asked, sipping on a lemonade like the world's most sophisticated almost-ten-year old that she was.

"I don't see why not—"

A loud horn went off, and stayed honking. Steve put his beer down and listened, trying to get a fix on it. One long, loud note. He turned in a circle and then realized that it was coming from behind his house, towards Dwight's farm.

"Tell your mom to call Uncle Dewey; tell her I'm heading over."

"I want to come with you," Amy said standing up.

"No, there's trouble. Stay here, I don't want you to get hurt," Steve said.

"Dad—"

"Do it," Steve yelled as he flipped his chair over backwards in his attempt to get away from the table.

He heard the back door open and for Angela to call out his name and then Amy talking to his mom just as he opened the back gate. He didn't pause to latch it, instead took off on a run down the path he took towards his friend's house. He patted his side, feeling the comforting weight of the compact .45 he'd taken to carrying over the Colt to see if it was still there. It was, and for the first time in years, Steve Taylor broke into a dead run.

It had been a while, and he'd forgotten about the alarm system he'd helped to ad hoc for Dwight. Bugs seemed to bounce off his face like they would splatter on your windshield when driving down the road, but he kept going. He made a left turn around a section of uncut corn and saw a figure in the most unseasonable looking white hoody running full out with two fuel cans, one for each hand. The figure was looking behind him, back towards Dwight's when Steve lowered his shoulder. The two hit just as Steve had planned, but what he'd forgotten in all his years, was how much it hurt to tackle somebody without pads.

The breath was almost knocked out of him as both men's feet left the ground. He heard a scream of pain as the man in the white hoody took the hit to his breadbasket. Both of them hit the ground with Steve more or less on top, his shoulder, chest, and neck sore from the full body impact. Shouts in the distance alerted him that somebody somewhere was coming, but all he could concentrate on was the sounds of heavy breathing, the snarled curses and arms that were swinging metal fuel cans at his head. One hit Steve in the temple, and he saw stars, but it didn't stop him from swinging a right fist into the hooded figures face once, twice, a third time, and the figure went limp, his arms dropping the fuel cans.

Steve stood up slowly, feeling his temple where he was a hit. His hand came back with a smear of crimson, and he sat down hard as the dizziness made his eyes cross.

"Daddy!" Amy screamed.

He looked up and saw Amy about a hundred yards in front of Angela, both of them running full out. A moan below him turned his attention back as the figure moved and pulled the hood back to vomit on the grass. He recognized the figure now. Billy Wilson, the neighbor's nineteen-year-old layabout. Two older metal fuel cans had been discarded, one of them dented pretty good. Steve flopped back onto his butt and drew the pistol, but didn't point it.

His bell was rung pretty hard, and he was seeing double.

"Don't shoot, Yankee!" Dwight's voice called out.

Steve looked up and tried to talk.

"That's all right—"

"Jesus, what'd he do to you?" Dwight asked, walking up close, almost out of breath.

"Hit me with the can," Steve said, holding his left hand up to his temple and holstered his pistol.

He could see two of the old farmer, and he had his broomstick with him.

"Daddy!" Amy yelled and slid to a stop a foot away.

"You ok?" Angela asked a moment later, a little out of breath as she slid to a stop next to Billy.

"Yeah, hit me with the can. Had to thump him to make him stop swinging," Steve told them, pulling at his shirt.

"No, Hoss, lay down," Dwight said, pushing Steve back and pulling what looked like a clean handkerchief from his center bib pocket.

It was still folded crisply, like it was new out of the package. Dwight folded it again and handed it to Steve. With sticky fingers, he took it and pressed it against the red-hot feeling wound on his temple.

Air whooshed out of Angela's mouth when he removed his hand. "You're going to need stitches," she told him. "I'm calling 911."

"Tell them to send two. I'm concussed, and I'm pretty sure I busted up Billy Wilson," Steve said, seeing double again.

He started slumping backward when Amy got behind him on her knees and pressed herself against her dad's back.

"You're going to get messy, Little Bit," Steve told her.

"Daddy, I got you. Just don't go to sleep. Remember in Ohio when I hit my head learning to ride my bike?"

"Yeah, baby," Steve admitted.

"Now, you need our help. Now, don't go to sleep, or I'll have Uncle Dewey and Mom turn the hose on you."

Dwight rolled Billy over, out of the growing pile of puke. He could see the entire side of his face swelling, his right eye a slit. Already the area around the eye and nose were turning purple.

"Sheriff and ambulance are on the way," Angela said smiling at the sight of her little princess doctoring her dad.

Steve wanted to be strong for the girls, but he was so dizzy. He knew he was scaring them, but trying to stay awake, trying to focus on Amy's murmurs, was taking every bit of concentration he had.

"Don't sleep," Amy said.

"Trying not to puke. Dizzy," Steve admitted.

"Then keep talking to me, Dad," she said.

"I'll open them in a minute," Steve said, his eyes closing.

The Sheriff and two deputies responded. The Sheriff took a general statement from Dwight and Angela, then left to go let the Wilson's know their son was heading to the hospital.

"We need to take your statement, Mr. Taylor," Deputy Lucy Javier said, a woman who looked to be of Italian or Greek descent.

Her partner was Deputy Ron Lewis, who had performed first aid on Steve while they waited for the ambulance.

"Sure," Steve said.

"Doesn't he need a lawyer?" Dwight asked.

"That depends. I just want a general overview, like the Sheriff got, but from your words."

"Can it wait?" Steve asked.

"Honestly, I wouldn't. That kid might be nineteen, but it looks like you broke his eye socket. I'd rather have something on record now, instead of letting the prosecuting attorney pick and choose who the aggressor was."

"It started with people stealing my fuel," Dwight started to tell her, but she waved him off.

"Ok, so it started with Mr. Abbott's fuel farm. People were stealing gasoline and diesel?"

"Yes," Steve said. "He got some locks, but they got cut once and I told him I knew a cheap way to make an alarm, so we did. I heard the alarm go off and ran over to see what's going on. That's when I ran into Billy, literally. He hit me with that metal gas can, and I punched him."

"How many times would you say?" Lucy asked.

"Twice as he was hitting me with the gas cans, then the third time to knock him out. I'm getting too old to take a beating like that."

Steve had twisted in pain and his shirt rode up. Deputy Lewis made a Pssst sound and nodded towards Steve's waist.

"Mister Taylor, you're armed." It was a statement rather than a question.

"Yes ma'am. I have a license for it. If you'd like to take possession for my safety or yours—"

"If you don't mind," she said looking at Amy who was still propping her dad up, though he didn't need it anymore, then looked to Angela.

"Go ahead," Angela said, "My husband is a gentle soul. He wouldn't have offered, if he didn't mean it."

Deputy Javier slowly reached over and undid the small strap over the top of the .45 and then pulled it out with two fingers and handed it back to her partner.

"So, while you were getting beaten with two gas cans, you didn't use a weapon? You didn't pistol whip him?"

"No, ma'am," Steve said. "But when I had him down I did draw it for a moment when I realized how bad a shape I was in. I know I've at least got a little bit of a concussion."

"How do you know that?" she asked, squatting in front of him.

"Because there's two of you," Steve admitted.

127

She held a finger up in front of his face, like she would a sobriety test and then stood up and walked back to her partner. They spoke quietly and then nodded. He removed the magazine, worked the slide and caught the ejected shell. He put it in the top of the mag and then walked over to Steve and offered the gun to Angela.

"Hospitals won't allow this inside, ma'am. He should be checked out. So far, looks like a case of self-defense on your husband's end, in my opinion. If for whatever reason we need more information. We'll be in touch."

"That's it?" Steve asked.

"Yeah, I think once we see how well William Wilson is faring, we'll be booking him for assault and battery, criminal trespass, and anything else I can throw at the little shithead."

"That's not a nice word," Amy said, though she was fighting off a giggle.

"Sorry about that, little ma'am," Deputy Lucas said tipping his hat in her direction. "I forget myself sometimes. That kid's a trouble maker, so you don't have nothing to do with him, you hear me?"

Steve could feel his daughter's chin on the back of his head as she nodded.

"Anything to worry about? We're neighbors with the Wilson's."

"Nothing specific, but he's been caught doing petty stuff: shoplifting, have a report that one of his high school teachers said he followed her and tried looking in her windows. Nothing horrible, just a boy who's not had enough parental guidance if you get my meaning."

"His parents are a menace, just like he is," Steve told him simply.

"Well, we'll sit here with you till the second ambulance comes."

"I'm riding with Dad, Mom, you should call Amber and bring her with you."

Steve tried not to laugh, it hurt too much. Gremlins were now working behind his eyeballs, forehead, temples, and the back of his brain, and they were all using supercharged jackhammers. Despite the nauseating dizziness and pain, it was still funny how bossy and protective the littlest of the family became when he got hurt.

"You know, Deputies," Angela said, as she could hear the approach of a new set of sirens, "we've had issues with Billy watching us out of his window upstairs, too. Could you talk to him about it?"

"Yes, ma'am," both chorused.

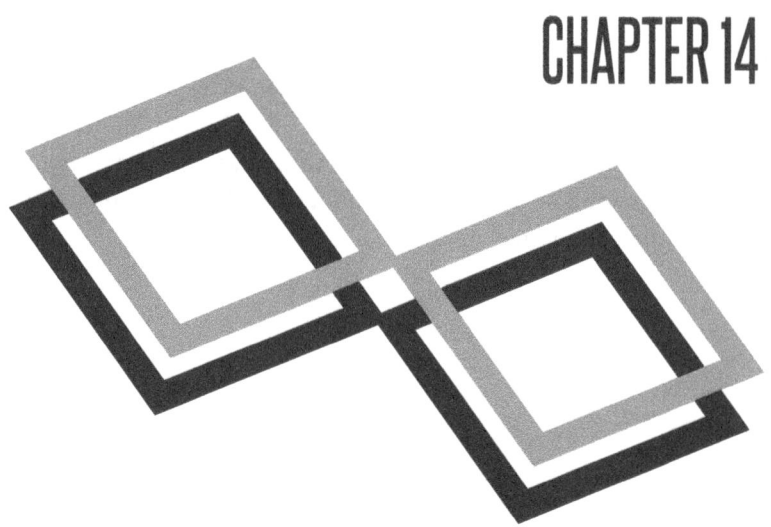

CHAPTER 14

Two weeks passed in a flurry. Pastor Johnson himself finished the pickups from Sam's the week that he was laid up while he recovered from his concussion, putting supplies at the church and the large storage unit. A nice set of stitches was put in and removed, and his temple went from bruised to now differing colors of yellow and brown in spots. Billy Wilson, upon discharge from the hospital, was arrested and taken to the county lockup. Twice, the Taylors had to call the police on Clark Wilson, who would go into screaming fits of rage whenever he saw Steve outside. The last incident, his wife Sarah had to pull him back from the Taylor's property where Steve stood patiently.

The Wilson's didn't understand the situation in any rational matter that Steve could get through to them. Their son had been trespassing on property he didn't have permission to be on, he was caught in the act of a crime, and was hurt when he attacked Steve. His clothing choice in the hot Georgia heat had all but removed any doubt that he wasn't a choirboy. He'd been clearly trying to hide his identity. That's why the Taylors weren't surprised to get another notice from the HOA.

This time, the four of the Taylors, Dwight, and another two individuals they invited were to meet up an hour before the appointed time. They had confirmed it with Jeff, because they didn't want any shenanigans of time changes, and he'd angrily confirmed the time of the meeting.

"So, who's your guest?" Dwight whispered to Steve as they sat in the mostly empty meeting room at the clubhouse.

"My lawyer, Sam Parish. The other's a surprise," Steve whispered back.

Sam had chosen to sit a few rows ahead of them. He was dressed in a business casual manner, with one leg crossed, a briefcase sitting beside his chair, and had a notebook and pen on his lap. He looked every bit of southern dignity personified. On top of his notebook was a copy of the HOA guidelines and bylaws. Steve and him had been talking nonstop for two days to see if they could head this off completely.

People filed in, a couple here, a couple there. Soon, it was standing room only, and the Taylors were having a hard time seeing over some of them. Matthew Fitzpatrick walked in and ordered everyone standing in front of the chairs to find a spot in the back of the room or leave. Some muttered at how short tempered he seemed, but they moved. Then the rest of the HOA senior committee or council came in a few moments later. After glaring at Jeff, Matthew took his seat behind the white folding tables.

A loud murmur rose from the crowd, and the buzzing wasn't friendly sounding.

"I'd like to thank the community for this turnout," Jeff said, and went on to give his monthly update on projects within the community before he got to the heart of the meeting.

"Now, I know a bunch of you heard about the problems we had here a couple weeks back in our community, where one of our kids was viciously attacked by another member here. I won't get into that overly much, but it sort of ties in with what I would like to get a consensus vote on. The Taylors, new to our community, have two violations against the HOA that have yet to be addressed, and they are defiantly refusing to come into compliance."

Angry murmurs from some of the crowd; a confused buzz seemed to come from the other.

"Furthermore, there are some ongoing concerns, and I would like to speak to you about some proposed rule changes. Steve and Angela Taylor have been members of this community for almost two years now, and the first violation I would like to address is the gate that has been cut into their rear brick wall separating their property from adjoining farmland."

"What's wrong with that? There's nothing in the HOA convention about that being against the rules," Steve shouted.

"You didn't get the Home Owner's Association permission before you did it," Doug Morris called out.

Jeff banged the gavel on the plastic table to quiet the mumbling from the two outbursts.

"I don't need to," Steve went on without asking them. "It's just like the constitution, anything not spelled out goes to the states like the Tenth Amendment. In this case, I pulled a permit to have it done, and I did have permission from the property owner to do it and go on the property whenever I wanted."

More murmurs.

"Can I go on?" Jeff asked dryly.

"This is going to take all night if you don't let him finish his charges against you," Cheryl Jacoby, the HOA's only female board member, said.

"Charges? Like you think you're going to fine me? Jail me? Throw me out?"

Jeff smiled. "Second violation that has been confirmed by Mr. Taylor's own lawyer, is that he's running a home business out of his residence. This is expressly forbidden under our convent." Jeff said with a wicked grin.

There was an angry murmur with that, and as Jeff looked around, about a third of the men and women in the meeting were talking to each other. Steve started to worry when a woman raised her hand.

"Yes? Mrs. Bacon, is it?"

"Yes. Mr. Arellano, if home businesses are against the HOA operations, how is it you're running a real estate office out of your house?"

The smug smile on Jeff's face slipped and his eye twitched.

"I'm not running a real estate office—"

"Your wife's business cards list your house with your house number," the woman said pulling something out of her purse and holding it up. "There's a ton of people here who've got home businesses. We were under the impression that as long as customers don't visit us here—"

"We're getting off the topic," Jeff interrupted. "My wife had those cards made up when she retired. She is not actively selling real estate in any manner. She keeps those for former clients so she can direct them to—"

"Mr. Arellano?" Matthew interrupted, slapping on the table till people quieted down. "Is your wife the connection to the developer that's trying to buy Mister Abbot's farm and your friend on the planning board who's trying to get a lot of the area rezoned for a new sub full of McMansions put in here?"

"That'll increase all of our property values," Jeff snarled, surprised to have been ambushed from behind the table.

"So," Steve said standing up, "it's ok if you break the rules as long as it's for the greater good, is that what I'm hearing?"

"That's not what—"

"I'd like to speak!" Doug Morris said, standing up.

His shout was thunderous, and even the lawyer looked up sharply at him. Steve sat down, but not before touching his side, an almost unconscious habit.

"Fine, go ahead...since there seems to be no order tonight," Jeff said dryly.

"Steve Taylor has willfully flaunted the HOA rules. He plants a garden in his flower beds, knowing that gardens are prohibited, he makes modifications to his property that makes it different than the others and no longer conforming to the look and standard of the community..."

Steve smiled, amused at the old gripes as they were being aired.

"He fires off his guns in his backyard, causing concern from neighbors in the area—"

"Excuse me," a man said shouting from near the back, "but since when has this part of Georgia become a liberal cesspool?"

Some clapping and a couple wolf whistles sounded off until Jeff banged on the gavel again.

"Let me finish," Doug said. "And to make matters worse, he refuses to quiet his daughter's jeep, which sounds like it has no muffler. Then he designed and put up a trap on somebody else's property, viciously attacked a community member's son to the point to where he's had to have surgery to repair the facial damage...and he pulled a gun on him. I'd like to see the council take action against the Taylors."

This time the murmurs didn't sound like they were sympathetic. That's when the woman who was sitting behind Angela rose to her feet and raised her hand.

"Yes ma'am...I don't recognize you. Can you give me your name and address please?"

"My name is Deputy Lucy Javier," she said crisply and watched as the entire room went silent, "When Mr. Taylor told me about the problems in this community, I thought he was joking. That's why he invited me here—"

"Surly this isn't a police matter," Jeff interrupted.

"But I can see right now that a statement from the Sherriff's department is in order."

"He tried to cave my son's skull in, and you didn't arrest him," Clark Wilson screamed from the front, as his wife Sarah tried to pull him back into his seat.

"Your son attacked Mr. Taylor with a weapon, causing a concussion and the stitches and bruising you see on him right now," she said, and the entire room turned to stare at Steve. "Mr. Taylor showed remarkable restraint in how he handled the situation. Concussed and losing blood, he elected to subdue your son with his fists instead of other means."

"Other means? My son needs surgery!" Clark yelled from his seat.

"Mr. Taylor has a legal concealed carry permit. He elected to take the hit to the head and not use his firearm in his own self-defense. This could have gone quite different, Mr. Wilson, and I think you know that. If a perp is running at an officer with a weapon, well, they better hope we have our taser handy, but I'm a righty and on my right hip is where I normally hang my gun."

The room was deathly quiet, and Sarah Wilson, with tears in her eyes, was holding onto her husband with both hands, whispering furiously to him.

"As I understand it," Matthew Fitzpatrick said, "the Wilson boy is being charged with numerous felonies and remains in lockup, is that correct?"

"Yes, sir," Lucy said, and sat down. "I just wanted to clear that up."

"I would like to propose a rule change, one forcing all community members into compliance with both structure and having a normal set of guidelines including everything from fences, planter boxes, noise ordinances, and some sort of reasonable firearms policy since it's apparent we have none."

"Excuse me," Sam Parish said, standing, "you do understand how this looks in the court of law?"

"Who the Sam hell are you?" Jeff said, losing his patience with all the interruptions.

"Well, my name is Sam Parish, not Sam Hell. I'm the Attorney on record for the Taylor family. You are the HOA President, Jeff Arellano?"

"Yes, I am?"

Sam pulled out a sheaf of papers and turned. Lucy stood and walked over and took them and walked them up to the white plastic tables and tossed them in front of Jeff with a thump.

"What is this?" Jeff asked, his voice somewhat quiet.

"Sir, you've been served," Lucy said and started walking back.

She dropped a wink, whether it was for Steve or Sam, the Taylors couldn't tell.

"Why is he such a meany head?" Amy whispered to her dad as Jeff started reading.

Jeff's face turned a bright scarlet and he passed it down the line.

"Shhh, be quiet, short stuff," Amber hissed to her sister.

"That," Steve said in a loud voice, "is a cease and desist. After researching you and your wife's background, your involvement with the zoning board, and the undisclosed fact that your wife's sister is the developer's cousin, I think it's pretty clear that you are not working for the community like you say you are."

"That's ridiculous!" Jeff thundered. "I have no—"

"Mister President," Sam said, standing up and pulling another sheaf of papers out of his briefcase as he did so, "I'd like to show the community some future site planning I was able to get—thanks to my friends with the county—on a proposed community expansion."

"You're out of order, and you're not even a part of the—"

"You mean the expansion onto my property that I own and haven't sold?" Dwight asked in a loud voice, making almost everyone turn to stare at him.

It was like a soap opera, an episode of *Colombo*, and a gameshow all rolled into one. The people who came here with one set of ideas were finding out the world had been flipped topsy-turvy, and nothing was what it seemed. At least, that was Steve's impression from the shocked look on people's faces, except for Matthew's. He was smiling. Shocked, but smiling.

"Yes. See, the portion of land they want to 'annex,'" Sam said, using his fingers to make air quotes, "is landlocked. They needed a new entrance to get in, and where else would be better than the back of a small cul-de-sac?"

"I don't; you didn't—"

His words were interrupted when Sam threw another packet of papers on the white table, this time in front of Matthew. He snatched them up before Jeff could launch himself halfway across the table sideways. Matthew stood up, held a hand out to stop him in case he tried to bum rush the big man and then paused to read. Everyone was staring, and when he flipped a page or two, you could almost hear a pin drop.

"This is bullshit," Doug said finally.

Several people threw their folded agendas at him, and he put his hands over his head as if to ward off multiple attackers.

"This is the most disgusting overreach I have ever seen," Matthew said after a moment.

"What's it say?" Thomas Durazo, one of the HOA leadership, asked from the other side of Jeff.

"It's exactly as bad as the Taylors and their attorney are implying," Matthew said, and walked it over to him and put it down.

Jeff snatched for it, but Matthew put a big arm out and put it on his chest and pushed. He put a little more oomph into it than intended, and the off-balance president went flying backwards as his chair folded up when his legs went over his head. Screams of surprise were shouted out, and Matthew turned to immediately bend over and help Jeff Arellano up. As he was pulling the older, much smaller, man to his feet, Jeff's arm shot out, hitting Matthew in the mouth. The blow barely moved the big man's jaw, but rage clouded the big man's features as pandemonium broke out in the crowd.

Lucy had seen that things had the potential to turn ugly and had stood and moved to the side of the left aisle when Matthew snatched the paperwork away from Jeff the first time. The second time Jeff tried to get it, she was already moving through the crowd. She saw the big man make a pushing motion knocking the president over and the punch. She made it to the front of the table as Matthew grabbed the front of Jeff's shirt in one palm, his right fist lining up on a shot that might very well kill him.

Her last step launched her across the table and she grabbed his arm just as he started moving. Her weight threw him off balance and he spun, toppling himself, pulling Lucy Javier over with him. They ended up in an undignified tangle of arms and legs as Jeff cursed and spat, the homeowners shouting, screaming, and dozens of phones out recording the fracas.

"Now you know why I hate to come to these things by myself?" Steve shouted to Sam.

"You're never going to one of these without me again," Sam said shouting back.

That's when the lights went out.

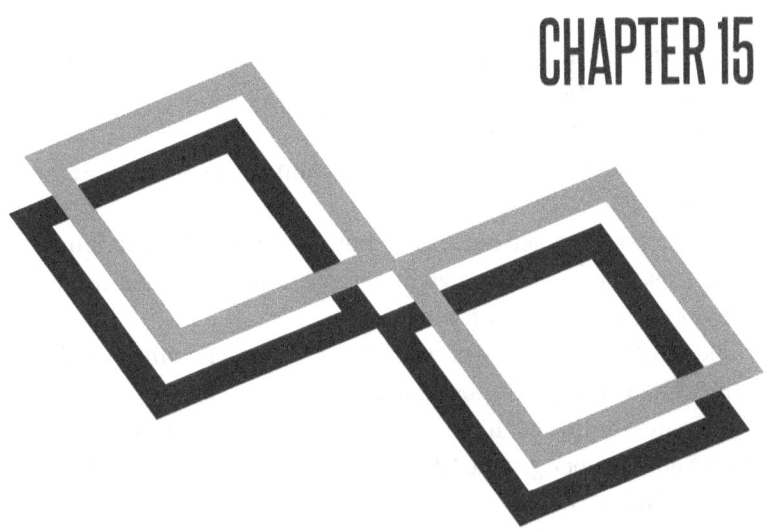

CHAPTER 15

"Dad, I'm sick of this power rationing," Amber griped.

"Yeah, sweetie, me too," Steve said, pulling his shirt away from his body and fanning himself.

In the last three weeks or so, rolling blackouts had hit almost every area east of the Mississippi. The news claimed a hot summer and everyone running their air conditioning caused rolling blackouts, much like what happened in 2012. What wasn't happening was that things came back on right away. There was a cascading effect that left a lot of the areas still without power. The short-term solution was to work on some sort of power rationing, giving home owners power long enough to have their freezers and fridges time to cool down enough to maintain the cooler temps and preserve food.

Some systems were given higher priority, such as utilities like the water and sewage plant and they were kept running by both generator and the power grid. Right off the bat, people flocked to their vehicles and RV's to fire up the air conditioning during the hottest parts of the day, but fuel prices seemed to double their already high prices. Food in the grocery stores went up in price as everything transported in had a sharp increase in cost to the stores.

There was less product on the shelf, but there was also fewer people buying last minute items at inflated prices.

"Can I go with you today?"

"To Home Depot, or to the community meeting later on?" Steve asked.

"I just want to get out of the house some. Since my job shut down, I really don't have anywhere to go, and Matt's dad has been having Matthew work with him."

"Really? I hadn't...I mean...why?" Steve asked, knowing Matthew's business had been pretty rock solid.

"Because he doesn't have to pay his kid the way he has to pay for union help," Amber griped. "But to be fair, Matt likes working with his dad...I'm just...bored."

"Hm...you must be, you hate going on prepping runs with me. Amy," he said turning to see both her and Angela walk in from the back yard. "Would you and your mom like to ride along with me today?"

"I'd love to," Angela said pulling her shirt away from her body, fanning herself, "Gives us an excuse to run the AC."

"I wanna go, Dad!" Amy said.

"Good, I'll take all the help I can get," Steve said, rubbing his hands together and making a good impression of a cartoon villain's laugh.

"Tell me again, why do we need two different types of solar panels?" Angela asked, a bit annoyed.

Money was tight, and although they had money in the bank, some of Steve's clients had quit paying as their finances and businesses crumpled.

"Well, what would you think if I could say...get you girls some air conditioning? Spend some money on making something that will run when the power is off?"

"How many solar panels do you need?" Amy asked, picking up a box nearly as big as she was.

"I've got all the big panels I need. These smaller ones are for the air conditioning," Steve told her.

"So we're good?" Amy asked.

"Almost. I need to pick up a couple of big coolers, a vent fan from the heating and cooling section, and a couple of lengths of galvanized ductwork."

Amy knew her husband read a ton and on topics that he wasn't an expert on, but she had no idea how he was going to build what he claimed he was going to. She watched as they piled supplies on two flatbed carts. One of them full of solar panels and a box he called a charge controller. She asked about batteries once, but he told her he wasn't worried about those yet...but he was buying what looked like furnace ductwork parts, a washable furnace filter, a large white cooler from an endcap and then they went to the plumbing department and found a very small pond pump that was the size of a fish tanks air pump.

Then he bought more odds and ends: hacksaw blades, jigsaw blades, hand tools. The girls were ready to revolt and steal his keys when he announced they were done. The store, much like everyone right now, was open, but whether or not they had power and when was anybody's guess. When the power was out, people had to pay cash only. This was one of those instances. Steve had been adding things up on a calculator and a piece of paper and when the clerk told him a price that was 20 percent higher than he figured he looked up sharply.

"Excuse me, but I think you're off. I've been keeping track right here," Steve said pulling out his notepad.

The clerk looked at it. He was in his mid-twenties and looked like the power outage hadn't been kind to him. He smelled like he hadn't showered recently, though with the heat and lack of air conditioning, everybody did to some extent. His hair was greasy and he had a nervous look about him that made Steve's spidey senses tingle.

"No, my math is right. It's one thousand, three hundred and twenty-seven dollars and thirty-three cents," the associate said.

Steve looked at his sheet, "One thousand, one hundred and thirty-two dollars and forty-nine cents is what I came up with."

"Four percent state sales tax and fourteen percent local municipality sales tax," the clerk said, his eyes shifting.

"No, that's not—"

"Steve, it doesn't matter," Angela said, pulling on his arm.

"Help you with something?" Another orange-aproned associate came up, probably noting the angry look on Steve's face.

"14 percent local municipality sales tax?" Steve asked loudly.

The head cashier looked between Steve and the cashier who suddenly found a spine and stood up a little straighter.

"That hasn't gone into effect," the head cashier said and took the pad of paper and the calculator.

After a minute of adding, he turned to the Taylors, "With tax, it's one thousand, one hundred and thirty-two dollars and forty-nine cents."

Steve peeled off money from the small wad he'd brought with him and paid the associate, who was giving his boss and Steve ugly looks. Without comment, he handed the changeover. Steve started to push one of the large carts away when the head cashier called, "Have a nice day."

Steve made it out to the truck without looking cross-eyed at anybody, but when he silently started slinging materials into the bed, it was Amy who spoke up first.

"What happened? You're mad?"

"Yeah, sorry. I am," Steve admitted.

"That guy in there didn't think his boss was paying attention and tried to rip us off," Amber said.

"So, he's like a bad man?" Amy asked.

Steve was putting the last box of solar panels in the truck and hesitated. "I don't think he's a bad man. I just think he's trying to make the best of a bad situation."

"Kind of like we are?"

Steve put the solar panel down and picked up Amy and sat her on the tailgate of the truck. She squeaked at being manhandled, and he had to grin. She was getting older, but she was still his baby.

"Yeah, kind of like that. The difference, is he was trying to do it in a dishonest way. I could be wrong, but he looked to me like he was taking advantage of the power outage to try to make some extra money off people."

"So he is kind of a bad guy," Amy said matter of fact.

Everyone looked at each other in an uncomfortable silence and then they finished loading the truck.

"Is Sam coming to the community meeting tonight?" Amber asked suddenly.

"Yes," Steve said starting the truck, kicking the air on.

They waited for it to blow cool air for a moment, and closed the doors when it was something less than ninety degrees.

"Good, what about Deputy Lucy?" Amy asked shyly, and then giggled.

"If Matthew Fitzpatrick is there, she'll be there," Angela said smiling.

Steve met her gaze a second and they both grinned. As awkward as it had been meeting each other, Deputy Javier and Matthew hit it off after the disaster of the last community meeting when she'd prevented the big man from knocking Jeff out. It hadn't been much of a secret, but the two of them hadn't tried to advertise the fact they'd had a couple of dates now.

"Good," Amy said. "Mr. Fitz seems to like her."

They talked about the budding relationship while Amber tried to ignore the fact hers was on hold on the drive back to the subdivision. Steve hit the button on the garage door opener and turned the truck around before backing into the garage. The explosive heat was almost oppressive, but they managed to pull the cooler out when the lights on the garage flipped on.

"Air!" Amber screamed, running inside.

"Amber...Amy...dammit," Angela muttered as the kids went running pell-mell into the house.

"They just want to cool down," Steve said.

"Yeah, but we have to—"

Her words were cut off with a kiss, and she hesitated a minute before returning it.

"How about you go cool off in the shower? I'm going to unload what I need for the project and then I'll join you."

"Don't make promises you won't keep," Angela said with a grin.

"I won't. Let's take advantage of the few hours of power while we have it. I hope it stays long enough for our meeting tonight."

"It will," Angela said as she walked away, her hips swaying, "just don't work out here too long."

In his best southern drawl, Steve told her, "Yes ma'am."

He dragged the large cooler, the ductwork and vent fan with him into the laundry room and put them up on the washer and dryer. Next, he went back out and unloaded the smaller solar panels he'd bought for this project and set the larger ones aside. He didn't have a use for those yet, but if things continued to go downhill, he had an idea on how to keep his fridge going. He'd ordered a part from Amazon that was made by Johnson Controls. The way it worked was you plugged in the freezer into the back of a plug on the controller, then the controller into the wall. Then you put the copper thermocouple in the freezer portion. Poof, a highly efficient fridge could be made for cheap.

He hadn't done the math yet, but he knew that he didn't have enough solar juice to run his freezer yet...but he was maybe halfway there.

✦

"What did you think of that?" Steve asked Sam as they walked out of the community center."

"Sadly, I'm sorta surprised the community voted to keep Jeff as the HOA president...but I wanted to let you know, I spoke with their lawyer earlier. They are going to drop their objections to you having a gate, if you drop the harassment suit," Sam said.

"Deal. Damn, that was easy," Steve said, a little annoyed even after getting exactly what he was aiming for.

"One more thing. They—and by 'they,' I mean Jeff—would like you to talk to Matthew about the pending investigation."

"I'll talk, but the big man is on the council. I'm not sure he's still over getting popped in the face."

"That one isn't a deal breaker," Sam said. "I have to run. Congratulations, by the way. Some people actually listened to your presentation. Don't be surprised if a few ask more questions."

"Thanks, Sam," Steve said and took his hand.

"That was kind of fun," Amy said, as the family started walking back towards their house.

"It was," Angela told her, reaching down to pull a string of hair out of her daughter's face.

"Do you think they are actually going to get ready?" Steve asked his family.

"Not the level we're at," Amber whispered, "but a lot of people paid attention when you warned them that prices are going up on things, and they should stock up now."

"I hope they do. Things are...weird," Angela finished for him.

"They better," Dwight said, startling Amy.

"I thought you left already," Amy said to him.

"Naw, I talked to a couple of people. After the last meeting when things got ugly, a couple people stopped me by the back of their fences to chew the fat. I was just catching up with them."

"Want to stay for dinner tonight?" Angela asked Dwight.

"Actually, that was another reason I was running behind, I was going to invite you all over to my place. I'm having Matthew and little Matt come out too, if you don't mind."

"I don't mind," Amber said, and quickly looked away at her mother's amused expression.

"I haven't been over there in a while. I want to see the baby pigs!" Amy said excitedly.

"Sounds good to me. Need me to bring anything?" Steve asked his neighbor.

"I think I got it all; maybe some beers?" Dwight asked.

"Sure thing. Cutting through at our place?"

"Yeah. Say, you still thinking about putting that handpump in?" Dwight asked suddenly.

"Hand pump?" Angela asked.

"I might, Dwight. Babe, it's the pitcher pump I got from Home Depot. I was going to drive a sand point for some backup water."

"You mean, we don't have to wait for the well pump to work if we have that?" Amy asked, squinting at her dad.

"Yeah, Dad, we don't have to wait for a shower if we have one of those? We could just...crank the handle instead of dying in the heat?" Amber piped up.

"You're not dying," Steve insisted.

"You've had this and you didn't tell me?" Angela asked, stopping and putting one hand on her hip.

"Well, yeah, as a just-in-case," Steve said, and turned to Dwight. "Looks like I am. Why?" he asked, trying not to grin.

All three ladies were giving him the stink eye and it was all he could do not to make matters worse by laughing.

"Good, I am gonna need a hand getting some more posts in for a fencing project, and while I have the auger on, I can get you down six feet or so."

"Oh man, that'll make it easy to start!"

146

"Yeah. I think if you open your gate up, I can get the auger in a couple feet off to the side. That way it won't be in the way."

"That sounds like a plan," Steve said as they approached the house.

With the power rationing and the well not running constantly, the automatic sprinklers were almost never used, and the lawn had started looking brown. That's why they immediately noticed drops of red in the grass. It was Amy who first called the alert.

"Mom, somebody dropped paint on the lawn."

"Baby, it's...oh. Steve? Dwight?" she asked, putting a hand out, stopping the younger girls from going further.

"That's blood," Steve said. "I almost didn't even see that. Good eyes, kid."

Dwight kneeled down and touched a small red fleck. He rubbed it between his fingers and then stood up, wiping it on his pant leg.

"Should I call—"

"Call Lucy, and go ahead and call 911," Steve said. "Dwight, I'm going inside the house to check things out. Can you sit with my ladies a minute?"

"Absolutely," Dwight said.

Steve pulled the pistol and held it at the low/ready position and opened the gate that led into the backyard. The blood was just a fleck here and there, but it was noticeable now that he was looking for it. He followed and saw that it led towards the back gate. He ignored that for now and headed for the back door. He switched gun hands to fish out the keys and unlock it and then switched back as he walked in. Had somebody broken in, got hurt and then fled? The lock on the back door was a deadbolt, so they didn't flee that way if they did break into the house somewhere.

He searched the downstairs, checking every closet and the pantry before opening the door to the garage. He headed inside, leaving the doors open so he could hear. Outside, he could just hear the muffled feminine voices and the deeper voice of Dwight. The truck was where he left it and for a second he felt foolish, but he still lowered himself to make sure there wasn't anybody under the Jeep or the Ford. Satisfied, he checked the lock to the mechanical room where he hid his preps and found it locked. Satisfied, he left the garage and headed back inside, closing the door behind him. He was halfway up the stairs when he heard a voice.

"Steve, Deputy Lucy Javier here."

"I'm on the staircase," Steve called back.

Her shout had startled him and he moved the gun to his left hand to wipe the sweat off before holding it again.

"Hold up," she called and he heard her walking across the tiled floor in his direction. "Hey, you don't do this. This is my job," she told him, an indignant look on her face.

"You clear houses much?" he asked her, moving to the side so she could go ahead of him.

"About as much as you," she snarked. "Put your gun up so I don't have to worry about you hitting me."

"What if—"

"I'm wearing my vest," Lucy said. "Just got out of work and was heading to Matthews when I got the call."

"Ok then."

✦

"The blood, it looks like it goes out the back fence," Amy said for the third time.

Dwight just gritted his teeth. His friend had put him in charge of their safety but it was killing him to wait outside while Lucy and Steve were checking everything out. The front door opening and closing had everyone spinning to see. Steve walked out after Lucy and locked the door behind him.

"Nobody was inside as far as we can tell," Lucy said. "In a couple minutes I'll have a backup here."

"Well, I ain't waiting for no backup. If somebody's hurt, maybe they're on my property and need help?" Dwight asked her.

Lucy looked at him and then shook her head.

"Come on Dwight," Steve said. "Maybe it was somebody hunting on your land and they took a shortcut out my gate?"

That stopped the old farmer and he tipped his ball cap back and rocked on his heels a minute before nodding to her. They didn't have long to wait. Her partner, Ron, pulled in with his personal car a moment later, and then a local police department car showed up. The neighbors on all sides of the cul-de-sac were stopping what they were doing and staring. Steve wanted to flip them all the bird, but most of that was because ousting Jeff had failed rather badly. People had given him a second chance, and as he was so close to making a juvenile example of his feelings he remembered that. Instead he waited and let Lucy explain things.

The locals seemed a little more agitated than the Sheriff's deputies about it and led the way. Steve kissed Angela and followed as Dwight started following the blood trail.

"You be safe," Angela said.

"I will be. The safest place to be: with four cops," Steve told her as he turned to follow.

Amy caught his gaze, and she gave him a wave with Amber following suit. He gave them a little wave back and started walking. They left the gate open behind them and Lucy started taking pictures with an iPhone. There was more blood near the back gate, more so than had dripped on the grass between the gates. Almost like something was put down....

"Looks like they left through his gates. Bet you we find a gut pile somewhere back there," one of the local cops said.

"That's my guess as well," Dwight told them.

It took them ten minutes to follow the blood trail and it didn't end in a gut pile as they expected, instead it led into livestock barn. Dwight cursed when he saw that and pushed open the big side door. A few chickens decided to inspect what the bipeds were doing and came running along like drunken velociraptors in a Hootie and the

Blowfish concert. They started picking at the more frequent blood droplets on the straw.

"Smells," Don told Lucy.

"It's a barn," Lucy hissed and walked in.

In the heat of summer, the air was more rank than Steve remembered, but he was expecting it. After a moment, his nose adjusted about the same moment his eyes adjusted to the gloom. The pigs were making agitated noises. Dwight approached the indoor, outdoor paddock and looked inside. Blood covered the handle on the barn side. He hesitated and instead got on his toes and looked over.

"Somebody got themselves bit," he said after a moment.

"What do you mean?" Steve asked as he leaned over to look.

"Blood's too high up for it to have been a pig. I have to go outside and see, but I'm worried I'm going to be one feeder hog shy."

"What? How can you...oh, those aren't that big," Lucy said as a pink pig poked his nose in the corral.

"Yeah, they're weaned and in a different pen than their momma. Come on."

They followed him, now more curious than nervous. He opened a side door, and when they went out, they found a bloody handprint on the outside of the barn. Lucy was quick to take a picture. They followed Dwight, who led them in a pathway between two sets of electric fencing. On the left, a boar hog sat in a mud hole, staring at the humans with a hungry intensity. Following the curving pathway to the right, they came to another mud wallow a good hundred feet back from the barn, part of it shaded by large poplar trees. Dwight started counting out loud and then cursed.

"That's what it was," Dwight said, pointing, "somebody took off with a feeder and got bit."

"Great, so now all we have to do is find somebody who's got what...an eighty-pound pig roaming around the neighborhood?" Lucy asked.

"You should go talk to the Wilsons," Steve told them. "I know they were at the meeting, but maybe they saw somebody coming and going before."

"Good idea, they're always spying on you guys," Dwight said, snapping his fingers.

"Isn't that the couple whose kid smacked you with the metal can?" one of the local cops asked.

"Yeah, my neighbors. Good news: they quit screaming obscenities whenever I'm outside."

A radio crackled and one of the local cops started talking into it as Dwight and Steve stepped off to the side.

"Would they have killed the pig first?" Steve asked him.

"No. They could have, but I don't think they did. Let's head inside the pen and see where the blood trail leads to."

"I bet you it leads into the barn," Steve said, "probably tried to boost a pig over the fence and got bit for his troubles."

Dwight nodded and both of them started walking back, not paying attention to the deputies and cops behind them.

"So they try to pick it up, one of them gets bit...."

"These pigs are so tame he could have walked it on a leash," Dwight said.

"So somebody who's bleeding, walking a pig somewhere...."

"Somebody had to see something," Dwight finished.

"Hey guys, I'll come back around later on for a statement," Lucy said walking up to them quickly, "We've got a call and all hands on deck. I'll be back around to finish later on today or when the situation resolves itself."

"What's going on?" Dwight asked, his curiosity piqued.

"Large riot," one of the local cops said.

"Are you going to talk to the Wilsons?" Steve asked as they were starting to leave.

"No time," They said starting to jog towards them and the barn in general, "Things are heating up. Damn, I wish I would have parked closer."

"We'll be in touch," Deputy Ron said as he went jogging by.

"I wonder what's going on?" Dwight asked.

"I dunno. I'm going to head home though and hose the blood off. Now that we're pretty sure it's human, I don't want to leave it...."

"I'll be out in a day or two with the tractor for your hand pump. You take it easy," Dwight said and gave a little wave.

Steve watched the old farmer leave. He wasn't sure why he wasn't more upset, but he had a feeling he was heading inside to listen to the radio or turn on the news. Maybe, Steve thought, he wasn't as worried or upset about the loss of a piglet as Steve thought he should be. Or...

"I wonder if he got the camera setup we were talking about," Steve mumbled to himself and headed back out the way he came in, the police and deputies leaving him alone as he slowly walked back to his house."

CHAPTER 16

The actual making of the air conditioner was more like a Rube Goldberg affair. Steve knew how he wanted to do it, but let the parts make the design. He had enough filter material to fold it in half and run it from the top to the bottom of the inside. About halfway up, he ran some small screws he had from a hinge set into the side and let the bottom drop, attaching the plastic filter media at about the halfway mark. He let it just hang free and brush against the floor of the cooler. Next, he marked and outlined the opening and the outlets using the vent pipe as a template. Both sides were cut out using a drill and a jigsaw.

He was pushing the fitting in to attach the inline fan when Amy came up.

"That doesn't look like it's going to work. At all."

"You don't know what I'm doing," Steve told her grinning.

"You're making an expensive mistake," she told him and then turned when a snort alerted her that she wasn't alone.

Steve turned to see both Angela and Amber sitting at the snack bar, both grinning.

"What? That's what you said, Mom?"

"Hey," Steve called out.

"I plead the fifth," Angela said.

The lights blinked off and everyone groaned.

"You stored a bunch of water, right?" Steve asked.

"Yes, Dad," she said with a dramatic sigh. "Can I walk down to Matt's in a little bit?"

"Yeah, I don't mind," Steve said. "See if Lucy is back from last night. I'm curious what went on. There wasn't anything on the radio or TV about any riot."

"I will, but I'm going to wait a little bit. It's too hot right now."

Angela and Steve had been talking about that and what was going to happen when school started back up. Prices for everything had gone up, but with the inflation and power outages, the news had remained oddly silent on the subject. With no power, there was little on the way of internet news that was reliable. It ran the gamut of wild conspiracy theories, alien invasion, to human interest stories about a dozen puppies from three litters that were rescued from an animal hoarder who'd died and was about to have become the next kibble for the critters.

"Ok, then you can see if this is going to work. Can you go set up the small panels like I showed you?"

"Yeah, you want them on the back patio, not the grass?"

"Yeah, the patio," Steve told her, "Then run the wires in here."

"Got it," she said and slowly untangled herself from the stool she'd been sitting on.

"What are you doing?" Angela asked as he drilled another hole in the cooler, this one in the back, under the lid near where the hinges were.

"This is going to sorta be like a swamp cooler. I don't know how good it'll work here, but I'm going to try," Steve said, taking the pond pump out and putting it on the bottom.

"Ok, I remember what those are. So the pump there is going to circulate the water?"

"Yeah," Steve said pulling the power cord out of the freshly drilled hole.

Angela grabbed the outlet hose and studied it for a second and then snapped her fingers. She was back a minute later with some golf tees. She shoved one in and Steve could see the cords of her arms stand out as she pushed. It wasn't a big pump, more for those little three-foot round ponds you make as a water feature on a walkway, but the golf tee worked perfectly.

"Do we need a clamp for it?" she asked.

"If it leaks a little bit, it won't hurt anything. We're going to be making holes in the line anyways," Steve said taking it and laying it out across the top of the filter media.

He strung it out, and then headed into the kitchen, coming back out with a handful of wooden clothespins and started pinning the two pieces of filter media and the now blocked hose across the tip. He took his Leatherman off his belt and opened the punch and worked it back and forth until he had small holes punched in the plastic tubing, mostly facing down or inside of the filters. Then he made sure he had enough line and cut off the excess before plugging that into the pump itself.

"Here's the power, is it safe to close the door with the uh...wires coming in?"

"Yeah, that's fine. I don't know if this fan is going to be powerful enough to do this, but we can always replace it with something else if it doesn't work."

"I still think Mommy is right," Amy said, having taken her sisters spot on the stool.

"Yeah, well, if this thing works, you and Mommy can sit in front of it last, how's that sound?"

"Hey, that's not fair!"

"Yeah well, how about you go run the rabbits and chickens some water real quick while me and your mom finish wiring this thing up, and I'll let you know before I kick it on?"

"Ugh," Amy said in her best Amber sound, and went stomping to the sink to get a large pitcher out of the dish drying rack.

"Is that why you froze a ton of water jugs yesterday?" Amber asked.

"Yeah, so we got two freeze cycles out of it, they should be rock solid. I'll make sure to keep it full so it doesn't run as much. Is the water in the tub cold?"

"Yes, but you said that's not for drinking...." Amber said.

"It's not," Angela told her. "Now I get what your dad is going to do. Go get those jugs and I'll get another pitcher while he wires this up."

Everyone scattered. Steve started wiring up the solar panels to an ACDC converter and tested the connections. He skipped using the charge controller that he was saving for the bigger system and then started plugging things in. Both the pond pump and the vent fan ran on 110, and as soon as he got water in it, it'd be plugged in. While he waited, he duct taped around the holes he cut for the vent, and the hole the pump plug came out of on the middle side. He stood and stretched, his tendon's popping when he felt something ice cold touch his back.

"Holy—"

"Shhh," Angela said as the cold was removed.

She grinned at him and put two one-gallon water jugs in the bottom of the cooler, followed by Amber who had a pitcher of water.

"How much more?" Angela asked

"Let's get another couple of gallons," he said as Amy headed out the door with a pitcher. "If this works, we can probably run this for hours and hours."

"I hope it works, this heat sucks."

"At least we don't live up north anymore. Can you imagine how cold it'd get with the power only being on a few days at a time?"

"So this is like, a nationwide thing?" Amy asked, heading back in to get another pitcher of water for the critters.

"Yes, it is now," Angela answered.

"This is kinda scary," Amber said pouring water into the cooler.

"Naw, nothing scary here," Steve lied to her and got up to go get a jug from the garage.

They worked on putting about six inches of water in the long white cooler, and with the animals fed and watered, Steve plugged in the fan to the converter. It started up and Amy immediately flopped down on the discharge side.

"I can feel the air!" she said.

"Well, is it any cooler?" Amber said flopping down and pushing her sister over half a foot.

"Hey, no shoving," Amy said and shoved back.

Steve gave Angela a quick grin and plugged in the pump. The effect was delayed, but they could hear water running somewhere in the cooler.

"Oh, Mom," Amber said, her voice dreamy.

"Is it...working?" Angela said, hurrying over.

"I think you both need to move over," Steve told them as both parents laid down in front of the six-inch outlet pipe.

They stayed like that for a good ten minutes, feeling the cooler air blowing on them.

"It's not going to cool a big area, is it?" Angela asked after a while of lying on her stomach, her face into the cool airflow.

"Probably not. This takes very little power to run. What we had before...I don't know if we have roof enough to run the big air conditioning unit. That's why we've left it cranked for when we have power—"

The lights blinked and then the power came back on. The air conditioning turned on and the younger girls shrieked in happiness, and Amber ran to the TV.

"I wonder if they're going to have..."

"I want to watch *Power Rangers*," Amy said.

"You're so 2005," Amber told her, pushing her back.

"Twice in a day?" Angela said. "Maybe things are looking better?"

"Yeah, I hope so," Steve told her, turning to kiss his wife who was still lying beside him on the tiled floor.

"Uh, Dad..."

Steve stood up and walked towards the TV. The images on the screen reminded him of the first gulf war, where smart bombs had cameras strapped to them. Instead of mere bombs, there were for images on what looked like a split screen on the local news station. One hit what looked like a concrete building, another hit a naval vessel with what had to have been a cruise missile before it went dark. The other two he only got a glimpse of, but it looked like their explosions were over land.

"The President has declared war with congressional approval, against both China and North Korea in retaliation for the sinking of the US Aircraft Carrier George H.W. Bush this morning. Rescue operations are underway, and it's too early to guess at casualties. Rumors of an underwater battle between the three nations by unnamed sources have told our news station that most of China and North Korea's first strike capable submarines have been targeted and are being hunted as we speak.

"The country is on high alert, and the emergency broadcast network will override all network stations if an attack is imminent. There is no threat to the homeland at this time. Let me repeat, there is no threat to the homeland at this time..."

"Dad?" Amy asked and walked over to her dad.

Steve was shaking as Amy walked up and hugged her dad and took one of his hands.

"Let's sit on the couch," Angela said as she pulled on Steve's other hand.

This was the thing he was dreading. With the currency already slipping, too many sabers had been rattled. It had been an on again and off again shooting naval matchup, but he hadn't seriously thought that the Chinese or North Koreans would start this. Unless nuclear weapons were used, the US Navy was larger than any ten nations combined and far more advanced. At least, that's what his research was telling him.

For the first time in weeks, he remembered the Russian satellite that had been hacked. Would this be the tipping point? Only about half of what the hacker had uncovered had been tried, but...

"...the DOW Jones and S&P Index were both sinking to new record lows and trading was halted at noon, Eastern Standard Time. In other news, Russia has pushed back against sanctions by turning off the gas flow into eastern and western Europe. Sources say it is only a temporary measure, one meant to make a political point. The US Stock Market fluctuations and now fears of instability may make this an interesting week. Power outages that have been plaguing the nation will soon be restored as a shipment of replacement parts have been flown in from multiple sources...as always, we will keep you up to date, right here."

The TV's logo flashed across the screen, but the ticker giving out information across the bottom continued as a commercial came on.

"Oh, shit," Angela said.

"Oh, shit," Steve agreed, sitting in the cooling air.

The goosebumps weren't from the difference the homemade air conditioner/swamp cooler made. It was fear. He had to get to the bank before it was too late. He still had close to four-thousand dollars left, but worried that wouldn't be enough to buy a can of soup. Monday morning, he would withdraw everything he could. There was little he could do tonight, and he was too morose to go talk to Dwight.

The tractor was the loudest noise for a long time. The auger on the smaller tractor and the fact that there was little to no traffic noise from the main road made it a beacon. More than a few times, Amber would see the curtains on the Wilson's house move and turned to flip them the bird. Steve stopped her the first time, but after a while, he considered joining her. The process was pretty simple, and it went much faster than Steve thought it would. Dwight backed his tractor up to the opening where the gate had been removed, stabilized the tractor and used a PTO driven auger to sink an eight-inch hole almost six feet into the ground. He would pause, every now and then for Steve or Amber to drag dirt out of the way with a shovel. It seemed to them it took less than a couple of minutes from when he started to where he was raising the leveler's legs and pulling the tractor forward and killing the engine.

"Will that get you going good?" Dwight asked as he walked up.

"That's going to save me a couple hours of digging," Steve said looking at the mixture of soil and clay.

"Let's hope you can get that sand point driven down into some water," Dwight told him.

"What happens if he doesn't hit water?" Amber asked.

"Well, then nothing comes up out of the pipe, genius," Dwight said nudging her with a callused hand.

"No, I mean, do you pull it, drive it deeper...."

"Drive it deeper," Steve told her. "Before the power and internet went wonky, I looked it up. Where we're at, I should have to go more than twenty, twenty-five feet down."

"Thanks, Dad," Amber said and then turned to Dwight and stuck her tongue out at him in a very immature fashion.

The farmer laughed at the young woman's antics and threw a finger flick at her nose. She ducked out of the way at the last second, but she was grinning too. Steve watched in amusement. Losing power and seeing the store shelves diminishing had a chilling effect on him. It was stressful, like watching a roller coaster that was under construction climb to the top, not knowing if the track down below was finished or not. Seeing Dwight and Amber goofing around was a relief. Sometimes he worried the stress was affecting everyone, but it wasn't evident today.

"Quit flipping off the neighbors," Steve told Amber, catching the motion as he was pulling a shovel full away from the dirt.

"Dad, that was Billy Wilson," Amber said.

"Oh, well, in that case," Steve said and turned, flipping off the general direction of the Wilsons.

He was joined by both Dwight and Amber who were grinning. The curtains opened and closed and briefly they saw him scowling.

"I wonder when they let him out?" Dwight asked.

"I don't know. He was being held on a low bond. I wasn't too worried; his dad's the loose cannon."

"Yeah, Billy is just creepy," Amber repeated.

"Yeah, well, he's going to be even creepier while you hold the pipe as I put the sections together I'll bet. Ignore him."

"You need a hand? I have to rotate the pig's pen today," Dwight asked after a second.

"I should be the one asking you. You just saved me a ton of time with your tractor," Steve said.

"Naw, I don't need a hand. I'm going to put them on the far side where it's kinda rocky. Away from the fence."

"Did somebody steal another one?" Amber asked.

"They didn't get a chance. They hit the new hotwire. I electrified some barbed fencing with a home charger. I heard the screaming and ran out, chased them off."

"You get a look at who did it?" Amber asked.

Steve had already fit the first portions of the sand point onto the first five-foot pipe with a special fitting and slid that into the hole, waiting on the old farmer to answer.

"No, but I don't think it was a guy. Had the wrong...profile," Dwight told them.

"That's...ok, that's a little bit strange," Steve said. "Food is hard to find, but it's not impossible."

"Yeah, but can you imagine what happens when most people don't have more than a couple days' worth of food in the house and then they go to the store and they don't have anything for a couple more days. What are they going to do?"

"Empty out the freezer?" Amber asked, trying to sound hopeful.

"Eventually, yeah. But this has been going on for a good while now. Hell, it was starting way back when your daddy was still working at the software company."

"How could you tell? I don't remember any shortages or big power outages back then?" Amber asked a little confused.

Steve placed the pipe and sand point in the hole, seeing that the point plus pipe had made it eight feet tall. In a six-foot hole, it was sadly two feet above ground level. He got the pipe wrenches out and put another coupler and then started on another pipe, listening, fascinated.

"The cost of commodities. The way the stock market was shifting, the way the price of corn per bushel was being traded."

"Farmers have to know about the stock market?" Amber asked in disbelief.

Another pipe put on, Steve stood on his tip toes and hand threaded on a driving cap.

"Hold this straight," Steve told her.

She did and he got the post driver over the top with a ton of cursing.

"Yeah, that's how we know what's a good price when we sell our corn or soybeans. Yeah, there's some lag to take into account, but when the prices were way off, it wasn't that hard to figure out when to talk to a different sales broker."

Amber was taking it all in, watching Dwight when Steve slammed the post driver down, the driving cap inside it ringing out.

"Ow...that hurts," Amber said after a second, but braced her feet and held the pipe tighter.

"Won't need you to hold it for long...." Steve said as he pulled it down, gravity assisting his muscles as it rang out again.

Amber let go and backed up, wiping her hands on her jeans, "That vibration..."

"I got it," Dwight said, and walked over and put one gnarled hand around it.

Several blows later Dwight let go and stood back. The pipe was more or less level and the tip of the sand point had been driven deep underground, giving them almost two feet of depth. Amber and Dwight talked about the aspects of farming that Steve had never imagined. Cashflow, budgeting, and even commodities trading. He was wearing himself out when he finally got the pipe down to the two-foot mark again and pulled the post driver off.

"Take a breather," Dwight said, taking the driver from the shaking arms of Steve.

"Let me get the—"

"You're not used to this," Dwight said and pulled a wrench out of his back pocket and turned off the driving cap.

Steve stood there, almost panting, his chest heaving and handed a special coupler to the farmer before handing over one of the wrenches he'd put in his pocket. Dwight put it on and then tightened the third five-foot section of pipe, the driving cap, and started pounding.

"I had no idea," Amber said, getting another section of pipe and coupler ready and leaning against the back gate.

"What's that?" Steve asked his older daughter.

"That there was so much to it. Soil management, pest management, banking...it's a huge business, and TV makes it look like guys like Uncle Dewey sit on a tractor all day."

"Want to know the secret, kiddo?" Steve asked, his breathing getting easier.

"What's that?" she asked, in between the rhythmic banging of the post driver.

"When he's on the tractor, he's planning the next thing out and learning something new."

⚏

The line at the bank confirmed Steve's fears. There were half a dozen parking spots left open and people were lined up to the door.

Steve got out and got in line and checked his watch. He knew his bank usually opened five minutes early, so he thought he'd go to get into the front of the line. Instead he found himself about the twenty-fifth person to come in and get in line. There was a lot of ugly words, people complaining about the lack of news. They confirmed to Steve that on the drive over that his radio hadn't died in his ancient Ford. The radios of others weren't getting broadcasts either. Steve was worried that the president would call for a bank holiday, and nobody would be able to do business in order to prevent a bank run like what had happened in the great depression. He knew withdrawing all of his money would further aggravate the problem, but like the great depression, the ones who got there early were the ones who ended up with more options.

The door was unlocked about ten minutes early, and the line started heading in. After the first ten people, the door was shut, with the manager barely able to be heard over people yammering in line.

"Excuse me," the mousy man said, "we're letting people inside in groups of ten. With the power acting up, we're doing a lot of this by hand, and it cuts down on the disruptions—"

"You expect us to stay out here in the sun? It's hot out here," a woman yelled indignantly, interrupting him.

Steve saw she was next in line and something about her looked a little bit familiar. He was puzzling that and missed the rest of their exchange but not the grumbles as he allowed her to go inside with him.

"Can you believe this?" A man asked Steve from behind him in line.

"They probably don't have much in the way of lighting in there," Steve said, hoping that there wasn't going to be any panicky people, "plus with the computers down, they have to use adding machines and calculators."

"My dad was telling me that they're talking about limiting the amount of money people can take out, so there isn't a bank run."

Steve turned to face the man. He was shorter, younger, with sandy-blonde hair, and a hint of stubble on his face. He had a weathered look with a half-unbuttoned flannel shirt tucked into a pair of jeans.

"I haven't been able to get online to do my banking," Steve lied. "So I figured I would come here and make a couple of deposits and get some money out."

"Is it true?" a woman in front of Steve asked, "They are limiting—"

The door ahead of the line banged open and two people came out, cursing. The manager pointed to the next two and the line moved up slowly.

"What business of theirs is it if I wanted to empty my account? It's my money," one man griped to another.

"Good thing I didn't have to worry about going over the limit," one said as they were nearing Steve.

"Limit? What kind of limit?" Steve asked.

"Oh, uh...they are holding cash withdrawals to ten-thousand dollars," one of the men said. "Not that I have that much in my savings, everything's so damned expensive nowadays."

"Thanks," Steve said, and watched them start up their griping again as they left.

"Ho boy," the man behind Steve said finally, "this is going to be a fun one."

"You have no idea," Steve said under his breath, rolling his shoulders, still sore from putting the hand pump in.

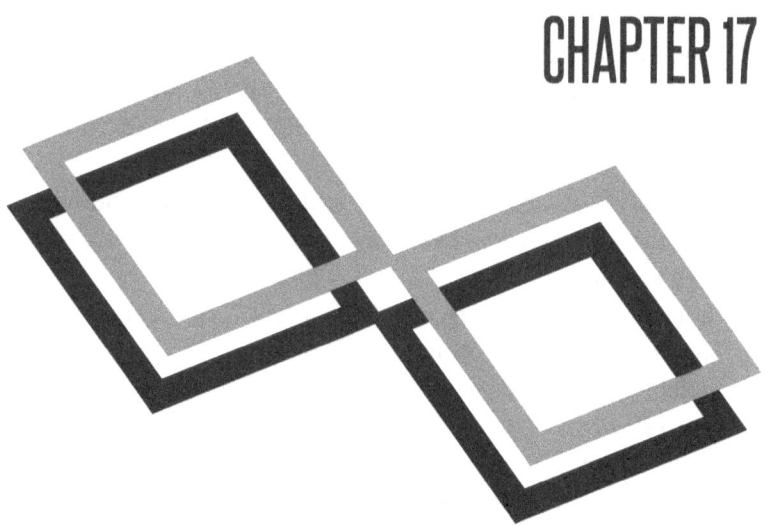

CHAPTER 17

Steve was able to come back every day for a week to withdraw money before the bank didn't open the following week. When the power was on, there were very few channels operating. When they did, it was government announcements and updates about the power status. Rumors were flying around about unrest in the larger cities, and more than once, Steve woke up with nightmares of people from downtown Macon or even Atlanta heading their direction. He felt like he was sitting on an anvil with a hammer hanging over his head.

School should have sent out notices for the kids to start, but nothing came. The grocery stores had less than one tenth of the products they had six months ago when the prices started creeping sky high almost overnight. Business had dried up, and having his bills paid in advance, the Taylors were better off than most, but not with everything. Living in the middle of suburbia USA, it wasn't like Steve could store a ton of fuel or run a generator nonstop without neighbors noticing. He had started working with Dwight more and more as he became at first bored and then depressed.

Angela noticed it first, and then Amy which surprised him. He thought for sure it would have been Amber, but a lack of things to do and McDonald's closing down had given Amber a lot of time to visit with Matt. What came as a surprise though, was when the Sheriff's Department car pulled in his driveway. Amy had heard it first, she'd been laying on the tiled floor in the laundry room, reading a book in front of the part-swamp cooler, part-air conditioning unit and had gone to tell her parents.

"Mom, it looks like Mr. Fitz's girlfriend is here," she said almost interrupting her parents trying to sneak some alone time in during the cooler part of the day.

"Oh hey, is she..." Steve started to ask but was interrupted by loud knocking.

"I've got this," Angela said, giving her husband a look. He'd had the least clothing on and she was still wearing a loose pair of shorts and a tank top.

"Ok," Steve said.

Angela closed the bedroom door. "Knock next time," she told Amy.

"How was I supposed to know you were taking a nap? The sun's been up for hours."

"It's ok—"

More knocking interrupted her, and on quiet feet, she hurried to the front door and looked out the side window first before opening it up.

"Deputies," she said, noting that both Deputy Lucy Javier and Lewis were both in uniform and in their cruiser, "want to come inside?"

"Sure," Deputy Lewis said. "Sun's hot today."

Angela agreed and showed them in and they headed to the snack bar just as Steve walked out of the bedroom.

"Hello, deputies," Steve said cheerfully.

"Hey, Steve," Lucy said.

"Mr. and Mrs. Taylor," Deputy Lewis said, "we've got some news."

"On what?" Steve asked, standing on the other side of the bar from them.

Lucy pulled a packet of papers out of her back pocket, something everyone had noticed when she'd come inside the house.

"The HOA is having kittens about your hand pump, apparently," Deputy Lewis told them, and nodded to the folded stack.

"I'm not really surprised," Steve said, taking an edge, pulling it to him, and unfolding the stack.

It was on letterhead from their attorney's office and notarized. It was a cease and desist, with a request for removal of the hand pump. Steve showed it to his wife who giggled like a schoolgirl who'd been passed a note. Steve waited a moment longer and started laughing out loud.

"What?" Lucy asked after a moment.

"It's not a permanent addition, structure or anything that requires permitting. Since we're not running the line into the house, we're not in any code violations and the most they can say is it's decorative. With the rules, this isn't anymore against the HOA conventions than a bird feeder being pushed into the grass," Steve told her with a grin.

"What do you mean?" Deputy Lewis asked.

"We installed the final section of pipe with a coupler just in case this came up. We disconnect the last few feet of pipe, cap it and tell them to kiss our ass. There's nothing they can—"

Both deputies were familiar with the chaos the HOA had caused and were familiar with the Wilson's and Doug Morris's antics. They had been called out on many of an occasion and were getting tired of dealing with the micro-politics of the HOA and the small-minded creeps who were trying to micromanage everyone's lives. Since they were expecting anything but the Taylors laughter, they were surprised when it happened. Realizing that once again the Taylors had stuck it to the HOA, grins popped out on their faces.

"Oh man, old man Morris and Arellano are going to be pissed," Lucy said, and then snorted before she could catch herself.

"Yeah, better to be pissed at than pissed on," Steve said.

"Language," the girls all chorused, and he shot his wife an innocent look as if to say "oops."

"You know," Deputy Lewis said, "with most of this area having wells, having a hand pump would be real convenient. I don't know why more of them don't? I know we have to run the water at our house while the power is on to get enough to last the next day."

"Yeah, it's a pain," Lucy said. "Matthew was talking about putting in one like yours...."

"So you are seeing him," Deputy Lewis said, and grinned as Lucy turned a bright red. "This girl," he said, using his thumb to point at her, "been my partner going on eight years; she still keeps stuff from me."

"Well, I don't think we really made whatever it is we have official," she said turning a furious shade of red, her ears looking like they had been badly sunburnt.

"Well, I can tell folks how to do it easy. It took us a couple of hours and if I had to dig the first six feet, it might have only added another half an hour or so. Cost me a couple hundred dollars for everything."

"Really?" Deputy Lewis asked.

"Yeah, let me go get you my list," Steve said and headed off in the direction of the garage.

"Is that all you two are doing out this way today?" Angela asked.

"No Mom, they're still investigating the pig thief," Amy said.

"Somebody stole Uncle Dewey's pigs again?" Amber said coming out of her bedroom, her hair plastered to the side of her head from the nap she'd been taking.

"Not that we know of," Lucy told her, "but the suspect that Mr. Abbott saw ran towards this subdivision. So we're still thinking it was somebody that lives in this area."

"You mean we have bad guys here?" Amy asked. "What are they going to do with the pigs?"

It had been something that she was deliberately being obtuse about, as they had told her where bacon and ham came from. Not that either had been available at the stores lately.

"Because somebody was probably desperate for food," Lucy told her.

"Got it," Steve said, coming back with a sheet he'd kept from the sand point that gave the basics and handed it to Deputy Lewis.

"Thanks," he said looking at it.

"Listen, there's another thing I'd like to tell you guys," Lucy said, cutting her eyes to Lewis who nodded to her. "There's going to be a broadcast later on tonight. The power is going to be coming back on between six and eight o'clock, if the rumors are right."

"Broadcast? Like when they told us that they'd declared war on China and North Korea?" Angela asked.

"Yeah, something like that. I guess until they get all the replacement transformer parts that it's a risk and a danger to energize a large area, but with the news blackout and radio stations going off the air..."

"What is it?" Steve asked them. "Martial Law? A gun turn in?"

"We don't know," Lewis told him. "But I'm guessing 'yes' to all of it at this point."

"You can't be serious," Amber said, surprising them all.

"Do you remember that big call we got called out on a while back, when we were at Dwight's?" Lucy asked.

"Yeah, I've been meaning to ask, what happened? It was an all hands-on-deck call." Steve asked.

"Large riot. Mix two kinds of politics and a bunch of broke, down-on-their-luck people... It was bad, we were stuck in Atlanta for a day and a half just helping with paperwork."

"Wow... I had no idea all that was going on," Angela said. "The news never reported anything like that."

"They can't," Deputy Lewis said. "We're kind of under martial law right now."

That bombshell had everyone who was jabbering quietly sober up and stand up. Even Amy knew what that was, having heard her father talk about it a time or two, and looked up in surprise.

"What?" Steve asked, the words almost coming out a whisper.

"Since the war started and the blackouts happened. That's why the bank runs weren't as severe as they could have been and why stock trading gets suspended so much. The government is quietly filtering the news and shutting down TV and radio stations," Lucy answered.

"How do you guys know this? I mean why doesn't everyone know this?" Angela asked.

"Because we're already at near riot points when the local grocery stores get trucks. The price on things keeps going up because the value of the dollar—"

"Keeps going down," Steve answered, and both deputies nodded.

"Why tell us now?" Amber asked, sounding far more grown up than she was.

"Because even if they dragged you guys into court, it might not have gone anywhere," Lucy said softly.

"It can't be that bad, can it?" Steve asked, "I've been to Macon off and on lately. It's not like I see roving gangs robbing people for food and—"

"Right now, it's fuel, but things are not as ugly because of the media blackout. If somebody panics and a large call out is needed...People have been walking off the job lately," Lewis said, interrupting Steve.

"You mean cops quitting?" Angela asked.

"Yeah, we haven't gotten a paycheck in weeks now," Lucy said. "If I didn't have some money set back in the bank and Matthew helping with things...it would be rough. You can't just walk into the grocery store and buy a cart of groceries anymore. I mean you guys have seen that, right?"

There was an uncomfortable silence and everyone looked back and forth.

"No, not really," Steve told them, "just for milk and bread and stuff."

"Definitely avoid Monday mornings and the first of the month—especially the first coming up."

"Why?" Steve asked, already having an inkling of what was going on.

"Because, the food stamps aren't going to work," Lewis said quietly.

"Are you spreading this info around or...?"

"No, actually we're telling very few. When we got the delivery for your papers we both talked. We were going to let you know one way or another, and it sounds like we're going to go talk to Lucy's boyfriend."

She turned slightly red in the face at that, but she nodded. They talked another ten or fifteen minutes, and then both said their goodbyes before leaving in their cruiser.

"Want to go to the laundry room and cool off?" Angela asked Steve, watching as both girls fled in that direction already.

"No, I was hoping to retry that nap you were telling Amy about," he said, stepping into her arms and pulling her close for a kiss.

"Ew...I'm sticky now. Besides...we need to talk. You, me, the girls. We haven't been out and didn't know about any of this. Those two seemed worried and it sounds like both of them are at their wit's end, not getting a paycheck."

"Yeah, I know, I just like being close to you," Steve said and then backed off a step. "What worries me is that I had no idea it was getting bad. I mean, it's something I guess we should know if everyone else is going through it and somebody mentions food shortages and we say 'what?' It becomes obvious that we're not even hurt by this. I mean we are—"

"But we aren't, because you prepared."

"It's part of my job as a husband and father," he said quietly.

They both entered the laundry room, a dark room that was between the garage and the rest of the house. The girls were playing a hand of cards but when they saw their parents, they scooted back to make more room. Both parents sat across from them.

"Teams?" Amber asked. "Or are you here to talk to us about not talking about what the cops told us about?"

"Mostly to talk, but how about a quick game of Euchre?" Angela asked.

Amy groaned, but Amber grinned and started shuffling the cards. "And then can I go to Matt's?"

"Sure," Steve told her, and watched as his daughter deftly shuffled the cards.

The game was a favorite in Northern Ohio and Michigan, and often confusing to people who weren't acquainted with it. While they played, they discussed what they'd heard, why it could be dangerous to share what they had heard and some things they were going to have to change. Amy was telling her dad how some of the kids she saw sometimes in the summer never really left their house this summer, and she thinks maybe their parents were still working in the city. They were about to play another round of cards when a knock interrupted their talk.

Steve hated to leave the air conditioning, but he headed to the front door, wiping the sweat from his forehead and then drying them on his hands. He was about to grab the knob when the knocking began again, louder this time. Instead of just opening it, he leaned to the side and looked out the window. His neighbors, Sarah Wilson and Billy were standing there, with Sarah holding her hand, blood dripping from it.

"Angela," Steve screamed over his shoulder and pulled the door open.

"My mom's hand, she slipped..." Billy said.

Three girls came running almost immediately, but Steve didn't look. He ushered them in and put one big hand around Sarah's wrist and held her hand up high.

"Ouch!" she shouted, tears in her eyes, but it was more in reaction to the pain than a rebuke to the treatment.

173

"Kitchen, get your mom her kit," Steve barked to Amy who took off at a run. "Get me two jugs of water," Steve barked to Amber, who took off back towards the laundry room where they stored the clean and sanitized water.

Being careful and ignoring Billy who was talking a thousand miles an hour, Steve led her to the kitchen where the stainless-steel sink was.

"What happened?" Angela said taking over and pulling the bloody hand towel back to look at it.

"I was chopping some half-frozen chicken and slipped," she said through gritted teeth.

"She needs to go to the doctor. My dad's at work, and we don't have fuel for Mom's car, and our phone is dead. Can you take us?"

"Don't worry, my mom knows what she's doing," Amber told Billy, trying to be a force for calming to the panic-stricken, young man.

"I just...she was going to be making me a sandwich when she slipped—"

Angela hissed and then clucked her tongue, thinking. Amy came running out with a plastic tackle box and put it up on the counter before thumping a cardboard box down next to it. Nitrile gloves waiting. She pulled two out and then gloved up. She'd been careful to avoid any of the blood, but now with the gloves on, she peeled the towel back more, showing a slice along the outer meaty part of her left palm, near the thumb.

"This is going to need some stitches," Angela told Sarah.

"I'm so sorry," Sarah said between tears.

"Can you give us a ride into town? Get her to the doc to stitch her up?" Bill asked.

The irony wasn't lost on Steve or Amber as they exchanged a glance. A while back, it was Billy who was in need of medical attention, by Steve's own hand. Then again, Steve mused, this might be a good opportunity for the Taylor family to mend fences.

"We can," Angela answered him without looking up. "Uncap that water and pour it over the wound," she said towards Amber. "Little bit, get me the gauze pad, tear it open, but don't touch it."

"Got it," Amy answered.

"I can take care of this for you," Angela said. "Or I can give you a ride into town. It's up to you," she told the neighbor softly.

"I can't...our insurance deductible... I don't know what to do. Money is tight," she managed to stutter out between tears.

"I can stitch you up," she told her, "I just need your permission, and you can't twitch. I don't have anything to numb you more than, say, a shot of whiskey...and then give you some antibiotics for it when I'm done."

"You're a doctor?" Billy asked suddenly, some of the frantic looks had gone out of his eyes.

"No, but I've worked in the medical field," she said taking the supplies her well-trained daughters started unloading.

"Go ahead," Sarah told her.

"You allergic to anything?" Angela asked suddenly and Sarah shook her head no, tears of pain running down her cheeks.

Amy pulled on a pair of gloves and started tearing things open as soon as Sarah had said yes. It had been a while since she'd helped her mom, but she didn't need much in the way of direction while Angela cleaned and checked the wound for anything foreign. Sarah winced but she held still, her breathing fast and heavy. She tore open a suture kit and got her hemostats ready. She met Sarah's eyes a second and the once enemy neighbor nodded, tears and sweat rolling down her face.

She held still for the stitching, and it was over in less than two minutes from start to finish. She spent some time cleaning around the wound a little bit, then dabbed it liberally with antibiotic cream, and then put fresh gauze over it and gently wrapped her thumb and hand to hold it in place.

"I'm sorry I was such a bother," Sarah said.

"No, not at all," Steve told her. "I'd like to think if it was my wife who got hurt, you and your family would help her."

Billy looked up at Steve and they locked eyes. The boy looked down at his feet and muttered, "Thanks."

"We're neighbors; we should look out for each other," Steve told him.

"Yeah, just not through the windows. That's creepy. Like a level of creep that makes my skin crawl," Amy told him matter-of-factly as Amber made a long sighing sound.

"I uh...won't," he said after a pause.

Sarah, Steve, and Angela shared a look and then they busted out into quiet laughter. Angela stripped out of her gloves and walked over to the fridge and opened it up, reaching back for the Tupperware container Steve kept his antibiotics stash in and came out with a bottle of pills. She closed the door before the cool air could all rush out and went over to the counter and got a Ziploc bag out and handed Steve the bottle of pills to crack open. It was fish antibiotics, but a kind they knew to be the same as the human variety.

"You're not allergic to anything, are you?" Angela asked as she started shaking pills into the baggie.

"No, you asked me earlier, I think," she said.

"Yeah, I usually do it multiple times," Angela told her.

Steve had been watching Billy with interest. When the fridge opened, the kid's mouth had fallen open, and he'd been staring, his eyes going back and forth to his mom and the fridge.

"Hey, Billy," Steve said quietly as Angela told his mom about how to keep things clean.

"Yeah?" he asked.

"How are you guys doing for food?" Steve asked in a low voice, almost a whisper.

"Things are tight. Dad had to get a new job and with the power issues...I can't work right now either to help. Not full time like I was."

"Trust me, I know how that is," Steve admitted.

Then the idea hit, he knew he was potentially inviting trouble, but he walked over to his kitchen pantry. It was fully stocked and refilled from their stores, but the door opened away from them and he slipped inside and hit the light switch a couple times before remembering the power was out again. He grabbed several boxes, an armload of cans and with two fingers left, snagged a couple of plastic grocery sacks. He frog-walked it back to the counter and put the armload down carefully.

"What's that?" Sarah asked, but Billy's eyes were big in surprise.

"Billy said some things are tight. With your hand hurt, I figured something like this would be easy for you to make ahead of time, and you won't pop stitches."

He'd gotten several boxes of instant rice, a few pounds of pasta, and the larger plastic jars of Ragu, along with a couple of cans of tuna fish. He started putting them in the bag when the tears came back, and he looked up after hearing a sob.

"I'm sorry we've been miserable to you and your family," Sarah said. "It's just...you were new and my husband was sure you were going to try to change the area..."

"No, no, it's not like that," Angela said.

Both Amy and Amber looked a little uncomfortable. Amy had been throwing away the discarded stuff from her mom's stitch job and then pulled her gloves off.

"Want to play cards again?" Amy asked. "Looks like grownups are going to talk."

"Sure," Amber said, wanting to get away from the fish-eyed stare of Billy whenever his gaze came her way.

They started a game of hearts and were talking quietly when Billy walked into the laundry room five minutes later.

"Listen, I'm sorry about...whoa," he said, rooted to the spot, looking at the big cooler on the electric dryer.

"It isn't as good as regular AC, but it works," Amber told him.

He held his hand in front of the outflow side and then pulled his hand back to his face, staring at it.

"Dad says it's like a swamp cooler. Pretty easy to make," Amy told him.

"Listen, I'm sorry about everything," Billy said, "and...um...can I talk to you...alone?" he asked, looking down at Amber and then to Amy.

Amber looked at her sister questioningly and then shrugged. Amy got up reluctantly and stomped out.

"Listen, I'm sorry if I was creepy. You moved in next door, and I didn't know you were that much younger than me till just now."

"Yeah, cuz you're like almost twenty," she said, a hint of snark in her voice.

"No, I get it. I was probably creepy. I was trying to build up the courage to talk to you, but now I find out you're total jailbait. I'm sorry. I'm just kind of awkward and apparently too stupid to know any better some days."

She looked up and met his gaze and stood up, so they were closer in height. More on the level and less intimidation.

"I've got a boyfriend, but I'm flattered, really. I just...how about you can lean out and say hi next time instead of staring from parted curtains? That really is kind of creepy."

"Sure. And the thing with your dad, I wish I hadn't done that. I was...things are tight. Dad had lost his job and didn't tell my mom for a long time. I was doing some stuff with him, getting him set up for an online business like I have, but he doesn't have the nose for it...I was trying to sneak him a couple of gallons of gas so he'd not stress so much."

"That doesn't even make sense. Dwight said somebody had been stealing his gas pretty regularly."

"Well, maybe I wasn't the only one?" Billy said, looking a little red in the darkened laundry room.

His words calmed her again, and she bit her lower lip while she considered his words and then nodded.

"I have to go, my mom was almost ready when I came in," Billy said and paused like he wanted to say something else, but didn't.

"Ok, take it easy," Amber said and followed him out of the room.

Angela was holding the bags of groceries and offered them to him. He took them and they both said their thanks and left.

"You were great," Steve told her, giving her a quick hug.

"Thanks. It's something you never lose. It's harder on animals, because half the time they don't understand you're trying to help them."

"Yeah. Are you worried...you know, the whole practicing medicine without a license thing? I could have easily driven them into town," Steve told her.

"They didn't have the money," Angela whispered. "Didn't you see how thin she's gotten?"

"No, I try not to check her out," Steve told her honestly.

"Good boy; I trained you well."

"Hey!" he said and reached out to poke his wife in the side.

Angela side stepped but she was smiling. Doing something to help neighbors had done a lot for her. She wasn't prideful, but she was feeling the glow of putting the animosity between them away. Neither of them heard Amy walk back into the laundry room as they talked in hushed tones.

"Did you see the scar on his hand?" Amy asked Amber.

"No?" Amber said.

"His mom is going to have a scar in the same place he did."

"Who cares. Solitaire? Hearts? Spades?"

"Let's get Mom and Dad and get the Euchre game going again," Amy said, surprising her sister.

CHAPTER 18

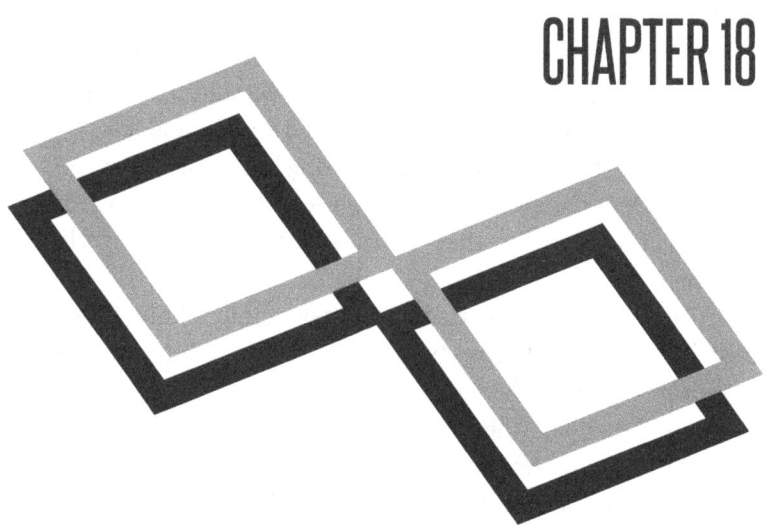

"My fellow Americans. We have been at war off and on for fifteen years. I have long harped on the Chinese for their currency manipulation and that was one thing I vowed to fight if elected President of the United States of America. The previous administration had done much to obscure the problems of our own here at home, and under bone crushing debt, the United States needs to work on our own backyards first before we continue on.

"Negotiations for a ceasefire have been requested of us and our ambassadors are now working on a deal to end hostilities so we can focus our time, energy, and efforts here. Most citizens are aware that a good portion of the country is suffering from terrible power loss, and the heat of this past summer has taken its toll. Fuel prices are sky high and many Americans find themselves with little to no food, gas to drive to the store, and many, many businesses have been shut down.

"As a country, we've been through two depressions already. The Great Depression was probably the worst, with what happened in the seventies hardly counting. After the housing bubble burst and banks had started to fail, we entered another depression, though with the bailouts and federal programs things have seemed to be getting better. They haven't. The printing presses were churning out Monopoly money and the Federal Reserve and the central banks were adding electronic zeros to their bottom lines.

"Today, that all stops. We are facing a natural disaster of our own making. To put a halt on this and reverse things, a series of executive orders are being enacted even as we speak. The Federal Reserve Act of 1913 is being placed on hold and we are moving the currency to a gold standard dollar. In order to expedite things, martial law has been enacted across the nation. Already, looting, rioting, thefts, and lawlessness has overtaken many of the larger urban areas.

"This will allow us to do two things: we can focus on removing regulations that got us to where we are while we re-evaluate things on currency and give our local police and national guard more room and flexibility to operate. I understand some locales have been operating without funding for a while. Until the currency situation is fixed, I've released many stores of supplies to our law enforcement officers and soldiers who seem to have left their stations to take care of their families or find employment elsewhere.

"I would strongly encourage every law enforcement officer and soldier who hasn't reported in to do so. I understand with power outages and poor communications that you may have been out of communication. Once you have checked in or returned back to the station, you'll be given your next set of orders that are being sent out as we speak.

"One last thing. I've ran on the campaign of 'America First.' We are the best at what we do, and what we do has been being the world's watchdog. Once we sign the cease fire and start working on our failing infrastructure that's led to our massive power outages and loss of services, we can start rebooting the country. I know things are hard, but they are getting better. "Two things to remember: the Martial Law decree is temporary, and the state governors will be coordinating with me in Washington to make sure the needs of the people are being met."

"Shit," Steve muttered, his head in his hands.

The younger girls chided him for language, but Angela started rubbing the back of his neck where the muscles had been knotting up, causing a headache.

CHAPTER 19

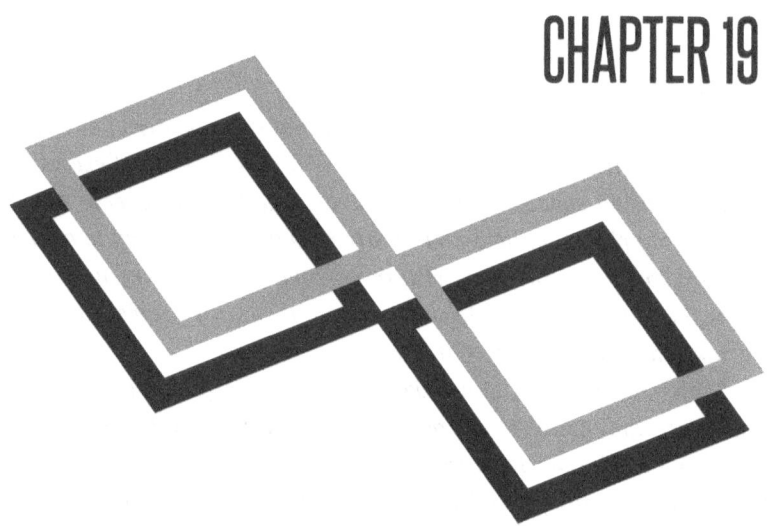

Neighbors began knocking on the door off and on the following day. Steve answered it to be surprised to see Billy and some of the folks he'd waved to down the street but never really got to know. A couple of them had buckets, the orange home depot specials.

"Hey, Billy. What can I do for you guys?" Steve asked, standing in the doorway.

"Listen, I was wondering if I could use your hand pump, so my mom can do some wash?"

"I don't...I mean. You guys want some water?" Steve asked.

There were smiles and nods and with a start he realized he recognized Richard Hunter, one of the HOA buddies of Jeff's, the one who had helped pull Matthew off of him.

"Wait, you're trying to sue me," Steve said walking out the door and pulling it behind him.

"It wasn't my choice," Richard said.

"What do you mean, sue you?" Billy asked.

"These lily-livered ass-clowns had me served with papers for the hand pump! Saying it's against the HOA conventions," Steve said, his voice rising in volume.

Somewhere behind all of them a door opened and closed, only audible because there was little to no traffic in their area. Steve didn't turn, but he knew with all the windows open, that one of the girls or Angela was coming around the house, to check on things.

"Hey, that was something Jeff and that Morris character pushed through. I voted no, along with Matthew for what it's worth."

Steve fumed a minute and then took a breath. If Steve had a "trigger" it was both the HOA and Doug Morris, a man who had been largely absent in the latest shenanigans lately.

"I guess I don't mind getting you folks some water. Come on," Steve said, walking around the house to see Angela coming their direction, the .45 she claimed in an open carry holster clipped to her side.

"Hey baby," she called softly. "Who're your friends?"

"Billy and some of the neighborhood folks. Looking to see if we'd get them some water from the pump."

Nobody said it, but when Steve opened the fence and closed it behind him, everybody was looking at his wife, and it wasn't only because she was nice on the eyes. A couple of them saw the large Colt and had correctly deduced that when Steve started getting loud, that she'd headed around the back to flank them as backup. Steve dropped her a wink and put his arms over the fence.

"Hand some over, I'll fill them up for ya," he said reaching.

"I can give you a hand," Billy offered.

"Naw, that's ok. Those chickens you and your parents complained about might poop on your shoes or something. I'm already getting dragged into court. Safer for me, if you stay on that side of the fence. Just in case," Steve said, and grinned when the teenager turned red in the face at his words.

"Oh, ok. Just trying to help," Billy said handing over his bucket.

Steve collected buckets from everyone, and Angela took a couple so her husband didn't have to carry so many.

"Thanks for the backup," Steve whispered.

"It should be them that's thanking me," she whispered back. "I figured you were about to come unglued when the HOA rep showed up."

"I nearly did," Steve told her, stopping in front of the pitcher pump.

He started working the pump handle until water started sloshing out. It was so muggy, that the water droplets that hit them both in the legs would have been barely felt, except it was much cooler than the air. After one bucket was finished, Angela took over the pumping and Steve changed buckets out and carried the water back to the fence. They repeated the process until everyone's was full.

"Now guys," Steve said, after Angela and him had finished pumping, "I'm not going to be doing this every day. My house and my property are likewise mine and off limits, despite what the HOA thinks or says." Steve looked pointedly at Richard.

"I uh...I told you, I didn't vote for that," Richard stuttered.

"I won't Mr. T," Billy said at the same time.

"I appreciate the help," another neighbor said, giving Steve an understanding nod.

"Ok, thanks for understanding. I still have my own stuff to do and I don't want the entire community here all the time. Now remember, you have to filter and boil that water, the well isn't deep enough and we live next to a farm," Steve told them, hooking a thumb over his shoulder.

"You mean, you won't do this...." one of the neighbors the Taylors hadn't officially met asked.

"All the time? Hell, no," Steve said. "There's a lake just south of us and to the north of us. Before the golf course is a couple of smaller lakes."

"Most of that property is privately owned," Richard said.

"But there's a stream that runs from one of them to the other. Walk to the main road, hook a left and you're at the stream in less than ten minutes."

"That sounds reasonable," Billy said hopefully.

"It is," Angela told them.

The men at the gate looked at each other and gave small waves goodbye. Angela and Steve watched them go.

"You did great," Steve said, after he heard Billy's front door close and kissed her on the side of the head.

"You did too. I didn't want them to see the rabbits and the solar panels. Ruffles had another litter."

"That's good. I am going to see if I can get ahold of Dwight and see if we can trade for some pork, next time he gets some butchered."

"I'd love that, Steve," Angela said and kissed him deeply.

❀

The sound of a bang had Steve jumping up, his heart racing. Angela heard the same and was already rolling off her side. The sound happened once, and seeing his wife's reactions, he knew it wasn't just a dream.

"What was that?" Steve asked her, feeling in the darkness for his shorts.

"I don't know, sounded like a door banging shut," Angela said, pulling her colt from the nightstand drawer.

Steve located his shorts and pulled them on in one smooth motion then got his own Colt off of his side of the bed, taking a flashlight.

"What are you going to do?" Angela asked.

"I'm going to check it out. Go upstairs with the girls. Get ready to call 911, if I start hollering."

"You be careful," she said, coming around the bed and giving him a quick hug before running off on nearly silent steps.

"I will be," Steve said, his adrenaline pumping.

Without turning on the flashlight, he headed through the downstairs on silent feet until he made it to the kitchen. Most of it had windows facing the backyard. The night was dark, but inside the house with no lights, it was darker. Moonlight reflected off the

185

white surfaces of the hutches, and a figure was briefly outlined as a lid to a hutch was opened who jerked its hand back, and the lid fell with a bang. Steve's blood was boiling in anger, and in the gloom, he checked the chamber on his Colt and then made sure the safety was off before he walked to the sliding door.

The glass panel had been left open, to let out as much of the hot air as possible and let the slightly cooler night air in. A small battery powered fan was on the floor, helping move things along. Steve barely heard its buzz, but he knew it was probably heard from outside as well. Slowly, he used his left hand to slide the screen open a couple inches. He led with the pistol, and then pushed it open hard, heedless of the sound.

"Stop!" Steve screamed as the figure opened the third hutch.

The moonlight silhouetted the figure for a minute, and he could see that it had to have been a woman based on the figure. He was already moving and nearly tripped on his head over the solar panels that ran the swamp cooler. He righted himself as the figure made a dash for the back gate going to Dwight's. Cursing, he hurried and as the woman fumbled for the latch in one hand, he could see a squirming rabbit to her left, trying to break free.

He leaped and hit the figure in the waist and felt the claws of the rabbit dig into his shirtless back as it used Steve as a springboard. All three fell and then a buzzing sound, a blue spark lit the night, and Steve started twitching as a taser unloaded on his bare skin. Agony ripped through his body as every muscle fiber flexed, and every nerve ending tried to shoot off at once. Just as it felt like he was going to crush his teeth by clenching his jaw so hard, the taser was removed, and the figure ran out the back gate.

Steve laid there a couple seconds longer when a flashlight illuminated him. A gun barrel came into sight next to the flashlight just as Steve was getting his muscles to relax enough to start moving his right hand. The gun had fallen close to him, and he was praying he was thankful his finger wasn't on the trigger when he was hit with the taser when the rabbit hopped into his view.

"Steve?!" Angela yelled.

"Fi...Fine..." he said, wiggling his feet and toes.

"Your...your back. Are you ok?" Angela asked rushing over.

"Yeah. Somebody tasered me," Steve spat.

A light turned on upstairs, one of the LED flashlights Steve equipped the girls with to only be used in the case of emergencies.

"Tasered? What were they..." Angela held her hand out and Steve tried to reach for it but he didn't have control enough to get it yet.

"Call 911," Steve whispered hoarsely, "they could still be out there."

Angela had seen he was already weak and moved to start checking on his injuries.

"What the hell happened here?" Angela asked again, mostly to herself.

Steve rolled over on his side, finally getting his muscle control back somewhat. Every nerve ending was still shooting bolts of pain, as if the electricity was still coursing through his body. Despite that, he made his way onto his butt while his wife checked his vital signs over, her flashlight searching for injuries, his back first and foremost the worst looking. If he was just hit with a taser, she knew to keep a feel on his pulse but the fact he was moving already told her he would be ok.

"Somebody was in here trying to get one of the rabbits, I think."

"I told Amy to call 911 when I saw you rushing at the figure. I told her to stay upstairs," Angela said.

Steve pulled his knees to his chest and then straightened back out, stretching. "Did you catch the rabbit, at least?" Steve asked.

"You're so silly, but I love you anyway," Angela said as the upstairs window opened, and Amber leaned out.

"Is everyone ok?" Amber yelled through the window. Amy's little face was in the curtain next to her older sister.

"Yeah, did you get a chance to call 911?"

"Yeah, they said to call back if someone was hurt."

"I wonder why the hell they would say that?" Steve asked his wife quietly.

"Probably because they have bigger things going on tonight," Angela said softly.

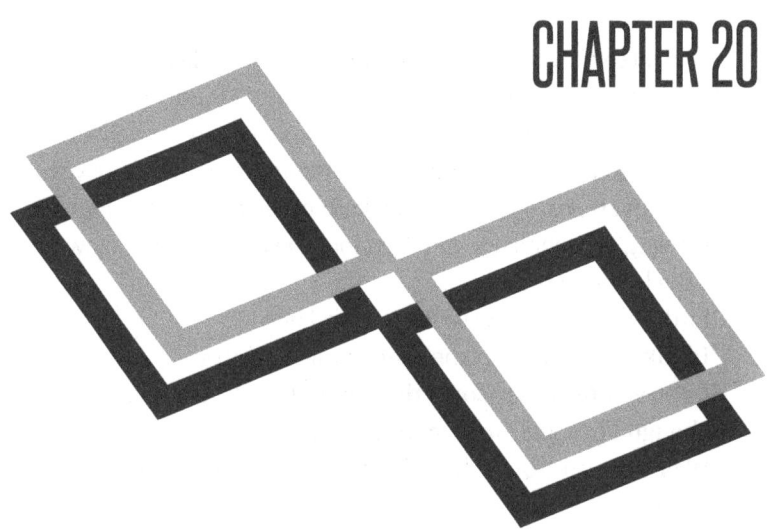

CHAPTER 20

It took the police four days to come out, and when they finally showed up it was the County Sheriffs, Lucy and Ron. Matthew walked over with Lucy, and they all talked about what had gone on and what actually happened. Lucy was in her plain clothes, but she still had her service pistol on her hip with the Sheriff's Department badge displayed prominently on the side of her belt.

"Did you come in the cruiser today?" Angela asked.

"Not today, and maybe not after this week either."

"What do you mean?" Steve asked her.

"I know the president gave the executive order, on top of the martial law, but there's no relief in sight. There's no help coming, and the promise of food and supplies was either greatly misinformed or an outright lie," Matthew told them.

"Oh man, so no paycheck still?" Amber asked, the curiosity of a teenager trumping her usual manners.

"No," Lucy said. "It's been rough. There have been rumors that they are going to federalize the Sherriff's Department but that hasn't happened yet. Even a case of MREs would be welcome right about now."

Steve was about to talk when Matthew's stomach rumbled.

"How are you guys set for supplies?" Angela asked.

Steve gave her a slight nod, as if to tell her to follow her instincts.

"We have food, but fuel...the last couple of tanker deliveries in town hasn't made it in. My boss isn't broadcasting it, but they think the fuel deliveries are getting hi-jacked somewhere on the highway."

"No way," Amber said, and then looked sideways as Amy walked out of the laundry room.

"Little ears," Matthew whispered to Lucy.

"It's ok," Angela said, "she's ten going on thirty."

"I also wanted to say sorry that I've not made it over here sooner, even though I'm spending a lot of time in the subdivision—"

"Well, I'm sure you've been busy," Steve told her. "Any news you can share?"

"Well, I've been busy, and I don't know if it's news or not, but two houses towards the front of the subdivision had home invasions."

"What?" most of the Taylor family chorused.

"Only two so far. They said men with Hispanic accents kicked in their front door and held the family at gunpoint while they took the food and anything of value they could find. One house had a few guns and ammunition, and they took that too," Lucy told them frankly.

"Oh god, did anybody get hurt?" Steve asked her.

"No," Deputy Ron said. "Just a little roughed up. Bumps and bruises, but it could have gone worse, much, much worse."

"Is there anything we can do to help?" Angela asked.

"There is a community meeting at the HOA clubhouse..." Mathew said, his words trailing off into dead air.

"Great," Steve said after a few minutes.

❖

After the cops had left, the Taylor family decided they did want to go to the community meeting after all. It wasn't that they wanted to look at the faces of the HOA leaders in the eye and talk to them, but the idea of pulling together as a community for mutual defense seemed like a good idea in light of the recent break-ins. The good thing they had going for them was that they had the Sheriff's deputy, Lucy, to work with them. Her relationship with Matthew had only grown and deepened in the month that they had officially been together. Steve had always wondered why Matthew seemed to have pulled away from the newfound friendship, he figured the situation was weird enough, without adding in the stress of a new girlfriend and what looked like a country doomed to collapse.

Weird in other ways, such as his own daughter, Amber, and Matthew's son are starting to get along in their own budding relationship. Mix that in with the fact that with a new girlfriend, he probably didn't have a lot of time to do things. And if he was being fair with himself, Steve was spending a lot of time over at Dwight's farm, ensuring that his family had enough food to put away. He replanted all his planter boxes, something that he'd been doing every time a crop finished in the Georgia weather, but his own small gardening endeavors weren't enough.

He knew he was pretty well set, but one thing you couldn't have out of buckets of freeze-dried food, rice, beans or whatever...was fresh greens. Sure, you could reconstitute freeze-dried food, but it didn't taste the same; it didn't have the same flavor. With the change in their diets, the girls were suddenly curious about vegetables and grains again.

The meeting coincided the night before the next Sunday service, something the Taylors had been skipping out on. They had gone a couple of times since the power had been going on and off, but without a steady and reliable way of telling time as all their batteries kept dying on them, they just got out of the habit. Yeah, Steve knew he could recharge them what his small solar set up, but they didn't want to get that out and get that all set, yet.

Neighbors, new and old, would start dropping over and asking for buckets of water. The days of reliable electricity were getting fewer and fewer. For a while there, they'd get up to a few hours a day to get power. Now if they were lucky, they got four hours every four days. It was never reliable, it would always happen at unexpected moments...almost like they were trying new things out. When the power was on, people would try to check the radio and check the TV, but there were no signals. More than a few times Steve had kicked himself for never getting into communications gear. He'd always heard about shortwave radios, CBs, and other stuff. He didn't have anything like that, and with the power being all wonky he didn't know if anyone else would be using it either, but that idea was still left open. It was still one checkbox left unchecked.

The Taylor family walked into the community building for the subdivision. It was already packed when they got there, but they were able to get seated. In another twenty minutes, it was so full people were standing in the back of the room. Jeff caught Steve's eyes, and a dark look crossed his face. Steve shot him a smile and a little jaunty wave. Matthew walked up with a LED, battery-powered lantern and turned it on and put it in the middle of the plastic folding tables that the HOA leaders liked to sit behind as if they were judges holding court.

Jeff spoke first, the weasel dick wanted to discuss the recent break-ins, and did so at length. He pointed out the two families that had been held at gunpoint and asked the community to see if they could help. That opened up the discussion when someone stood up and pointed out they didn't hardly have anything to share. That talk went on as other people went off topic and took turns standing and speaking, with the HOA leadership board throwing questions in here and there.

Lack of food, lack of transportation, lack of fuel, and lack of medical attention were all topics that were brought up. Steve sat between his wife, Angela, and little Amy. Little bit. Early on Angela's hand snaked into Steve's right and as people were describing how dire the situation was getting, Amy's hand snaked into her father's left. The girls and Angela kept shooting Steve looks, but he shook his head slowly, as if to say this isn't the right time. Surveying the crowd, the Taylor family saw a lot of people were starting to look on the thin side. That's when someone said something that made Steve sit straight up, as if a bolt of electricity had zapped him in the ass.

"How about we go and talk to that farmer on the backside of the property?" someone shouted from the audience.

Steve tried to pick out who'd called the question but he couldn't find them in this sea of faces. Jeff looked over at Steve. Jeff looked at Steve thoughtfully and steepled his fingers together, touching his thumbs to his lips a couple of times in a tapping motion. He looked over at the Taylor family and spoke.

"Steve Taylor, you know Dwight Abbott the best, do you think he would be willing to help the community out? Provided of course, we can pay for it."

Steve stood up. "Dwight is a reasonable man, I think he probably would. I don't think he gives it away for free, but who knows what's in a man's heart. I can ask him for the community," Steve said, but kept standing.

Matthew spoke. "I've gotten to know Dwight a little bit myself, and here's something I think needs to be said, and I don't care if it pisses any of y'all off. This foolishness that this board has perpetrated against the Taylor family and the Abbott farm needs to be talked about. We look like hypocrites if we suddenly go over looking like beggar princes after raising hell, trying to get them shut down, trying to even get him to sell the land off for some kind of real estate bullshit," Matthew said, looking angrily at Jeff. "So my advice to you guys, is to make your apologies. Be damn humble about it, especially before you ask him what the price is going to be. You never know, he might be a better Christian than all of you. Steve, will you ask him?"

Steve nodded. "I said I would."

"All things considered," Jeff said, "that's damn kind of you."

That admission looked like it had to have been forced out, the way a kidney stone was passed. From the back of the crowd, someone shouted, "Yeah, but you're still a Yankee," and the tension in the crowd broke a little bit as people started chuckling.

Steve sat down. Amber stood up, looking more like Angela with every passing day. "Do we know anything more about the people who broke in?" she said and then sat down. That seemed to have gotten everyone's attention, and then the board member started sharing what they heard.

The next part of that discussion on the break-in seemed to go on for an hour. When asked if anyone had any ideas for a solution, Steve told them why not put together a neighborhood watch. Except, for a watch that could run 24/7, it would require people to stay awake or work third shift. In the community center, there had to have been 200 people. Three people stood up, and said they would be willing to help. Steve said he would help also, but at this point they would get together after the meeting or Sunday to talk about things and discuss how to react to an armed home intrusion.

Professor Toodles stood up and started berating the volunteers, telling them they couldn't do a neighborhood watch, especially if it was going to be people that were going to be armed.

"Why should I disarm if I'm volunteering to keep an eye on the community as I walk around?" Steve asked him in a loud voice.

"What you mean disarm? You're carrying a gun right now?"

Steve stood up and turned to him and just smiled. He really liked the subcompact .45 he'd taken to carrying, a newer purchase in the last couple of months. You couldn't even see the outline with him wearing his jean shorts white shirt and a short-sleeved button-up that was left unbuttoned.

"I've got a permit to carry, there isn't any law or any ordinance for any HOA guidelines saying you can't carry."

"I can just see something happening right now! You'll pull your gun, and something will happen. It'll be just like that...that...that kid in Florida who bought the skittles."

"That was an unfortunate case," Steve said, "but...that nineteen-year-old 'man' attacked someone with a concealed carry permit. Only after the permit holder had his head smashed into the concrete a few times, and the nineteen-year-old man," Steve said, emphasizing the M, "went for his gun, did the concealed-permit holder use it in self-defense. I'm not saying we're going out to shoot people, but having someone walk around in the afternoons and evenings as an extra set of eyes might be better off armed. Besides Professor Toodles, what do you think those home invaders had? Kitchen knives and good intentions? Are we going to rush in there to help, or are we going to rush in there when something happens and be hurt or killed because we're disarmed?"

Doug Morris sputtered something, but his wife, who seemed to have the better judgment of the two, stood up and talked to him in harsh tones and yanked him back down in his seat. Her face was bright red, and from across the room, Steve could tell that her fury was directed at her husband and not at the Taylor family that Doug seems so intent on pushing buttons with.

Amy gave Steve's hand a squeeze, Steve looked over to his eldest daughter.

"Daddy," she whispered, "now should we tell them about the church?"

Steve's mind was torn on that. It's not that he didn't want to help them, because he really did. He just lost touch with the pastor while they were busy just getting on with their day-to-day business of flying under the radar. It had made Steve feel guilty. You never get too busy to go to church. You never get too busy to go see friends. Yet in his own mind he did just that. Hell, for a little while there he thought Matthew didn't want to be friends, but Steve hadn't gone over to Matt's house, not even once. The guilt Steve was feeling doubled.

"Tomorrow, I will go talk to the pastor about it."

"I think that's a good idea, maybe they can help," Amber told her dad in a hushed tone.

"What church? What help?" someone from behind the Taylors asked loudly.

Several heads turned from the other side conversation, startled.

"Time to go," Steve said, giving his wife and daughter's hand a squeeze. Amber was the first one to get to her feet, sitting on the outside of the row.

Jeff and Matt's eyes both turned to see the Taylor family stand up and start walking out. Matthew gave Steve a nod, Jeff just glowered. Some people turned to look and see who was leaving the meeting early, most of them were watching everything else that was going on and all the side conversations in the meeting room. Getting outside, everyone took a deep breath.

"God, it stank in there!" Amy said, making her sister let out a surprised bark of laughter.

"What's so funny?" Angela asked her daughters. "Most of these people don't have running water. Now that the banks are closed, nobody's working. Probably don't have any more soap and shampoo."

"Or deodorant?" Amber said getting her giggles under control.

"Or toilet paper?" Amy said and busted up in the giggles herself.

Turning to Steve, Angela looked at him and said, "You gotta help me out here."

"Well I don't know if he's out of toilet paper. Seems to me that Jeff and Doug Morris are full of shit. I just figured all that stench was coming out of their mouth."

"Daddy!"

"Steve!"

Steve just laughed. Tomorrow would be a better day since they would be at the church. They would find out how much the supplies had lasted the past two months.

CHAPTER 21

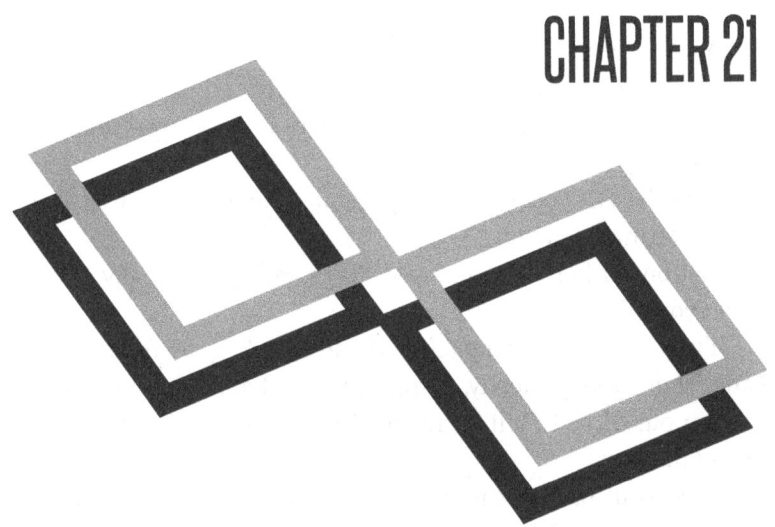

Now that Steve was conscious of his decision to go to church, figuring that not making a decision was in essence making a decision... he made sure he was going to be up on time. He got out his wind-up clock from a storage bin in the garage, one that he'd inherited from his father from years ago. He had set it the night before, and when it went off first thing in the morning, surprised shouts came from upstairs directly over the Taylor grown-ups' bedroom.

"Oh God, I forgot how loud that thing is," Angela said, pulling a pillow over her face.

"Don't worry, I got it," Steve said, reaching over and hitting the button to silence it.

Feet came thundering down the stairs, and Amy ran and launched herself and landed on the top sheet in between her two parents.

"Guess who we get to see today?" Amy said brightly, being one of those annoying people that don't need caffeine to get the day going.

"I don't know, who're we going to see today?" Steve said, sitting up letting the sheets fall to his waist.

"We get to see..."

"Her boyfriend," Amber said from the doorway.

"He is not my boyfriend!" Amy said loudly.

"You've been excited ever since Dad said we were going to church today."

"Well, let's go you guys. Get up; get up," Amy said, pulling at the sheet covering her mom.

"Get out of here," Angela said. "Let's get up and ready. Amber would you—"

"I've got the little camp stove already working on boiling some water," Amber said sweetly, despite the fact that she looked like she just ran out of bed. "It'll be ready and in the percolator in about twenty minutes."

Steve smiled. His daughter was almost seventeen, and she already appreciated the finer things in life. Honesty, integrity, jeeps with big engines, and most of all...coffee.

⬦

The sermon had gone on a lot longer than any of the previous services the Taylor family had sat through before. The pastor was joined at the altar with his wife, and they read off community news by candlelight. Then the pastor launched into a sermon, was a little bit of book of Matthew, and all of the revelations thrown in.

Steve sat through it all, almost wondering if other churches were having the same type of sermon and discussions going on. Looking around the congregation, he noticed the people weren't in as poor of shape as the folks from his subdivision. They didn't stink as bad either. There were still some individual families where you could tell things had hit them harder than it had some of the other members there.

After the sermon, everyone waited in line to say their goodbyes and then gather out on the front lawn of the church to continue talking. With no TV, no phones, no Internet, no radio, no news... everyone was hungry for gossip, for new information. As usual, the

Taylor family was the last one to say their goodbyes, deliberately holding back even though the Taylor girls wanted to run out to the crowd on the lawn and join in on all the discussions.

"There was a great sermon," Steve said, shaking the pastor's hand.

"Thank you, I didn't want to go all doom and gloom in there," the pastor said with a smile. "I'll leave that for the Baptists."

The pastor's wife busted out laughing, she gave her husband a playful punch in the shoulder. Their son was nowhere to be seen, Steve figured he was probably outside playing with the other kids and catching up on the news himself.

"Are you guys getting to come here for the community dinner now?" the pastor asked them.

"What community dinner?" Angela asked.

"Well, it's a good thing we bought all the supplies we did. Instead of just handing out food, what we've been doing is using the church kitchen and kind of making a mass meal. It isn't much, but we can make sure everyone in our congregation gets one good big healthy meal a day."

Steve was about to say something, but the pastor's wife spoke up first.

"And we've only dipped into the food that the church purchased for this reason so far, I just wanted you to know," she told Steve and Angela.

"Oh no, that's what we bought it for. We might need to come and start taking from the community store ourselves someday, but we're still sitting in really good shape. Is everyone here doing all right?"

The pastor looked at Steve for a moment and shook his head.

"We've had some unfortunate news. Some of our older members of our congregation have run out of their medications. We've heard rumors, but we lost three so far to heart attacks. Mrs. Bertie was insulin-dependent and passed away yesterday, and we lost a few more due to heatstroke or heat exhaustion, whichever it was."

Steve's mouth dropped open in shock. He knew there was going to be losses, he was just surprised that he hadn't seen or even heard of these losses before. Then again, they've been staying real close to their house. It was one of the only ways he could think of to feel safe. He looked the pastor and his wife over, noticing the changes in them. Before things got rough, the pastor hadn't exactly been fat, but he hadn't been a skinny guy either. His wife as well was full figured, and they looked like they had been losing weight.

"Are you guys eating enough?" Steve asked them bluntly.

"Oh yes, probably better than we ever have. You're talking about quantity not quality. Our diets changed, we're exercising more, we're doing what we need to do. I've never felt so good in my entire life."

"I'm really glad to hear that. How is your son doing?" Steve asked, a sly grin directed at the littlest Taylor in the family.

"Daddy..." Amy interrupted.

"I'll take her outside to go find him," Amber told her parents.

The four of them watched the girls nearly run outside, Amy's laughter and giggles belying the fact that despite the world changing drastically it was still one she could find happiness and joy in.

"He's doing really good," the pastor's wife said, "he was getting a little lonely, but people started coming back to church. When the power first started getting really wonky, people stayed at home for a little while. You would think all those post-apocalyptic and zombie books had everyone all freaked out."

"But he got used to it; how have you guys been?" the pastor asked Steve.

"We've been doing pretty good, actually. We just kind of...we've been staying close to the house. Members in our neighborhood aren't doing so well, and we helped one neighbor out with food. Also helping folks out with water every once in a while, and I think while I'm now the first one in the community to have a hand pump there's two more from the rumblings I heard at the meeting. The hard part of all of this is realizing that trying to stay in the house, and out of everyone's public view...I mean they are suing us...again...We've been trying to fly under the radar. I was wondering—"

The pastor interrupted Steve. "I don't mind if you want to take some of the supplies to go towards the community you live in. We bought this is a safeguard for all of us, you more so than anyone else, and contributed to the food pantry we set up here at the church. I know the prepper mantra is, 'two is one, and one is none,' so why not have three, so if you like to do this, whatever you want," the pastor told him with a grin. "The only thing I ask is that you don't do it in front of the whole congregation while they're out here waiting."

"Yeah, I can see how that would make things look weird. I don't know if I really want to do that, or maybe set something up so—I don't know what to do, Pastor."

Angela looked over at her husband and put her hand in the crook of his arm. "That's because you care what happens, even if you don't like a lot of the people living around us."

"Why didn't you guys move?" the pastor's wife asked her, "with all of the ongoing trouble?"

"I don't think we ever really thought about it," Steve said. "I mean, as long as we were staying within the law, the HOA notices were annoying more than anything else, and when they sued us...I think I kind of dug my heels in and...this is gonna sound horrible."

The pastor looked up to Steve and nodded. "Go ahead Steve, it's confessional time," the pastor said with a chuckle.

"I mean, they sued us. They went public saying we did something wrong, that's all on record somewhere. I'd like to go on record of at least being right, and if not right, at least have it show that we weren't guilty of whatever trumped up charges they were saying. I mean the last time they sued us, it was for putting in a hand water pump. Then the next day the neighbors started showing up looking for water," Steve said, shaking his head in disgust.

"But you did help them; you did give them water," Pastor's wife said.

"Yes, he did," Angela said, with a note of finality in her voice.

"So, you want to go outside and hang out with everyone? They usually do this for about an hour and then supper will be ready at... well, at about suppertime."

"I think we'll have to call it a maybe," Angela said looking out the doors of the church and watching the kids chasing each other.

Amy and Amber were being chased by several of the boys, both parents looked on in mild surprise and amusement as their older daughter played like she was ten again. Despite some of the bad news, some of the horrible news, they were still having fun. "Let's go," Angela said taking her husband's hand.

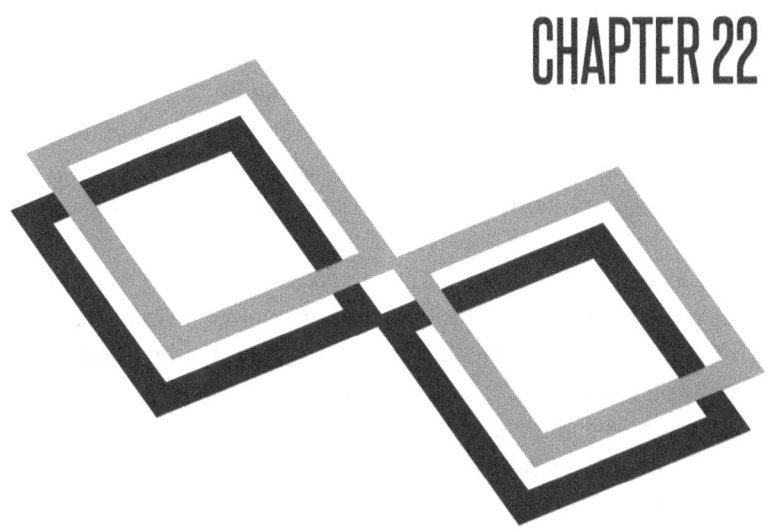

CHAPTER 22

Not wanting to wait all day to get the food from the church, Steve took the entire family to the storage unit. The gates were locked. He'd forgotten about the electronic code access. With the power out, it wasn't working. Now a chain and padlock were across the front, and the office of the mini storage dark.

"Are they even open?" Angela asked.

"God, I hope so. I paid for at least a year in advance. Paid cash."

"You want me to go check, Dad?" Amber asked.

"No, I got this," Steve said, getting out of the truck and slamming the door.

They had taken the truck to church, because it had the most fuel in it. There wasn't any conscious decision to take or not take Angela's BMW, and the way the Jeep guzzled gas everyone naturally just piled into Steve's truck. It also hadn't been driven in a while. Steve remembered his father's advice that the quickest way to kill a car is to park it for a long time.

Walking up to the door to the office, Steve stopped to look. There was a note on the door that said "knock hard."

Steve knocked hard, trying to be careful not to crack the tinted glass door. He wasn't expecting anything, his hopes shot, but within a couple moments he heard footsteps approaching from the other side of the glass and a deadbolt turning. The same young woman who rented him the unit opened the door and gave him a smile.

"Hey Mr. Taylor, you need to get in your units?"

"I do. What's with the lock?" Steve asked her, curiosity in his voice.

"Well, it's something new I had to do. When the electricity goes off, it keeps the main gate locked. I dug out the electronic lock in it, and now I just use the chain instead of the electronic deadbolt to keep people's stuff safe."

"You not keeping me out, are you?" Steve asked with a grin.

"I wouldn't keep you out, Mr. Taylor," she said, little blush hitting her cheeks.

"I meant, I might need to get some stuff out of my unit," Steve told her looking back at the truck and seeing Angela watching him intently.

Oh great, Steve thought to himself, Angela probably thinks I just flirted with the kid when it was the opposite. Or maybe she didn't mean her comment to come out the way it did, and it was an embarrassment? Steve looked back at the young woman who barely met his gaze, the red creeping into the tips of her ears.

"I set aside a key for you, Mr. Taylor," she said with a grin, and then followed his gaze to the truck and saw three blonde ladies staring at her from within the truck's windows.

"What you did, renting those units in cash...it helped me out of a bad financial situation. I don't know if you realize it, but I go to your church. I listened the day that you and Pastor first talked about being ready for something like this. I took that money you gave me for the units after I got my bills paid up, and I went on a little bit of buying spree in Costco."

"Sam's Club?" Steve asked, a grin breaking his features.

"Same thing, right?"

"I guess so," Steve told her with a grin.

"I'll go get you that key, and use it to open the gate, but could you lock it behind you?" she asked, all business like now,. "With the power out more often than not, I won't have my security cameras and alarms working. I'm hoping somewhere to scrounge up one of those mechanic's bells."

"Mechanic's bells?" Steve asked her.

"You know...this thing with a rubber hose that has a plug in the end, it runs by your car driving over and it makes it sound."

Steve slapped his forehand and grinned. "Yeah, I know exactly what you mean. I had a blonde moment there."

The girl let out a laugh, and gave him a raised finger as if to say be right back, and went inside. A moment later she was walking back out and pressed a key into his hand.

"Thanks," Steve told her.

"No problem. See you around sometime?"

"Yeah, I'll be around now and then. Not too often, though."

Steve gave her a little wave and headed back to the truck, opened the gate, and got in.

"So, Daddy," Amy asked in a singsong voice, "who's your friend?"

"I told you not to!" Angela said, her voice sounding irritated.

"It's not like Dad was flirting with her or anything," Amber told her mom in a sarcastic tone. "I mean, did you see her playing with her hair, Dad?"

"What?" Steve asked almost throwing the kids into the front seat's headrests as he slammed on the breaks.

Angela looked at her daughters and made a motion with two fingers pointed at her eyes and then back at the daughters, who were sitting in the back of the truck. Message received: "I'm watching you."

"I think I'm lost here," Steve said.

"We joked that that girl over there is your girlfriend," Amy said, happy to be helpful, "but mom didn't sound very happy about it."

"Oh, crap," Steve said.

"Yeah, what was that about?" Angela asked, turning to Steve.

"It wasn't anything," Steve said with a dramatic sigh. "I paid for each of our units with cash. She's part of our congregation, and was there the day that me and Pastor talked about what we think might be coming. It was when we talked about putting together the community food bank. She was just..." Steve said the last word drawn out as he struggled to find the perfect way to phrase it, to say it in such a way that his wife couldn't use it against him at a later date, "telling me how much she appreciated it."

"Yeah, but she still has the hots for you," Amber snarked.

"Shut up," Angela and Steve chorused.

Everyone busted up laughing. Everyone except for Steve, who joined up a moment later.

⊶

Steve pulled up to the HOA community building and turned off the engine. The whole family got out, and Amber stayed back to see if the tarp in the back of the truck had stayed in place. They didn't want to advertise the fact that they had loaded about 200 pounds of dry rice, beans, lentils, and some freeze-dried TVP in it and then left it unattended. Happy with the tarp job, Amber followed her family into the community center, which was unlocked.

Jeff was sitting in a chair near the desk with his feet propped up and a paperback closed on his lap. The door closing behind Amber startled him awake. He must've been catching an afternoon nap in the community center, keeping it open for the residents.

"Mr. Taylor," Jeff said, a blank look on his face, "what can I do for you." He wiped his eyes to rub away the sleep.

His question sounded like a statement, which was an indicator of how hard things had been for Jeff lately. He couldn't even fire up his usual ire in the face of the family that had thwarted his plans.

Rumor had it, according to Matthew, when it was exposed that Jeff and Jeff's wife might have had less than stellar motives for trying to run the Taylors out, they tasted a little bit of backlash of their own.

There were rumblings in the community that some people didn't trust him, they'd been there for so long that as long as he wasn't actively going after the Taylors like he had that town hall meeting that turned into a brawl, they were willing to let the status quo go. Taylors – 3; HOA – 0

"Just come back from church," Steve told him, "and there's something that we were doing with our church that maybe would help out the community—I mean the subdivision," Steve said.

"Oh yeah? What do you mean?" Jeff asked, his voice more quiet than it ever had been before.

"We're Lutheran, and much like the Mormons, our church tries to be a little bit prepared. Our church family and our church community started putting together a food bank for those in need."

"Are you saying...wait a minute, what are you saying?"

"We notice that this community's folks seem to be going through some really hard times. We'd like to help," Angela said, chiming in before Steve had a chance.

"Well, sure. What can I do to help you help the community?" Jeff asked after a moment.

"Well," Angela said after a moment's hesitation, "you think you can help us carry about 200 pounds of food in here?"

Jeff's mouth just dropped open in shock.

"Before anyone else spreads this info or food, maybe we should approach this community dinner thing like our church does. They do a communal meal every day. I don't know how many people are in the community here, but we probably have enough to get people one or two really good meals," Amy said, looking up at her sister Amber.

Amber nodded. "I don't know how many meals we can actually make out of this, but we felt it was the right thing to do."

"Steve, I..." Jeff said, his eyes starting to water. "I don't know what to say. Of course, I'll help you unloaded. What about helping those that need the most help first?"

"We thought about that," Steve said, "that you're always going to find some people that are going to hoard food if you just give it out. Maybe some don't need it so bad. What if the volunteers from the community offered to do like the subdivision cookout, or the one that you guys do every summer. Except for this time, it is for the HOA members instead of a big massive block party where everybody is invited."

"That way, only the people that really need the food come get it and the people that don't need help yet...."

"That's...it's very charitable of you guys. Your church is ok with you bringing all this food?" Jeff asked.

"Yes," Steve said fibbing a bit, because what was in the truck hadn't technically come from the church, yet. "I talked to the pastor and his wife about it. Our agreement with the church, what we're doing, is trying to help. Some of the church family and I helped set up the food bank. It wasn't meant to be for everyone, forever, but so far, it's a little bit to stave off starvation. Supplies won't last long, and the food doesn't get restocked, so supplies are limited."

"Almost everyone here is without jobs, money is worthless, really," Jeff asked, "You brought 200 pounds of food?" he repeated.

"Yes. Do you want to give us a hand unloading it in here into the community center? We can spread the word and start whenever you want. Since I'm starting to help out with the neighborhood watch, I don't know how much cooking and volunteering time I'll be able to do."

"Yeah, let's go get that in here, put it up nice and safe," Jeff told them as they headed out.

❖

Word spread throughout the community as Steve started talking to neighbors. Since they had cut out of the meeting early, he was hoping to find some of the volunteers for the neighborhood watch and get that organized. It was with more than a little amusement when he knocked on Doug Morris's front door, to let him know about the community meal that Jeff was already getting the water going for. After a moment, his wife answered.

"Mrs. Morris, I'm—"

"I know who you are Mr. Taylor. Came here to gloat?" she asked, a tired anger emanating from her voice.

"No ma'am. I'm here to let you know that there's going to be a community meal at the HOA clubhouse in a few hours, if you and Doug would like to come out."

"I would love to," she said, the anger draining away from her expression.

"Thank you, ma'am," Steve told her. "Would you mind spreading the word a little bit to the neighbors you know, and ask them to do the same? I'm also looking to set up a meeting with the neighborhood watch volunteers after the meal."

"I'll help spread the word," she said and shot him a small smile.

"Thank you," Steve said, giving her a wave and already starting to back up.

"You know, I don't always agree with him with how he's treated your family."

Steve turned back to look at her.

"For a long time, I didn't know what it was about, but he really is trying to look out for the community. He has this idea of justice and working in the college has done little to quiet the activist he always wanted to be. I'm sorry, for what it's worth."

"I...." Steve's words trailed off, shocked into silence.

"No, it's ok. I am sorry I didn't sit on him two years ago when he started causing a ruckus," she told him, a smile tugging at the corner of her mouth.

"It's...ok," Steve told her and gave her a smile back, and half a wave.

She returned it and shut her door. Feeling conflicted, he started walking. Steve had two more families to let know and hoped that people talking to their neighbors this way would go viral like the way a post on Facebook used to.

-¤-

Steve walked to Dwight's farm, having a couple days in between seeing him last. He hadn't relayed the communities question and tonight he was sure he was going to be asked about it. Steve changed his mind about helping cook and feed folks. There was so much animosity and festering dislike, every time he tried to help and be a part of the community it felt good. He felt like they were even starting to accept him. His neighbors, the Wilsons, Doug Morris's wife, even Jeff Arellano had all changed or softened their stances. Plus, the dinner would be a good chance for him to catch up with everyone that was going to form the neighborhood watch.

"Hey, Steve," Dwight said, seeing him walking towards the house.

"Hey, yourself," Steve called back, seeing the old farmer walking out of his barn with a grease stained set of coveralls on, unzipped down to his waist in spots, the fabric damp with sweat.

"What can I do you for?" Dwight asked, grinning and offered a big hand as Steve closed the distance.

They shook and Steve had to smile. Of everyone in the community, right here, Dwight and Matthew had become fast friends.

"Got a minute to talk? This might take a few?"

"Sure," Dwight said. "Want to head into the house? I got sweet tea."

That made Steve's mouth water, "Yes, sir," Steve muttered.

"No ice, but it's still good. C'mon son," Dwight told him, turning and starting to walk, his back turned.

After glasses had been poured and both men were sitting at the table, Steve told him about the home invasions and how he was going to start sort of a neighborhood watch, to at least warn people.

"You going to get Lucy involved in that?" Dwight asked.

"Yeah, if she'd like. I just haven't talked to her and Matt much lately and—"

"Oh, you don't wanna be talking to them too much," Dwight said with a grin.

"Huh?" Steve asked, sobering immediately. "Why's that?"

"Matthew has been coming around here, helping me with little things—"

"Wait, Junior?" Steve asked, trying to catch up.

"Yes, Matty Junior has been coming around and helping me with stuff. He volunteered when Matthew and Lucy started living together to give them some privacy, plus the kid was going crazy. I've been teaching him how to work on some of the implements and do tune ups on the tractor, little stuff like that."

"Is that why you haven't needed a hand as much lately?" Steve asked.

"Partially. With my son god knows where... it's nice having somebody around to teach stuff to. I sort of... I'm sorry I didn't—"

"Oh no, I was feeling the guilts too," Steve said. "I've had my head down so much while things are hard."

"No blood, no foul," Dwight said, and they both took a long swig from their tea.

"So, what else?" Dwight asked after a moment.

"Some folks in the community were wondering if you'd be willing to sell some stuff. Food: corn, soy, even a butchered pig, or part of it. I guess they're asking—"

"Sure, but I don't want to deal with anybody on the HOA 'cept you and Matthew," Dwight said. "The rest of them can kiss my hairy ass."

Steve almost burst into a choking laugh, but managed to hold it in, if only just.

"I don't mind being the go-between. I figured I'd ask because tonight the HOA is going to have a community dinner. That way we'll get a feel for how many are—"

"Where'd the food come from?" Dwight interrupted, his voice soft but serious.

Steve looked down at his tea and Dwight nodded, understanding.

"Do they know it was you?" Dwight asked.

"No. It's stuff I took out of my backup stores but my church has agreed to help."

"You mean all that stuff that you spent weeks buying, moving, and hauling?" Dwight asked.

Steve nodded, taking a long drink.

"Well then, if they think it's the church and not sitting in your garage or something...."

Steve winced. "Yeah, I thought of that. The thing is, there's a lot of people who're going through some really difficult times."

"I want to help the community out," Dwight said, "but I can't feed everyone. I don't have enough of the crops ready to harvest, plus now I have to save some for seed and feed for my sows. I could use some help around here though. How about this...I send you to the dinner tonight with a nice fat ham to do with whatever you want. Spread it out tonight, let everyone get some. A gift. All I ask is that in the future, I get a hand around the farm. Kind of the same deal I am already doing with you and the Fitzpatrick boy."

"That's..." Steve said his words trailing off a second, "that's pretty generous."

"Yeah, my son would have my ass if he was here, but he isn't. I figure I'm the guy who has the tools, equipment, and know how to grow food. It has occurred to me more than once I might need the community to help me keep it from being removed from the area."

"You mean, like FEMA coming in and—"

"Exactly that, or people like the home invaders who kicked in the doorways of those houses...."

Steve took another long drink and thought about that. He nodded and then finished off his glass of tea and put it down.

"You want to buy a little goodwill?" he asked the old farmer with a grin.

"Damn straight," Dwight replied. "I've been running people off the farm off and on for weeks now."

"Are they coming through my gate?" Steve asked, a hint of alarm coming into his voice.

"No, usually over the wall, or walk in from the road. I've set up more of those noise makers you showed me how to wire up. One battery and a bunch of horns."

"I haven't heard that many horns lately...." Steve said.

"Yeah, one night I had two of them go off, one right after another. Almost like I had two guys coming onto the property at once...."

"Or two groups?" Steve asked, finishing the thought after Dwight's words trailed off.

Dwight finished off his tea glass as well, wiped his temple with his wrist, and put the glass down.

"That my friend, is a scary thought."

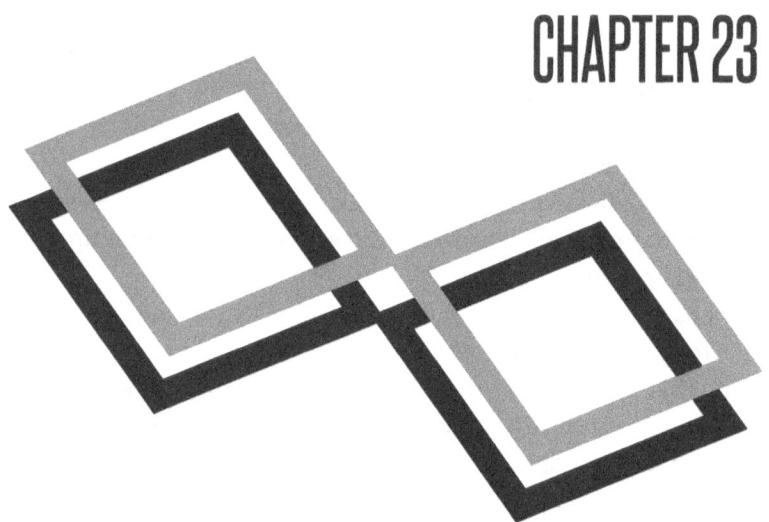

CHAPTER 23

The smell of cooking food brought people out of their houses almost as well as the visiting with people up and down the block. Chunks of a salt-cured, smoked ham were added to the water the beans were boiling in along with a large section of the bone. Rice, beans, lentils and the chunks of pork in broth took close to three hours to prepare in several large pots. People started lining up with bowls and their own spoons. For the first time in a while, the Taylors saw smiles.

It had been Amy's idea, but Steve had brought down in her little red wagon, four five gallon buckets of water, sanitized, from the hand pump. He had a few party packet sized pouches of Gatorade to mix in to get rid of the chlorine smell, if any was left. At the start of the long line of his community when the food was finally ready, he mixed the mixture and started dispensing it in whatever containers people brought with them. Cups for the most part, but there were more than a few coffee mugs.

"Thank you," was given out to the volunteers scooping food from the large pots holding the ad hock mixture by what felt like hundreds or even thousands of people. Steve watched and talked with anyone who would want. Up line, near the beginning of the white folding tables the HOA leadership usually sat behind, but now were being used in a real community outreach... Jeff explained to everyone coming up that Jeff and Steve would be addressing everyone on the front lawn of the community building so please sit down afterward.

It took them almost an hour to get everyone fed, and Steve didn't bat an eye when he saw somebody come through the line twice, especially when it was a kid. More than a few people had taste tested in the line waiting to get to their drinks and had commented how good everything was. Finally, the pots were emptied and a cold bowl was handed to Steve. He thought about giving the foam bowl and plastic ware to somebody, but as he turned and really looked, he was sort of blown away by the community.

Everyone was sitting in the grass, and the only place on the front of the property that was open was the cement sidewalk that was probably over one hundred degrees and would be uncomfortable to sit on.

"Thank you," a man's voice shouted from the crowd and everyone began clapping. Steve stood there looking poleaxed and when he turned to look at Jeff, he was clapping too, smiling. After a moment, Amy came running up from the crowd, leaving her mother and sister sitting in the grass about halfway back to his left. She ran up and hugged her dad around the waist tightly.

"You're supposed to say something," she said over the thunderous applause.

"What are you doing up here, little one?" he said, hugging her back with his free hand.

"You look like you swallowed a frog," she told him.

Steve tried to give his daughter a smile, but of everything that was going on today, this wasn't what he expected. He wanted to have a chance to get with the volunteers for the watch and then go home. Suddenly he was at center stage, and there would be questions about the food that he didn't really want to answer, couldn't answer, and realized the folly of his mistake. It all led to his tongue feeling like it was cemented to the roof of his mouth, but as his gaze ran around the gathering, he saw kids he'd seen a day or two back with dour expressions...and now they were smiling. The neighbors who once shunned him were now giving him smiles and thanks. Steve found Doug Morris in the crowd with his wife, and even there a smile touched the side of his mouth, and he gave Steve a polite nod.

"Wow, uh thanks," Steve said and then handed his bowl to Amy, went to the table and got some Gatorade in a plastic cup and turned back to everyone.

"I uh...a long time ago our church talked about being ready for hard times. We put together our own food bank to help other members in need. I contributed some to the bank and when I told the church about the needs of the community, they shared what they could," he told them, the words not entirely a lie but not the whole truth. "With what was brought today, we probably have enough left over for what," he turned to Jeff, "a week's worth of food?"

"Yes," Jeff said, his voice carrying well over the crowd. "It went a lot further than I expected. It's a good thing Doug's wife knows how to cook this stuff, or we'd have leftovers going bad!"

Chuckles in the crowd gave him a little confidence.

"Now, I talked with Dwight Abbott today, he's the one who provided the ham and soup bone. He's having troubles of his own, but nothing like the families that have been robbed at gunpoint—"

"What are the cops going to do about that?" somebody shouted, the voice shrill and hard to determine if it was a male or female.

"I don't know, I haven't seen any—"

"Fitzpatrick's woman is a cop," a different voice interrupted and the crowd erupted in murmurs.

"Hold on a second," Steve said putting his hands up. "Let me get through this, and then I'll let Jeff handle the discussions."

After a few more moments of hushed conversation, they quieted enough for Steve to continue.

"Like I was saying, The Abbott Farm has had its own problems. Everything from fuel theft to somebody stealing the livestock, some of what you're eating now came from his farm," he said, and he could see several people look into their bowls. "You asked me to talk to him, and I did. What he can use in return is some help. Everything from security to people turning wrenches. There won't be enough jobs for the entire community, he just doesn't have enough. So if you're in a bad way, out of gas, out of food or out of medicine, we need to figure out a way to keep going."

"Is your church going to send more food after this runs out?" a young woman yelled, probably barely eighteen-years-old, but it was hard to tell as hunger had left its mark on her features.

"There's only so much to go around, but this is what I could do right now. You have to remember, there are more problems out there than just the ones we're having inside here. The police and local governments—"

"They're folding up," Lucy said standing up, ignoring Matthew who was pulling on her hand. "Which is why I'm going to be assisting Mr. Taylor there in the community watch. I know police procedure and the laws, but with no communications and no help, we've essentially been cut off. I know Steve Taylor there threw the idea out and had some detractors," she said and people looked pointedly at Morris, "but it's a good one. I've taken emergency management classes and I have an idea on how ugly this is going to be if we don't organize now."

She sat back down and a few people clapped politely. Steve looked over at Jeff and then finished. "I'd like any volunteers for the watch and for the Abbot Farm to talk to me once we're done here tonight, so we can organize. That's all I got. Jeff?"

Jeff stepped up, and he held up the book Steve had found on his lap when he was napping.

"I've had my world view rocked. The last two days have really changed my view on things. For a long time, I fought Mr. Taylor on planting beans in his planter box and now six months later I'm reading a book about converting my front yard into a sustainable garden. You want to know why?"

Nobody said anything, their words were quiet.

"Look around. We've all lost weight. The fuel is gone, the power is out. A few 'unauthorized,'" he said, using his fingers to air quote, "hand well pumps are the reason that many of us survived. I've heard of a few passing away and seen firsthand that emergency services are not timely if you can even get ahold of them. Things are different now. Like it or not, we have to change and adapt."

"But if their church helped us out once, they probably can again!" a voice shouted.

"Yeah, maybe we should head over there!"

"Steve, where do you go?" another shouted.

A car horn went off in the distance, and then a second. Gunfire erupted. Steve got to his feet, his bowl flying out of his hands. He knew the direction of the gunfire and turned, catching Lucy and Matthew's eyes. They were already rising.

"That's Dwight," Steve said stepping over Angela and Amber who was already trying to raise herself.

"Steve—"

"Keep Amy safe," Steve commanded as his youngest was already trying to rise too.

He took off at a dead run, hearing the whip crack of gunfire from multiple locations. He'd fired enough rounds from his carbine to recognize the gunfire wasn't from only handguns. He heard the occasional boom of return fire that signified Dwight's .30/06 and the fact that he was still in the fight. Knowing he had to hurry to make a difference, he started running, his eyes sweeping side to side to make sure he didn't fall into the trap of tunnel vision. He'd done that once already and had a concussion and stitches to show for it.

"Meet you there," Amber said breathlessly and then took off like a streak.

Steve couldn't keep up with his daughter, she poured on the speed only the way a sixteen-year-old who ran two miles before breakfast could. He pounded the pavement, hearing the larger and heavier Matthew cursing and Lucy shouting encouraging words. Amber got two blocks ahead of her father and he saw her stop briefly, unlock the front door and head in. By the time his feet hit the pavement the garage door was already opening.

"Dad," Amber yelled, not realizing he was close.

Her hair was plastered to her head and sweat ran down her temples, her shirt just starting to stick to her, a stark contrast to Steve who was breathing heavily and drenched in sweat. She had two of the ARs from the gun safe. After she had startled for half a heartbeat, she held one out to her father and then hurried back into the "mechanical" room. Steve was breathing too hard to hear her, but she came back with his AR-500 vest with magazine holders and a hanging dump pouch. Steve handed her back the AR and started putting the vest on just as a cursing Matthew came rushing in.

As soon as he'd gotten the vest mostly strapped in, Amber shoved the AR back into his hands and turned.

"Wait—" Steve said, "Give the other one to Matt or Lucy," he said panting.

Amber didn't hesitate and shoved the carbine past Steve's body and rushed back into the mechanical room. Steve bent over a second with the extra weight of the metal plates in the vest and half a dozen magazines and breathed in deeply, filling his lungs, praying it was enough. After what seemed like an eternity but probably was five seconds, Amber ran back up with a double handful of already loaded magazines.

"I'm getting my pistol out," Amber said.

"You're not joining the fight," Steve told her sternly.

She nodded. "Mom and Amy will be over soon, I'm getting things ready for them also. Come back safe, Daddy," she said and then wrapped her dad in a big hug.

Steve gave her a squeeze back and then led Matthew and Lucy past the mechanical room and through the house to the back door. Until this point both Matthew and Lucy had been silent.

"I told Matt to come here with the ladies," he said, his own face beet red from the insane dash through the neighborhood.

"Thank you," Steve said. "I'm sure Amber will keep him safe."

Lucy snickered as they opened the back door and rushed out. Steve wasn't sure, but he thought he heard the big man whisper "asshole" before following him to the gate. Shouts from the community and people yelling back and forth to each other could be heard, punctuated by rapid-fire from smaller calibers and then the booming of the old man's deer gun.

"Slow down," Lucy hissed.

She took the AR from Matthew and then checked the magazine he held out to her.

"Green tips?" she asked.

"Yeah, steel core. I have one mag of black tips if we...I mean...." Steve stammered.

Lucy didn't hesitate, she inserted the mag, pulled the charging bolt and put it on safe like she'd been born with one in her hands.

"Nice sights," she said.

"My wife's," Steve told her and then walked through the gate.

"Sounds like four shooters," Matthew said.

"Five," both Lucy and Steve said in unison.

"Oh yeah, Dwight," Matthew said, pulling his shirt up and pulling a black pistol out.

Steve couldn't tell what it was with a quick glance, but it looked like a Glock to him and wasn't surprised when Lucy elected to take the longer-range gun. She'd done more training than any of them with it and if everybody was shooting rifle rounds, the only thing the big guy could do was watch for somebody running a pincer behind them.

"Let's move along the fence line, towards the shooting backstop. He's got some tall weeds left from his last corn crop that'll probably break up our profile," Lucy said.

"I agree, but stay down. I don't think at this distance Dwight can figure out if we're good guys or bad guys."

Matthew nodded and followed. Lucy took point, something Steve almost argued about because he was wearing a vest, but the way she moved told him she'd done this before. He realized he didn't know much about her past and made a mental note to ask politely at some point. They made it to the back of the shooting backstop, a large mound of stumps covered with rocks and topped with soil.

Lucy hissed, and Steve looked around.

"Oh, we're in the shit now," Matthew said.

CHAPTER 24

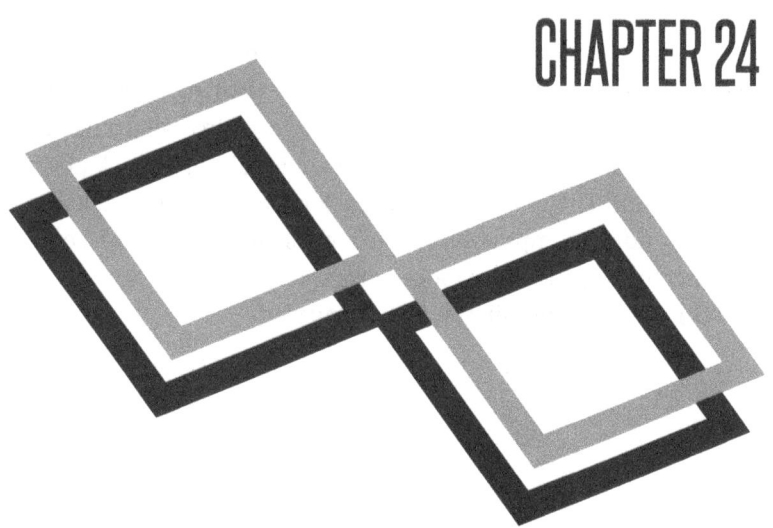

Amber was closing the garage door when she saw her mom and Amy running down the block. Angela had one hand holding onto Amy's but the other was holding onto her side, where her .45 was bouncing around. She waited, seeing Matt Junior running behind them with somebody hot on his heels. It made her twitch and she tried looking beyond Matt but couldn't make an identification.

"Where's your father?" Angela asked in a gasping breath.

"Him and the others went out the back gate. They're shooting at Uncle Dewey," she said, breathing easy.

Amy was a little red in the face from her run, but she was probably in almost as good a shape as her older sister.

"What did he say, do they need—"

"My dad said to come help you guys," Matt Junior said, running and panting.

Angela looked at him, then back at her daughter who wore her own pistol on her hip and then back at the young man and nodded.

"Downstairs," she said, and turned to start pulling the garage door down as Billy Wilson came barreling in.

Angela hesitated, if she hadn't, the closing door would have taken his head off. Instead, he barely cleared it and came to a sliding stop, almost into Amber.

"I came to check on..." he said, and then knelt down and started to dry heave.

"We're fine," Amy said. "If you upchuck on our floor, Momma's gonna be pissed."

"Amy," both Angela and Amber chorused, one a hint of a laugh, the other voice a hint of surprise and annoyance.

"We're fine," Angela said. "You should go check on your parents."

"They're at the community center. Almost everyone is. There are half a dozen people heading this way to help. I think they are the volunteers for the—"

His eyes widened as he saw the open door to the mechanical room and the boxes piled up. What caught his eye was the open hatch that led down into the storm shelter, where food wasn't disguised.

"Move," Amber said shoving him backwards and slammed the door to the mechanical room.

"You have a panic room?" he asked, a hint of wonder in his voice.

"Tornado shelter. Go on now, I need to check on my husband and I want to shut the garage door."

Torn, Billy looked between Amber and Angela for a couple moments and then shrugged and started walking. As he passed Angela on his way out, her nose wrinkled. Once he was out, she pulled the overhead door and then turned to her daughter.

"How much did he see?" she asked.

"I don't know. The safe was open, but Mom, the food down there isn't..." her words trailed off as she pointed to the boxes and Rubbermaid totes that concealed the food storage they had at the house.

"We'll just have to pray. Get everyone in the tornado shelter and I'm going to make sure the house is locked up. I'll join you in a second, so don't lock it."

"Ok, Mom," Amber said, and Angela was almost tackled by both Taylor daughters in a big hug.

"Come on, Matty," Amy said, taking Matt's hand and pulling him towards the closed door.

"Tornado shelter?" he asked.

"He would find out sooner or later," Amber said. "Lead the way, sprat."

"I am not a brat, you're a meany head!"

"No, I said sprat...you know what? Never mind. Move," Amber said, a note of authority in her voice.

Amy moved, and Matt followed, shooting Amber a confused look.

"You see them?" Matthew asked.

"Yeah, I got three, no four by the blue tractor," Steve said.

"And a group of two to the left, near the tailgate of his truck," Lucy told them.

Steve cursed silently and put his carbine up to his shoulder and sighted in.

"Don't we need to coordinate—"

"I'm trying to see what we're dealing with," Steve said, and a moment later Lucy brought hers up as well.

"Wait, those look like police or government...."

The black BDUs and vests looked like something straight out a Hollywood Swat Team, except there was no identifying patches or lettering on their clothing. Two of them looked like they were wearing baklavas bunched up on the top of their head like a watch cap. Steve saw one raise an AR and take aim towards the farmhouse, where most of the shooting had been concentrated.

Pink mist exploded and the man's head seemed to split in two just as Steve was trying to time his shot between heartbeats. With the man dropping, several of the gunmen turned to see him fall, blood and unmentionable things splattering them. One of them screamed a curse and stood up and began firing rapidly at the house.

"Fuck this," Lucy muttered just as Steve started firing.

A moment later, probably half a heartbeat later, Lucy did as well. The NATO rounds with the steel penetrators ripped into the first men who had no idea they'd been flanked. They had their backs mostly to the group, with part of their sides showing. Steve aimed for their sides, a smaller target than the back, but if they were wearing vests too, there was less likely of a chance they had the side armor also.

The first two men crumpled before the last one at the tractor realized he was now under fire from two directions, and moved to try to protect himself. The two by the truck threw themselves flat and crawled out of sight. As one man maneuvered too far, another shot boomed out from the house and almost like in a movie, he slapped his hand over his heart before his legs buckled and he fell out of sight.

"Reload," Lucy said. "Even if your mag is full."

Steve did it automatically, realizing that one or both kills had come from him, but in the heat of the shooting he couldn't tell whose shots hit who, or who even missed entirely. He looked back to see Matthew waving off a group coming up towards their back. With his blood up, Steve swung his AR in that direction to have Matt grab it by the hot barrel and point it straight up.

"It's our people," he hissed and let go, shaking his hand.

"Dumbass, you grabbed it by the hot end."

"'Tis only a scratch," Matthew said, putting a couple fingers in his mouth where they'd been on the barrel.

"The Black Knight?" Steve asked incredulously. "That didn't work out too good for him, Monty Python."

"I'll bite yer ankles, get over here, ya two-legged freak," he said and then ducked as a shot boomed out from the farmhouse.

"Who the SAM HELL is out there?" Dwight's voice boomed out.

Everybody looked at Steve, he stood up slowly, his barrel in the air and walked out from around the shooting backstop. He kept his head on a swivel and yelled as he came in sight of the farmhouse, "It's me, Steve."

"You got anybody with you?" Dwight asked.

"Yes, Matthew, Lucy and further back some folks from the community."

"You three, come up slow. Be careful, I saw two of them running for the hills. Tell the rest of the people to get out of here for now."

"We heard you. You need anything?" a voice shouted from behind them.

"Yeah, somebody get me a god damned medic. I took a hit."

Lucy and Matthew did what they could to get in touch with the authorities with no luck. Instead, they took the bodies and loaded them into the bucket of the front-end loader for a later burial. They didn't know how to drive most of the equipment and Matthew wasn't about to let Junior on the farm till things had settled down.

Steve had passed word back and then walked his wife to the farmhouse where Dwight was swaying in the doorway, his shooting stick and Remington within easy reach. He'd taken his shirt off and had wrapped it around his left arm. Steve was cursing at the old man as soon as he saw him, a red anger at the dead men almost consuming him.

"I got this, how about you go check on everyone," Angela said, knowing her husband needed to be elsewhere while she worked.

"The girls?" Steve asked hoarsely after his dismissal kicked in.

"Locked in the shelter, with the house, mechanical room, and garage locked. They're safe. How about you go get some information before I have to sit on the old man here."

Steve cursed again, but Angela let it go without comment and watched her husband storm out of the house.

"You'd think he was the one shot, not me," Dwight said after a pregnant silence.

"Right in the ass, too," she snarked and they both laughed.

"What happened?" she asked, unwrapping his arm.

"I was going to go put down one of the feeders and start processing him for the smokehouse," Dwight said and winced as the sticky cloth pulled away from his arm.

Angela was ready for that and had her mobile kit ready with some of the antibiotics with her.

"Are you allergic to anything?" she asked as she got the final layer off.

"No, I can take anything," Dwight said.

"You got a graze on the outside of your left arm. I can clean it up, but I don't think it's going to need stitching, but it's bleeding pretty good. I could always cauterize it to stop the bleeding faster though," she said looking at the three-inch groove on the side of his arm.

"Is it gonna hurt?" Dwight asked in a quiet voice.

"You ever branded cattle?" Angela asked.

"Oh, Momma," Dwight murmured to nobody as Angela pulled the gauze back and then started cleaning the wound. "Go ahead. I got a white gas stove on the counter."

"Good, saves me from having to go get mine," she whispered back.

Steve looked at the corpses. He knew he should feel something other than this cold anger, but he couldn't. All of them had been stripped of their vests and those had been lined up against the tractor next to three ARs.

"How's the old man?" Matthew asked.

Steve shrugged and hunkered down in front of the bodies, one of them having two extra holes in his grossly deformed head.

"None of them were carrying ID. The gear I thought at first was mil-spec, but it looks like civilian stuff, like yours. Didn't stop Dwight's last shot though," Lucy said.

Steve got up and went and checked out the vest. There had been a hole neatly punched through it.

"Ceramic. Mine has steel plates. Heavy as hell. I'm no expert, but most armor won't stop a .30/06 though."

"Yeah, well, these guys are dressed up like mall ninjas and from what little I heard from Dwight while you were getting Angela, they opened fire on him as he started walking to the barn. He made it the four steps back into the house and returned fire. He was pretty pinned down 'till we came along," Matthew said, his voice soft and horrified.

"This one," Steve said, pointing to a man in the bucket. "Should I know your name? I'm pretty sure most of that torn flesh is my fault. Should I—"

"Steve!" Lucy snapped and pushed Steve.

She was half his size, and her shove wasn't as hard as she could, but he looked up at her sharply.

"You don't know if it was me or you. In fact, all of your shots missed."

"Bullshit," Steve said.

"If it lets you sleep at night, believe that. I can't have you going into shock right now," Lucy snapped, her voice harsh.

"Why not?" Steve asked, the anger he felt still glowing red hot in his stomach, but he policed his words well and only some of the anger and horror seeped out.

"Because when everyone else panicked you and your family worked like you'd practiced for something like this. You had a plan you fucking executed. You saved Dwight's life, and if you hadn't fucking pulled the trigger, your pasty, white-boy ass would have been hamburger the moment that no-good, cock-sucking, pencil-dicked, puss-nutted, no-load, monkey-fucking son of a whore's little pimple on his mommy's ass after his daddy shot the best part of his offspring off all over—"

A bray of laughter erupted from Steve's mouth at the angry tirade. He never had heard of a woman talk so vulgar, and although he knew she was a Sherriff's Deputy and a badass, this wasn't what he expected. It hit him funny, and he realized Matthew was laughing so hard he was crying as well, which made Lucy's face turn even brighter.

"You're a bunch of fucking no-good, pieces-of-monkey—"

"Stop, stop," Matthew begged, both hands up.

Steve had to set his carbine down, his stomach was hurting as the adrenaline he'd held back flooded out of his system. It left him in a rush, slightly light headed and he fell onto his ass hard, almost knocking the wind out of himself.

"Oh man, you...I didn't know you could use the word...I mean... oh my...."

"I will end you if you so much as snicker," Lucy said pointing a finger under Matthew's nose, and he started braying all over again.

She stood there, red-faced as both men got themselves under control, which took a lot longer than either of them expected.

"Pencil dicked...." Steve muttered and they were laughing again.

"Puss nutted," Matthew said a few moments later, and they were off again.

"I'll wait until you're both done. I'm a southern woman of a gentle upbringing, and I won't be made fun of," Lucy said with a mock sniff then looked at the men and grinned.

"Thank you," Steve told her getting up and brushing the dust off his ass and held his hand out.

She stood there looking at him for a second and ignored the hand. Instead she slipped into his arms and gave him a hard hug. Steve started hugging back when he felt her punch him right in the bread basket. His breath left him in a whoosh and he stumbled backwards, half laughing half gasping.

"And that's for laughing at me!" she said pointing a fingernail at his eyes.

"I'm sorry. Where did you learn to swear like that?" Steve asked her.

"If I told you, I'd have to kill you. I wasn't always a Sherriff's Deputy you know."

"Yeah, I saw that. Where'd you learn to handle an AR like that? I know the cops don't get a lot of—"

"And I'll be getting you later on!" she said, turning and pointing at Matthew's face as the smirk left his face and he turned white as a sheet.

"I'm sorry, ma'am, I don't know what came over me. I do hope you take my apology as earnest and genuine as it surely is," he said.

If he would have been wearing a hat, Steve was sure he'd be wringing it between both hands.

"No ID, good equipment, but not military. Opened fire without warning. There's somebody operating around here, and I don't like the look of it. You're going to need to organize the watch after this. These might or might not be with the same groups that were kicking in doors."

"Let's find out how Dwight is, and then I'll ask him where he wants me to dig a hole."

An old man's muffled scream erupted from the house. Lucy started walking, but Steve held up a placating hand.

"Did you see she brought a little old-fashioned iron?" Steve asked her.

One of Lucy's eyes got larger, and she tilted her head, her mouth dropping open.

"Savage as f—" the breath left Matthew's mouth, cutting off his words as Lucy rapped her knuckles just under his sternum.

⚒

"How long are we going to stay down here?" Matthew asked.

Amber looked at him and gave him her best smile. To conserve the batteries, they had lit an emergency candle. The fire would draw out some of the moisture and give them some light in the process.

"Until my mom comes back with the all clear."

"I'm scared for Uncle Dewey," Amy said for the thousandth time, tears still streaking her face.

"He'll be ok. They would have brought him here if it was bad," Amber answered.

"So we just wait?" Matthew asked.

Amber shrugged, her shoulder movement caused the shadow behind her to move exaggeratedly.

"We could always play monopoly?" Amy said, wiping her eyes.

"I don't know how to play...."

Amy hopped up to get the game.

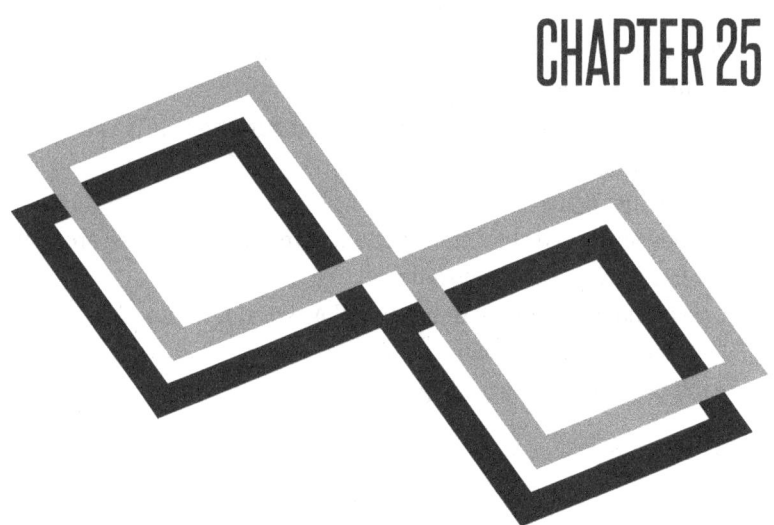

CHAPTER 25

The graze on Dwight's arm wasn't severe, but it pained him. When Steve wasn't organizing the community watch, which he hoped to dump on Lucy soon and just show up for his patrols, he was working with the cranky old farmer, him and half a dozen others. The days got long, though the heat wasn't so insufferable as October came and went. It was almost harvest time and there was equipment to fix, and a one-armed Dwight was a cantankerous, old bastard. Everyone avoided him and let Steve be the go-between. In all, he fed them and sent food back for their families.

Steve had borrowed Dwight's smaller tractor with a four-foot tiller on it one day and with a jerrican of diesel, he took it to the neighborhood. Jeff and him had spoken about it, and when somebody shamefacedly admitted to being a poacher of some repute, they put him to work on thinning off any wild game they could find for the community meals. Steve once more took some food out of his storage unit, but had skipped the church for a couple weeks. Every time he left for there, somebody would try to follow. He didn't blame them, but he didn't want to lead somebody to the food stores either.

A bit of paranoia set in. Nobody knew who the four men in black ripstop BDUs were, nobody came to collect them, and nobody asked about them. The community knew the day it happened what had happened and the rumors were swirling. Everything from government agents to an underground bunker of people who had popped up to randomly raid people in the area. The neighborhood watch stopped an attempted break in, but the two men who tried kicking in a door were armed with a cheap .38 special, the chrome almost worn off.

Like most folks of the south, the house they tried to rob had an owner at home who had a gun. The first man died in the doorjamb and one of Steve's volunteers who lived next door and was taking some downtime, heard the shots. He arrived in enough time to see the man turn to run away, before he turned to stop, turn, raise his own gun at the doorway. He never saw the man who killed him, the shot taking him at the base of the throat.

The two weren't known by anybody in the subdivision and were buried on the farm, somewhere near where the other bodies had been placed. Everyone in the area got thinner as food was tighter and tighter. Almost daily, Steve would be woken up by somebody knocking, asking for water or food. At first, he shared, but when he took a tally, he saw that unless he made a trip to the church or the storage unit, something he didn't want to do, he was running out of wiggle room. The first time he turned somebody away because the food was too tight almost broke him.

Community meetings happened almost daily. People would all gather at the community center daily to share news while they waited for food. Jeff spent most of that time talking or introducing somebody to talk. There was a lot shouted back and forth and more and more people were wanting food. The hunting had been good for a week, but the game didn't stretch. More than a couple people wondered aloud if they should go and take what Dwight had. Steve kept silent, but Matthew and Lucy didn't. They told in very great and gory detail what happened to the last four men who went up against Dwight.

More than a few people looked at the Taylors with something like hatred in their eyes again. They weren't losing weight as fast as the others and all but Amy were volunteering for extra activities for the community. Maybe they were getting food from the church on a regular basis? When Steve overheard that, he knew it was almost time for them to pull a fade for a while, but he couldn't leave anybody high and dry. Surprisingly, Matthew, Lucy, and Matt Junior, and those who worked at the farm were left alone, the focus seemed to once again, be on the Taylors.

"That was a waste of time," Steve muttered under his breath as the family walked back towards the house.

"At least we know what they're thinking," Angela said. "Though it might be good for us to go back to the house and pretend like we're not there for a month or two."

"And let the leeches die off," Amber said sullenly.

"Leeches? Ew...." Amy piped up.

"That's not nice," Angela piped up, cutting off all talk.

"Let's stay in tonight," Steve said.

"I figured that, since the food hadn't been made yet."

The community center had turned into its namesake. Before it was a building that was big enough to hold small meetings, had a community kitchen, or could be rented to have parties. Most of the time it sat empty, but the HOA fees had paid for it and it had been there when most of the houses had been built. Now, they had walked away from it and headed inside their own house before continuing the discussion.

"Yeah, I want to lay low. We're going to ignore people at the door unless we know it's a friendly."

"Like Matt Junior?" Amber asked, then turned red in the face as her father looked at her, curious at her tone.

"He's a friendly. Unless he gets too friendly, and then I won't be a friendly—"

"Steve," Angela said with a hiccupping laugh.

"Yeah, Dad, not funny," Amber said, her tone sulking.

"Yeah, Dad," Amy said in a sing-song mocking version of her sister's voice, "totes not funny."

"I'll—" Amber started talking but a sudden banging at the door interrupted her.

"Can't these...." Steve said and yanked back the curtain near the front door to see Billy Wilson beating on it, casting a fearful glance over his shoulder.

"Is he a friendly?" Amy piped up.

Steve slapped his side, almost in an unconscious manner to feel his concealed piece against his hip, before making a stand back motion and opening the door.

"Mr. Taylor, there's people...." Billy said panting.

"People? Who? Is somebody getting broke into?" Steve asked.

"No, they just walked in. There's fighting...." His words trailed off and looked over his shoulder again.

He could hear shouts, screams, but no gunfire.

"What do you want me to do?" Steve asked him coldly, closing the door enough to where only he could be seen in the cracked opening.

"You're in charge of the watch, they're beating up old people and are trying to take the food—"

"Steve," Angela said, putting her arm on his back, "don't let—"

"I'll be right there," Steve said and shut the door in Billy's face.

The ladies were silent as he stalked to his bedroom and opened his closet. Instead of keeping his gear locked up, he was now keeping it closer. Only his daughter's youth and quick thinking had saved him precious moments when they counted. Now, he kept it close by his side as much as possible. Steve strapped on his vest and reached in for the AR.

"You're going to be careful."

"Yes," Steve answered without turning.

"There's no gunfire so far," Amber said.

"I want all of you to be ready to head to the shelter or bug out to Dwight's."

"We know, Daddy," Amy piped up.

"I love you," Steve said turning to see the three ladies.

Amy rushed him and hugged him hard, then Amber who had a mischievous grin on her face. Last was Angela who walked up and kissed him hard on the mouth and then touched her own hip, to make sure her pistol was secure before breaking contact.

"Love you, too," they all chorused.

Steve walked out and grinned as he heard the deadbolts behind him being engaged. Billy was nowhere in sight, but he could follow the sounds of shouts and the smell of a cookfire. There wasn't any pork ready, but the smell of cooking food traveled far and the starchy smell of the pots full of supplies was heady. He thought of hurrying, but considering how heavy his vest was, he didn't want to rush to a threat to be too tired to be much help.

He didn't have the adrenaline to aid him as he had in the fight at Dwight's farm, but unlike that fight, he had twice the distance to travel in full gear. So instead, he settled on a fast walk that allowed him to let his eyes roam and wander, looking for threats. Almost everyone in the neighborhood seemed to be at the community center. That left a lot of open and empty houses behind him, though he knew that not every house was empty. Blinds rustled as he moved past as an odd person here and there looked out to see him walking down the middle of the street.

Steve could see the commotion long before he got close enough to make out individual sounds. He made sure his magazine was seated properly, a bullet in the chamber and the safety on before starting to walk up. From almost two hundred feet away he saw two figures dressed in all black, similar to the four men that had been killed, but with them were about a dozen figures wearing camouflage, though they were emaciated. Only the two men dressed in all black seemed to be carrying any visible firearms.

As Steve approached, he saw a couple of the volunteers of the neighborhood watch, Johnathon and his wife Justina give him a nod and stand up. He could see they had side arms on, though neither of them carried long guns like they were won't to do during the night shifts they took, so they could help Dwight out at first light.

"Steve," Justina said, "they just walked in from the street, we sent your neighbor's son to come let you know."

"He found me, thanks. Any word? Do we know what they want?" Steve asked.

"No," Johnathon said. "They are too far off, but it has something to do with the food. They want us to share it out or something."

"So they're not from around here," Steve asked.

"Never seen them before," Justina answered.

They kept walking and after a dozen steps, Steve muttered a curse. "Yeah, well I recognize those two in the black."

"From Dwight's?"

"Yeah," Steve hissed, tempted to bring his carbine up and take them out now, but he didn't know who the other figures were in camouflage. The ones who looked like extras on a zombie set, but put in clean clothing.

"That's far enough," one of them yelled, putting a hand up as Steve approached, his carbine low and ready.

Steve didn't answer, but brought his AR up and sighted in on the figures who were caught flat footed. Justina and Johnathon spread out and as he passed, somebody else sat up from the grass and dusted his pants off. Matthew. The big man was wearing his sidearm as well and pulled it. The two men in black pajamas stood there, their guns still slung, but their hands twitching as if they wanted to make a sudden move.

"Easy friend," one of them called, "we don't want to have any accidents here."

"I've been watching to see if they had anybody else sneaking in around us," Matthew hissed without moving his lips. "So far, nothing," he finished, nothing sounding like "muffing" as he tried to speak without appearing to.

"There's not going to be any accidents," Steve said, his voice almost a snarl. "I recognize you two. You're lucky I didn't have an angle on you at the farm."

One of them looked to the other man and whispered something. Steve had closed the gap to within fifty feet and saw that the group had stopped in front of the cookfire that Jeff and others had been getting the supplies ready and the water was starting to boil.

"You?" the man asked, looking Steve over.

"Me," Steve answered, and saw the volunteer watch were almost all accounted for and had fanned out into a semi-circle.

Community members were moving out of the watch's way and people started crowding the sidewalk leading up to the building, all bunched up. Steve wanted to tell them that they were making themselves easy targets if the shooting started, but he couldn't take his focus off the front sights and the nearly fourteen men and women that had walked in.

"The farmer shot at us first," one man offered, the one who had whispered before.

"Why didn't you leave when you set off the alarms then?" Steve asked, moving the safety off.

"We didn't know what—"

"They want us to share out what little food we have," Jeff yelled.

A dozen figures in camo turned to look at him and the large bags of rice and beans on one of the folding tables, ready to go into the water.

"What about you people?" Steve asked, walking closer towards that group, though his gun remained on the twitchy men dressed in all-too-familiar black ripstop BDUs.

"We're from another community. We came to ask for assistance. We're here to help carry anything, and those men were supposed to protect us from roaming gangs and raiders," a feminine voice said.

Steve couldn't tell if it was a feminine sounding young man, or a woman who was so thin she was all but indistinguishable by gender.

As Steve's gaze found theirs, several put their hands up showing they were unarmed.

"These two are responsible for shooting Dwight," Steve said, jerking his gun at the men dressed in black, "so you hanging out with them and asking for assistance kinda sounds fishy to me."

"If they just wanted a bowl to fill their stomachs, there wouldn't have been a disagreement," Jeff called to Dwight.

"You seem well supplied, we were hoping you could be encouraged to share," the man in black BDUs said, the one who'd first spoken to Steve.

"Encouraged? Forced? How many of your people have been kicking in doors around here lately?" Steve's voice thundered.

Several of the men and women in the camos looked at each other, one of the men in black looked down at his boots for a moment. It wasn't lost on Steve nor Matthew who yelled next.

"If you came here to encourage us to share, why come in with demands?"

"You folks have so much more than we do!" the same feminine voice in the camos screamed back, making one of the men in black look at her.

"This is it!" Jeff screamed at them from the side.

One of the men's self-control slipped and his hand reached for the stock of the carbine that was slung over one shoulder. Steve had the man's center mass already in his sights. He hesitated half a heartbeat and several people in front of him screamed and flattened. Steve fired and watched as the man's legs buckled and he fell backwards on his butt.

People screamed in response, but Steve started stalking forward when a movement behind the man in black who was still standing made him move his gun off him. He was half a breath away from pulling the trigger when Lucy ghosted behind the man and leveled her service pistol.

"Keep your hands where we can see them," Lucy said softly.

"You killed him—"

"No, I didn't," Steve said walking up and kicking the dropped rifle away from the still twitching and convulsing body.

The man cursed, his breathing wheezy and Matthew walked up, holstering his gun and pulled the man on his back. The shouting from the other man cut off as Lucy held him and the group in camo watched as Matthew slapped the man's hands away and undid the Velcro straps on one shoulder and the side and pulled the vest off. He stuck his finger in the hole made from Steve's round and then looked at the inside, showing everyone it hadn't penetrated.

"I hit him in the ceramic plate with a hollow point," Steve said loudly. "Even though you two opened fire on my people once, I'm not going to murder you in cold blood."

Johnathon let out a low whistle as Matthew picked up the downed man with one arm and ignoring the squeaks as he wrapped a big arm around his neck for a grip. Then he patted the man down as Lucy started doing the same with her captive, relieving them of a pistol apiece and both ARs.

"Damn, that hurts," the man gasped, rubbing his chest, tears running down his face.

Steve finally lowered his rifle and finished closing the distance.

"Johnathon, Justina, can you keep an eye on these green camo mall ninjas for us?"

"On it," Justina answered.

Steve saw she had her gun out and Johnathon was drawing his. They seemed to have everything under control.

"You two are in a world of shit," Lucy said. "You have the right to remain silent, anything you say or do will be used against—"

"Oh shit, she's a cop," the one she had disarmed cried.

"—in a court of law. You have the right to an attorney. If you cannot afford an attorney—"

"We're under martial law, there are no courts," he interrupted again as she roughly pulled his arm behind him as if to cuff him.

"Well then, I won't get in trouble for this, will I?"

"In trouble for—"

The man dropped when her boot connected with his lower extremities and he started gagging. Matthew hunkered down next to the man Steve shot and looked at him.

"Who sent you?" Matthew asked.

"Nobody sent us," the man gasped, rubbing his chest.

"You don't just show up out of the blue and start demanding food, no matter how nicely you were asking. Where are you from, and don't make me ask again."

"The subdivision," one of the people in camo yelled.

"And you two?" Steve asked, holding his AR at the low and ready.

"We're from around," the man holding his balls said.

"You got anything to add to that, or should I give you a kick to get your memory working?" Matthew asked the man Steve had shot.

He sat up and took several deep breaths, his hands rubbing his sternum.

"I swear, we're from around here. We sorta banded together. We've been helping others, you know, for the community."

"Not our community apparently," Steve said. "You've been leading raids on locals. It's more than the farm, isn't it?"

Both shut up, but in his mind, he already knew the answer.

"I don't know what you think you were going to do with that gun," Jeff said, "but I think Steve over there is right; you didn't have good intentions. My god man, you were going to shoot one of us. I don't know how Steve knew you'd live—"

"Because we killed four of his buddies when he tried to assassinate Dwight," Steve interrupted.

Several of their people blanched. It was one thing to hear about attempted crimes, but now they had seen what almost happened to them.

"What do you think we should do with them?" Lucy asked.

"Shoot these two," Steve said, pointing with his muzzle, "they were for sure at..." Steve's words trailed off as several people around them started shaking their head at Steve's words.

"We just wanted food, we're all hungry," one of the folks in camo begged.

"We can share out a little bit wider, but we cannot give up everything we have here," Jeff asserted.

Matthew roughly pulled the man who'd been shot to his feet. He still rubbed his chest, and when his gaze met Steve's, it was full of anger and pain. The other man was roughly pulled to his feet by judicial use of an arm behind his back and cursing by Lucy.

"These two," Lucy said. "You sure?"

"You were there Lucy," Steve told her. "Recognize these two as the ones shooting from by the truck?"

She nodded. "We can't just kill them," she said softly. "That's not right. I might not be wearing my badge right now, but I can't condone just gunning them down."

"Yeah, you should listen to the lady, man. I have rights." The man she'd forced up started sputtering when Steve took a few steps forward and butt stroked him.

He slumped to the ground, and Lucy cursed.

"I don't care what you do with this trash," Steve said, anger in his voice, "just remember, I was at home when somebody came and got me. Last time these assholes opened the dance, I was the first one to respond and held back to let you two come along—"

"I'm on your side," Lucy interrupted. "I just can't. There's still a constitution to uphold and these two deserve to be judged by a jury of their peers. I took an oath."

Steve swore again softly. "Then you figure it out," he whispered back to her hoarsely and started walking.

⁘

"You know she's right," Dwight said to Steve who was still fuming.

"Things have changed. I mean, these were two guys who shot at you, probably one of them was the guy who winged you."

242

"I know, but it's one thing to shoot a guy when you're in the heat of battle. To execute somebody when you're not...it isn't that easy."

"What do you know about it?" Steve asked, trying to keep the anger out of his voice.

"Two tours."

"Oh, sorry. I didn't—"

"Don't be sorry, I'm just saying. To those who took an oath, it isn't that simple. Why didn't you splatter that guy's head when you knew he was wearing a vest and you weren't gonna kill him with a shot to the plate in his vest?"

"I..." Steve's words trailed off as he thought about that. Why had he not followed up with it? He could have easily kept firing and then gone on to the next target.

"See, it isn't that easy, even when your blood is running hot."

"Well, shit," he muttered.

"Daddy," Amy complained.

They had set up in Steve's back yard. Dwight had brought over some cured ham, enough slices to make a single serving for each of them, and Steve had done what he could with some of his own pantry items to make it a full meal. Potato pearls into mashed potatoes, rice, green beans, and a glass of warm lemonade. The power had stayed out for a long time now, and everybody was worried that it was finally out for good.

"Sorry, baby."

"Don't get worked up," Angela said. "You told Lucy they could figure it out. Let them."

"Well, they certainly don't need my permission. The only thing I was good for was startling them when it looked like they had the drop on most of the community."

"Lucy would have probably had them," Amber said. "She's a badass."

"Amber!" Steve and Angela chorused, while Amy and Dwight started laughing.

"As far as role models go, she isn't a bad one," Dwight said around his laughs.

"Neither is your mother," Steve said, shooting him a look, but Dwight ignored it and playfully swiped at Steve.

"So what else is needed around the farm?" Steve asked him.

"Nothing really. I wouldn't mind knowing where those guys came from though," Dwight said, "The only other community in the area, concentration wise, is the subdivision half a mile north of us, on the other side of the golf course."

"You think they came from there?" Steve asked.

"Who knows. I'm surprised things have held together for so long now, to be honest."

"What do you mean?" Angela asked him, swatting lazily at a fly that was trying to land on her shoulder.

"We live outside of a big city. You'd think they'd either have things together already, or the golden horde heading for the countryside, looking for more food."

"Well, maybe they have? I mean, we're still in the Macon limits, but we're in the outskirts."

"Yeah, this isn't really right in the middle, is it? You know what scares me though? What happens if, say, a hundred people show up at the farm all at once, wanting food? Who stays? Who goes? That might wipe me out completely, but I can't defend against that. Not with you and the handful of others who help keep an eye and ear to help me."

"Yeah, I hope you never have to make that kind of decision. To be honest, I'm surprised that there haven't been more people trying... stuff." Steve said his gaze briefly resting on his daughters before turning back to Dwight.

"It's always hard to tell, especially when civilized society isn't quite so civil," Dwight said and finished off the last of his food.

Steve chewed on that for a few moments. "Who's watching the farm?"

"Matt Junior is out there with some of the volunteers. I've been paying them in grain and cured pork."

"Any chance you can teach me how to cure it?" Steve asked.

"Well sure," Dwight said. "Just come over on a butchering day, and I'll get you started on the whole process. Why? What are you thinking?"

"All the local game seems to be hunted out now. We've got the winter migration of ducks and geese, but that isn't for a while and—"

"You can't salt cure everything safely," Dwight said. "Some of it, you have to smoke it also."

"Yeah, I thought so," Steve said with a grin, "but we're not really doing any trapping around here. I thought the area was lousy with feral hogs too?"

"It is sometimes, but I have a feeling that we're not the only ones that have been hunting. I'm sure everyone with a gun has been hunting to put food on the table."

"Think we've missed the boat on some things?" Steve asked him.

"Why would we?" Angela asked her husband. "We've been ready for these kinds of things. I might have argued with you about this at first, but I feel like we're in far better shape than most. It's not our fault that we've survived in better shape than some."

"Yeah Mom, but shouldn't we be helping people more?" Amy asked.

Everyone went silent and chewed on that. A shout from somewhere went up, but it was so far off, the words were lost. Everyone waited to see if a whistle blew, a signal for help from one of the volunteer neighborhood watch, but none went up. Another shout, this one closer, asking if somebody had seen somebody else, the names lost to the light breeze and the coming twilight.

"We can help more," Amber answered for her mom, "but then we won't have as much. If we gave the community center all of our food," she was whispering now, "it would only last them a week or two, then we'd be starving too."

"There's just too many people to feed?" Amy asked.

"Yes," Angela said. "We can't help everyone. We just don't have enough."

"This sucks," Amy said. "It seems like they should have been ready, like Daddy and Uncle Dewey were, for this kind of stuff."

"Not everybody believed that hard times were coming," Steve told her softly.

"But they always do," Dwight told her. "History always repeats itself one way or another, little one."

Amy let out a sigh and wiped at her eyes. She was the sensitive one in the bunch, but she was also the most accepting, especially when Steve was prepping for an unknown disaster.

"With that, I'm going to get started on the dishes," Angela said.

"I'll help," Steve told her rising.

"No, you and Dwight take a seat. I've got two helpers if I need them," she said, looking at the girls.

They piled plates and the three ladies headed into the kitchen. Amber came back out a moment later with a holstered pistol on her jean shorts.

"Expecting trouble?" Dwight asked her.

"No, sir," Amber said truthfully, "but it's like you said, 'hard times are coming and history repeats itself.'"

Steve looked at his daughter and realized how much she had grown and matured in the last year.

"I hope I'm wrong about that," Dwight told her, "but it doesn't hurt to be ready, for anything."

CHAPTER 26

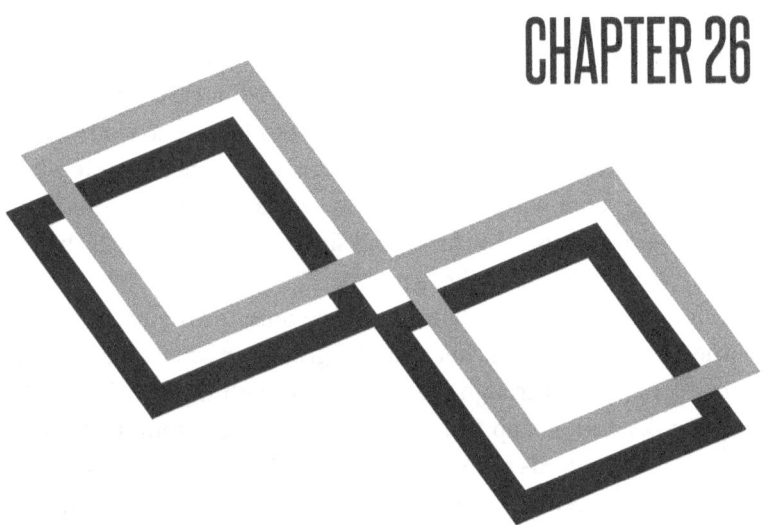

A thumping noise awoke Steve. He lay in the dark, trying to figure out what it was that had startled him awake. It hadn't been the first time that a night noise, or an animal had scared the crap out of him. Angela rolled over, still breathing slowly and wrapped an arm around his chest. Had he heard her roll over, letting her arm thump against the—

Above him he heard a startled exclamation and a shout by Amy.

"Wha..." Angela slurred as he pushed his wife's hand off him and reached for his holster on the bedside table.

Something had awakened Amy. It wasn't her sister's snoring, Amber always snored, and murmured in her sleep. Usually about Matt and lots of lovey-dovey stuff. If Matt knew the kinds of things that flew out of her sister's mouth in her sleep, she'd be so embarrassed that she'd... there was the sound again. They kept the windows upstairs open and the rest of the house locked while they slept. Her dad had explained that heat rose, so the room she shared with her sister was always warmer than the rest of the house.

That's why they kept the screen in place but left the two big windows open. They were large tall windows that cranked out to the side, and if Amy angled them just right, they helped scoop fresh air into the hot room. When it was too hot, they took their blankets into the laundry room where it was always darker and cooler, but her parents were always being gross and she didn't want to hear that, so they suffered the heat on those nights.

She sat up slowly, her hand reaching onto the nightstand to try to find the LED flashlight her dad had given her when a dark shape seemingly stepped through the window. Something crunched as the figure took another step and Amy made a choking sound. The dark figure moved towards her just as she flicked the flashlight on, and a large hand covered her mouth and face. A hoarse voice whispered for her to be quiet.

Steve was creeping up the stairs, but when he heard Amber scream, he ran. He'd been trying to be quiet in case it was another false alarm or a nightmare that had startled one of the girls awake... and he didn't want to scare his girls. But hearing Amber let out a surprised or pained scream gave him a full adrenaline dump. The door to their room was cracked open, and a harsh white light seeped out from the edges.

He hit the door with his hip, his finger already finding the safety and flicking it off. A dark figure was wrestling with a wild Amy. Despite screaming, Amber was already reaching into her bedside stand where she kept her own concealed piece when Steve saw a second figure in the leftover glow of what looked like Amy's flashlight. It had been coming in the window when he'd hit the lights.

Both wore black hoodies, and both had what looked like dark scarves or masks over most of the face. Steve didn't hesitate and put a round center mass into the figure coming inside. It looked like an old cowboy movie where the bad guy got shot and the figure's arms

248

pinwheeled backwards and fell out of sight. He barely heard the thump over the ringing in his ears from the .45's discharge.

The shot had given Amy a moment when the figure that was trying to silence her had looked up sharply when Steve rushed in and fired off his round. She was already rolling off her bed sideways when the grip that was holding her went slack. Amber jumped at the figure from her own bed, abandoning the urge to get the gun apparently. For a moment, Steve had a clear sight but hesitated, and then both daughter and the figure were wrestling.

He didn't realize who was yelling at first, but he knew it was him when he grabbed the figure in the black hoody by the back of the neck and yanked. He was almost in a rage, and when Amber saw her dad yanking, she let go. The figure screamed in pain as Steve used every ounce of strength to pull them away and then with what looked like one hand, shoved the figure towards the window.

They stumbled and for a second he had a chance to try to look. A wisp of blond hair trailed out from the bottom of the hood, the shape was familiar, slender...then the hand went to the waistband in a fast movement and Steve started pulling the trigger. After five shots, he realized that Angela and the girls were screaming too as that figure slumped backwards, their legs barely hitting the wall as they tumbled out the window.

"Get them to the shelter," Steve snarled.

"No, Daddy. Reload," Amber said, wiping her eyes.

"Are you ok?" Angela said at the same time.

"The bad man, I heard something bump, but I thought it was a nightmare," Amy said. "Then I saw it move. He must have been pulling the screen out."

"I'm ok," Amber said. "Bitch got me with her nails though," she hissed, showing furrows on her arm from where she had been wrestling with the figure.

"Bitch?" Steve said, his mind working faster than his body.

Steve stared at her for a minute and then looked down at his boxer briefs, all he had been sleeping in and walked over to her nightstand. He pulled out her pistol, ejected the magazine and took her spare. In the heat of the moment, he had just taken his gun. He changed his partial out for a full magazine.

"Go to the shelter, now. I'll throw on some pants and see what's going on outside. If everything is all clear, I'll come get you right away."

"Let me come with you," Amber said right away.

"No, you need to look out for your sister. I'm going with him," Angela told her.

"None of you—"

"We're a team," Angela said, cutting off all further conversation.

The gunshots and then Steve blowing the whistle had people running. Angela had ensured that the girls were safe and that Amber was rearmed while Steve pulled on some basketball shorts and got his Maglite. He made it around to the side of the house even as two figures carrying flashlights came running his way. For a moment, he saw the ladder pushed onto the side of his house, one of the screens carefully placed on the ground, leaned against the house, and two figures on the ground.

One had a huge pool of red underneath them, almost looking black in the harsh light of the flashlight and the other with a smaller pool, their legs kicking carefully.

"Steve, that you?" Lucy's voice yelled, just as the flashlight hit him in the face.

"Yeah, and Angela," his wife said, shining her own flashlight at the running figures.

It was Matthew and Lucy. Her flashlight moved and lit up the figures Steve had been looking at. All held their guns at the low and ready, seeing a handgun a few feet from the figure under the largest pool of blood.

"Help...." the figure writhing on the ground said.

Steve handed his flashlight to Angela and walked over, his gun trained. He knelt down and pushed the mask up. Billy Wilson laid there, blood coming from his mouth, his skin already pale and getting paler. He looked and saw his round had hit the neighbor in the chest, just off center.

"What were you doing?" Steve asked.

"What the fuck is going on?" Clark Wilson's voice came out of the dark. The flashlight Lucy held swiveled to light him up.

"Oh man, get him out of here," Steve said.

"Da..." Billy's eyes closed, and he let out a rattling breath, a large bubble of blood breaking on his lips.

"Who are you shooting...." Clark was in his boxers and saw the face lit up from one of the flashlights.

"No...." he screamed and went running towards his son.

Steve moved to the side and walked over. The next figure had several holes in the same center mass area but he got a better look. The fall onto the concrete had done as much damage as the bullets, but he could still see the slender figure beneath the black, and the slight feminine curves. With a shaking hand, he pushed the mask up. A girl, no more than twenty-two or twenty-three looked up at him sightlessly. She'd probably been dead as soon as she'd hit the ground. Her teeth were partially rotted out, but she didn't look emaciated like so many others he'd seen lately. A chemical smell came off her clothing and a small taser was in her left hand.

Voices behind him, Steve turned to see Matthew holding back Clark and Lucy talking to Sarah Wilson. There were more screams, wails, and more people shouting. More lights coming their way.

"She was just a kid," Steve told her.

"Smell that?" Angela asked softly.

"The chemical smell?" Steve asked.

"Crack or meth. I can't tell. It's been forever since I volunteered at the County—"

"Steve!" Matthew shouted and then he was tackled.

251

He was hit while he knelt, and it bowled him over sideways. He tried to get an arm up, but fists pummeled him and a cursing, spitting, and biting Clark Wilson did everything in his power to kill Steve. Angela screamed and beat at him with the butt of her pistol before holstering it and swinging with Steve's Maglite.

Matthew was half a heartbeat behind that and pulled at the neighbor. His arms were locked on Steve and he bent his head in as if to kiss him and Steve screamed in agony. Matthew grabbed Clark by the hair and tried pulling him off before losing his grip. A single gunshot went off and Clark stiffened, Matthew grabbed him by the hair again and yanked. Clark flipped over on his back, a blackened hole, now gushing, was in his sternum. Sarah started screaming harder, but she had her arms wrapped around Lucy, who was holding her up more than holding her back.

Steve sat up, holding his throat. It was inflamed, red. There were scratch marks and the bottom of his jaw was bleeding from a crescent-shaped bite. His hands shook as he put the Colt on safe, rolled over, and started vomiting.

The community meeting was a circus. Word had gotten around to those who hadn't shown up in the middle of the night. In one fell swoop, they had learned that the Taylors had wiped out two-thirds of the Wilson family and killed the Wilson boy's on-again, off-again girlfriend. That much they could get out of Sarah who kept crying and picking at her hand. At some point, one of the Wilsons had removed the stitches, but she worried the scar there till it was angry and red.

"I'd like to ask the volunteer neighborhood watch to disband," Doug Morris shouted over the din of shouting.

People turned to look at him and he stood up. "Not only should they disband, but we need to elect our own arm of law enforcement. Not anybody who wants to help and has a gun. You see what happened here last night? You saw what happened two weeks ago? Death. People have suddenly gone gun crazy, and human beings are dying!"

Somebody else shouted, "I was one of the first ones there after Deputy Lucy, those two that were killed were breaking into the Taylors house, and he caught one of them messing with his younger daughter! The dad went insane and tried to rip out Steve's throat!"

"That doesn't give him the right to remove their rights to a fair trial. By blowing them away...." a woman's loud cries shattered the otherwise silent crowd who was watching intently. Somebody put their arm around Mrs. Wilson, and she buried her head on the woman's shoulder, "By taking matters into his own hands, he denied those young adults of their constitutional rights to a fair trial. Since when does breaking and entering get a death penalty? I would like..."

Linda Morris stood up angrily and started walking away. Doug grabbed her wrist when she was almost out of his reach. He pulled her back to him and for a brief moment it looked like she was going to be manhandled in front of everyone, but she instead stepped in close to him. He dropped her wrist, and they spoke angrily. The words lost, but the tone wasn't. Quick as a lightning strike, her hand shot out, slapping the taste out of his mouth. A shocked sound came out of Doug's mouth, as her knee came up and caught him in a delicate place.

Doug dropped to the ground, both hands holding onto his family jewels as she stomped away, in the direction of their house.

"That was kinda funny," Amy whispered.

"Yeah, I'm trying not to laugh," Steve croaked, his bruised throat sore.

"Don't talk," Angela whispered. "You'll hurt yourself."

"Dad's a badass, he can handle some bruising," Amber said.

"Hey!" Steve said, his voice sounding like Kermit. "Don't—"

"Your dad is kinda badass. Doesn't give you permission to say it out loud. You two girls held your own by the way. I'm proud of all of you."

"You had our backs," Amy said, smiling at her mother's words.

Angela smiled back, her daughter's words making her seem far older than she was. She was ready and she had been ready to back whatever play her husband did. She'd been as shocked as anybody to discover the figure who'd been trying to keep Amy quiet was a woman, though she'd never seen her husband bodily throw somebody across a room before.

Both parents had worried about Amy and how she was going to react to it. She slept between her parents to finish the night off, but she didn't seem any worse for wear. Both girls had slept in the tornado shelter a bit, while the worst of the cleanup happened and were spared knowing everything that had happened. Now, Morris's words were sinking in a little bit, but they didn't seem to be hurting the kids, only confirming their convictions in the family.

"I'd like to propose that we do the opposite of what Doug said," Matthew said, his voice thundering. "I'd like to expand the neighborhood watch. I'd like to have a group head north and see if that's where those dozen folks came from, and I'd like to have more eyeballs at night. Especially when we have neighbor on neighbor issues."

People murmured, and Jeff stood up next to Matthew. "There's something else we need to discuss. Food is almost out again. Hunting has not been going well. There's also the matter of our gardens and watering them and a hundred other things."

"Why don't you ask Steve Taylor about food?" Sarah Wilson screamed, her voice cracking at the end. "That's what my family died trying to get!"

"What are you talking about?" Jeff asked her. "He brought some bulk from his church for us—"

"He has a storm shelter full of food! Look at him, look at his whole family! Yes, he's been nice and kind, and he's slowly letting all of us starve to death while he's killed anybody who has gone after his food or his friends."

Her words were half true, but nobody knew why her son and his girlfriend were breaking into the house next door. The crowd murmured at that, realizing the truth in some of that. Many looked at the Taylor family. Like the pastor, they had lost weight, but they weren't unhealthy. In fact, of everyone there, they seemed to glow with health, and they were better groomed, cleaner and all around in better shape.

Steve and Angela must have realized the same thing at once, because their eyes locked.

"A shelter full of food?" Jeff asked her.

"My son saw it when the farmer was attacked. He ran over to help. If he had shared his food out, my husband and my son might still be—"

"What kind of shelter?" somebody else screamed.

Doug Morris stood up, his face red. "He's got a tornado shelter, same as a few of the other houses in this subdivision. We all had the option to get one when our houses were built. We all didn't have the option to fill it full of food though....How about it, Steve?"

Steve stood up, but Angela reached and took his hand and pulled herself up as well. She shushed her husband, gave his hand a tight squeeze and turned to Doug and the rest of the crowd who stared at them with hate-filled eyes.

"I'm speaking for my husband and my family. Last night our house was attacked by two people who put up a ladder, removed the screen from my daughters' room and then tried to silence her when she woke up. In the fight, both my husband and my oldest daughter were injured, not badly, but this wasn't flat out murder like some of these ass munchers are saying!" Her words were biting, and Amber stifled a giggle hearing her mom use "ass muncher" in a sentence. "As far as what they were getting into the house for...who knows? The girlfriend was a known drug user.

"Sarah Wilson—I am sorry for your loss, I really am. I was there when your son and husband were shot. There was literally nothing else that could have been done. Your husband was choking out my husband and bit him in the face. Only then did my husband defend himself. Now I don't know what you think we have food wise, but any of you ever been through a harsh winter? One where there were feet of snow and ice?"

The crowd looked at her, but nobody spoke.

"We come from Ohio. In Ohio, we did have snow and ice storms that would shut down cities for days or even weeks depending on how bad it got. When we bought our house, we found out it had a tornado shelter. Just like you, Doug Morris," she said pointing at him, "and like we would do in Michigan, we put in some food and water in case we got stuck down there. Say a tornado came through and knocked the house down, and we were buried underneath there.

"Now I don't know what you think we have, but you all aren't entitled to anything of ours. Not our food, our privacy within our own home, not our possessions, not our kid's feelings of safety and security, and not our lives. None of you deserve any of that. We've already helped this community out, and we always planned on doing it as much as we can. What you all need to do is put this incident to rest—"

"How about we go over and take inventory for ourselves?" Doug Morris asked.

Steve pulled his .45, his hands almost a blur. Not everybody in the crowd heard the hammer click back as he cocked it, but later on, many would claim to. Nobody spoke, except the man with the bruised throat.

"Socialism only works until you run out of other people's stuff. Unless you want a terminal case of lead poisoning, Doug, I wouldn't encourage you to try it," Steve said and then coughed and spit.

There was a splatter of red in the grass, and Angela turned and whispered to her husband. "Don't, he isn't worth it."

Steve held the pistol at arm's length, the barrel unwavering as he aimed it at center mass at the man who'd made his life hell since moving to Georgia. He ignored the shouts of alarm, the whispers, and the people moving out of the line of fire. More than anything else, he wanted to pull the trigger. He could have dismissed Sarah's words because she had lost everything, but Doug rabble rousing to have people come and by force... inventory his family's food? He would die stopping them if that was what was needed. Dwight would take care of his family. Slowly, his finger started squeezing—

"Daddy, let's go home," Amy said, breaking Steve's concentration as she took his free hand, having gotten up while he was lost in his own thoughts.

He let out a startled breath and lowered the hammer, before holstering the pistol. He held out his free hand to Amber who took it and pulled herself to her feet.

"We're going to do what we can to help," Angela said. "We had planned on going to the church to see if there was anything else we could do. As you just saw, trying to come after us or forcing us... it won't end well for you."

"I wouldn't suggest folk to try to turn into Venezuela or North Korea, we see how well that ended up for their people," Matthew shouted.

"As somebody who spent a lifetime in 'Law Enforcement,'" Lucy yelled. "I wouldn't suggest you try that either. You all saw what happened to the neighbor who tried to break in. No, they didn't get a trial, but as soon as they went into the house and tried to silence little Amy, the homeowner, Mr. Taylor had every right to defend his family against any and all threats."

"You're just saying that because y'all are friends. Hell, he's probably feeding you too!" a man shouted angrily, standing up.

The situation was getting more than a little tense, and Steve gave everyone a look and jerked his head behind him as if to say "let's go." Angela nodded, and they all started moving as one.

"I don't think so," Doug Morris screamed and started stalking towards them in a lurching gait, "you're holding back on everyone here. I knew you were up to something, I just didn't know—"

He hadn't been all that far, but Steve was out of patience. When people had moved out of his way when he'd pulled his pistol on

Doug, they hadn't filled the gaps back in yet. It was through these where Steve strode forward. Somehow, Doug's face impacted with the outstretched fist from Steve's hands. The results were not to be unexpected. Doug Morris flew off his feet, a spray of blood as his nose bore the brunt of the impact.

"Damn, that felt good," Steve said shaking his hand and turned to walk back to his family.

"Feel better, Daddy?" Amy asked.

"Actually—"

"Steve!" Angela admonished.

"Dad!" Amber said. "How did that...I mean, I've never seen you... only the...."

"He had it coming," Steve told them and turned to look behind him.

Doug was working his way to his feet, the lower half of his face a mask of blood. Nobody had moved to help him and equal parts of the crowd were looking at Doug and the departing Taylors in horror. Steve resisted the urge to wave to them, but instead put one arm around Angela and his right arm around Amber.

"Next time," Angela said to him softly, "don't hit anybody in the face. You can break your own bones, and it's too tough of a target. Get them in the gut, the solar plexus or kidney next time."

"Mom's a badass, too," Amy whispered to Amber, who promptly snickered.

"I heard that," both parents chorused.

CHAPTER 27

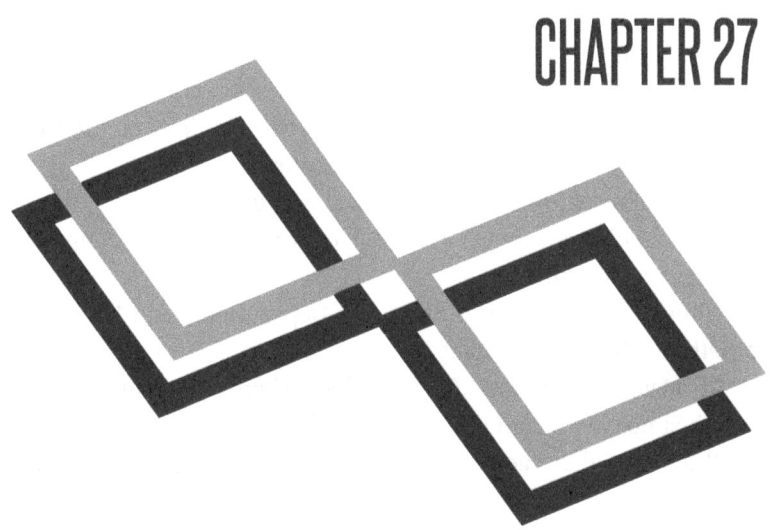

Angela was taking her turn at the neighborhood watch. She'd paired up with Lucy, despite Matthew and Steve's objections that the ladies participate in the watch. They told them how sexist that was, which shut them both up. They'd left their men at home and both were walking together through the community. Lucy had her service pistol with a borrowed AR and Angela carried her own AR and .45 1911 on her hip.

"I had to get out of the house," Lucy told her.

"You and me both. Thanks for having my back," Angela told her.

Lucy made a fist, and they bumped knuckles before laughing. They were two extras tonight, with two other volunteers that had been working into the rotation. They were new, but had been more than willing to help. As much animosity as Doug and others had caused after the death of the Wilsons, people didn't turn down the Taylor family's offer to help. To keep things on the up and up, at least for appearance's sake, men were paired with men, women were paired with women.

"Anytime. I was going stir crazy. Junior and his dad are so full of testosterone sometimes that I think I get stuck on the hormone roller coaster with them."

"God, Steve gets like that too. He gets so overprotective sometimes, but I love him to pieces."

"What do you think of the guy's idea to travel beyond the sub a bit? Those guys we turned loose headed north."

"You followed them?" Angela asked, a laugh escaping.

"I could kick Matthew's ass, I just let him think he's a tough guy," Lucy said with a smirk.

"Plus, you were in the Sherriff's Department, and Steve said something about the military too."

"That was forever ago," Lucy told her. "There was plenty of beach sand, just no water...and it was hot as hell."

"I thought about getting into the military, but I got married and had kids right away."

"You? What did you want to do?" Lucy asked.

"Something in medical, like what I was doing. I wanted to help people, to make a difference. Don't get me wrong, I have no regrets about my life, but I always wonder. You ever think about the 'what-ifs?'"

"I always wonder what if I met Matthew before I joined the service. Would we already be married with a ton of kids of our own?"

"Yeah. Kind of like I'm wondering...what if we headed north up the road and tried to get a look at the subdivision north of us."

"It would piss off our men," Lucy said, a smirk implied by her tone.

"It's dark. Just a walk along the roadside."

"Just a walk in the dark. Let's go," Lucy said with a grin.

⚡

"Dad, I wish you would chill out," Amber said.

"I will. It's your mom's first time patrolling," Steve told her in the candle light.

"Even Amy didn't last this late," Amber said nodding to the softly snoring Amy who went face down during a long Monopoly game.

"I know, I know. I'm usually in bed by now. You don't have to stay up with me."

"It's cool, Dad. Even though Mom will be pissed that you didn't trust her enough to do this on her own, it's cool you worry."

"Dammit, it's not that," Steve said softly.

"No?"

"I'm... I haven't slept alone at night since we've been married," he admitted. "I tried."

"Would you feel better if you went out there and helped her? I can stay here and guard the house. Uncle Dewey says I'm a better shot than you are, anyways."

Steve grinned at that and chucked his thumb at the tip of her nose. She took the mild abuse and stuck her tongue out at her dad.

"No, I'm not that worried. I just don't feel... I dunno."

"Want me to carry the sprout upstairs, so you can hang out on the front porch and watch?"

"Naw, she's fine on my floor," Steve told her.

They had camped out in the space between the bedroom door and the hallway where most of the moonlight was filtering in.

"Ok. I'll probably camp out here too, then," she said simply.

Steve stood, leaving the game the way it had been and checked his side. It was a habit now. He made sure his holster was secure, then he patted his left pants pocket and felt the heavy magazines he kept there. Lastly, he felt in his back pocket for his wallet, though that truly was an old habit. No ID required, no debit or credit cards needed. The little cash he had left was worthless. It would take a mountain of hundred-dollar bills to buy anything, if the rumors were accurate.

Instead, he took one of his kitchen stools and headed out to his front door and went out, leaving the steel door open so he could listen if Amber or Amy shouted out. As much as they went through and as scared as Amy was the night of the shooting, it was Steve who had the nightmares. There was no doubt about who got who, and he was so close to Clark Wilson when he shot him he saw the lights go out of his eyes. Nobody attempted CPR on any of them. For some reason, that bugged him. Not that he was upset about them dying, but had their humanity been so stripped away that—

Two gunshots in the distance made him jerk upright, as he was sitting down. He waited, holding his breath. Nothing was repeated. No whistles were blown. Somebody jack lighting deer? The sound was the wrong direction to be coming from Dwight's. When nothing was repeated, he got comfortable on the stool again and leaned against the brickwork in the alcove of his front door. The roof came out over this spot, so even in the great off chance that it rained, he'd be mostly dry unless the wind picked up.

He heard a new set of snoring start up and realized it was Amber who must have fallen asleep. It was soothing, it was—

⚙

Angela's heart was racing as she ran along the roadside, her sneakers barely making a sound on the pavement. She was keeping up with Lucy easily, having longer legs. They had crept out of the area as quietly as they could, but somebody in Black BDUs had popped up. Lucy threw a rock far over his shoulder and when it hit in the dirt, the man had spun and fired two shots. They slipped out into the darkness, thanking heaven that even though he'd been wearing all black, he silhouetted himself in the moonlight.

They were both breathing hard and starting to sweat as they got into the subdivision, finally stopping at the community center. They flopped on the dead grass and laid on their backs. Lucy started snickering, and soon, both women were laughing.

"The look on his face...." Lucy started.

"I smelled him, as soon as he shot."

"I heard it, he crapped himself—"

"He smelled like...." Lucy paused and laughed deeply.

A flashlight blinked on and both ladies put a hand up over their eyes while they giggled. Both went for their pistols but stopped.

"You two cackling hens all done for the night? I was getting worried," Matthew said stepping out of the darkness.

"Yeah, why were you worried?" Lucy asked, sobering immediately.

"It's almost sunrise. I thought you were staying out until 4:00 a.m.?"

Lucy held up her wrist and looked. "Oops."

"Sorry," Angela said, "I wasn't paying attention either."

"So what was so funny?"

"How about you go get Matt and meet us girls over at my house," Angela said. "I'll cook up some eggs."

"You've got eggs?" both of them chorused.

"Shhhhh, yeah. We still have our hens."

"You know, I forgot about that," Lucy whispered.

"Meet us there, we have a lot to talk about," Angela told him.

"Looks like he was doing his own watch," Lucy whispered, poking Angela in the ribs.

"At least mine didn't come looking for me," she snarked.

"Yours fell asleep on guard duty," Lucy snarked back.

Steve was leaned in the corner between the door and the brick wall in the enclosed portion the front door was in. The brick would have still held some of the previous day's warmth. It wasn't hot, but it had cooled in the night. With his arms folded, Steve snored softly sitting up.

"Hey, slugger," Angela whispered, running her hand along her husband's shoulder.

"Slugger," Lucy snickered.

Steve startled awake all at once. He blinked his eyes widely twice and looked at the ladies. Then he wiped his eyes with his hand and opened them again, seeing they were still there.

"Hey you," Steve said.

"Hey, playing doorman?" she asked.

"Doorman...oh, yeah," he said, sliding off the stool, picking it up, and opening the front door.

In the distance behind them the sun had started coming up across the horizon. It was still dark, but not black, out. The ladies followed Steve in who returned the stool to the kitchen bar where he grabbed a pitcher of water and poured it into the percolator. Then he played with the camp stove and got it lit, putting the pot on to start the process of it warming while he dug for everything else.

"Where's the coffee?" Steve mumbled.

"Top shelf on the right, how about you sit on the stool and let me take over."

Steve mumbled something and went on the other side of the bar and slouched down. Both ladies leaned their long guns against the wall, and Angela went to work. Steve came awake, watching Angela working her magic on the two-burner stove. Just as the coffee smell was starting to drive Steve insane with cravings, there was a quiet knock.

He got up and answered it. A sleepy Matt was standing there and a larger figure loomed behind him. Steve grunted and waved both of the Fitzpatrick men inside. They followed him in soundlessly. Matt slowed as he saw two sleeping forms in the bedroom doorway, but kept walking. Both fathers watching to see the boy's reaction.

"So why don't you have to put those in the fridge?" Lucy was asking as the three guys walked into the kitchen.

The smell of eggs and corned beef hash permeated the kitchen, but it took second place to the five steaming mugs of coffee that awaited them.

"Coffee and eggs?" Matthew said. "If you weren't already married—"

"Sorry bub, I got you beat by almost twenty years," Steve said, wrapping his hands around a mug and sat down at the bar.

"This smells really good, Mrs. Taylor," little Matt said.

"Dig in," Lucy told them. "While Angela and I fill you in on what happened."

"What happened?" Steve asked, dumbfounded.

"Drink up, big guy, you're going to want to be awake for this," Lucy told him and dropped Matthew a wink.

"Is this some sort of psychosexual, malarkey, shenanigans thing that I'm not supposed to get?" Matt Junior asked.

He turned red in the face when everyone busted up laughing softly, so not to wake up the girls.

✠

The community to the north of them had turned into an armed camp. All access points from the lake to the south, the golf course in the middle, the western wall surrounding the subdivision, to the hastily erected guard shack were all new. There was a surprising amount of people walking around armed, and many of them were dressed in the camo looking clothing the twelve men and women who came to ask for food with the black shirts wore. It was the men in the black ripstop BDUs who seemed to be armed without fail, but there were those in the dark camos who were as well.

The moonlit night had helped some, but a generator had been running near the front where a barricade had been erected. Smoke rose from what smelled like a large cookfire. Some sort of meat must have been cooking, and the ladies had both wondered what they could be cooking or smoking in the middle of the night. There was a lot of people there and awake. Until the nervous guard had popped up, they had been able to travel three-quarters of the way around it to take note.

Steve and Matthew didn't seem happy about it, and Lucy wasn't wild about it, but they all had to admire the security measures and had immediately talked about what they could do too.

"So you think that's where the raiders came from?" Steve asked Lucy.

"The ones at the farm? Yeah. Yeah, I do. What I don't know is if they were acting under orders. Same way I don't know about the ones we turned loose, and I followed back to that direction."

"You what?" Matthew asked loudly.

Behind them, there was a stirring and a loud yawn.

"Oh my god!" Amber shrieked and yanked her sister into her parents' bedroom and slammed the door.

"If you make one crack about bedhead, she might shoot you," Steve told Matt Junior mildly.

"I wasn't—I mean..."

They laughed again, and watched as he turned red in the face.

"So we have an armed group that is nervous and patrolling the area. We think, or at least suspect, that they are the ones who've raided or tried to raid people in the area. The only proof we have is the damned weird way they are all dressed," Angela said.

"Like somebody there had a stockpile of stuff or it was an element of the state or federal government?" Lucy asked.

"Or something," Steve finished and took a long drink of coffee.

"You guys better not have drunk all the coffee," Amber yelled from behind the closed door.

Steve and Angela looked at each other and busted up laughing again.

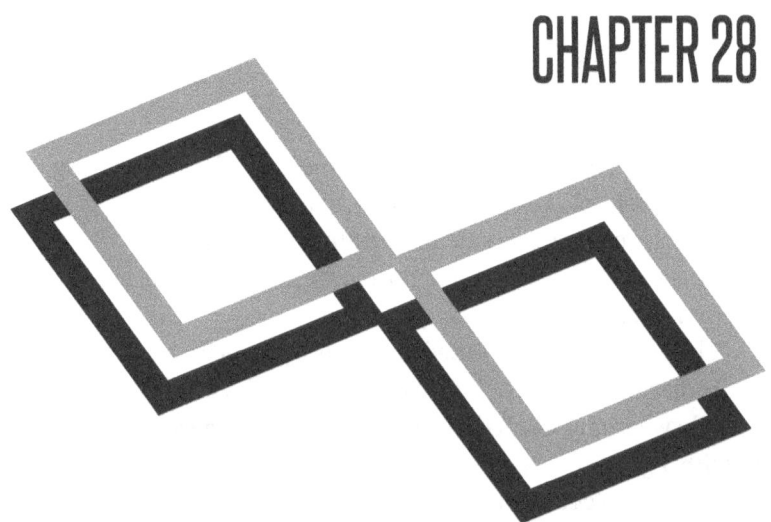

CHAPTER 28

On Sunday, they all went to church. The congregation was smaller than at any time Steve had seen it. The brief ice storm last year had halted a lot of people from coming, but this was worse than even that. Joseph had sat in the back row, and nobody said anything when Amy, who had been sitting at the end of the row by her mom, slipped out of the pew and headed back to sit by him.

"To be young and in love...." Angela whispered to Steve.

"She's too young," Steve growled in a voice that was all but a whisper.

"Right now, it's harmless. Joseph is a good kid; besides, he's still pining for Amber," she whispered in his ear as the pastor finished.

He just let out a warning grumble and Angela smiled, patting her husband's leg. Her own father had been much like that and had more than once threatened to run Steve off with a shotgun when they had first started dating, though she was much, much older than Amy. It was a guy thing, one she knew they were biologically incapable of helping. It was annoying when it was her father, but it was endearing when it was her husband being protective of her daughters. She found the irony especially delightful.

"I'm heading out with Amy," Amber said, scooting past her parents.

"She's already—"

"Yeah, I'll keep an eye on her. Don't worry," she said patting the side of her belt in a gesture Steve was all too familiar with.

"Thank you," Angela said before Steve could protest.

Steve stood up as the rest of the congregation did and made their way to the center aisle.

"They grow up too damned fast," Steve growled.

"Swearing in church?" she asked, an eyebrow arched.

"I'll swear any darned place I rootin' tootin' please," Steve told her with a grin.

"Go on, you goof," she said and gave him a play shove.

He had to grin. They had been through good times and bad. Angela had been more than just a wife, she was also his confidant and best friend. After twenty years, she still saw the humor and didn't mind sharing the jokes with him. As always, they waited to be the last in line.

"Steve, Angela Taylor, how are you?" Pastor James said, taking them each by the hand in a firm shake.

"Good, how are things with you and the fam?" Steve said grinning.

"Good. Mary is feeling a little under the weather, so she stayed back today. Joseph is full of energy, just like always."

"Oh no, is everything ok?" Angela asked, concerned.

"Mostly allergies. Sinuses. She should be on her feet tonight, but felt better staying away from the congregation till she makes sure that's all it is."

"That makes sense," Steve told him. "Where is everybody?"

"I know you haven't been here in a couple of weeks, but we've had...some losses."

"But the food—" Angela started.

"No, no. It's not that. Our congregation is largely made up of the elderly. Medications have been running low or out, plus there's been a lot of groups that have been going through the area lately. I'm guessing that people are keeping their heads down or..."

"Somebody has been going after them to rob them?" Angela asked softly.

"Yes," Pastor James said, his eyes boring holes into the floor. "You guys are probably safer than most, living in a community that's off the main drag."

"We've had issues of our own," Steve said, "but I don't think anything like this. We've only had a few break-ins, but nobody was really hurt except..."

"The people who broke into our house," Angela said.

"Oh no, is everyone ok? I saw Amy sneak out with Joseph a little while ago..."

"Oh, we're ok. It's just been... awful, to be honest," Steve finished.

"What happened to the people who broke into your house?" Pastor James asked, already guessing by the expressions on the Taylors faces.

⬥

"...that's why they were insisting that somebody come and inventory our house," Steve told them.

"I can understand why you don't want to do that," Pastor James said patiently as they all sat on the lawn in front of the church. "But you probably don't have enough food there to feed the community for more than a few days, I'm willing to bet."

"You'd be right," Angela told him, though she wasn't for sure how long it would hold out.

"Well, we still have the bulk of the food you bought for the pantry, and as you can see, our numbers keep dropping," Pastor James said sadly.

"Would you mind? It would go a long way to getting some heat off of us and giving the community a fighting chance, in case we have to be strong enough to defend against..."

"You have another group in the area, competing for resources. Kicking in doors and hurting people?"

Steve and Angela both nodded and then watched as Joseph went running by them, laughing hysterically as Amy made kissing noises, followed by Amber who was dying the death of the easily amused... and also laughing hysterically.

"You want to stop that?" Angela asked.

"Truthfully? I'm glad he's running. Makes it easier not to shoot him."

"Steve!" Angela said shocked.

"No, I know he's kidding. I hope," Pastor James said grinning, "besides, Joseph can run about three times that fast. He's not trying to lose them all that hard."

"You're not helping my itchy finger," Steve said, and earned an elbow to the ribs.

"Oof," he said and rubbed his side. "For the record, I am kidding. Joseph is a good kid. He's not some leech like that..." Steve's smile vanished as memory hit, and a cloud darkened his features.

"Yeah, I understand," Pastor James said. "It wasn't your fault, you know."

"Pastor, since everything went to... uh... heck...I've probably had to kill three to five people. I don't...I mean...am I eternally damned?"

It had been an issue that had been gnawing at Steve, and his former Catholic upbringing had left him feeling conflicted on the issue.

"You know, the Ten Commandments were written in Hebrew?"

"Sure," Angela said.

"So the whole 'Thou Shall Not Kill' thing?"

"Yeah?" Steve asked.

"The actual translation is more like 'Thou Shall Not Commit Murder,'" Pastor James said quietly.

"You didn't murder them in cold blood, Steve," Angela said.

Steve let out a big sigh and looked at the dirt that was peeking through the trampled and sparse grass of the church's lawn.

"Can I load up while we are here?" Steve asked.

"Yes, I don't see a problem with that. Most folks here...they get what they need and we've got quite a bit right now. Nobody is dying of hunger," Pastor James's voice sounded sad.

"I'm sorry," Angela told him softly.

"It is what it is. I wish I could do more, but I do often wonder what is going on. Do you guys have any news? From...outside the area?"

"No," Steve said simply. "Communications equipment is not something anybody I know has. I thought about getting some ham radio stuff, but I just never got the time, or never took the time, to do it."

"That's too bad. You would think that after all of this, there would be something. Somebody. I mean, in all the books FEMA comes through or big huge convoys of military vehicles. It's like..."

"Everyone is dying out quietly?" Steve asked.

The pastor didn't answer, he just looked away and stared off into the distance. That's the moment three tired and sweaty kids flopped down on the grass in front of their parents.

"Hey Dad," Amber asked. "Can Joseph come hang out at our house for a day or two, if it's ok with his dad?"

Steve's eyebrows went up and Angela let out a little snort at the hopeful expression on Amy's face. She had a pretty good idea what it was that Amber was up to. Steve was kind of lost, but shook his head.

"I am not sure that'd be a good idea right now. We've had so much happen, and I'm worried that Doug or some of his cronies will want to make some sort of play. I don't think it'd be safe right now."

"Oh, ok," Amber said. "But when things aren't so crazy?"

"We wouldn't mind," Angela answered, and looked at Pastor James who answered, "I wouldn't mind either. He needs to get out more."

"See, that's how you do it," Amber said to Amy who picked up a handful of dead grass and chucked it at her sister.

That elicited a scream and then a small turf fight, before the three of them were off and running around again.

"If things are that rough, who's watching your house right now?"

"Deputy Lucy," Angela told him.

"Ah, it'll be nice and safe then."

"Safe for Lucy. We told her we wouldn't be gone that long, so—"

"I'll give you a hand loading some stuff up, go ahead and pull your truck up to the back door, nobody here will give us a problem. Hell, I've sent food home with some of them now that things have really...well... you know."

"You mean you don't feel safe here with all of it?" Angela asked.

"Oh no, it's not that. I just think I'm going to run out of people to feed long before I run out of food."

"It can't be that bad, can it?" Steve asked.

Again, the Pastor didn't meet his gaze and shook his head, "Just... not feeling as hopeful as I let on sometimes," he finished, his gaze finding the running and laughing kids.

"I told you, that's where he's been getting it," the man whispered as the three of them watched the Taylors loading up the pickup truck.

"I always knew you'd come through for me. I never doubted it."

"Thanks, Alan."

CHAPTER 29

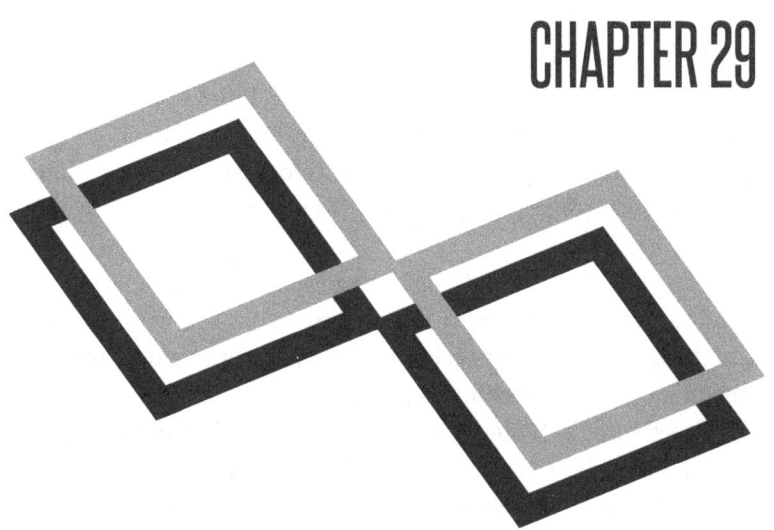

The food was dropped off at the community center with very little fanfare. People saw the Taylors back up to the doorway to unload, and they started walking and sitting down on the grass. Some of the residents had gone in, but there wasn't very much being done. Steve grouched that it didn't look like many people were making an effort.

"They might not have the energy," Angela said simply.

That sobered everyone up. Jeff wasn't there to help them unload, but Cheryl Jacoby, one of the HOA leadership was there. She seemed shocked, but she had problems moving the fifty-pound sacks. The Taylors took over that part, all except for Amy, who watched the front door as everyone started filing in.

"Where's everyone at?" Steve asked Cheryl.

"They're...I don't know. Jeff asked me to watch the place. I'm glad you came, we really didn't have anything to feed people today. The gardens aren't doing so good, and I was worried about what we were going to do."

"I didn't know you ran out, I knew it had to have been getting low." Steve told her.

"Yeah, yesterday was smaller rations. A couple of groups showed up earlier asking directions to your house, but I told them you'd already made it clear that you weren't...I mean, wouldn't..."

"No, I don't have much, and what I do have, is for my family," Steve said softly, "but I did bring this. It's part of what my family put away for hard times."

"I know, I just... none of this is easy. Especially as you watch your friends and family all slowly starving to death. You want to do the right thing, but the hunger gets you and when your babies are crying nonstop and there's nothing to eat—"

"I need some air," Steve told her, interrupting her and pushing by.

"I'm sorry, did I say something?" Cheryl asked Angela.

"Yes, you did," Angela said, and put the last bag inside the door. "Tell Jeff and whoever else that there isn't much more left for us to share. We're probably going to be avoiding the meetings for a while. We're still going to do the neighborhood watch like we did before, but this whole big community dinner...I don't know. It hasn't gone well for us the last few times we've come here. It seems like everyone hates us and that isn't fair to my husband and my daughters."

"If you'd only share out a little more—"

"Why didn't you buy your own food?" Amy interrupted.

"I did, but the stores are closed now and there's no fuel to go anywhere if the money was any good," Cheryl told her, a condescending note in her tone.

"I meant like before. Isn't that your job as a parent to make sure you're always ready and prepared to help your family and feed your kids?" Amy asked, oblivious to the woman's tone.

A look of pure hatred crossed Cheryl's face and she took one angry step towards Amy. Before Angela could react, Amber got in the middle and pushed the mid-thirties woman hard. Cheryl's feet went out from under her and she slid on the slick floor of the community center for several feet before she hit the edge of the doorway into the meeting room. Amber advanced with a clenched fist, held close to her waist.

"Amber!" Angela warned. "That's enough."

"If she comes anywhere near my little sister like she was going to, I'll knock her block off. I don't even need to use my gun on her."

"You fucking brat," Cheryl said getting to her feet. "I'll teach you some manners, you no good, slut of a whore."

"Now you did it," Angela said, putting her hands over Amy's ears. "Go ahead, Amber."

Amber made a feint and Cheryl put her hands up to protect her face when Ambers uppercut took Cheryl in the stomach. She made an 'Ooof' sound and sat down.

"Take it back, or I'll use my knees next time."

"You can't do this, you fucking—"

Amber took half a step forward and her knee shot out. At the last second, she held it back as Cheryl cried out. The knee never connected. Amber grabbed the woman by the hair and yanked it savagely.

"My dad isn't the only one who's a badass. Nobody talks to us like that. Nobody," Amber said, starting to pull the woman across the floor.

Cheryl had been screaming bloody murder as soon as the knee fake to the head happened. Steve walked in the door to see Angela holding her arms around Amy, covering her ears as filth fell out of Cheryl's mouth. Amber didn't hurt her so much as she humiliated her. Steve locked gazes with his wife, seeing his daughter deftly avoiding slaps, kicks, her grip never letting up on a handful of hair.

"What in the—"

"Shh, she deserved it. Amber is being nicer than I would," Angela finished.

"I hope you all die," Cheryl screamed.

Amber got a second handful of hair and dragged Cheryl into the center of the floor, spitting and screaming, away from the wall and kicked her hard in the side. Then she let go of her and stepped back.

"What...." Steve asked, surprised at the brutality his daughter just showed.

Cheryl was curled up on the floor, dry heaving, her feet twitching.

"She got ugly and was going to go after Amy. I gave her a polite shove and..."

"Let's go," Angela said, "We'll explain when we get home."

"I don't..." Steve said, his words trailing off as he saw a few scratches on his daughter's arm.

⚙

"So, let me get this straight, you let Amber fight a grown woman?" Steve asked, a tumbler of whiskey perched on his knee as the girls fought over how to spice dinner just inside the house, but within earshot of their parents and Lucy.

"Yeah, she said some pretty stupid, hateful things. You know how I feel about language. I was going to let Amber stop after the shove, but when she started calling my baby names even after getting put on her ass...I told Amber never mind, continue."

Steve chuckled. "In another lifetime, that kick to the kidneys might have caused her some legal issues."

"Well it's a good thing it isn't in another time. It's this time. She needed to be taught a lesson, and if she has to have a little blood in her urine, so be it."

"I've never seen her act so..."

"Brutal?"

"Yeah," he said reluctantly. "I mean, I never saw her move like that, it's like she's a scrapper and I didn't even..."

"Come on, she knows how to fight. We used to have her in Krav Maga classes with me, back in Ohio," Angela said.

"Yeah, but she was barely a little older than Amy when she quit. It's been years and years..."

"Some things you never forget, you just get a little rusty at. Like target practice," Lucy said, chiming in.

"Yeah, I suppose that's true," Steve admitted. "Does Amy know how to—"

"No, but she wants to learn. Me and Lucy will show her, right Sis?"

"Sis?" Lucy said with a grin. "Sure, we will."

"Are the guys going to come out for dinner?" Angela asked her.

"I don't know. I can walk home and ask them if you'd like. What's on the menu?"

"Rabbit," both Angela and Steve said at once.

"Is that how you're keeping the grass cut back here?" Lucy asked with an amused grin.

"Yeah, we let the grow outs munch on the lawn some, plus I have pellets. The trick is to not let them dig out. It's time to get some on the grill. I figure two or three grow outs will feed the seven of us, and I'll do something veggie wise."

"Want me to bring anything? I made some flatbread the other day while I wait on my sourdough."

"What the...yes!" Steve said at once.

"Easy there, carb monster," Angela said, playfully closing his jaw.

✦

"Why was she so mad at me?" Amy asked Amber as they rubbed spices into the rabbit sections.

"You weren't trying to be mean to her, but your words must have made her feel guilty. That came across as her being mad."

"That's when you went all Jackie Chan on her. That was pretty cool," Amy said.

"I thought so too, at first," Amber told her, "but now I sort of feel bad."

"What do you mean? She was saying all this hateful stuff. Even though Mom covered my ears, I heard what she said."

"Well, that's just it. The only one she really hurt in the end was a couple of scratches she gave to me. I might have hurt her really bad."

"You did it to protect me," Amy told her.

"Yeah, but I could have done it a little less hurtful. Sometimes you have to act and worry about it later. That's all I'm doing. Worrying that I went too far."

Amy walked up and with grimy hands, hugged her sister hard. "Well, I don't worry so much with having so many badasses around me."

"I heard that!" Lucy said, breezing through the back door.

"Doh!" Amy said in an almost perfect Homer Simpson impression.

"Don't let your parents hear you. I'll be back, I'm going to get the Matts."

"Yes," Amber said, making a fist pump.

Amy just sulked a moment. "But Joseph can't make it. I wish he could."

"He's too old for you," Both Lucy and Amber chorused.

"DOH!" Amy all but yelled at them in a louder repeat performance.

CHAPTER 30

It was midweek, and the Taylors had been avoiding the nightly food and meetings at the community center. The only time they left the property was to go to Dwight's, or do the volunteer neighborhood watch. Things had been quiet. They were all sitting in the living room when Amy shot upright.

"Dad, a whistle!"

Steve bolted upright. Another whistle sounded and a gunshot.

"Don't move my piece," he said motioning to the never-ending Monopoly tournament.

"You're not going out there alone," Angela said. "Amber—"

"I know," she said and rotated to see her sister, "let's go get ready."

"I hate this, sometimes," Amy said.

"I do, too."

Both Steve and Angela put on AR-500 vests and had several magazines already loaded and in the ammo pouches. Then they both got the spare magazines for their side arms.

"I wish you would stay here with the girls," Steve told Angela.

"No, we're a team. Amber has proven herself more than capable—"

Gunshots rang out, a long stream of them coming in from several directions. People screamed.

"Get in the shelter," Steve bellowed in the direction the girls had been in.

"Locking it down," Amber's muffled scream came to them from the direction of the garage.

"Good girl," Angela said softly, and both of them made sure their ARs were charged and on safe.

The community center was on fire when they got there. Several people were laid out on the grass, either bleeding or dead. Neither Taylor could have counted the number of shots fired, but it sounded like a small war had gone on. They had hurried as much as they possibly could, but with that much lead being thrown around, they had to be careful.

"Is somebody putting that out?" Steve shouted to Matthew who stood off to the side, looking shocked.

"I don't... I can't," Matthew said and sat down hard.

Angela rushed over to him and started checking him over and he pushed her away as gently as the big man could and pointed.

The cries of half the volunteer community watch group were loud. Several of them were among the dead, but a lot of them were wounded. Steve didn't try to pay attention to any one injury, because most of them looked like they'd been used like a large pincushion. Angela was good at patching people up, but she wasn't that good.

"Lucy, Matt Junior?" Steve asked him.

"Safe; I made her promise to get him to safety."

"Who did this?" Angela said standing up.

"I don't know. They shot from ambush. I just had my pistol, I ran back to my house to get my rifle and when I came back, they were almost all gone. Carried off food and somebody torched the inside. It's gonna burn down the whole block...."

"You're ok," Steve told Matt, "are you hurt anywhere?"

"No," he said and took a big breath. "I just..."

"You went inside the center, looking for survivors. You're dehydrated."

Matthew nodded, and Steve looked at his wife questioningly.

"He smells like gasoline and ashes. His arm has burn blisters. He won't feel it till the adrenaline wears off. It doesn't look bad. Not like—"

"Matt!" Matthew screamed and lumbered to his feet.

"Dad!" Matt Junior yelled back.

They both started running and met in the middle, the big man wrapping his son up in his arms.

"What can we do for gunshot wounds like this?" Steve asked.

Angela looked at the people on the ground and didn't meet her husband's gaze. "I don't know, not without an ER. These people aren't just winged. There's damage here that I can't fix."

Steve was expecting that and nodded.

"Let's get everyone comfortable."

"Mom and Dad would be so pissed if they knew we didn't lock ourselves in," Amy said from their upstairs bedroom.

"You watch the back windows. In case Uncle Dwight comes through."

"Uncle Dewey," Amy insisted.

"Sometimes, it's ok to grow up a little bit, kiddo," Amber said, scanning to the south and east windows that made the corner of the bedroom.

"Like deciding not to listen to Mom and Dad?" Amy asked.

"I didn't think of it before they left. What if this was a distraction to get Mom and Dad out of the house? Remember what people said? They wanted our stuff."

"Is that why you got one of Dad's long guns out?"

"Yeah squirt, because pistols are only good for close work. You know that."

Amy shivered and wrapped her arms around herself, despite the warm air and open windows.

"I don't see anybody."

"Keep watching Amy. I left the doors opened all the way to the shelter. The locks are already turned. If we need to, we can pull them shut, locking them behind us if we see somebody coming."

"If we're going to run, why did you get a long gun out?" Amy asked.

Busted, Amber stayed silent.

"There's nothing more we can do here," Angela said.

"I know, I just...we need to get together and talk about going after—"

"With what, a handful of people? They shot ours from ambush and then a couple dozen people popped up to steal the community's food before torching the place. We'd be outmanned and outgunned."

"I know, it's just..."

"You're feeling survivor's guilt, same as Matthew. Running back for his rifle saved his life. Us living so far from the point of contact saved ours," Angela said as they started walking.

"It didn't save LINDA!" a grimy and bloody figure said standing up.

Doug Morris was covered in drying and crusting blood, his wife's form crumpled in front of him, or what they assumed was his wife. She'd taken a shot to the head and chest. Steve let out a small gasp as recognition hit.

"I'm so sorry Doug," Steve said, grabbing his wife by the arm.

"This is all your fault, Taylor!" Doug shouted.

"Let's go before I have to do something I'm going to regret," Steve whispered to Angela who nodded, and she matched his pace when he broke out into a jog.

Doug's screams and shouts were louder than anything else. They had stayed and helped who they could, gave comfort to those who were close to passing, and prayed for anybody who needed it. They would need to have that meeting, but today was not that day. They weren't even worried about the community center burning the block anymore. While they held onto an elderly man's hand who'd been shot in the chest, the roof collapsed into the brickwork of the building. Barring any high winds, it'd burn itself out.

"Mom and Dad are coming," Amber said.

"Should we stay out or—"

"Naw, let's go lock ourselves in."

"Wait, there's somebody coming through the back gate!"

Amber rushed over and put the AR up to her shoulder and looked through the sight. Dwight's face popped up in profile and she dropped the gun, "It's Uncle Dewey!" she said and took off running for the back gate.

"I thought you said it was Uncle Dwight?"

Amber let out an exasperated sound as she raced downstairs.

"It looks like it's Dwight coming through the back gate," Steve told Angela.

They both heard the back door open and Amber call out to him. Steve fumbled with the keys and got the door unlocked. Angela almost knocked him over, getting inside. She rushed to the back door to see Dwight standing there, his chest heaving, sweaty.

"I was on the tractor, I didn't hear it till one of the guys got me...I got here as fast as I—"

"Sit down," Angela said. "No heart attacks in my house."

Amber rushed over and took his deer rifle gently and leaned it against the wall as the old farmer slumped onto the couch.

"Mom!" Amy yelled, "You and Daddy..."

"No, hun, it's not ours," Angela said, getting a pitcher of water out and stoppering one side of the sink.

"What is happening?" Dwight gasped, color starting to return to his cheeks.

"Somebody attacked the community center. They shot up a bunch of people and set fire to the building," Steve answered.

"The food?" Amber asked.

"Taken or burned up," Angela answered.

"Matt, Lucy, Mr. Fitzpatrick?" Amy asked.

"They're all fine. The fighting was done when we got there. We live too damned far, we should have taken the—"

"I told you, don't you be borrowing blame when none of it is yours," Angela chided. "Now, go rinse off as best as you can and then come bring me a bucket of clean water. I want to wash up with warm water. I want you to do it also, we have blood from many sources on us. We need to be—"

"I'll help," Amy said, unflappable as ever and pulled at the only clean spot on her Dad's arm. His elbow.

While Steve went out to clean up some, Angela got a pot out and started trying to light the camp stove when Amber made a shooing motion and did it.

"You're covered in grodyness. You need to go rinse off with Dad. I can handle this."

"We're going to talk about why you girls were out of the shelter..." She saw Amber's mouth open to complain, but she cut her off. "But not right now. I don't think your father even noticed. He feels guilty because he got there too late, and he's kinda creeping me out," she finished, and turned to Dwight. "Can you talk to him? I explained survivor's guilt, but he's still too dazed to listen."

"I know a thing or three about that," Dwight said, "but once he gets washed up, he's gonna need some liquor in him. It's going to make him easier to persuade."

Angela nodded and headed out.

"So, alcohol will make my dad feel better?" Amber asked.

"No, but he'll listen better," he said, feeling mostly better, "and I've been there before. I might have a drop or two to calm my nerves as well."

"Thank you," Amber said softly.

"For what?" Dwight asked, his voice hoarse.

"For being a good friend of my dad's and our family's," she said, and turned back to the camp stove and started pouring water into one of the many pots.

Dwight listened, and both men became slightly slurred in their speech. At one point, Matthew and Matt stopped out with Lucy, but they all went out on the back porch and let Steve talk to Dwight. Lucy had served, and she'd told Angela in passing that Matthew had gotten over the shock faster than she'd expected.

There was a lot of anger, and more than a few groups of the community who were arming themselves to go after those who attacked them. Nobody could have talked them out of it. More people just sat and stared at the community center, long after the fire burned low and asked anybody who'd listen where they were gonna get their next meal.

Steve though, he talked to Dwight. Vietnam was the anvil that had shaped and forged Dwight into the man he was. He poked and prodded Steve's feelings. Sometimes they were loud, sometimes they both cried at their perceived failures. Twice, Amber or Angela tried to give them food to eat, but both sandwiches were still sitting untouched.

"...and that's all you can do," Dwight said with a slight slur to his words.

"I still feel like I could have done more, should have done more," Steve told him.

"Eat your damned sandwich, then let's go rejoin the rest of the party out back."

"I'm not hungry," Steve said.

"Yeah, but you're gonna be hung over if you aren't. This isn't my first go-round with the bottle, if you catch my meaning. Just make sure it don't become a habit."

"Promise," Steve said, crossing his heart and then pulled the sandwich made from some of Lucy's flat bread, some fresh cut greens, homemade mayo made from oil and an egg, and some smoked, shredded rabbit.

Dwight dug in, and his eyes opened up wide. "Damnation, you eat like this all the time?" he asked around his mouthful.

"You know I do, you eat over here half as often as not," Steve said around his own bite.

"Oh good, you're finally eating. I was thinking I was going to have to take those for myself," Amber said, walking in.

"Mine," Steve told her in a joking tone.

"You want another drink, Dad and Uncle Dewey?"

"No," both Steve and Dwight said together.

"Well, alrighty then," Amber said and walked back out with a pitcher of lemonade she took from the counter.

"You know, what you told me about the church...with the rest of the families not showing up...do you think they're getting hit by the same group?" Dwight asked.

Steve had the folded flatbread sandwich halfway to his mouth and dropped it.

"Oh shit. What if they hit the church?" Steve said starting to stand, his plate and food flying.

"Oh hell no, not tonight. Not now!" Dwight said, putting a hand out and pushing Steve back down onto the couch.

"But... people know some of the food came from—"

"Do they know what church you go to?"

"No, nobody other than Matthew really got to know us around here—"

"So they don't know where you go to church, they just know it's not theirs?"

"Yes but—"

"Pick your food up; it's the apocalypse. Eat up. We can go check on it in the morning."

"I'd feel better if... wait, you want to come with me?" Steve asked, slow on the uptake from the drinks.

"Why do you think despite having some fun gear like you got, I still carry my old deer gun?"

"You... I dunno. Because it can punch through the body armor these guys wear?"

"No stupid, because it gives the advantage of range. Sure, your AR is basically the same platform I used in 'Nam, but I spent half the damned war using something a little heavier."

"Sniper?"

"Everybody has to be good at something. Law of averages," Dwight said and shoved the rest of his food in his mouth.

"Let's figure out somebody to watch the farm and I'll have the ladies here hold down the fort. Maybe we can talk Matthew and Lucy to ride shotgun with us?"

"I'd like one or two more people, but that sounds like a good start. You ready to go outside and see what kinda shape this party is in?"

"Yeah," Steve said, but in his heart, he was worried.

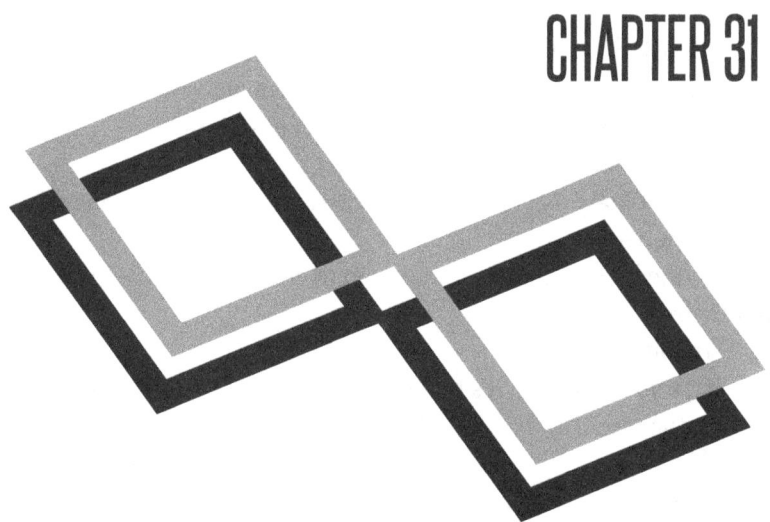

CHAPTER 31

They saw the smoke long before they were going to drop off Dwight. They had taken Amber's Jeep, knowing the larger engine and frame built for mudding and climbing gave them more options if they had to get away than Steve's truck or Angela's BMW. The rumble of the motor was a big disadvantage, but they felt it was worth it in the event they had to escape in a hurry.

"Aww, shit," Dwight said from the back, his rifle butt between his feet.

"Oh lord, no," Angela said.

Steve didn't say anything. He almost wished Lucy would have come after all, but she was feeling slightly under the weather today and stayed back at the Taylor's house to watch over the girls.

"You don't think..." Matthew's words trailed off.

"No sense in dropping me off, let's roll in," Dwight said.

Steve didn't turn his gaze from the road, but nodded grimly. As soon as the thought had hit yesterday evening, he couldn't get the cold certainty out of his mind. They pulled into the parking lot and found the smoldering remains of the church. The outside was littered with bodies. Many of them wore camo and a couple wore the black BDUs. As soon as Steve saw that, he jerked the Jeep to a stop and turned off the motor. Everyone exited.

Dwight got out last and stretched, then started walking slowly. Nobody questioned that the old farmer had a point. He started moving differently. Deliberate and slow, his head on a swivel. Without turning back to look, he made a hand motion to his right, pointing and Steve moved more to the right as directed. Matthew was already moving to the left when the signal was given and Angela brought up the rear. All of them carried carbines except for Dwight. All of them had side arms, but they elected to keep the vests at home, to give them more flexibility and space.

"How many?" Angela asked quietly, over the sound of flames still licking at the remains of the wood.

"I see seven down. Looks like buckshot," Steve said.

"Picked the bodies clean of gear, even the armor by the look of things," Matthew said, kicking at a corpse wearing all black.

Steve didn't say anything. He was looking intently at the bodies, trying to pick out James or Mary's features. So far, all he saw were strangers.

"I wonder if they got out of the church?" Steve asked after a moment.

"Let me make a sweep," Dwight said. "See if anybody is holed up, ready to pick off first responders. Grab some cover."

"I smell something other than smoke," Angela said walking towards the front of the church.

"Wait, it could be a trap," Dwight told her.

A cry erupted from her mouth and she rushed forward, past the men who suddenly were left in the dust. They followed her to the steps leading up to the church and saw what made her upset. Part of the interior wall that separated the front room from the main portion of the church had collapsed. Sticking out of the smoking rubble was a badly charred set of legs. The shoes were unmistakable, even to Steve. A woman's flats, a pair they'd seen Mary wear more than once.

"Mary?" Steve asked.

"Yes, it has to be," she said and tried to walk forward, but was stopped by the heat radiating out of the structure.

She put a hand up to shield her face and tried again, but it was too hot. After a moment, Steve put his arm around his wife's waist and pulled her back. She tried to pull free at first, but then started sobbing. With tears in his own eyes, Steve pulled her off the concrete steps and back. That's when he saw a body along the side of the church he hadn't notice before on their angled approach. They had come in from the left front, but most of the right side of the church had been shielded from their view.

Steve pointed and they started walking. Pastor James lay crumpled on his side, wearing his street clothes. His body looked as if it had been used as target practice by a dozen men. An ugly looking shotgun lay discarded at his side.

"Oh god, where's Joseph?" James asked quietly. "Joseph!" he shouted, making everyone wince.

"Joseph!" Angela echoed herself.

"You two, we don't have the area clear. Be quiet," Dwight said and then grunted as they both took off around the church, looking in what windows they could.

Most had been sucked in by the hungry flames, but a couple that was intact were black with smoke residue. Steve smashed those with the butt of his AR and tried to look inside. Matthew hung back, and being much taller, spent more time looking in the windows, mindful not to get too close to what felt like a forge.

"Let's check the house," Dwight said after a moment, "they live in the little house behind the church, right?"

"Yeah," Steve said, and then changed directions.

The house looked as if it too had been used for target practice. The front door was shattered, as a boot print near the handle and the splintered door jamb told the story nobody wanted to hear. Pushing it open, Dwight went in first.

"Shit," Dwight said.

Steve and Angela's hearts dropped and they followed him inside.

"I'll wait out here," Matthew said and turned to cover their backside.

Steve saw what had made Dwight swear. Blood splattered the back wall of the living room as soon as the front door was opened and bullet holes were evident in the wall. They checked room by room, but other than the front room, that was the only evidence of blood they found. No Joseph. With a heavy heart, Steve walked outside. When they were all out, Dwight took his hat off.

"If that was his momma in the church, chances are...."

"I know," Steve said, "I was hoping I was wrong."

"How are we going to tell the girls?" Angela asked.

Steve couldn't answer her; his eyes were watering too bad.

"If there was anybody still in the area, they would have made their move by now, don't you think?" Matthew asked Dwight.

"Yeah, I reckon."

"Let's get out of here," Matthew said.

"Shouldn't we bury them?" Angela asked her husband.

"I'm not gonna bury the asshats who did this," he spat, "but I don't have tools with me. If we go to my storage unit, I have a couple of shovels. It'd be faster than going home. Maybe it'll be cool enough for us to be able to get to Mary and Jo...." His words trailed off and his chest hitched.

Food. This was all food. This group to the north had killed and burned relentlessly. Sure, it was circumstantial, but they were all dressed and armed the same. They were less than a mile away. They were slaughtering people needlessly. Steve kept his eyes peeled, but he was furious and that made the tears fall faster as he made his way to the Jeep. Everyone piled in. Without speaking, he fired up the Jeep when they were all loaded.

"You got the key your girlfriend gave you?" Angela asked pointedly.

Steve let out a sigh and rolled his eyes as Matthew leaned forward.

"Girlfriend?" he asked, disbelief in his voice.

"She's not my girl—"

"She's pulling your chain to get you to quit dwelling on everything," Dwight growled from the backseat.

"I've got the keys," Steve said, and smiled faintly as the old farmer's words sank in.

He left the Jeep idling and walked up to the gate, pulling his truck keys from his pocket. He unlocked it, and pulled the chain through and pushed open the gate. He walked back and opened the door to the Jeep when the side door opened a crack and a double barrel shotgun pointed at the Jeep. Steve paused and everyone turned to look where he was.

"That's his girlfriend," Angela said with a grin as a young woman appeared in the doorway, holding what looked like an old coach gun.

"Mr. Taylor?"

"Yeah, it's me," Steve said, his mouth suddenly dry.

"Sorry, I didn't recognize the Jeep. Thought somebody was trying to break in or stole your key."

"No, this is my daughter's Jeep. I just need to get a couple things. Has...has there been any trouble here? Break-ins?" He was curious, because she mentioned it, but now he wondered if this place would be targeted. How much of a target did it really look like?

"No, it's been really quiet. Nobody has tried it, but I still stay in the front office during the daytime. It's got windows on three sides and they are all tinted so I can see out, but nobody can see in."

"You take your job seriously," he said with a grin.

She smiled. "Naw, it's a family business type of thing. I won't hold you up. Say hello to the missus, and maybe I'll see you at church soon!"

"I uh...."

"Steve," Angela hissed.

"See you soon."

He got in and drove the jeep back to his unit. From his truck keys, he opened the large storage unit. Before he closed it up last time, he'd put in a folding ladder, a ton of gardening tools and some extra hose reels. They were all things from his garage, but they were not only cover, but they were also extras that he wanted to put in a separate location in case he ever needed them. He got the door unlocked and rolled up the door. He walked over and grabbed the shovel and was about to turn to leave when he realized that it wasn't where he'd left it.

He deliberately left it to the left of the step ladder. The ladder had been placed underneath the attic stairs as part of his ruse. That meant it had been leaned up against the secret doorway. He checked the floor, but nothing seemed disturbed, nothing looked like it had been dragged. He felt around and then pushed the door open.

"Please Mister, don't shoot!" Joseph yelled from the dark.

"Joseph?"

"Mister Taylor?" Joseph said coming out into the light.

His clothing smelled of gasoline and smoke and soot still smeared his features. He held a gallon sized jug of water, but he hadn't found the electric lanterns inside by the look of things.

"How did you...?"

"Amber showed me the escape hatch into the other unit. Did... have you been to the church?"

"Joseph?" Angela screamed, having gotten out of the jeep as soon as the hidden door opened and saw the grimy boy emerge from the darkness.

The boy started crying as Angela closed the distance and wrapped her arms around him. They cried together like that for a long time.

"I guess the boy got away," Matthew remarked from the backseat.

"I wonder how he knew to come here?" Dwight asked.

❈

The story slowly came out as they drove back into the subdivision. Steve listened to Angela talking to Joseph from the backseat. She'd traded places with the much larger Matthew so everyone could fit. He was silent as Joseph described how after the service Sunday night and the communal dinner that his dad had changed and was cleaning up when several trucks pulled up out front.

They couldn't see it at the time, but they had been full of men. As soon as the group saw his dad, they opened fire. His father was hit in the arm and told James to leave out the back door and get to safety. He tried to argue, so he could go warn his mom, but his dad said to get safe, and then got out a big shotgun. Joseph grinned at that mental image. It wasn't a pleasant sight.

"Did...did my parents make it out?" Joseph asked.

"No," Dwight said softly.

Steve saw the boy's facial features harden and the muscles around his jaw tightened as tears squeezed their way out again.

"I knew, somehow I knew. I was going to try to go home, but I told my dad where I was gonna hide and when he didn't come to find me...."

"I'm so sorry." Angela said.

"Everyone, get ready," Matthew said in a loud voice.

"What?" Dwight asked.

"There's a crowd around my house," Steve said through gritted teeth.

"Let me out, I can't do nothing from back here," Dwight told him, "Steve, you and the kid stay in here."

"Hell, no. Angela, I want you driving," Steve told her.

"Chinese fire drill?" Angela asked, the humor in her voice wasn't mirrored by her eyes.

"Yeah. Some of them just noticed us. Let's do it," he said and threw the creeping Jeep into park and then opened the door.

They quickly got out and Angela made Joseph sit in the back seat.

"You know how to use this?" Angela asked, showing him her AR.

"Yeah, my dad has...had...."

She handed it back and he took it. She could hear him work the bolt and then the safety click on and off.

"What are you doing?" Steve yelled over the rumble of the motor.

If the people weren't looking at them before, they were now. The three men advanced down the road in a rough line with the jeep bringing up the rear. People started shouting in two directions. One way was towards the house and somebody ran toward the door. A shot rang out and everybody shouldered their guns, but several people in the front door turned and started running backwards.

That's when Matthew pointed with his left hand at the upstairs window. Two rifle barrels were poking out.

"Hey, assholes!" Steve shouted.

The crowd seemed to part and Doug Morris came out of the middle, screaming.

"You catch that?" Dwight asked.

"No, you?" Matthew asked Steve.

Steve lowered his carbine and let it hang on his sling as his former nemesis walked towards him.

"Slow down, I can't understand you," Steve told him and held out a hand to slow his approach.

"This is all your fault, Taylor," Doug snarled.

"I didn't do anything," Steve told him, yet Morris kept stalking towards him.

Steve pulled his pistol and left his arm at the side as Doug stopped five feet away from the group, forcing them and the jeep to come to a halt.

"You refused to share your food with the community and let us grow weak. When those men came in to take what little we had, they killed my Linda! This is all your fault, because you think you're so much better than all of us. I know your kind, the smug dot-com, want-to-be-rich, little—"

"You do realize the food that the raiders stole from the community came from me and the Taylors?" Dwight interrupted, his gun held at waist level.

"And if you hadn't been letting us all slowly starve we could have stopped the slaughter—"

Another gunshot from the house drew everybody's attention. Somebody dropped what looked to be a glass bottle with flames coming from the top.

"Everybody move!" Matthew said and started charging forward, ignoring Doug who had eyes only for Steve.

Not everyone in the throng of humanity moved fast enough and Matthew started pushing his way through till somebody threw a punch. He took it across the side of the head, and then he started using the butt of his carbine. People started pushing in on Matthew as Doug started screaming and charged Steve.

His gun barked and the top of Doug's head split open. He fell as Matthew started falling under the combined weight of people attacking him. Dwight saw the bottle of flaming fluid picked up, and in a heartbeat, he knew what he had to do.

The voice of his instructor, almost a ghost, seemed to reverberate inside his skull.

You will shoot the fucking target. You will not miss. You miss and your men will be killed. In return, I'll fucking stick my boot so far up your miserable ass you'll taste the polish I used on it this morning. Do not fucking fail. Sight, acquire, fire. Motherfucker, I said fire!

Dwight had a split second, but with the angle he was standing he knew that he had one of Steve's windows behind the bottle and the bullet would enter approximately six feet above the floor. It would exit almost eight feet on the other side of the house. Even if somebody was on the first floor, none of the ladies were that tall and odds were, the littler girls were in the shelter or in the upstairs. This all happened in half a heartbeat as he lined up the shot in one motion and fired as the bottle was drawn back to throw.

The bullet shattered the bottle just above the neck, dousing the man holding it with something that immediately ignited, turning him into a human torch. The gunshots did two things. It made everyone pause, because they weren't warning shots from the house and made people start to turn in the direction of the five of them. That allowed the screams of the man on fire who tried to run through the crowd to scare and scatter them. He made it half a dozen feet and collapsed. People started breaking and running.

All except several who were piled onto Matthew and pummeling him. Steve stalked over and debated on butt stroking them, but he heard Matthew cry out in pain. He grabbed what he thought was a neighbor from Doug's side of the community back by his greasy hair. He screamed in pain and his eyes went wide as Steve put his pistol to his temple.

"I'll stop, I pro—"

The gunshot was angled down away from the bodies writhing on the ground but that shot, and the spray of gore more than anything else, had men up and scrambling to their feet. Steve shot another one in the stomach as he turned towards him and then raised his pistol to point in the face of the last man who paused. Matthew made his way to his feet slowly, blood gushing from the center of his nose.

"We're just trying to—"

Matthew pulled his own pistol and ended him where he stood and reached down, getting his dropped carbine.

"When they rode me down, I didn't want to lose control of the gun," he said, by way of apology.

"You guys ok?" Amber called from somewhere inside.

"Yes," Dwight said, walking over to the grass and stomping at the flames that had lit on the patches of grass that hadn't been tilled under.

"Garden didn't make it," Steve said looking at the ruined plantings.

That's when everyone was startled when the Jeep roared and tires squealed as it tore into the driveway, the horn blaring suddenly.

Steve looked around at the bodies, the singed grass, the bloody work on Matthew's face, his ruined garden, and the furious looks Angela was throwing at the bodies on her lawn. She shut it off and got out, holding the door for Joseph.

"You ok?" she called to Steve.

"Yeah, you ok?" Steve called back, walking her way.

"Yeah. Did they really try to burn us out?" she asked, looking at the man who now resembled a crispy critter and had quit screaming, unlike the gut-shot man.

"That one did," Steve said.

From above, a gunshot went off and the moaning man holding his stomach went still. They both looked up to see Lucy lower a carbine, a grim expression on her face.

"I need a drink," Dwight said suddenly.

"I do, too," Steve said.

"You might want to wait till you hear who Joseph saw in that group there," Angela told them.

They all turned, puzzled and horrified at how the day had effectively turned to shit.

"The one man, near the back? The one who ran? He was at my parents' house. He was next to the guy who first shot my dad."

Steve's face went dark.

"Would you recognize him if you saw him again?"

"Yes," Joseph said, though his tone made it sound like he was numb, going into shock.

"Let's get everyone inside and get Matthew cleaned up."

"Tis only a flesh wound."

Dwight groaned, but they went inside where the two younger Taylors had been running down the stairs.

"Mom, Dad? Joseph?" Amy called, her look confused.

"We have a lot to talk about," Angela said.

"Yeah, y'all do," Dwight said, "after this fracas, is it gonna be safe for any of you all to stay here?"

"What do you mean?" Lucy asked.

"You and Matthew just defended this place, and they were already sore at Steve here. They tried to burn them out. Now that there are dead bodies...theirs...you think they are gonna call it quits?"

"I hope they do," Angela said.

"Well, I do too, but we need to make a plan, in case they don't," Dwight told her.

"Well, shit," Amber said and then looked shocked when her parents didn't even correct her.

"I'm glad you're here," Amy told Joseph. "Has it been crazy at your house too?"

Joseph's eyes filled with tears. Angela pointed towards the living room and Amy and Amber took him by the hand and led the way, a girl on each arm.

"You got a plan?" Steve asked Dwight.

"Oh yeah. And if that don't work, we'll see what my son thinks."

"Your son?" Angela asked. "I thought he was deployed somewhere?"

"Got back this morning," Dwight told her, as he continued to scan the bodies on the ground.

"Shit. We should've brought him along with us," Matthew said, putting a handkerchief Lucy provided across the bridge of his nose.

"Nope. Didn't want him to know the shenanigans I was up to. He and some buddies finally made it back to the farm. If I would have known all this was gonna happen...let's just say that they are probably already scoping this place out."

"You got that right," A big man said walking out from the kitchen.

He was dressed in jeans, a white cotton t-shirt, and a cowboy hat. He carried a Mossberg 12 gauge loosely in one hand by the middle.

"God dammit, Carter," Dwight said.

Angela was the closest and could see that the big man was in his mid-forties. He had a scar that ran across his neck on a diagonal, and his right hand was horribly scarred across the top like he'd had it pressed into hot coals and it healed badly. The face and look in the eyes were unmistakable: it was Dwight's boy.

"How'd you get in here?" Dwight asked.

"Came in the back door. Lock sucks, ma'am," he said tipping his hat to Angela. "When I saw the fracas y'all were in, I ghosted in the back to make sure nobody came in the bottom to flush y'all out. Monk, Bear, and Loki are out back, covering the other sides."

"Excuse me?" Steve asked, confused, disarmed, and not keeping up.

"We knew this had to be your place by dad's description this morning. When the shooting started, we made our way over and got into position. Glad to see the old man still has good aim, thought he was gonna wing me when that shot went through the house. I was ready to make my presence known when y'all showed up."

"God dammit, Carter!" Dwight said angrily.

"Carter, thank you," Steve said holding his hand out.

After a moment, the soldier returned grips with him.

"You got a plan?" Steve asked him.

"I have a feeling he does, look at that shit-eating grin!" Dwight said, suddenly chuckling.

"Dad was pretty good back in the day. I'm still pretty good now, and I brought my fire team with me."

"They any good?" Steve asked.

"They're deadly."

"Good, I have a feeling the neighborhood just went to shit. We have to figure out who here is working with the guys in the black BDUs."

"We'll recon that later on, let's get the leakers off your front lawn."

"Leakers?" Lucy asked.

"Inside joke with our boys. The guys out front."

Lucy nodded and smiled and turned to Matthew. "You should go get Matty, and we should sit down and make some plans."

"That sounds like a good idea," Matthew said.

"He's still at the farm," Carter told them. "I'll radio one of the guys to run back and escort him here."

Amy walked out of the living room, having listened to part of the conversation. She had tears in her eyes from Joseph's story he told in part, and she kept looking between Carter and Dwight.

"Is it going to be ok?" She seemingly asked Carter.

"Yes ma'am. I promise you," Carter told her, tipping his hat to her.

From the living room, they could make out the soft sobs of Joseph, and the quiet murmuring voice of Amber.

The End

ABOUT THE AUTHOR

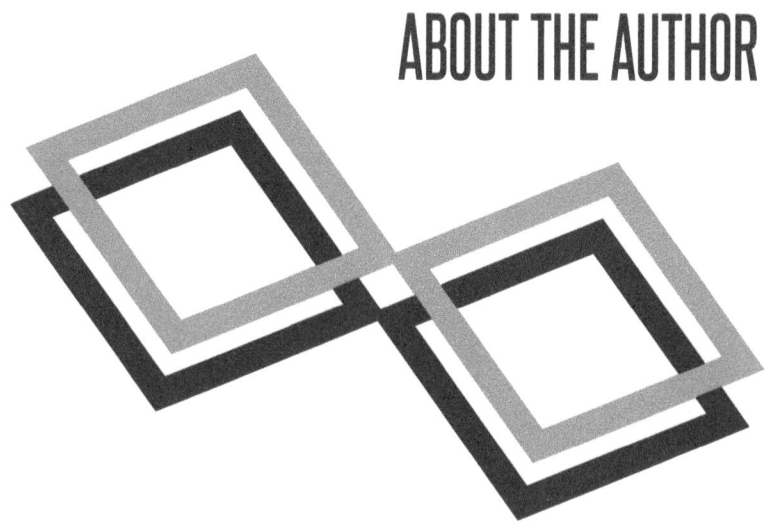

Boyd Craven has penned over twenty books over the last two years, only recently deciding to take the plunge into publishing. His *The World Burns Series* has hit the top ten in the Dystopian Genre in the USA, the UK, Canada, and Australia. Boyd has made his home in Michigan with his wonderful wife and about a million kids, but travels to Texas to visit family as frequently as possible.

PERMUTED PRESS
needs **you** to help

SPREAD (THE) INFECTION

FOLLOW US!

ｆ | Facebook.com/PermutedPress
𝕐 | Twitter.com/PermutedPress

REVIEW US!

Wherever you buy our book, they can be
reviewed! We want to know what you like!

GET INFECTED!

Sign up for our mailing list at
PermutedPress.com

PERMUTED
PRESS

KING ARTHUR AND THE KNIGHTS OF THE ROUND TABLE HAVE BEEN REBORN TO SAVE THE WORLD FROM THE CLUTCHES OF MORGANA WHILE SHE PROPELS OUR MODERN WORLD INTO THE MIDDLE AGES.

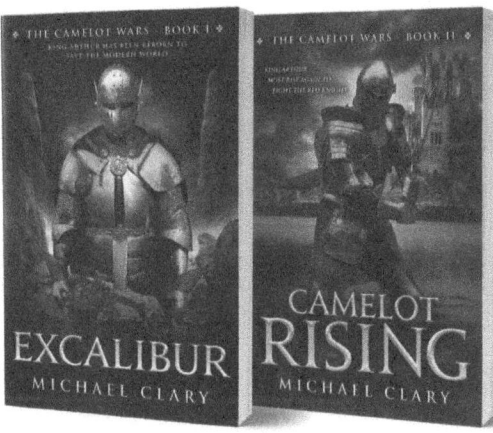

Morgana's first attack came in a red fog that wiped out all modern technology. The entire planet was pushed back into the middle ages. The world descended into chaos.

But hope is not yet lost— King Arthur, Merlin, and the Knights of the Round Table have been reborn.

PERMUTED
PRESS

THE ULTIMATE PREPPER'S ADVENTURE.
THE JOURNEY BEGINS HERE!

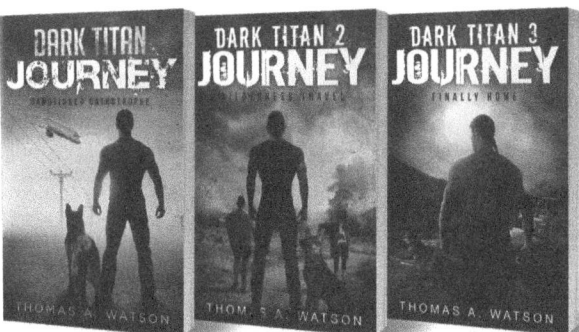

EAN 9781682611654 $9.99   EAN 9781618687371 $9.99   EAN 9781618687395 $9.99

The long-predicted Coronal Mass Ejection
has finally hit the Earth, virtually destroying
civilization. Nathan Owens has been prepping
for a disaster like this for years, but now he's
a thousand miles away from his family and
his refuge. He'll have to employ all his hard-won
survivalist skills to save his current community,
before he begins his long journey through
doomsday to get back home.

PERMUTED
PRESS

THE MORNINGSTAR STRAIN HAS BEEN LET LOOSE—IS THERE ANY WAY TO STOP IT?

An industrial accident unleashes some of the Morningstar Strain. The

EAN 9781618686497 $16.00

doctor who discovered the strain and her assistant will have to fight their way through Sprinters and Shamblers to save themselves, the vaccine, and the base. Then they discover that it wasn't an accident at all—somebody inside the facility did it on purpose. The war with the RSA and the infected is far from over.

This is the fourth book in Z.A. Recht's The Morningstar Strain series, written by Brad Munson.

PERMUTED PRESS

GATHERED TOGETHER AT LAST, THREE TALES OF FANTASY CENTERING AROUND THE MYSTERIOUS CITY OF SHADOWS...ALSO KNOWN AS CHICAGO.

EAN 9781682612286 $9.99   EAN 9781618684639 $5.99   EAN 9781618684899 $5.99

From *The New York Times* and *USA Today* bestselling author Richard A. Knaak comes three tales from Chicago, the City of Shadows. Enter the world of the Grey—the creatures that live at the edge of our imagination and seek to be real. Follow the quest of a wizard seeking escape from the centuries-long haunting of a gargoyle. Behold the coming of the end of the world as the Dutchman arrives.

Enter the City of Shadows.

PERMUTED
PRESS

WE CAN'T GUARANTEE
THIS GUIDE WILL SAVE
YOUR LIFE. BUT WE CAN
GUARANTEE IT WILL
KEEP YOU SMILING
WHILE THE LIVING
DEAD ARE CHOWING
DOWN ON YOU.

This is the only tool you need to survive the zombie apocalypse.

OK, that's not really true. But when the SHTF, you're going to want a survival guide that's not just geared toward day-to-day survival. You'll need one that addresses the essential skills for true nourishment of the human spirit. Living through the end of the world isn't worth a damn unless you can enjoy yourself in any way you want. (Except, of course, for anything having to do with abuse. We could never condone such things. At least the publisher's lawyers say we can't.)

PERMUTED
PRESS